ABOUT THE AUTHOR

Helen Paris worked in the performing arts for two decades, touring internationally with her London-based theatre company, Curious. After several years living in San Francisco and working as a theatre professor at Stanford University, she returned to the UK to focus on writing fiction.

As part of her research for a performance called *Lost & Found*, Paris shadowed employees in the Baker Street Lost Property Office for a week – an experience that sparked her imagination and inspired this novel.

LOST
PROPERTY

HELEN PARIS

PENGUIN BOOKS

TRANSWORLD PUBLISHERS
Penguin Random House, One Embassy Gardens,
8 Viaduct Gardens, London SW11 7BW
www.penguin.co.uk

Transworld is part of the Penguin Random House group of companies
whose addresses can be found at global.penguinrandomhouse.com

Penguin
Random House
UK

First published in Great Britain in 2021 by Doubleday
an imprint of Transworld Publishers
Penguin paperback edition published 2022

A CIP catalogue record for this book
is available from the British Library.

ISBN
9781529176339

Typeset in Sabon LT Std by Integra Software Services Pvt. Ltd, Pondicherry.
Printed and bound in Great Britain by Clays Ltd, Elcograf S.p.A.

The authorized representative in the EEA is Penguin Random House Ireland,
Morrison Chambers, 32 Nassau Street, Dublin D02 YH68.

Penguin Random House is committed to a sustainable
future for our business, our readers and our planet. This book
is made from Forest Stewardship Council® certified paper.

For darling Leslie, with all my love

PROLOGUE

It's church-like down here, shadowy with unlikely con-
gregations: wine bottles, prams, a funeral urn. As the
overhead fluorescents hum into life, the colours glow like
light through a stained-glass window – yellow, amber,
taupe, turquoise, more fuchsia than you might imagine. It's
the yellow that hits you first. Mustard yellow. Dijon, rather
than Colman's powdered. You have to be precise in Lost
Property. You have to find the exact right words and fit them
on to the modestly sized Dijon-coloured labels tied to every
single lost item stored here. If you write 'Woman's Handbag,
dappled burgundy' rather than 'Woman's Handbag, red',
it can make all the difference as to whether that bag is
reunited with its owner or languishes in Lost Property for
ever. Leather handle, you say? What kind? I ask. Looped?
Stitched? Buckled? Chewed? Admittedly, it's a challenge to

1

make one black collapsible umbrella stand out from another, but I do my best. I pay attention to the details.

Amidst the aisles of the mislaid, forgotten and walked-away-from is me, Dot. You'll hear me before you see me, mind; I have my father's feet (flat) attached to my mother's ankles (slim). I'm generally down here, shelving and tagging, and sometimes, when the other staff have gone home, you'll find me rooted on my family-tree feet, staring at the rows and rows of loss.

1

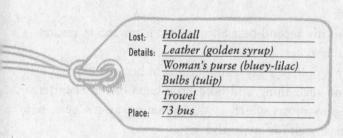

Lost: _Holdall_
Details: _Leather (golden syrup)_
Woman's purse (bluey-lilac)
Bulbs (tulip)
Trowel
Place: _73 bus_

It's seasonal, loss. Outside, autumn rain buckets down full force; inside, a deluge of brollies all need logging and labelling. We're jam-packed in Customer Service. A damp line of people queue the length of the counter, steam gently rising off woollen coats, seeking temporary sanctuary in Lost Property, in search of what they have lost, or delivering what they have found.

I'm sitting at the far end of the counter tagging the lost umbrellas while Anita deals with customers, though when I look over she's rootling through her bag as per.

'Bugger, where's my pen?' she says. _Staff possessions are strictly prohibited from the public area._ 'It's in here somewhere.' She digs deeper into the vast recesses of her handbag. A large flank of matted brown-and-white suede, it is permanently attached to her, clanking her bits and bobs around like Marley's ghost. Whenever I look at Anita she is

3

elbow-deep in that bag, as if birthing a cow, forever groping for one of her slimmer's bars or a squirt of perfume. I have considered suggesting she might be better off with something smaller – a buckled satchel, perhaps? I am always picking up after her – scarf left in the Ladies, hairbrush abandoned on the counter. 'Ta, Dots! Lose my head if it wasn't screwed on.'

Indeed.

I unclip my second-best Sheaffer from my jacket pocket and hand it to her.

'You're a doll,' she says, and returns to her customer.

I am no such thing and hold little hope of the Sheaffer returning to roost, which is disappointing as it's new, a present to myself for my birthday.

When she first started working at Lost Property, I asked Anita what had drawn her here – seeing as it's clearly a challenge to keep hold of her own things, let alone other people's. 'I told the job centre all my skills,' she confessed over a frothy coffee at the Italian next door, firing two white pellets into her mug from a small tube retrieved from her commodious bag. 'Showed them my cosmetics certificate and business plans and they sent me here! What about "Level 3 Diploma in Nail Services" makes them think I'd be good at dealing with people's crap every day?'

She's been here almost as long as I have now. Unlike the others who come and go, Anita stayed. Perhaps the nails never worked out. She didn't say and it's not my place to ask – we've all had our dreams. When I was young I longed to be a librarian. I often sought sanctuary in the quiet order of the public library, delighting in the assured way the librarian splayed my book open, the crinkle of the cellophane jacket. Most of all I loved the confident stamp of the date and the

4

soft slither of the pink ticket leaving the cardboard pocket, knowing the librarian would keep it safe in her file for me till I returned.

They've closed most of them now, the libraries, and Lost Property was the right place for me after all. We are the repository for all the items left on London's buses, black cabs, tubes and trains; we get hundreds of items a day. Loss never stops; it's reliable like that. And the hours are good. Occasionally we have to go on Transport for London 'Awaydays' to stare at flip charts and listen to Lynx-doused lads in their machine-washable suits say 'not a problem' ad infinitum. What do they know of the intricacies of Lost Property? Of loss and its myriad problems? With them, it's all staff development and recruitment. Mind you, we do rather well in recruitment. Recruitment is 'not a problem'. *Ha*. It's an endless procession of temps – students mostly – passing through, wanting a pay packet and a job in the city. Whatever the employment agency finds them will suffice.

I applied.

You see, I know about loss. I know its shape, its weak spots, its corners and sharp edges. I have felt its coordinates. I have sewn its name into the back of its collar.

When I've finished labelling the brollies, I start on a crate of items that came in yesterday from the depot at Victoria coach station. Beyond Customer Service is the back office, and as I sort I am lulled by the comforting thrum that drifts through the doorway as Gabrielle (French exchange student) and Sukanya (drama school) field telephone enquiries.

'Six long-stemmed glasses from John Lewis? Exactly as you described, madam. Your taxi driver brought them in yesterday.'

'You changed from the Central Line to the Northern Line at Tottenham Court Road? . . . I know, those escalators have been out of order for ever, haven't they – it's terrible, too totally tragic.'

Truth be told, Sukanya could try to be a tad less dramatic and a tad more sotto voce – I understand she's practising her acting skills, but there is such a thing as too much projection.

In my crate, there's a woman's cardy in an appealing periwinkle. Looks handmade – that row of pearl buttons sets it off splendidly. I'm guessing she's elderly, an ice-cream whip of hair and an archipelago of liver spots. Mind you, could be a teenager experimenting with a retro look . . . but no, a quick sniff reveals a powdery lily of the valley. I was right first time, usually am. I complete the Dijon label and securely loop it around one of the pearl buttons, then move on to a grubby pond-green man's anorak with half a packet of Polos in one pocket, a pencilled shopping list in the other. The odour this time is less definable – a mélange of mint and mildew with a dab of gravy. Much loved though, the jacket; he'll be upset he left that behind. I fill out the Dijon, double knot it to the zip. What's next? A handbag, rather a nice one to boot. She was asking for trouble, the owner, with that broken clasp. It's only a matter of time before something falls out and gets lost. You have to respect someone, though, who doesn't throw a handbag away at the first sign of wear and tear. Most people don't have that sort of loyalty any more.

Not much inside – Anita, take note – hanky, lipstick, till receipts. Any money or credit cards have already been removed and locked up in Valuables. Mind you, what, I always ask, is the true value of an object? The bag is fine leather, worn but cherished. I can spot quality. I'm not boasting. When you spend all day handling other people's property, you get to know these things.

Mostly it's a parade of phones, plastic travel-card wallets and dog-eared thrillers, so when something special turns up, you take notice, bask for a moment in the glow of its patina. The hanky is a treat – linen and one of Liberty's original prints, I'd argue their best. But the lipstick is a surprise. I don't wear make-up – never really got the hang of it – but Red-Hot Poker? It just doesn't go with the handbag or the hanky. I remove the lid and roll up a few jarring crimson centimetres. Hmm, no pristine diamond tip – it's rounded and smudged with use. Oh, that mismatched lipstick is going to bother me for the rest of the day, like a poppy seed in my teeth.

'I see your admirer was in again, Nita.' Ed nods at a customer tottering out with a walking stick. Despite his actual place of employment being Baker Street station next door, Ed spends a vast amount of his working day propping up our counter, swapping double entendres with Anita and drinking alarmingly milky tea from a chipped red-and-white Arsenal mug.

'Give over, he's not my admirer,' Anita says, unearthing a tub of strawberry lip gloss from her bag. *Staff possessions are strictly prohibited from the* . . . I'm fighting a losing battle. Ed watches transfixed, like a figure in Botticelli's *Adoration of the Magi*, as Anita coats her mouth with slow back-and-forth swoops of shimmering gloss.

'A repeat offender then,' Ed says, breathing unattractively through his nose.

'Takes one to know one.' Anita pouts her lips into a kiss shape at him. 'Quick smoke?'

'Don't mind if I do—'

'Hiya.' Sheila, our latest from SmartChoice Temping Agency, clops in from the back office on heels designed to induce altitude sickness.

Ed's head whips in her direction.

'What are you chatting about?' Sheila SmartChoice shimmies her tiny bottom up on to the counter, liquorice-twisting her stockinged legs.

Ed stares.

Anita pelts the tub of gloss into her bag.

'Nothing, just an old chap who comes in every couple of months, reporting the "loss" of his walking stick.' Anita pauses to punctuate the word with her index fingers, one distressingly sticky.

'He must be ever so forgetful,' says SmartChoice, giving Ed a wink that causes him to slop his tea on the counter.

I staunch Ed's milky ablution with the hanky I keep safety-pinned inside my jacket pocket. The customer in question can give you a precise catalogue of the test scores since the England and Wales Cricket Board took over from Marylebone Cricket Club in 1997. He can also tell you the best time to plant asparagus and broad beans, and knows the complete taxonomy of *Turdidae*. He is not one jot forgetful. He is, I fear, lonely.

'So, what do you do when the man comes in for his stick?' pursues SmartChoice.

'I go get him an unclaimed one from downstairs,' Anita says.

'Oooh, is that allowed?' asks SmartChoice, rabbit-eyed.

'Why not!' says Anita. 'We're buried in sticks, crutches, canes – you name it. Got a fair number of false limbs too,

8

not to mention false teeth and false eyes. How, I ask you, is someone able to get up and walk off the train *without their prosthetic leg*? Miracle cures on the Metropolitan Line? No wonder TfL charge so much for the bloody tickets.' She gives a husky chuckle that has Ed back in her thrall.

I glance at the door; there's a lull right now, but a customer could come in at any moment searching for a lost item and find us dilly-dallying the day away. Clearly, I am the only one concerned.

'Bet the Brolly Dollies were in today, eh, Nita?' Ed says.

'Too right,' Anita says. She flashes Ed a conspiratorial smile, bends forward and says in a querulous voice, '"Excuse me, dear, I seem to have lost my umbrella."'

Ed laughs and, encouraged, Anita continues: '"Could you describe your umbrella?"'

'"Oh, yes," they say. "It's black, and has a handle."'

'"Black with a handle?" I say. "I believe one matching your exact description was handed in this morning. I'll get it for you."'

'That's amazing you knew we had it,' says SmartChoice. The girl is as vacuous as an open window.

'Coming for that smoke, Ed?' Anita says.

'I better shift and get myself back to work,' says Ed, showing no sign of shifting. Anita stands for a moment, bites her glossy lip, then hoists the beast of a bag on to her shoulder.

'Dot, cover me, will you? I'll only be a quick five.'

Knowing it's going to be more like a long fifteen, I leave my crate of lost items and take her place at the counter as she struts off to join the soggy smokers on the fire escape.

I turn to SmartChoice.

'Unless you want to be filed under miscellaneous, may I suggest you return to work?'

'Laters.' SmartChoice untwizzles her legs and teeters back to the office. Ed gazes after her, sighs and slinks out of the door.

I neaten a pile of Lost Item forms and straighten my jacket in readiness for the next customer. I do not condone Anita's laissez-faire attitude with the walking sticks and umbrellas, handing them out willy-nilly, but she has been facing some trials of late. After years of putting up with her porcine husband's dalliances and semi-permanent state of intoxication, she has finally given him his marching orders. He recently showed up inebriated and covered in Elizabeth Arden's Provocative Woman, and she threw him out on the spot, followed by a tray of crispy pork balls. 'I spent the weekend on the sofa getting intimate with Gordon and his best mate Tonic,' Anita said when she regaled me with the news, panda-eyed. It transpired she had also made the acquaintance of Harveys Bristol Cream and faced the silent watches of the night with Napoleon Brandy. I pass no judgement. On occasion, I have entertained myself similarly. I brewed her a cup of Lapsang Souchong and popped *Exploring the Greek Islands* (a truly first-rate travel guide) into her bag.

The door opens and an elderly gentleman in a soft, putty-coloured raincoat and tweed cap slowly approaches the counter.

'How may I help you, sir?' I say.

'I come more in hope than expectation.' Rainwater traces the wrinkles in his face, beads his thick, grey eyebrows. 'Quite my own fault,' he continues. 'The holdall.'

I lick my finger and thumb, peel a Lost Item form from my stack, unclip my silver Sheaffer from my jacket pocket.

'A holdall?'

'Yes. Leather. Sort of a golden-syrup colour. Old, but in pretty good shape, better than me.' He gives a dry chuckle that turns into a cough.

Three small darns in his cap; whoever did them matched the thread exactly.

'Excuse me.' He unfurls a crumpled handkerchief. Raindrops from his coat splatter across the counter. One lands on my jacket sleeve.

'Last Friday I was on the bus,' the old man continues.

'Which one?'

'Stoke Newington to Oxford Street.'

I nod, write '73' on my form.

'What was in the holdall?'

'Let me see . . . the purse, tulip bulbs, a trowel . . .'

'Can you describe the purse?'

'It's blue.'

'What shade? Sky? Sea? Squid-ink?'

'Sort of bluey-lilac, with a little gold snap closure.'

'A woman's purse?'

'Yes, Joan's. My wife.'

'And how much would you say was in it?'

'How much?' His forehead puckers.

'Money.' My hand hovers over the form.

'Oh, quite empty. Her favourite, you see, so it's nice to have it close.'

'I see.'

I do.

'You mentioned tulip bulbs? A trowel?'

'I often visit Abney Park Cemetery. I take *The Times* and do the crossword. I prefer the concise but Joanie was a devil for the cryptic. Always spot on with the, er . . . whatsits . . .'

'Anagrams?'

'Yes!' Such a kind smile he has. 'Anagrams. A real dab hand. Fifty-four years and she never made a mistake . . .' His Adam's apple bobs. 'So, if I'm wrestling with a tricky puzzle, I hop on the bus to Abney and we do it together.'

I look down; the word 'holdall' blurs on the page before me.

'It's really just Joanie's purse I'd like back. It's small, like this . . .' He cups his hands gently, as if holding a tiny bird – opens and closes them. They shake a little but I can clearly see the shape of the purse, hear the bright chirrup of the snap closure.

Sellotape. Superglue. Safety Pin. My special words. I repeat them in my head while I concentrate on breathing. Substantial, aniseed balls of words, dependable, safe.

'I'll do my best, sir. Let me take your contact details. Your name?'

'Appleby, John Appleby.'

After Mr Appleby leaves, I manage to deal with the next two customers but am glad when the loud clanking of an overfilled handbag behind me heralds the return of Anita.

'You're a star, Dots.'

'Must get these things shelved,' I say, grabbing the crate of brollies, desperate for the sanctuary of the stacks.

I search the shelves for the holdall, even though I know we don't have it. I look because I know what it is to need something the way Mr Appleby needs that chirruping purse.

I still have Dad's pipe. Dunhill. Tortoiseshell body, ebony-black stem, and when I dip my nose into the bowl, that tug of cherry tobacco . . . I ration myself to one small sniff a day. Once, I followed a man from Baker Street to Marble Arch because of that smell. Occasionally, I slip the stem of the pipe between my lips – we have the same slight overbite, Dad and I. My teeth settle into the ridge made by his and, anchored, I inhale. I try to breathe him back.

2

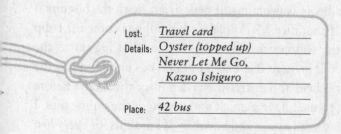

Lost:	Travel card
Details:	Oyster (topped up)
	Never Let Me Go,
	Kazuo Ishiguro
Place:	42 bus

My commute consists of one train, two buses and a brisk clip up Baker Street. On my way to work I'm always on the lookout. I can't help myself, it goes with the job. I can tell when something is about to go, about to be lost. There's a kind of silence. A pause. I catch myself waiting for it. The woman in the coriander-green coat four seats in front of me on the bus might very well be holding on to her bag but she is paying no attention whatsoever to her silk scarf, which slips from her shoulders and flops over the rail of the seat behind her. Thankfully her neighbour, a girl sporting impressively large headphones, notices and returns it. Then there's that young chap with his brand-new briefcase, the square of his lunchbox pressing its shape into the soft leather. He'll abandon the lunchbox after a few weeks, realizing that to fit in with the boys you have to go to the pub at lunchtime and buy the first round, not sit by yourself eating your sandwiches. But right now, he's new, hopeful. Gripping that briefcase too tightly though, that's often when things get lost.

As usual, I'm first to arrive at work. I let myself in and make a cup of Lapsang in what passes as the staff kitchen – it's just a nook at the far end of the back office with a kettle and communal box of tea-bags (I bring my own leaves), but our boss Brian is generous, if pedestrian, with the biscuits. I wonder if that nice Mr Appleby's holdall has come in? I slip behind the counter in Customer Service and log on to the computer. If an item is left on a London bus and found by the driver, it is held at the Arriva bus depot for three days before it comes to us. I have a quick scan through the online files. I confess it's a tad above and beyond – if I did this for every lost item, where would we be? Drowning in a sea of unstacked brollies, that's where. It's just that . . . well . . . it would be rather splendid if I could call him with good news. I search under 'Appleby', then 'holdall', and then for good measure 'bag' ('kit-' 'shoulder-' and 'carrier-') then 'tote', 'leather' and 'luggage'. My travails reveal a leather belt with a buckle in the shape of Texas, and a lady's beaded evening bag. Nothing for Mr Appleby. I log out, deflated. It is possible the holdall was found by another passenger on the bus; if so, it might come in this week. If something's going to come to us it usually comes quickly. Purloin or proffer is the modus operandi of the general public, for better or worse. Mind you, I can't say a bad word about the people who return lost property. Last year over 13,000 keys were handed in, though only a fraction were claimed – this discrepancy speaks to: 1) a heartwarming desire to help, and 2) an absolute lack of hope.

It's barely 8.30 a.m. and the doors don't open to customers for half an hour, so no other staff are in yet. I take the

16

service lift down to the stacks and spend a very relaxing twenty minutes shelving yesterday's logged items. I find it quite meditative, shelving. The lady's periwinkle cardy goes to stack five – 'Women's Clothing: Jumpers and Woollens' – offering cheery company to a faded yellow ribbed sweater. At stack seven – 'Assorted Bags, Briefcases and Trollies' – I slip the handbag with the broken clasp alongside a rather outré cork shoulder bag with the words 'Made in Portugal' stamped on the strap, thus collating a shabby chic/ cosmopolitan/bohemian fusion which I think rather works.

It takes me a moment to find just the right spot for the anorak with the half-packet of Polo mints in the 'Coats and Outdoor Wear' stack. Quite wrong to put it next to that heavy-duty army camouflage flak jacket. No, no, no. You see, there's an art to organizing loss; it is a world not without its heroes. My *héroïne véritable* is Phyllis Pearsall, who, on becoming lost in London with only a sub-par map to hand, conceived the *London A–Z*. What a pioneer! A true pathfinder. She made such a worthwhile contribution to ameliorate loss, to help us find our way around this metropolis. Of course, then people started to lose their copies of the *A–Z*. We used to have two whole shelf stacks of them: hardbacks, paperbacks and – less attractive but admittedly handy – spiral-bounds. They rarely come in any more though, because nowadays people prefer to navigate the city in head-bowed deference to a moving blob on their phones, which, in turn, now line the shelves of the Valuables lock-up. Like I say, loss never ends. But when I think of Phyllis walking 3,000 miles in order to ascertain and note individual house numbers on main roads in her quest to stop us getting lost, I am eternally grateful for her care and attention. I snuggle the anorak between a cherry-red cagoule and a shiny azure belted raincoat, and stand back to admire the triptych. I hope, in my own way, I make a small difference to the lost charges in my care.

'How are we this morning?' From the bumptious use of the plural it can only be Neil Burrows.

I turn and sure enough it is he, lurking behind me.

'You're in early,' I say, searching for an escape route. The aisle between stacks six and seven is looking good, save for a tartan shopping trolley adrift.

'I'm off to a rather important meeting with Bri,' he says. 'Some pretty interesting stuff going on with TfL at the moment.'

Puffed up and on patrol, jiggling the six-key set hanging from his trouser belt and acting as if the whole of Lost Property is under his purview rather than just one moderately sized Valuables cage, Neil Burrows puts me in mind of Miss Hyde's Derbyshire Redcap cockerel, Chaunticleer.

For a few discordant years, I was sent to Miss Hyde for piano lessons. In the garden of her 1950s semi, Chaunticleer shuffled despondently, scratching bleakly between the cracks of the pink-stoned patio. Alopecia had taken most of his neck feathers, revealing long tracks of yellow, scarred flesh. I'd often stare out of Miss Hyde's French windows as she berated me over a wrong note or incorrect answer ('B sharp? I wish you would *be sharp*, young lady!') and watch Chaunticleer bothering one of his scabs, consoling myself that his lot was worse than mine.

One day, steeled for an agonizing hour of 'Clair de Lune', I found Miss Hyde transfixed, looking out at her garden.

'Dot! Come and take a look at my girls!' Sensing a reprieve from Debussy, I rushed to join her at the window. Her patio was pulsing with the fluffy brown, white and orange bodies of half a dozen newly acquired chickens.

'Named 'em after the suffragettes,' she said, a noble arch to her brow. 'Thought it might give them something to aspire to, you know.' I eagerly followed my piano teacher's dewy gaze out on to Emmeline, Christabel, Sylvia and Adela Pankhurst, Lady Constance Lytton and General Flora Drummond. Miss Hyde's girls were a sprightly bunch who gave her a frisson of excitement I had not previously noticed. Her transformation, however, was nothing compared to that of Chaunticleer. I barely recognized him. His sullen stoop was gone, replaced by what one could only call a shimmy as he squawked and sashayed around *his* girls, bright-eyed, expectant and erect.

Yes, Neil Burrows was a dead ringer for Chaunticleer.

'Me and Bri are like this,' Neil Burrows says, wrapping his middle finger tightly over his index. He steps closer and says on a stream of hot halitosis, 'I could put in a good word for you if you like?'

'Thanks, but no need.' Yes, nipping past that tartan trolley is definitely going to be my fastest route, then down to the end of the stacks, up in the lift back to Customer Service.

'Well, think about it. I can see you in a more managerial role. Perhaps a drink one evening to discuss strategies?' His hands jangle his Valuables keys and he steps forward.

At exactly the same moment, as if we are in a meticulously timed square-dance, I sashay to the side and past him.

'Must get back upstairs,' I say, and make my escape.

'All right, Dots?' Anita clanks in and takes her seat behind the counter seconds before the doors open to the public. The woman certainly lives on the edge. 'Do anything exciting last night?' she asks, already well into her bag obstetrics.

'Just a quiet night in.'

'Any plans for tonight?'

'Nothing special.' I admire Anita's fortitude. She makes these exact enquiries of me every day despite always receiving the same response.

'You don't fancy coming to a dance class with me, do you? There's one in Camden in a few weeks' time that looks fab. Thought I might try it out.'

I'm about to nip this startling variant in the bud when I notice that Anita is no longer ensconced in her bag but looking at me, a redness to her eyes, an extra layer of gloss on her lips. That added upholstery to get through the day.

I used to love to dance, old-fashioned numbers – the foxtrot, the Viennese waltz, the cha-cha. My feet balanced on Dad's slippers. Once he danced all the loose change out of his pockets; a spill of silver spraying behind us as he twirled me around the room. I haven't danced in a long time.

'Please, Dots,' Anita says.

I nod, hoping when it comes to the time she will have forgotten.

After lunch I give SmartChoice an induction into the procedures of Customer Service. Having spent her first day in the back office doing online data entry, today she becomes privy to the intricacies of labelling and logging. I'm keen to teach and she seems equally keen to learn – she is certainly rather taken with my uniform.

'So, you actually wear that *by choice*?' she says.

20

The Lost Property office has not officially had a uniform since 1947. However, my chosen livery consists of a pleated skirt and matching jacket. Felt. Felt knows its own shape, doesn't languish and loop like all those cheap synthetic fabrics. Felt stands up for itself. The thing that would make my uniform perfect is a belt. Something solid. A cummerbund? Next to Anita, glamorous in her Lycra trousers and billowing see-through blouses, and SmartChoice, who today sports a postage stamp of a skirt with skyscraper heels, I suppose I am somewhat the outlier. But still.

'Yes, Sheila, because a uniform shows respect: for yourself, for your job and for other people's possessions. This way, please, let's get on with your orientation.'

I lead her behind the counter and pick up a pile of the Dijons.

'Found items are handed in by black-cab drivers, by Overground and Underground train staff, and come to us from the London bus depots. Members of the public also hand items in. Whenever you receive an item, whoever you get it from, the first thing you must do, *every single time*, is fill out this tag.' I hand her a Dijon. It feels like quite a moment, almost akin to the bestowing of a bequest, handing over the mantle. She holds the tag at arm's length, dangles it from its string and wrinkles her nose.

'Why don't we just do it all online? Or a phone app?'

I whip back the tag, take a breath.

'Found items are manually tagged before they are shelved. Tagging is *extremely* important. You write the date the item was found here' – I point to the appropriate place on the Dijon – 'the location where it was found here, and then

21

you write a very precise description of the item in the space remaining here. When you have completed the tag, you tie it to the item. I strongly recommend a double knot – like so. Once you have labelled the item, you do the data entry so it can be easily looked up on the computer, and then you take it down to the stacks and shelve it in the appropriate place. Follow me.'

SmartChoice clip-clops behind me through Customer Service to the back office, past the kitchen nook and the staff cloakrooms.

I lead her to the service lift at the far end of the room and press the button down to the stacks. As we step out I flick on the overheads. She gasps and stands open-mouthed. I admit I'm surprised yet delighted by her reaction.

'I know' – I nod – 'takes your breath away.'

'Gucci!' she squeals, pointing to a shelf of bags. 'Who'd leave that behind? Real too, not one of those fakes!'

'The stacks are ordered and organized in specific categories.' I swiftly stride down the aisles of shelved items, pointing out the different sections: 'Men's Clothing', 'Walking Sticks and Crutches', 'Prams and Strollers', all the way to 'Miscellaneous' at the far end of the room. 'As you can see, it is the size of a small aircraft hangar down here, so the sooner you can become familiar with the layout, with what goes where, the better. Can't have staff getting lost!' I turn to see if she appreciates my little joke. She is several aisles behind, staring every which way, agog.

'OMG. I literally can't believe there's so much stuff down here. I mean, I never even knew this place existed till the agency got me the job.'

'Lost Property has been here in this exact spot dealing with loss since 1933,' I say, standing a little taller in my uniform.

'It's sort of like a TK Maxx, isn't it? Just with some really minging stuff mixed in,' SmartChoice says, pointing to the pond-green anorak.

Phyllis Pearsall, where are you?

'Sheila, your responsibility is to diligently log and shelve every object. I strongly recommend spending some time down here, getting to know the layout so you can do your job to the very best of your ability.'

'Totes. Ooh, what's this?' She trots over to the 'Children's Toys' stack and picks up a plastic bag from the shelf, reads out the Dijon tag. '"Slime kit, coloured-in colouring book." Who's going to come looking for that?'

I go to her, retrieve the bag and return it to its place, quite firmly.

'If someone has gone to the trouble of bringing an item in, be it a single glove, a mediocre English essay or indeed slime, we label it, we log it and we shelve it. Once here it is under our care, our protection. Once here it is Lost Property.'

Although I had been rather looking forward to it, I admit it's a relief when SmartChoice's orientation is over and I finally get back to Customer Service. I don't think her heart is really in the work. She does not, I fear, have the makings of a Phyllis.

The afternoon passes in a comforting blur of forgotten phones, brollies and scarves. My last customer of the day is a schoolboy who sports a pair of distressingly smudged spectacles. All bones and angles, he jiggles nervously at the counter.

'Hello there,' I say.

He stares at me through the foggy lattice of his fingerprints. I resist an urge to proffer my hanky.

'I . . . I . . . left my travel card on the bus.'

'What was it in? A wallet? A holder?'

'Never let me go.' My Sheaffer hovers. 'Our set text,' he adds. Clarity is no nearer my grasp. 'Our book for GCSE English? Kazuo Ishiguro?' he says, ending on that upward questioning tone the young are so prone to, as if everything is obvious and utterly confusing at the same time.

'Ah.' I add this vital information to my form.

'I put it in my book,' he says, 'sort of like a bookmark.' Across the counter his hands mime placing a small flat object inside a book shape and then closing the book shape by pressing his palms together – just in case I don't know what putting a bookmark in a book might look like. I take no offence. I find these small choreographies of loss rather moving, the gestures that carve an object out, retrace its presence to the moment just before it is lost. The boy's hands are large, rangy; he has yet to grow into them.

'I put it there to keep it safe,' he adds glumly, hefting his glasses up the mountain of his nose.

'To clarify, you have lost both your travel card and a novel?' I ask.

'The book doesn't matter – English is pants – but Mum'll kill me if I lose my Oyster. She just topped up the balance.'

I grip my sturdy Sheaffer.

'Books are your friends,' I say. He shrugs, bites a piece of skin from his thumb and swallows. 'Without books where would we be?' I persist. 'They take us to all sorts of places.'

'I dunno . . . but without my Oyster I'll be . . . nowhere.'

Before he leaves, I slide a slim column of card across the counter.

'Safer than your Oyster. It's from World Book Day.' He peels the bookmark up from the varnished wood with his gnawed fingernails.

'To keep?'

'Yes, to keep. Now you won't lose your place.'

'Thanks.'

I see myself at his age, half unfurled, in my hand-me-down clothes from my sister, Philippa, nothing quite fitting, especially me. Never getting it right, not like the other girls with their bright white knee socks and sharp triangles of sandwiches, their flashy bags of crisps and glinting pierced ears. I'd sit solo in the playground with the domino sandwiches Dad made me – half white-bread, half brown-bread rectangles – wrapped in greaseproof paper, tied with green garden twine.

I glance down at my uniform, my sturdy brogues, and wonder for a moment how much has actually changed.

I still make Dad's domino sandwiches, bring them in for my packed lunch. Before we moved Mum into The Pines, I'd make up a parcel for her as well and leave them in the fridge. This morning, I wasn't thinking and made two.

Well, no need to worry about tonight's supper.

3

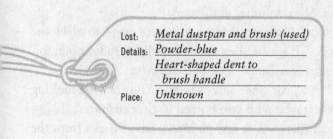

Lost:	_Metal dustpan and brush (used)_
Details:	_Powder-blue_
	Heart-shaped dent to
	brush handle
Place:	_Unknown_

Thursday after work: Philippa has summoned me to 'discuss' arrangements for Mum. I glimpse her first, through the bobbled diamond pane of glass in her front door – a discombobulation of silver, pink and blue particles. Like that, she seems possible. Approachable. Then the door opens and my sister comes sharply into focus. She wears ice-pink lipstick and matching nail polish; silvery half-moons dome her eyelids. The overall ensemble approximates chilled prawn cocktail.

'Not today, thank you!' She taps the ceramic sign on the front of the door and squawks with laughter.

NO COLD CALLERS –

NO SALESMEN –

NO RELIGIOUS GROUPS

Apparently, according to my sister, my uniform makes me look as if I'm from the Salvation Army. Thankfully it turns out that Philippa is on the phone, so I am saved more of her bon mots. She waves me into the sitting room.

'Make yourself comfortable.' A challenge rather than an invitation, as her house is all hard lines and angles – not unlike her. She continues with her call.

'Only Dot.' She's got her phone voice on – total Home Counties RP. It's as if she's a wartime RAF radio operator. *Hello Tonbridge, Tango, Oscar, November, Bravo . . .*

I head towards the only vaguely comfortable-looking armchair, arrayed with two pursed leather cushions.

'Don't sit there – I've just plumped,' she shrieks from the hallway before resuming her phone call.

I perch on the end of a long, liver-hued sofa, its sides chrome-armoured. Eventually, with a graze of powder and sharp nip of L'Air du Temps, Philippa knocks her cheek to mine.

'How's life?' she says, in a tone that suggests she's not entirely sure I have one.

'Tippety-top.'

Her fingers twitch. She's always moving, my sister. A jangling bracelet, a jigging foot. Eager to be up and off, on to the next thing. Or maybe that's just when she's with me.

'And the "job"?' I see the inverted commas shining like two well-polished knobs. Philippa is ever ready to point out that my chosen career is renowned neither for its remuneration nor its prestige. I've worked at Lost Property for well over a decade, yet my sister is still on the lookout for a 'proper job' for me. She has sent me advertisements for a tranche of unsuitable roles for which I have neither interest nor skill:

bank clerk, nutritionist, radiologist. *You should try it, Dot – it's just taking a photo with a really large camera. And it means you can tell people you work in medicine!*

I know that Philippa lies to her friends about what I do. At one of her drinks evenings, I spent a very long gin and tonic talking with a stockbroker friend of her husband Gerald. My sister had been on a quest to align me romantically with Gerald's pal Stafford for some time – my single status being even more embarrassing to her than my career. Stafford ticked all the boxes: big salary, big house, big ego.

He wedged me up against a glass-and-chrome display cabinet in Philippa's sitting room and enthused about how exciting my job must be. Though vexed by his proximity, I admit I was somewhat pleased to have such an interest taken in my work – a rare occurrence in my sister's house.

'What with Crossrail and the new links all the way out to Reading, you must be going from strength to strength,' he said.

'Well, we certainly keep busy.'

It was only when he said, 'Tell me, is it true what they're saying about Catford being the new Hackney? Is this a good time to invest?' that I realized we were talking at cross-purposes.

'I didn't lie!' Philippa protested when confronted. 'I just said you worked in "property management" – same thing, give or take. Honestly, you can be so pedantic.'

Needless to say, I have not attended one of her drinks parties since.

'The job is fine,' I say.

Philippa's laser gaze patrols the coffee table for dust motes then swivels to my right hand, honing in on where the oval pads of my fingers make contact with the buffed chrome of her sofa. I take a firmer, smudgier grip and see her wince.

'And how are you?' I concede.

Then she's away: next-door's extension (too big), Gerald's promotion (not big enough), Melanie's A-level choices (maths, double maths, computer science).

'And Sam?' I ask.

That gets the arms going. She has this thing that she does with her arms. In the middle of a conversation she'll start waving them about. She's doing Spray and Wipe. Can't help herself. She's never happier than with a tin of cleaning spray and a duster, removing evidence, clearing up a mess. So, whenever she gets caught in a challenging or emotional situation – a Labour candidate at the door, or having coffee with me – off go the arms. It's quite balletic if you don't know its origins. If you do, it's an assault.

'The boy is impossible.'

'Still doing his drama?'

'Oh, the humanities!' she decries, defining my nephew's love of theatre as a disaster of equal magnitude to the Hindenburg. The arms rev at double speed. 'Where on earth will *they* get him?'

'He's only twelve.'

'You always take his side, Dot. You're such a softy. You're just like—'

The arms freeze mid-spray. The word hangs between us.

Dad.

That's how we are, Philippa and I, always bumping each other's edges, bruising each other's corners.

'Coffee?'

Before I have time to respond she escapes to the kitchen, finding balm in a barrage of matching china. When she returns, the conversation is on an even keel for a while as I steer it through the trusty waters of Melanie's Oxbridge potential, and Philippa and Gerald's recent cruise.

'Our state room had the biggest balcony *by far* and we were invited to the captain's table every night. So embarrassing! And the staff! Nothing too much trouble. All Polish or Romanian, but still ever so nice. Big pours with the vino.'

It isn't long, though, before we are wind over tide. I confess, I start it.

'I meant to ask, do you have Mum's dustpan and brush set?'

Initially reluctant to be dragged away from the heady delights of the captain's table, she flaps the question away with a light Spray and Wipe, but I stand fast.

'Her old powder-blue metal dustpan set – have you seen it?'

'Why on earth would I?'

'When we packed up her things to take to The Pines last month?'

'Why would we have taken that? One of the reasons we chose The Pines was its excellent hygiene rating. You did tell Mum she's not expected to clean her own room, didn't you? Honestly!'

'I think it's more to do with the object itself. She kept asking for it all that day we were moving her in, remember? I want to bring it when I visit.'

'The one she used to keep in the spidery cupboard under the stairs?'

I nod.

'Ugh.' Philippa shivers. 'No, I don't bloody have it. Why can't you just take her something normal? Something she actually needs? What's wrong with a pot of hyacinths and a nice dried-fruit platter for her bowels?'

'Nothing, of course. But I think the dustpan is about wanting something familiar. Having her old bits and bobs around—'

'Something *familiar*? What about photographs? Books? Ornaments – like that pair of china King Charles Spaniels that used to sit on the mantel. Ugly as sin, but surely a step up from the dustpan?'

'Seeing the dustpan and brush might make her feel more like . . . her old self.'

'How on earth could it do that? Why do you have to be so . . . so . . . ?'

Here we go. I watch her rifle through the arsenal of words she stockpiles for me.

'Anomalous? Perspicacious? Sagacious?' I offer – we Salvation Army types are ever keen to help.

She shakes her head despairingly. 'There you go again, see. Saying things like that. You're just . . .'

Careful.

'Odd, Dot. Just so . . . odd.'

Odd? A new recruit.

Philippa refills my cup and turns the handle of the milk jug towards me. Whatever my sister's faults, she has perfect table manners. I imagine when she flies off on her jaunts with Gerald, she waits until all the passengers on the plane have been served their meal before she takes the foil off her rectangular dinner tray and bursts the plastic cutlery free from its cellophane pack.

'Last time I visited, Mum was going on about somebody called Maria – one of the staff, I presume,' Philippa says, pinching a cube of sugar between silver tongs. 'She doesn't have a clue who her daughters are but clearly remembers her old dustpan fondly.' In the silence that ensues, the sugar cube falls into her coffee cup. We watch it break the surface – a small cannonball – before it sinks to the bottom.

It was always Mum and Philippa, Dad and me. Philippa has Mum's light colouring and breakable slim build. I have Dad's brown eyes and thick dark hair. Two light, two dark, like domino sandwiches. At the weekends they went shopping, we went on adventures; Friday evenings we listened to his 78 rpm records, they watched TV; family games nights we were in charge of Chance and Community Chest, they had Properties and the Bank. Philippa would lick her forefinger and thumb and dole out the candy-coloured banknotes just like the lady at Barclays. She liked being banker even more than she liked playing Monopoly.

That's just how it was: Mum and Philippa, Dad and Dot.

'Anyway, we need to discuss visiting hours, get a regular schedule timetabled,' Philippa says. 'What about if you do Saturdays, Gerald will come with the kids Sundays, and I'll pop in as and when on my flexi-days.'

Not so much of a discussion, then, more of a fait accompli.

'And we need to talk about the house,' Philippa continues, opening and closing the sugar tongs as if she is trying to catch something.

'Are you thinking of getting something else done?' With its new wraparound deck and kitchen 'island' I'm unsure what there is left to do to my sister's house, except perhaps crack a bottle of champagne against its side and launch it.

'Mum's house,' she says.

'What do you mean?'

'Well, I don't see her coming back, do you?'

'I suppose . . . probably not, but—'

'There's enough money in her account to cover the cost of The Pines in the short term, but we need to make plans . . .' The tongs snap, searching for the right words. 'And right now it's a sellers' market, excellent potential to get a significant dividend.'

I recognize her husband's lingo.

'So you've already discussed this with Gerald?'

'I may have mentioned it. He does know about finance, after all, and this could be a great opportunity for you.'

'For me? To my mind it leaves me homeless.'

'Well, yes, but you could put down a deposit, buy something. Perfect time.'

'I thought you said it was a sellers' market?'

She sighs. 'I knew you would be difficult about this.'

'But I live there, remember?'

'I know, I know.' The tongs snap faster now. 'But surely you never thought that was going to be permanent? People don't recover from dementia. We knew we'd have to make other arrangements sooner or later. And then when she broke her hip . . .' A pause before she delivers her closing statement, just long enough to remind me I am the guilty party, that Mum's fall happened on my watch. 'Well, it's just ended up being sooner, that's all.'

A silence. The tongs hover. Philippa resets her face into what she thinks is an encouraging smile. 'Think about it – this could be an exciting opportunity for you, a chance to buy your own place . . . Fresh start! What about something on the coast, or further afield? Nothing to stop you from making all kinds of new choices.'

'Apart from the fact that my job is in London.'

'What about a flat in Paris?'

'Paris? Well, that would be a significant commute to Baker Street.'

'I mean, go back and do something with your languages – you were so good at all that. And you were happy there.'

The hem of a damson-hued winter coat, the city heart-breakingly beautiful in its lacing of frost. The woman at the greengrocer's blowing on her beetroot-stained fingers: '*Fraîchement!*' she would call, stamping her feet on the icy pavement. Then spring and Paris at her most lovely, the window-box of sharp-scented geraniums on the balcony of my apartment in the 14th arrondissement.

'That was a lifetime ago. I hardly remember.'

Philippa sighs.

'Well, I'm scheduling Greenridge, Cooper and Price to do the valuation. They're highly professional.'

'I need more time—'

'Got to get on. Unless you can afford to pay Mum's board and lodging?'

A pause. Then the tongs give a final triumphant snap.

'Good,' Philippa says, 'that's decided. Time to make a change. Can't sit around for ever.'

In unison, we stand up.

She comes to the door to see me off. Another knock of L'Air du Temps.

'Take care, Dot.' It sounds like a warning. At the end of her driveway I turn and see her standing silhouetted in the door frame, spraying and wiping delicately in the evening light, as if I am still there, annoying her, making a mess.

*

I feel a bit shaky on the journey home. Seeking sustenance and solace, I stop at the corner shop to replenish my soup supply. Today they're doing a two-for-one offer on 'Soups from Around the World', and as I have never been one to turn down a bargain or a cultural experience, I include two tins labelled 'Tandoori Nights'.

In the tiny kitchen of Mum's maisonette, I ignore the ring pull and get out my tin opener, warm the soup on the stove and bring my bowl into the quiet sitting room. The last puzzle Mum bought is on the table, unfinished. It's an Alpine scene, a challenge with all that white. Perfect to focus an anxious and agitated mind.

I assemble the slanting sides of the mountain, appreciating the nuances of grey-white, blue-white and white-white, but to tell the truth, even the majesty of the Alps can only partially distract. A book? A book might help take my mind off Philippa's news about the house sale. My travel guides are my salvation. I have a carefully curated selection of cast-offs from work. They almost never get collected, the guides, yet they are such gems. I confess that over the years I've amassed quite an archive – well, that's the Piccadilly Line from Heathrow for you! I love their pencilled marginalia, dog-eared pages folded to remember beloved cafes, favourite parks and gardens underlined, sites of interest decorated with exclamation marks, with little fireworks of stars. The occasional cautionary frowny face for the cafe/hike/hotel that disappointed.

I peruse my travel guide library – it covers all seven continents and the entirety of Mum's bookcase. I run my finger along the spines and stop on *Discover India!* Perfect. An entirely fitting intellectual buttered roll, as it were, to my soup.

I read that the lotus is the sacred flower of that venerable country. Apparently, the lotus seed waits in a muddy bog for thousands of years before it blossoms. What stubborn belief in one's own existence! How admirable!

Despite the fortitude of the lotus, I can't concentrate. The thing is, it's so quiet without Mum. I moved in with her a year ago when her dementia became more pronounced: spectacles frozen in the ice cube compartment of the fridge; the smell of Camembert oozing obscenely from the bathroom medicine cabinet, announcing a distinctly unsterile environment. Although, come to think of it, I can see the advantage to storing specs in the fridge: one would always have a fresh icy stare to hand. *Ha*. I could have used that on Philippa today – a chilling glance might have frozen her in her tracks with all that talk of Greenridge, Cooper & Price and sellers' markets. Whoops, a cold spoonful of Tandoori Nights puddles at the foot of the Alps. Perhaps soup wasn't the best choice for this evening's repast, as I seem to be a tad shaky still. Luckily I'm in my uniform, so it's just a whisk of a hanky unpinned from my jacket and the mountainside glistens, pristine once more.

I didn't know how it would be, just Mum and me living together, but I felt it was my duty. Since Dad, we've not been what SmartChoice might refer to as 'besties'. I'd see her at Christmas, her birthday, occasional family get-togethers, but that was about it. Philippa lives nearby and the two of them were thick as the proverbial. She deliberated over taking Mum in to live with her when the dementia took hold, but the stress of Melanie's private maths tutorials coincided with the pressure of Gerald's 'targets' and the drama of Sam's rehearsals for Jem in *To Kill a Mockingbird*, and it seemed their household could not tolerate such a domestic balancing act. And Mum wanted to stay in her own home. My landlord was threatening to double the rent on my flat, and a new-build multi-storey monstrosity across the street seemed to grow a floor each week.

And of course, I wanted to help.

Mind you, it means a significant commute to work, not to mention the closer proximity to my sister. Although my old flat wasn't up to much, I'd become quite partial to the silver birch outside my bedroom window, the soft curve of the original Victorian banister in the communal hallway. I miss my Fridays, when I'd hop on the number 74 after work and spend a couple of hours ensconced in the velvety darkness of Ciné Lumière in South Kensington, treating myself to a supper of salade au chèvre chaud in the cafe-restaurant afterwards.

But there you are.

I didn't have much to bring when I moved in. Mostly it was just my travel guides.

'What's all that tat?' Philippa asked, when she came to pick me up and found me with one suitcase, double belted with a leather strap, and a cardboard box full of guides.

'My book collection,' I said, with the merest sliver of pride. She snorted.

'Collection?' she said. 'They're worthless. Most of them haven't even got covers!'

I resisted 'Don't judge a book by its cover,' but did allow 'They are collectors' items by dint of the fact I collect them.'

She wrinkled her nose and picked up *All Things Andalucía!* – one of my favourites – by its corner. 'Do you actually plan on going to any of these places again?'

'There are many ways of circumnavigating the globe,' I said, rescuing poor Andalucía. 'I see myself now as more of a literary flâneur, mentally traversing whitewashed pathways and taking in breathtaking vistas. It's amazing where one can be transported to if one puts one's mind to it.'

She had her special Dot look on her face, the one that shows she despairs of me, so I said no more.

I left behind my small breakfast table to be collected by the Samaritans. In fact, I think I bought it from them originally, so there was a prosaic poetry in that. Completely unmarked, except for a single ring from a cup of Lapsang left alone one day.

Everything in my new life with Mum was meticulously timetabled by Philippa:

6 a.m.:	Dot wakes Mum with tea in bed. (No sugar!)
6.30 a.m.:	Breakfast of lightly boiled eggs every other day, yoghurt on the in-betweens.
7 a.m.:	Dot hands over to Admiral nurses.
Noon:	Meals on Wheels.
1–2 p.m.:	Nap and tablets. (Philippa will call from work to check.)
2–4.30 p.m.:	'Memory Club' or similar excursion with Kent Dementia Support.
4.30–6 p.m.:	Home Help cleans house and makes tea. (Dot: remember to leave money in envelope every Friday.)

| 6 p.m.: | Dot home. |
| 7.30 p.m.: | Supper. (<u>No cheese!</u>) |

Philippa took Mum at weekends.

Mum's maisonette is all white surfaces and reflective sheens, nowhere to hide. Mum and I moved between the kitchen and the sitting room, and tried to ignore the silhouettes of ourselves flitting like ghosts. A mother who did not know her daughter and a daughter who no longer recognized the woman her mother had become.

And yet, I miss the strangest things: the rasp of her slippers on the rattan mat in the hall, the middle-of-the-night loo flush, the rattling of the front-door chain lock when she fancied one of her late-night constitutionals. Poor Mum. I feel the absence of her presence, miss the balance of taking two cups of tea down the hallway, lopsided now with just the one. I miss the vocal sliding scale of her yawns, the creak of her bones, the gurgle of her stomach. I miss the sudden chortle of her laugh in the other room, and the accompanying Tourette-like swing of her crossed leg as she watched her programmes. The ones with storylines began to upset and confuse her, so in the end I left the television on a channel that played a range of baking and home improvement shows. The TV glowed cosily; egg whites folded into creamed butter and sugar, thick coats of paint slathered on dark wood. The sight would comfort us both. Highly informative too, those programmes.

Sometimes I'd leave the room for a moment and not realize the programme had changed; I'd find myself mesmerized by a close-up of a lathe knurling a pine table leg only to realize it was actually a spatula layering icing. Perhaps there was a relief in becoming like Mum, sliding into a world where a man in overalls frosted buttercream on to a wall, a baker knifed putty on to a Victoria sponge. A release in taking up residence in a blurred landscape of cakes and carpentry and the intoxicating oblivion of forgetting.

There are a few relics here from our old family home. It still gives me a jolt to see them, strangers marooned in an unknown land: the Murano glass vase, a wedding present from Mum's brother Joe that used to adorn the breakfast table, full of flowers, but which now sits empty; the antique china King Charles Spaniels that perch precariously on the thin mantel above the gas fire; the Monopoly box that lurks forlorn under the TV. Dogs, board games – everything a family room needs, apart from the actual family. Perhaps I should take the Spaniels when I next visit Mum, as Philippa suggested. What else? A puzzle? A two-by-four, a bag of icing sugar and some quick-dry cement?

I got used to coming home at night to the map of Mum's day, in abandoned biscuits on the stairs, a tea-cup cast adrift from its spoon, a saucer unmoored on the windowsill. Once to a wobbly tower of my travel guides leaning, Pisa-like, in the sitting room. I don't know what she was looking for, but it took me an entire evening to recategorize them. She sat and watched me, humming one of her tunes, shaking her head. I told her it didn't matter. Now when I come home, everything is exactly as I left it.

Tandoori Nights has congealed in the bowl; I have lost my place in *Discover India!* and all track of time. Pitch-dark outside now; I stare out of the blank-faced windows at nothing, and wonder how Mum is in her single bed in an unfamiliar room. I wish she was here, rearranging my guides, remembering who I am.

I rinse my bowl, upend it on the draining board. Then I get another out of the cupboard and place it next to mine. I switch off the light and go to bed.

4

Lost:	Bottle of champagne
Details:	Mumm Millésimé 2008
	In Selfridges bag
Place:	~~Black Cab~~ Lost Property, the stacks

The amount of loss that has passed through my hands this Monday morning, and it's not even elevenses! A floral washbag, an imitation Oscar statue with the inscription *Martin, Forever My Star*, a Silver Jubilee mug in a British Home Stores carrier left on a train from Paddington to King's Cross – goodness knows how long that has been doing the rounds on the Circle Line. What else? A pair of men's shoes. They can be devastating, shoes; the obedient line of side-by-side toes pressed into the leather, the larger hillock of the big toe. All the items handed in to Lost Property bear the imprints of their owners, but none more so than the lost clothes. Look at the hope suspended in socks still arching the shape of missing feet, the cardigan cuffs aching to close around absent wrists, questioning elbows in the sleeves of a lost shirt! Feel the idiosyncratic knot of a shoelace, smell the trace of perfume on a silk scarf.

All of this but still no holdall, no bluey-lilac purse with a gold snap closure.

During my lunch break I nip downstairs to the stacks to see if I missed either of them coming in. I fine-tooth comb 'Assorted Bags, Briefcases and Trollies', take a gander in 'Luggage', and even a quick nip along 'Miscellaneous', which boasts everything from a Chinese typewriter to a jar of bull's sperm and a Tibetan bell – ours is not to reason why – but no holdall to be found.

I'll keep vigilant. Because I know that some days, having a totem, a talisman, holding it, pressing your lips against it, can be a salve in the face of grief, if only for a moment.

I eat my domino sandwiches and watch the beams from the fluorescents play on a huddle of forgotten shopping bags, see them radiate, the light catching the corners of the shiny plastic, making their hunched shapes sparkle. Shining, ecclesiastical, three wise men.

The tinny sound of the Bee Gees' 'More Than A Woman' whines up through a trapdoor-sized hatch in the floor that leads down to the pit. The pit is a long low-ceilinged basement that runs the length of the building and is dimly lit by lights permanently on the blink. It is home to the detritus, the no-longer wanted. After three months, unclaimed items – single gloves and shopping bags and overcoats – are pushed through the hatch down a wide metal slide into the pit. Once a week these things are sorted and shipped off to Snagsbey's auction house in Tooting, where they are sold to the highest bidder. The pit is almost solely Big Jim's terrain. Not a loquacious individual; I can't tell you too much about him, except for his tattoos – covered in them: neck, scalp, even his earlobes. Anchors, dragons, swords running up and down his arms, on one fist a scorpion, on the other a fork-tongued snake. For such a silent chap, he's a boisterously loud eyeful. He comes in once a week to crate the next load for auction. You always know it's Monday because a soundtrack constantly thrums through the open hatch from Big Jim's vintage orange Toot-a-Loop transistor radio, hits from the seventies, the decade in which, I suspect, he felt most like himself and to which he forever tries to return. There are those of us who feel similarly out of our own time. Dad. Me. Lost Property itself has something of the past about it, like a museum, a depository of memories, a library of loss. I think that is why I have always felt at home here.

I peer down through the hatch.

'Halloo?'

'*And if I lose you now, I think I would die,*' the Bee Gees intone back.

I crouch down closer and poke my head through the hatch. A faulty fluorescent flickers over a mound of coats and jackets at the bottom of the chute, leather carcasses of bags heaped on a table, a metal crate in which tangles of scarves cling to each other; polyester and silk, cheap and fancy – all equal now, no longer property, now just lost.

'A plentiful consignment this week,' I call down over the music.

Big Jim appears below. In the tremulous light, his tattoos quiver, wraithlike.

'Yup,' he says. I don't recollect ever having seen Big Jim outside Lost Property in the light of day. I imagine if I did it would be like catching sight of Boo Radley: amorphous, spectral, someone from another world.

'Saved these for you.' Big Jim upturns a crate, stands on it and reaches towards the hatch.

I stretch out my arm to retrieve my haul of books. *Exploring the Canaries*, *Hiking in the Highlands* and *Scopri Londra!*

'These are super, Jim,' I say, 'thank you!'

'Only three. Sorry.'

'Please don't apologize! Autumn is such an in-between time, isn't it? Too late for people's summer holidays but still too early for their winter ones. These guides are excellent. One in Italian, I see – *splendido*!'

He nods, returns to work.

The collapsed face of a handmade sock puppet stares out from a crate. I remember the much-loved little fellow coming in, a chequered bow tied with panache around his neck. His rosy cheek suddenly mashes against the wire mesh as Big Jim pushes a few more unclaimed items into the crate before closing it. Tomorrow, if someone comes to collect that puppet, it will be too late. I say 'much loved', but why didn't his owner come? How could they have forgotten him in the first place? Why were they so careless? There's a difference, though, I know, between being lost and being left.

I hug my rescued guides to my chest and take the lift back up to Customer Service.

The following day, Lost Property is abuzz with what I am secretly calling The Mystery of the Missing Millésimé. A week ago, a bottle of Mumm champagne in a Selfridges bag came in, having been left in the back of a black cab. October can be eclectic. As well as the flood of brollies there's always a tranche of 'back to school' items – pencil cases feature highly. Treasured in September, they start to go astray as autumn advances, not to mention the swathes of woolly scarves that people haven't quite got used to wearing, unwrapped on muggy bus rides and left behind. But a bottle of champagne, so long before Christmas? It was almost too much.

Then the bottle mysteriously went missing at close of business yesterday! Now, the rule – unwritten but commonly comprehended – is, of course, that nothing may be taken from Lost Property before the requisite three-month waiting period is over. This rule is generally followed – Anita's cavalier attitude to walking sticks and brollies aside. So, when a bottle of high-profile bubbles goes walkabout, suspicions and deductions abound.

Ed, who has been taking noticeably longer sojourns from Baker Street station since SmartChoice joined our ranks, starts running a betting book. He gives Anita odds of 7/1 on her supposition that the bottle must have been accidentally broken, the mess mopped up in secret shame by the culprit. SmartChoice, sporting an outfit that seems to be made entirely of macramé, puts forth a dramatic scenario wherein an accomplished heist team – including twin Mormon getaway drivers and a Chinese acrobatic 'grease man' – combine their varied skills to pull off the job. Anita disqualifies this theory on the grounds that it is the plot of something called *Ocean's Eleven*.

To the astonishment of all, this afternoon the champagne, still in its Selfridges bag, turns up back on the shelf like a magician's trick. While my colleagues wonder at the turn of events, I nip down to the stacks and privately examine the returned bottle, ascertain that it is a 2012 vintage as opposed to a 2008, and piece together the clues of the case as I see them:

Clue one: Gabrielle has been skipping lunch recently – decidedly un-French – making do with a handful of garibaldis from the kitchen nook.

Clue two: The other day I overheard her telling Sukanya she wanted to make a nice dinner for her boyfriend's birthday, but could barely afford a jar of olives let alone a bottle of wine.

Clue three: Yesterday (the day the champagne went missing, and also the day of said boyfriend's birthday) I was just popping down to the stacks at home-time to double-check that the holdall hadn't come in, when I bumped into Gabrielle coming out of the service lift carrying her jumper in a way that struck me as *un peu suspect*.

Clue four: Today is pay day. Restitution of funds into Gabrielle's bank account and of *a* missing Millésimé to its shelf in the stacks. But not *the* Millésimé.

I categorically do not condone the theft of lost property in any way. Whatsoever. But Gabrielle is a diligent worker, scrupulously polite with the customers and assiduous in recording lost items. And – oh, the romance of it! I know that if she . . . *borrowed* the champagne last night, it was because she wanted to celebrate the birthday of her amour in style.

These things are so important to the French. They don't overindulge, but do like things done *avec finesse*: the coup

48

de champagne aperitif, the espresso digestif. I visited Champagne during my time in France, saw the magnificent wine caves where riddlers lovingly rotate the bottles every six months. I sampled delicious varietals, appreciated that hint of apricot, of lemon, of brioche. I only have to reread my *Guide to North-East France: Forests, Beaches and Vineyards* to imagine myself back there; *Champagne proffers an abundance of riches. Visit in spring for the wildflowers, but for wine connoisseurs autumn is the time to catch the harvest, when verdant vineyards are pungent with the musky scents of Chardonnay, Pinot Noir and Pinot Meunier grapes.*

None of the other staff has noticed the discrepancy of the vintage, so *Mumm's* the word. *Ha.*

At home-time, I pop into the Ladies cloakroom to discover Anita staring at herself in the bathroom mirror, her hands stretching back the skin either side of her face.

'Blimey,' she says, 'I spend a fortune on face cream and it's doing sweet F. A. Organic calf liver, meant to make you look ten years younger. Might as well have used Princes Beef Paste for all the good it's done me. You're lucky, Dots, you've got such beautiful skin.'

Have I? I join her gaze in the glass. Dad's chocolate-brown eyes look back at me under industrious eyebrows. I compare Anita's glossy bud of a mouth to my quizzical frown, her elaborately painted lashes to my long, straight, bare ones. Anita has old-fashioned Hollywood glamour: Rita Hayworth, Sophia Loren. Next to her bouncy energetic curls, my fringe is more 'duck for cover' than 'bob'.

Anita lets go of her face and we watch as the skin settles back to its familiar mooring. She retrieves a mascara wand from her bag, and ferociously bangs it in and out of the tube a few times as if tamping gunpowder into a muzzle – talk about warpaint.

'What about the news, eh?' she says.

'What news?' Has poor Gabrielle been discovered? I do hope not. Anita layers black paint on her lashes with quick strokes. It's really rather magnificent to watch.

'Brian's leaving. Going back up to Scotland. His mum's taken a turn for the worse and is all alone, poor thing. To be honest, I think he's been wanting to make the move back home for a while; he's been seeing a chap in Glasgow and it looks pretty serious. But guess who's been put in charge in Brian's place?'

Anita stares at me in the mirror, the mascara brush more of a baton now, poised mid-air as if conducting a tiny orchestra, Puccini maybe.

I shake my head.

'Only bloody Neil Burrows,' Anita says, the make-up brush slashing through the air. Definitely not Puccini; we're in the dark turmoil of Wagner.

'No!' I meet my own shocked eyes in the mirror, picture Chaunticleer, cockier than ever.

'He is going to be an even bigger tool than usual.' Anita reads my thoughts, then adds, 'But more than that, it's not fair! It should have been you, Dots. I mean, you've been here *for ever*, right?'

'Well, not that long, only a couple of years more than you . . .'

'Like I said, for ever.' Anita abandons the mascara, delves into the nosebag and retrieves a chocolate-flavoured slimmer's bar. She tears off a strip of wrapping with her teeth and spits it out viciously. 'It's going to be a nightmare.' She sinks her teeth into the bar.

Neil Burrows in charge. I can already see the extra appendage of keys at his belt, hear his voice crowing through the stacks. I stare at my startled reflection, watch a shadow of foreboding cloud my face.

5

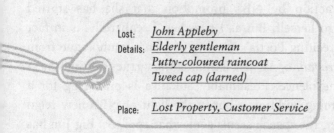

Lost: _John Appleby_

Details: _Elderly gentleman_
Putty-coloured raincoat
Tweed cap (darned)

Place: _Lost Property, Customer Service_

The following Monday is marked by two office emails. The first one, from Brian, apologizes for his swift departure and promises he'll be back for a proper goodbye as soon as he is able. His missive is closely followed by one flagged IMPORTANT, from Neil Burrows, requiring all staff to attend a meeting just before closing.

'This better not take long,' says Anita, as we make our way to Brian's old office.

On NB's orders, SmartChoice has been left in charge of Customer Service. It is usually quiet at the end of the day, but still, I am not at all sure it is a prudent decision. This morning she was in the back office 'helping out' with phone enquiries, and her level of assistance was highly debatable. When I checked on her she was talking to a customer about the merits of something called a 'highlighting cap', and I'm certain we have not had one of those handed in. My doubts are confirmed now, as I spot her lolling against the Customer Service counter in a chilblain of an outfit, cleaning her nails with a Lost Item form.

Sukanya and Gabrielle are already in the office when Anita and I arrive. I worry that Sukanya has been so driven to distraction by NB's promotion that she has started talking to herself. But as I pass her, I realize she is in fact quietly reciting Portia's 'quality of mercy' monologue from *The Merchant of Venice*, extolling the virtues of forgiveness and benevolence. Presumably Sukanya is practising for a forthcoming audition – but in the light of NB's new reign of power, the speech seems somewhat apropos. Big Jim has also been summoned, standing sombre in a corner of the office where his tattoos really pop against the white walls.

Even though NB's takeover occurred less than a week ago, there are already noticeable changes afoot. Gone are Brian's piles of papers and his whimsical collection of Matchbox cars. A silver filing cabinet now glints like a knife in the corner, and when he bustles in, the amendments to NB's own person are no less noticeable. His everyday button-down white shirt has been replaced by a sharp-creased pink one. He has done something different to his hair, making it shiny and slick to his head, as if Chaunticleer has come into close contact with an oil spill.

'I have gathered you here today . . .' he starts.

'Blimey,' Anita whispers, 'we're not getting married!'

'. . . to talk about the future,' he continues. 'We've been using outdated tagging systems, holding on to property for too long. From now on things are going to be different, modern, with state-of-the-art storage and digital tagging.'

He licks his lips excitedly. 'We're going to be efficient, working together like a well-oiled machine . . .'

'He certainly looks well oiled.' Anita nudges me, causing her bag to rattle gently.

'. . . striving for the same goal. A machine that works smoothly, without waste. This is a challenging time for TfL. The boys at the top are doing all they can to make this the most streamlined travel system in the UK.'

'My arse,' whispers Anita. 'Doing their very best to keep counting their bonuses is more like it.'

'So, we must all play our part,' NB drones on. 'Man and, er – woman – the ropes, and pull together.'

We have suddenly gone from a well-oiled machine to a boat crew. Shall we hold hands and sing shanties now, or must we keep pace with yet another metaphor of collective industry – a hive of busy bees, perhaps?

'There are going to be some changes. As we all know, living in London comes at a price and there is no commodity more valuable than space. Our current policy is to retain items for three months. This means that we are always operating at full capacity. 'Fraid we just don't have the room. Going forward, we will be limiting the holding time to one month.'

Anita and I exchange a horrified look. Big Jim shifts against the wall, the tattooed blades of his swords quivering. This hugely lessens the chance of items being reunited with their owners. The ferocity of the cut feels like an actual wound; my hand flies to my chest.

'Neil, may I suggest—' I say.

Neil Burrows holds up a finger, wets his lips and continues.

'In addition, although it has been the policy to charge members of the general public one pound when they come to reclaim their stuff, we will now be instituting a nominal fee of five pounds to cover our overheads.'

'To keep you in new shirts and hair gel,' Anita hisses.

'Finally,' NB continues his dastardly discourse, 'it has been brought to my attention that umbrellas and walking sticks are being given away. I am sure I do not need to tell you that this is against protocol, and things will not look good for any member of staff discovered in such activity.'

'That bloody Sheila snitched on me,' Anita rasps. I try not to judge but it does seem likely.

'And now, can we all hold hands . . .'

Please, no.

A damp palm adheres to mine.

'So glad you're on board,' whispers NB, pumping my hand as if he is trying to resuscitate it.

He is enlivened. Happy. He turns to the assembled throng.

'To TfL!' he cries, rippling the arms to either side of him (mine and a tragic-faced Big Jim's) in a flaccid attempt at a Mexican wave.

Looks like Anita might jump ship.

Back at the counter, SmartChoice is serving a customer. Kind face. Tweed cap.

'Mr Appleby!' I cry.

He turns to me. Smiles.

'What a good memory!' he says. 'I hope it's all right to come in again. Don't want to take up your time, it's just that I was in the vicinity . . .'

The Times is neatly folded under his arm. I picture the graveyard.

'Absolutely, sir, but I'm afraid the holdall hasn't come in.'

'Ah, well.' He nods. A slight droop to his shoulders.

'But there is every chance it still might.'

'Really? I rather worried if it hadn't been handed in by now—'

'It's still early days.' I forgive myself the lie when I see the hope light his face.

'Oh, that is good to know. Also, while I am here, perhaps I should update my address.'

'Sheila!' I turn to SmartChoice who is gazing vacantly into space, fiddling with one of her earrings. 'Could you be so kind as to get Mr Appleby's form?'

'No worries!' she says, and saunters off into the back office. I turn to Mr Appleby.

'Are you moving?' A draughty bedsit, miles from anyone he knows? Or a care home, like Mum, with none of his old familiar possessions to comfort him, no bluey-lilac purse to nestle in his palm . . .

'I'm going to the coast. My grandson and his wife have invited me down for a long visit.'

'Oh, that's brilliant!' I cry, relieved. Mr Appleby looks at me, somewhat startled. At that moment SmartChoice reappears. 'I mean . . . oh, look, here's Sheila with your form!' I say. 'We will update your details pronto.' I unclip my Sheaffer. 'The coast – how lovely. Nothing nicer than an ice cream at the seaside, is there?'

'Not a thing.' Mr Appleby smiles. 'John, my grandson, has a place up on the West Hill looking down over the fishermen's huts. You can see all the way across the Channel on a clear day. And there's a funicular railway . . .'

57

'Dot, quick word?' NB is suddenly beside me.

'I'll be with you directly, Mr Burrows. I'm just dealing with a customer . . .'

'Let Sheila take it from here,' NB says, gesturing to SmartChoice, who has started doodling on Mr Appleby's form. 'She is in training after all, good to let her have the experience. Carry on, Sheila. Dot, my office? Nice one.'

I reluctantly bid Mr Appleby farewell and follow NB back to his office. He closes the door and I am overwhelmed by claustrophobia. Though only moments ago the room was filled with the crew of the Lost Property sloop, now it seems to have telescoped to the size of a cuddy cabin.

'Meeting went down well, didn't it?' He grins. 'Good team, good team. I've got big plans for this place. Big plans. The changes I outlined today are just the start.'

Although keen to get back to Mr Appleby, I can't lose the opportunity to seize my moment.

'About those changes,' I say. 'I really do think that we should retain the three-month holding period; people need ample opportunity to reclaim their possessions. It's the heart of what we do. Could you reconsider?'

'No can do, I'm afraid.' He waggles his finger. 'The boys at TfL want a brand-new system: cost efficient, time efficient, labour efficient.'

'But it won't be labour efficient, will it? No sooner than we have stacked the shelves, items will be going down the chute. Jim will be working overtime shipping things to Snagsbey's—'

'Let's leave me to worry about that, shall we? I wanted a quick word about *you*.'

'Me?' What on earth could NB want to talk to me about? Instinctively I take a step back.

'Now I'm in charge, the head honcho,' he sniggers, 'I want to look out for your prospects, take you under my wing.' He raises his elbow suggestively and reveals a damp oxter. Chaunticleer.

'I'm sure you have many more things to occupy your time,' I say. 'I'm tip-top as I am, thank you.'

'Let's make a date, shall we? Get something in the diary, yup? Terrific.'

When I finally extricate myself, kind-faced Mr Appleby is gone.

6

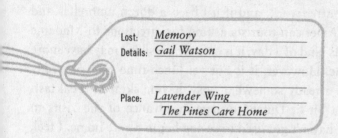

Lost: *Memory*
Details: *Gail Watson*

Place: *Lavender Wing*
      The Pines Care Home

Philippa chose The Pines Care Home for its excellent hygiene. I rate care over cleanliness, don't mind a bit of clutter as long as the staff are kindly. *Care is in the name, Dot, but there's no mention of clean – that we have to ascertain for ourselves.* The other reason for the choice, unstated but abundantly clear, is the proximity of The Pines to my sister's house in Kent. Her county, her rules.

The signage reads, in bulbous letters:

At The Pines,
You're Always Welcome

Which I find a jot unnerving.

A dark-haired man clad entirely in white exits the main entrance as I enter.

'Visiting?' He smiles.

I restrain myself from responding, 'Joining,' and instead nod.

'I'm Adison Chang, on Rosemary and Basil.'

'I'm Dot Watson, on Gin and Tonic.'

I confess I stopped for what Anita refers to as an 'adult beverage' en route to visit Mum. I often have a drink in the evening after work, and if it's been a dozen umbrellas and several American tourists asking for directions to Madame Tussauds kind of a day, it is entirely possible I may have more than one. However, it is not yet lunch-time on a Saturday and I'm already somewhat tipsy, having skipped breakfast. I need a bit of Dutch courage in advance of the visits to Mum. I haven't got used to seeing her in a care home. I feel, somehow, that Philippa and I have let her down.

The man looks at me quizzically, then beams warmly.

'Those are the wings I work on.'

Ah.

A loud snort of laughter erupts before I can stop it.

'Whoops! How embarrassing,' I say, clamping my hand over my nose and mouth.

He shakes his head, his smile broadening. 'Not at all.'

The silliness lifts my mood. I smile back at the amiable chap and continue on into The Pines.

Lavender Wing comprises a row of matching rooms with matching occupants set along a pallid corridor that smells of decay and air freshener – sharp citrus rather than lavender, which, to my mind, shows poor follow-through.

Mum was officially diagnosed with early-onset dementia a year ago, but things went awry some time before that. Familiar names left trailing. My own started to go quite near the start – a case of last in, first out, I suppose. Yawning gaps

62

appeared in her ability to trace what she had done, where she had done it and/or why. She had to stop driving – she kept getting lost and then one time she just left her car in the middle of the road, the keys still in the ignition. More than once I found her at the bus stop at the end of the street, waiting to catch a number 13 to take her to our old house. 'I want to go home!' she had cried when I led her back to the maisonette. One morning she got up and went out in her nightie. It was still dark and the pavement was slick with rain, and she had slipped and broken her hip. The doctor at A&E had been reassuring, telling us that what with her age and the osteoporosis she had been dealing with since menopause, a broken hip was quite common. But still. I was supposed to be looking after her. A fact Philippa was not shy about reminding me of. While Mum was in hospital recovering from the hip operation, Philippa came round to the maisonette and stated in no uncertain terms that we had to put Mum in a home for her own good. I felt relief and guilt in equal parts.

Mum declined so swiftly after the fall I could hardly keep up with the changes in her. Most days now she can't remember a thing. She thinks Philippa is someone called Edna who used to clean for Grandma when Mum was little, which might afford me some small amusement if it wasn't so sad.

No clue at all who I am.

Philippa is in Mum's room when I arrive, a sobering surprise.

'Philippa. This is a surprise.'

'Hello, D.' She shortens my name when she's trying to get the upper hand. 'The children are both at friends' and Gerald is spending the day playing mixed doubles with some of the chaps from work. I knew you wouldn't mind me sharing your visiting hours.'

Fifteen–love.

Although apparently, it's *l'oeuf*, not love. Interesting fact gleaned from *Travels Around Wimbledon* (District Line, last July). A zero on the scoreboard resembles an egg, you see – *l'oeuf*. But owing to our mispronunciation, it's become 'love'. An egg becoming love has its own poetic licence, I suppose.

Mum's room has a single bed and a chest of drawers in an unappealing 'wood-effect' laminate, on which Philippa has arranged silver-framed pictures of Sam and Melanie. There is also a small vanity, though what vanity remains at this stage I do not know, especially when the rest of the room is decked with various reminders that disease and death are ever present: a red panic button on the wall next to resuscitation equipment, her walking stick in the corner. Not to mention the bedpans.

Residents are permitted personal items such as lamps, rugs and easy chairs. I insisted we bring the two wingbacks from the maisonette – sweet Harris Tweed chairs that Mum and Dad have owned for ever, which used to sit either side of the fireplace in our old house. Philippa, meanwhile, went to John Lewis and bought chrome lamps and a glacial-white sheepskin 'floor throw'. 'Personal items means things from home, things to imbue a sense of familiarity,' I said when I saw her purchases. 'Don't be ridiculous, D,' Philippa batted back. 'Why on earth would Mum want all that old junk? She needs something new, nice and fresh.' Philippa took a dim view of my armchairs and the pink chenille coverlet from our parents' bed. Mum had clutched on to it as I helped her into Philippa's car to go to The Pines, muttering, 'I can't leave Rosie behind.'

I give Mum a kiss. She looks different. Her hair. Lips. Something odd on her cheeks. It turns out they've had girls in from one of the local salons to give everyone a 'new look'. I'm not sure what look they were going for with Mum. I detect some very questionable lip gloss that veers to the brassy.

Philippa has brought Mum a tropical fruit platter and an Elizabeth Arden Skin Essentials gift set, with a 'brow shaper' and 'SPF 15 Lip Protectant Stick' – I don't know what she thinks Mum will do with any of it.

Philippa shows what she thinks of my gift – a jigsaw of 'Hop Picking in Kent' – with a disparaging arch of an eyebrow. No need of a brow shaper for her then.

'A puzzle can provide stimulating mental activity,' I say. 'This one also offers nostalgic recollections of pastoral Kent. And anyway, Mum likes them.'

Fifteen all, I rather think.

Mum ignores us both and busies herself unpicking tufts of fabric from the bedspread. Her glossy lips shape words that sound like 'kettle', or maybe 'petal', and she is quietly humming one of her tunes.

I sit in Dad's old chair, Philippa sits in Mum's, and across the faded, plucked expanse of Rosie we try to hold the family together.

At first a silence sags between us, a slack sail. Quickly, we man the ropes.

'What about that time when—'

'Remember that stray tabby we adopted, Mr Tibbles?'

We retrace our steps, fall in line with each other. I defer to Philippa, of course.

'I remember coming back from a week in Dorset and finding the carpet full of cat fleas.' Will she ever let go of that?

'It was Devon,' I say, 'because we had a cream tea and I thought that meant tea-cups full of cream. Remember, Mum?'

'Definitely Dorset,' says Philippa.

'Open the curtains, Edna,' says Mum.

Rising and falling like the winds and seas on the Shipping Forecast, Philippa's face loses its identity for a moment. Tyne. Dogger. Fisher.

'It's me, Mum. Philippa.' Then she gets up and opens the curtains anyway. 'I was just telling Mum about the pressure Gerald is under after his promotion. Global finance is no walk in the park, I can tell you. It's good for him to take the weekend off, knock a few balls about . . .'

I look out of the lavender-curtained windows. Despite its name, the nursing home is sparse on foliage. No pines at all, just a dear old apple tree with outstretched arms that sag like a Chelsea Pensioner. The focus is on paved patios and wooden boardwalks, presumably for an easy wheelchair turn about the lawn. The thought depresses me.

We used to live in a house surrounded by trees; I wonder if Mum can remember it. A dense, towering forest. Dad loved it. 'Isn't this perfect, Dot?' he said, out on the darkening lawn the evening of the day we moved in, gesturing to the black shadows looming about us. 'So secret. Hidden.' Privately, I agreed with Mum's decree that the trees were too tall, creepy. She wanted a smaller garden with a nice wooden fence that she could train her honeysuckle up; she had seen just the thing in another house for sale a few streets over. That house also had a marvellous attic, converted into a bedroom that boasted a porthole skylight. If that was your room, you could lie in bed and stare at the moon, imagine you were steering a ship on the high seas, trace the constellations. Traitor to my own desires and to my mother, I said I wanted the house Dad liked. It was cheaper, which in the end Mum couldn't argue with. From the day that we moved in, the house made her feel sad but it made Dad feel safe.

I'd do anything to make him happy. It was a challenge during the week. He'd leave early for the City. Middle management: his parents' career choice, not his. He worked in a big office on Threadneedle Street and would come home late, all buttoned up. I'd rush to meet him, make him loose-leaf tea in the sturdy brown tea-pot. I'd make it nice and strong with two sugars, and fill his pipe, tamping the cool fronds of toffee-coloured tobacco with my thumb like he taught me. Occasionally I'd get a smile, but mostly he would just pat my head and sigh. But Friday nights he glowed. He would rub his hands together. 'What adventures shall we have, my dearest Dot! What shall we discover? Where shall we roam?' Weekends, Philippa was barely home, always out with friends. Dad and I had our own private world. He was far more comfortable in the past than the present. An idealized past, before his time, where he felt safe. I was happy to join him there in a world filled with black-and-white films and crackly records. Dad loved opera – *La bohème*, *Carmen*, *Madama Butterfly*. He also liked stirring, passionate duets by two men called Jussi Björling and Robert Merrill. And there were the musicals – Gilbert and Sullivan, Rodgers and Hammerstein. The happy, funny tunes by George Formby were my favourite, especially when Dad would join in, pretending to play the banjo, and I would jig and jump about, get one of the napkins from the dresser and act as if I was cleaning really big windows. At the end of the evening he would always play a song called 'Beautiful Dreamer'. It was such a sad song and always seemed to make Dad melancholy, so I didn't understand why he played it. It made me glum too, because it meant I had to go to bed.

If he hadn't brought home any work from the office, he would play with me all weekend. Sometimes he would do magic tricks with a 50p coin and his white cotton handkerchief, making the coin disappear, but my favourite was when we made up Sherlock Holmes mysteries. Occasionally Mum would seek us out, wearing a nice dress, her hair freshly curled, and ask Dad if he fancied popping next door to the neighbour's barbecue. 'Would you be awfully disappointed if we just stayed here?' he'd say. 'Darling, we will never get to know anyone if we don't go out,' she'd answer, already slipping off her outdoor shoes. He didn't like to go out, to socialize. Once he was home from work he loved to escape into our secret world of make-believe. In the end, Mum stopped asking him.

She's smiling at Philippa now, her fingers still carefully plucking tufts of pink from the bedspread. A sudden ray of sunlight catches the – is it bronze? – gloss on her lips, making them flicker, as if she is quivering to say something.

'. . . Melanie is going from strength to strength, Mum.' Philippa's solo volley continues. 'We are cautiously optimistic; if her A-levels go as well as her GCSEs did, it's beginning to look a lot like Oxbridge. Gerald's boss said he would put in a good word when the time came, old boys' network and all that. They love Gerald at work, such a team player . . .'

Dad was never part of the old boys' network, knowing the codes, playing the game. The only games he liked to play were our made-up ones, our mysteries and adventures. He eschewed the swaggering, swearing, stubbled machismo of Mel Gibson and Bruce Willis for the nostalgic gentility and integrity of Gregory Peck and Jimmy Stewart. He sought sanctuary in a sepia past, an imagined world of chivalrous men scented with a light almond pomade. Their gracious dignity gave him another language, another way of being, far removed from the brash, testosteroned thrust and pull of the 'greed is good' world around him. He was a true gentleman and I loved him for it. I wanted to be just like him.

In the films we watched together, the men wore felt hats, smoked pipes and whistled jolly tunes. They did their hair like Dad, using twin brushes to swoop it back at the sides like bird wings. Those men would set off for work in the mornings, smiling happily, jackets slung jauntily over their shoulders. But Dad never went to work like that.

'Dot?'

Philippa's icy radar tracks me across the no-man's land of pink chenille.

'Yes?'

'I was saying we should have a little get-together, celebrate Gerald's promotion. You could bring . . . somebody?'

'No plus one. Just me.'

Philippa maintains her crusade.

'What about at your . . . work, anybody there?'

I have a momentary vision of turning up at Philippa's, arm-in-tattooed-arm with Big Jim.

A snort of laughter reverberates in my nose.

'No, no one.'

'Well, I'll have a dig around,' she says – ever game – as if she's going to rummage through Gerald's old gum boots and find me something; faded, rubbery, but still reasonably watertight.

We lob a few more random memories of our family life across the bedspread and the woman who used to be our mother, until eventually Philippa stands up.

'I'd better be off. Dot, quick word?' She dabs a particularly fierce smear of blush from Mum's cheek. 'Bye, Mum.'

'Don't forget to do the windowsills next time, Edna,' Mum says.

I follow Philippa out of the room into the corridor. The usually perfect isosceles of her shoulders slopes to one side. I reach out towards the sharp corner of her elbow but she turns, blinking swiftly.

'Greenridge, Cooper and Price are confirmed for a valuation next Wednesday. Then photos, probably the following day. You don't need to be in, they've got keys.'

She stalks off down the corridor, hard heels sparking off the institutional tile.

The ghost of L'Air du Temps lurks on the laminate surfaces of Mum's room.

She is looking out of the window, singing softly, a hymn I think. I wait till she finishes, turns to me, smiles.

'That was lovely, Mum.'

She nods. Suddenly alone with her, I feel awkward. Not enough. I wish Philippa were here, filling in the gaps.

'Who fancies a spot of Hop Picking?' I say eventually, my voice booming in the new silence. The puzzle pieces clatter on to the dinner tray attached to Mum's bed. 'Straight edges first?'

Mum's hands take shelter in the nest of pink tufts from the balding chenille bedspread.

'Where is Maria?' she says.

'Do you want me to call a nurse, Mum? What is it? Do you need something?' She shakes her head, plucks more fiercely at the bedspread. Gently, I lift her hands on to the dinner tray. They are cotton-flecked and dry as tissue paper. 'We had a box of Rose and Honeysuckle from Yardley handed in at work the other day. It looked rather nice. I'll buy you some if you fancy.'

Her fingers tap over the jigsaw pieces like Braille. Then they close on one, a middle piece, part of a man's face, the edge of his beard.

'Speaking of work, it's been all systems go as per. A man came in the other day looking for his wife's purse – you would have liked him, Mum, such a nice gentleman—'

'Where are my dustpan and brush?'

'I haven't found them, Mum, but I'll keep looking, I promise.' I try again to change the subject, fill the silence between us, ease Mum's growing distress. I scan the drab room for inspiration but find none. I pick up the lid of the puzzle box, point to the picture of golden hops in a sunlit field. 'Did you ever go hop picking, when you were little?' My voice has become primary-coloured. 'With Grandma, perhaps? We went blackberrying, didn't we? Remember, Mum?' She doesn't, of course, and when I think back she never came.

71

'What about Reg the fishmonger, remember him?' Desperate now, I pretend to sport a pair of braces and snap them to my chest. 'I've got a nice tail for you this week, Mrs Watson. Remember Reg, Mum?' She gives a little laugh. Hope in the dark. Encouraged, I go on. 'And what did you say? Remember what you said, Mum?' Another smile. She nods and together we chorus, 'If you don't mind, Reg, I'd rather have a piece of fish!'

We succumb to some loud chortling and spend the rest of the morning with me being Reg the fishmonger. It keeps her entertained and it feels like such a wonderful achievement to get her to smile, let alone belly laugh. Even if she doesn't know who on earth I am.

I force myself to stay for lunch. The diners shimmer and glow, and I feel as if I have stepped into a church of saints or a Renaissance painting of the Annunciation. The salon girls have been industrious with their metallic colour palette.

The decor of the dining room resembles a two-star hotel and everything is done in an unappetizing green bean and cream: the chair backs, the swathes of ruched curtains, the carpet, the lampshades, the place mats. Mozart's Serenade No. 13 in G major is playing, rather a robust choice for this time of day.

In general, the other residents are older than Mum. Most manage to feed themselves, and one woman in a jaunty lemon jacket wheels her husband to a table. Her hair is as burnished as a new penny.

'What's today?' the husband says, as his lemon wife tucks him in at the table as if she's putting him to bed.

She peers at the menu card, her hand patting at her chest for her spectacles, which hang around her neck on a sensible chain.

72

'Let me see,' she says, propping her glasses on her nose. 'There's soup or there's a ravioli – don't you sometimes like a ravioli?'

'What is it?'

'Rice.'

'Oh. Is it? Right you are. I'll have the ravioli then.'

'Hold on.' She taps the side of her head with her fingers as if trying to shake something loose. 'No, it's not rice. I'm thinking of risotto. Ravioli is like spaghetti but in the shape of little pillows.'

'Oh. Is it? Right you are. I'll have the ravioli then.'

I choose a table by the window for Mum and me. Prop her stick against the wall. Help her into her chair. We sit, both lost for words. I stare out into the garden for inspiration, though there is little to inspire – a patio with a scattering of brown plastic tables and chairs, a couple of grey wooden benches looking the worse for wear. Who, I wonder, made the aesthetic choice to install the stone bird bath held aloft by two naked, generously buttocked cherubs? Sister Gloria passes by with a crackle of starched cotton and forced jollity.

'Well then, Mrs Watson, I see you had both your daughters visiting today. Now, isn't that grand. You two look like you are having a lovely old knees-up.'

Either Sister Gloria lives in a world of her own imagining or she has a very sub-par grasp on reality; a silent order of nuns would create more of a ruckus than Mother and me at this particular moment.

'Do you like my hair?' Mum, suddenly animated, pats her crisped coiffure and beams at Sister Gloria. I stand corrected. Clearly Mum has plenty to say now. Just not to me.

'Gorgeous, Mrs Watson. You look like that Adele or a Spice Girl.'

Mum gives an unfamiliar tinkle. I search for her in her face, but see only disappointment and a smear of butter on her chin.

After lunch, I lead her back to Lavender Wing and settle her into her old armchair, pull the pink bedspread over her knees, tuck her hands in.

'I'll be in next weekend then, Mum.' I kiss her cheek. It smells tomatoey.

As I get to the door she calls out, 'Dear?'

I quickly turn. 'Yes, Mum?'

'Can you close the window, nurse?'

After I shut her door behind me I lean against it for a moment, winded. I'd prefer an 'Edna' to nothing at all. But then again, as Philippa has told me on more than one occasion, she was the surprise. I was the mistake. Maybe that's why Mum forgets me. I was never supposed to be here in the first place.

Outside, rain collides with my tears in damp solidarity. A headache presses at my temples. Rushing to catch my bus, I careen into something warm and solid.

'Sorry!' I rub my sleeve across my face.

'Oh, hi again. It's Adi, Adison Chang,' he says. 'We met earlier . . .'

'Ah . . . yes.' I hadn't noticed before, but now I see that *Dr A. Chang DPT* is emblazoned on the pocket of his uniform. 'So you're a doctor here?'

'Well, I am a doctor in that I have a PhD in physical therapy. Which isn't the same as an MD. Which sometimes confuses people.'

'Do I detect a North American accent?'

'I'm from California. I'm over here running a clinical trial.' He smiles. How delighted Philippa would be with all this medical banter! 'So you were visiting someone . . . ?' he continues, still smiling. Excellent teeth, very American.

'Yes, my mum, she's on Lavender.'

'I start on Lavender next week. Right now I'm on Basil—'

'And Rosemary, yes, you said.' Any more and we will have cultivated a whole herb garden between us. Involuntarily, I press my fingers to my forehead, trying to release a vice of pain that is slowly tightening – a combination of tension and the upset of not being recognized by my own mother.

'May I?'

Suddenly an intense heat warms my temples. Adison Chang DPT holds his hands either side of my face. Despite the gross intrusion on my personal space, I stand for a moment immobilized between his palms.

His eyes are closed. The light catches the soft stubble on his cheeks; he looks as if he has been dusted with cinnamon. The heat travels to further territories of my body. I pull away, lose my balance, tumble forward.

'Sorry. Must dash. Bus.' I hurry off.

All the way home, I feel a tug of guilt at leaving Mum behind. I also find myself rather preoccupied with thoughts of herbaceous borders and unsettling sensations of warmth around my face. So forward, the sudden healing hands. So Californian. I press my flushed face against the cool of the bus window.

The rest of the weekend stretches before me. Unlike Philippa with her drinks do's and dinner parties and girls' nights, I don't go in for entertaining. Neither am I currently what is known as a 'people person' – rather an unhygienic turn of phrase, I've always thought. Mum mistaking me for the nurse still rattles in my chest. Perhaps I'll re-catalogue my travel guides. Applying order to chaos is always soothing. Just what the doctor ordered. *Ha*. That and a sizeable bar of cacao-rich dark chocolate.

I have experimented with a variety of organizational principles for my guides, including the order of countries I would most like to visit, and climate (coldest to hottest). Ordering them alphabetically by author has, I'm afraid, been rather a non-starter. It elicited some superb surprises and lovely geographical collisions, such as seeing *Exploring the Emerald Isle* by Aoife Aherne nestled right next to *Kazakhstan: Travel Tips and More!* by Amir Aliyev, but it made finding anything on purpose tricky. Today I shall put my best foot forward and reorganize, curating for myself a round-the-world trip, journeying from west to east. This means some significant changes to the current iteration – countries from smallest (Vatican City) to largest (Russia) – but I am happy to do it. The weather is dank and broody and it will distract me.

I set to my task with brio, and spend a couple of hours shifting tectonic plates, aided by large squares of chocolate washed down with cups of Lapsang. As I stand back to admire my work, rubbing an ache in my lower back, I spot a faded shoebox squatting on a high shelf.

The box once housed the pair of Netley Rose brogues that preceded my current ones. Now its contents are a medley of old postcards, letters, birthday cards – missives from another time, a time as unstructured and freeform as the jumble of photos and post that document it. I pull down the box, open it, and take out a card covered in bright blue forget-me-nots signed by lots of people I've completely forgotten from university, despite the wording on the card: *Keep in Touch!* I pick up another card, this one for my twenty-first birthday, a picture of a wrinkly walrus on the front, and inside the words, *You're older and not wiser but love you for ever!* signed by Louise in her big looping hand.

Louise. I met her in a queue during freshers' week. I was standing in line to enrol for something called the JOY society. I chose it because it sounded upbeat, and I imagined a plethora of games nights and a general feeling of bonhomie. Also it had the shortest queue. It turned out that Louise, standing just ahead of me, had been drawn to JOY for exactly the same reasons. It wasn't until we got to the front of the line and an earnest-looking girl in an Alice band gave us the clipboard that we realized JOY was dedicated to spreading the word of Jesus. Although a worthy endeavour for many, Jesus wasn't the new friend either of us was hoping to meet at freshers' week, and instead we bonded over a feast of tea and biscuits back in Louise's room. Happily, we discovered that we were both studying modern languages and would be taking the same French literature class. We stayed friends all the way through our BA, both went to Provence for our year abroad, both applied for graduate school in Paris.

She still keeps in touch, always a newsy letter at Christmas. Lives in Marseilles now, very happily so it seems. Full of joy. *Ha.* She always signs off inviting me to visit. I send her something with a robin or a snowy fir and keep it short.

Tucked away at the bottom of the box, tied with ribbon, are the hand-drawn cards from Emile.

Je t'aime xxxx
Tu es la femme de ma vie xxxx

Always so many kisses for me.

Fanning out the letters and cards in my hands, I see my time in Paris in full glorious Technicolor: dashing down the Boulevard Saint-Michel in a bright red skirt in the pouring rain; posing against the mint-green Art Deco letters of the Métro sign at Saint-Sulpice; sauntering across the Pont des Arts in the glow of a crushed-orange evening light, the bridge alive with the thrum of guitar and saxophone, and the overlapping chatter of friends passing around a bottle of Bordeaux, their legs dangling over the Seine; tumbling to Marché Mouffetard to buy bread and salty cheese on a sun-drenched Sunday morning; shopping in the bustle and flap of the Saint Ouen flea market, Louise and me trying on hats, admiring antique jewellery heavy as a canteen of cutlery; sitting on the ornate seats in the Jardin du Luxembourg; riding the silver lift that rattled me up to my wooden-floored *appartement*, which smelt of coffee and milled soap and the garlic that wafted up from the bistro below.

I pick up a photograph of a short-sleeved black dress hanging out of my window high up on the fourth floor. It looks like it was dancing, as if it had taken flight. I had hand-washed the dress, hung it out to dry and forgotten about it, lost in my studies. Emile spotted it there, spinning and twirling, on his way back from the university that evening, and took a picture of it.

When he gave me the photo he said, 'I will always remember you like this. Dancing high above, so free. *Ma belle Dottette.*' My name became two syllables in his mouth, like musical notes, lingering, as if he wanted to hold on to me a moment longer. I could have fallen in love with him just for that.

We made plans. I'd stay on in Paris after my Master's – plenty of opportunities for jobs as an interpreter – we'd rent a place in Grenoble for Christmas . . . The Alps! A whoosh of energy with each new day.

I put the lid on the box, slide it to the back of the shelf, and with a seismic shift it is covered by South America.

7

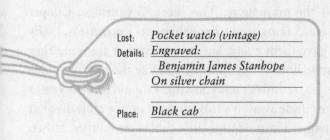

Lost: _Pocket watch (vintage)_
Details: _Engraved:_
    Benjamin James Stanhope
    On silver chain

Place: _Black cab_

'I swear to God I don't know why we bother to shelve these things,' Anita says, hoisting a crate full of lost items on to the counter. 'We might just as well send everything straight to Snagsbey's.'

NB has been in charge for almost two weeks. Gone are the biscuits in the kitchen nook, gone indeed the kitchen nook, which he has requisitioned as an 'administrative auxiliary annex'. The five-pound collection charge has been implemented, which almost led to fisticuffs this morning when a man who had clearly left his manners at the door chose to walk off without his grandfather's cufflinks rather than pay the fee.

'Poor Jim said he was in at the crack of dawn today,' Anita went on. 'He can't get it all crated and carted off to Snagsbey's fast enough. I was going to pop down with a cuppa for him – worked right through his tea break – but then I remembered there's no bloody kettle. Do you know what, Dots? I wouldn't be surprised if Burrows isn't up to something. He's always on the phone with some jobsworth tosser at TfL talking about Human Resources challenges and opportunities, or— Dot, are you listening to me?'

'Sorry, what?' It's true I have wandered off. I'm preoccupied with the maisonette. This week Greenridge, Cooper & Price are coming to do the valuation. I understand why Philippa gave them a key, but am alarmed at thinking they could just walk in at any time. I don't like the idea of people in Mum's house and her not knowing. I should probably clear the Alpine puzzle away, it's still lying out on the table. I've left the best part till last: a family in a cable car; mother, father, son and daughter, all wearing red woolly hats and carrying skis. The silver cable car carries them up the mountain. The family are the only real splash of colour in the picture, bar a few emerald-green firs scattered here and there. The father points up towards the mountain peak and the girl's blue eyes follow his hand. They are all smiling, eager to get to the top. I'd like to finish it.

'What's on your mind?' says Anita. 'Tall, dark, handsome stranger? Because we've already had one of those in today, so I doubt we'll get another, unless they're like buses! Wait for them all your life, then when you've just about given up, not done your hair or bothered to put on your lippy, three come at once.'

Anita is referring to a brief encounter that took place earlier this morning, which I have had the pleasure of hearing her re-enact several times since. I indulge her retelling as it seems to be giving her a bit of a lift. Even SmartChoice has been treated to the tale.

'So this woman comes in, and I said, "What have you lost, madam?" and she said, "My husband."' (At this point Anita pauses for the general eyebrow-raise and snigger that ensues. SmartChoice offered neither but Anita proceeded regardless.) '"Well, I'm very sorry to hear that, madam," I said, "when did you last see him?" "Debenhams Women's Casual," she said – apparently when she came out of the changing rooms he was nowhere to be found. So then I said, "What does your husband look like?" and she said, "George Clooney."' (Anita takes a dramatic pause before following through with the punchline.) 'So then I said, "Well in that case, madam, if I find him, I'm keeping him!"'

SmartChoice simply made a little moue of her lips, saying, 'Why didn't she just text him, or track his phone?'

'If people really want to get lost,' Anita snapped, 'you can be sure they'll find a way.' Then, as if to prove a point, she turned on her heel and disappeared.

During my lunch break, I nip to the stacks to see if Big Jim needs assistance in the pit. I peer through the hatch into the flickering depths. Anita was right: the place is overflowing.

'Looks like all systems go and full steam ahead,' I call down. 'Is there anything I can do?'

Big Jim appears below, his snake and scorpion tattoos glistening with sweat. He shakes his head.

'No, thanks. Hold on.' He slips a tattooed paw into his pocket, steps on a crate, reaches up through the hatch and hands me *Frommer's Guide to Forty-Eight Hours in Rome*.

'Thank you, that's wonderful, how thoughtful, especially when you are so busy. Are you sure I can't help?'

He shakes his head and returns to work.

I don't tell him I already have *Frommer's Guide to Forty-Eight Hours in Rome*. That's the thing with the popular places – most of the European cities, Manhattan and all the ski destinations – we tend to get them in droves. But have I managed to get my hands on even one copy of *Travels Around East Timor* or *Discover Dominica*? Not yet. But I live in hope.

Whenever Big Jim gives me a guide I already own, I am thrilled because it means it's time for my Travel Exchange Programme. I secrete my duplicate guides into various coats, handbags and suitcases waiting to be collected. You could see it as a form of recycling, or even upcycling – I hear that's very *au courant* – but for me it is more diagnostic than that; homeopathy for the soul, if you will. I take my time, consider the cut of a coat, the contents of a handbag, the grain of a leather suitcase. It's important to deduce the type of person and find a destination that will be the exact right fit.

Often, it's obvious. The other day, a man's aubergine overcoat demanded Amsterdam so directly I was quite taken aback. It was evident in the belt, kinked and worn from being pulled too tight, as if the poor chap was forever trying to bolster himself up. I had only to take that coat in my hands and the canals of Amsterdam rippled before me. The relaxed attitude of the locals, the whizz of a bicycle, its wicker basket full of flowers, the invitation to wander at will along winding waterside pathways, made it the perfect choice. Strolling along the Herengracht canal eating a stroopwafel might just remind him of life's possibilities. Often it is straightforward like that – Barcelona for the battered suitcase that smelt of lemons, Berlin for the anorak with the Polos.

If I don't have a strong initial hunch, it helps to hold the bag or put on the coat. I did that recently with a lady's suede jacket. Initially, when I saw the jacket in the stacks I thought Venice. But when I slipped it on to double-check, something about the feel of the pockets stopped me – it seemed as if the owner's hands, unheld for too long, had burrowed deep into the soft comfort of the dark. There is far too much at stake in being on one's own in Venice. Gondolas, like tandems, are built for two. Spain then, instead? *Sí!* Much better, the clean ochre light of Seville . . . or Madrid. Hours at Del Prado in front of the Bosch, strolling the wide plazas in the late afternoon, a supper of piquant cheese and charcuterie washed down with a cold glass of dry Albariño in one of the little wine bars where a woman can sit alone and feel in good company.

I dithered for some time with a man's raincoat in a dark-roast coffee shade. Paris or Florence? It could have gone either way. The arthouse cinema ticket in the pocket and that whiff of tuberose on the collar made me lean towards Paris, but the quality of the fabric and particular shade of cappuccino said, *Portami a Firenze.*

It's not about what they want; it's about what they need. For example, I might select *Exploring the Cornish Coast* for Mr Appleby. I think he would like the vistas, the warm breezes, stopping to whet his appetite with a nice cream tea. And for Big Jim, my trusty tattooed supplier? Tahiti, of course.

I know exactly where the guide Big Jim has just slipped me needs to go. For the bag with the Liberty-print hanky and the mismatched lipstick?

Rome, by all means, Rome.

*

Back in Customer Service, I am filling out a Dijon for a fetching emerald bike helmet when a short, middle-aged woman in a cream coat and woolly spearmint-coloured hat and scarf looks at me anxiously across the counter.

'I telephoned and reported it but then thought I'd just come in, seeing as I was still in town,' she says breathlessly. 'We've been up for a week, to take in the sights and visit our nephew – he's just started at LSE, so proud. Saw *The Mousetrap* – brilliant – then went out to dinner. That must have been when I lost it.'

She pauses for a moment, catches her breath. I nod, smile encouragingly, let her take her time. Peel off a fresh Lost Item form, unclip my Sheaffer.

'We took a cab,' she continues, 'such an expense – I said the bus would do me fine – but my husband insisted, he knows my legs. The pocket watch has been in the family for ages. Proper silver, good quality, beautiful chain. It's probably not actually worth that much but it's ever so valuable to us. It was a present for my nephew, I got it engraved with his name.'

'Let me just take down a few details about the item, madam. What was the name?'

'Mary.'

'Mary?' My Sheaffer hovers.

'Oops no, sorry, you mean the engraving! Benjamin James Stanhope. Lovely, isn't it?'

'Very nice. I'll see if anything has come in.'

Mary waits while I go to the computer and type in 'pocket watch'. One is listed, having come in two days ago. Not marked as engraved – thank you, SmartChoice – but it might just be the fellow. It's in Valuables. I'll have to go to NB for the key.

He is slipping something into the filing cabinet and jumps when I come in.

'Mr Burrows—'

'Neil, please.'

'I need to check if we have a pocket watch in Valuables.'

'Sure, sure.' He fumbles excitedly with his keys. 'Let's walk and talk. We still need to book in our one-to-one.'

'I can just nip down on my own.' I hold out my hand for the key.

'Not a problem, happy to come with. How's Wednesday looking for a window?' His keys remain stubbornly clipped to his belt.

'Busy, I'm afraid.'

'What are you up to?'

(Clearly 'completing an Alpine jigsaw' isn't going to cut it.)

'Dance class.' Actually, I'm hoping to heaven Anita has forgotten about the class, but in any case, it might provide me with an excuse to dodge NB for another week.

'Dance class?' NB smiles excitedly. 'Don't mind a bit of a boogie myself.'

I watch in horror as he puts his hands on his hips and swings them from left to right, keys penduluming wildly.

'You and I could—'

Whatever heinous invitation NB is about to issue is interrupted by his office phone. He ignores it, and I fear he is about to resume exhibiting his dance prowess when the answering machine clicks on.

'Neil, Trev here, from Snagsbey's,' a voice says. Neil pounces.

'Be right with you, Trevor.' Holding the receiver against his jacket with one hand, he rootles at his belt with the other, unclips the keys and hands them to me. They are warm. 'Dog and Duck next Monday for our one-to-one, Dot? Terrific.' I feel him watch me leave before he resumes his call.

The plethora of leather wallets, metal and money in the Valuables lock-up smells like blood. NB has instigated a new filing system down here, eliminating the Dijon tags entirely and instead stacking each item in a grey box printed with long indecipherable codes, so the only way to know what each box contains is to open it. Hardly streamlining! He is the only one who understands what the codes refer to. I will have to be more hands-on for my search. I push back my uniform sleeves and dig in. Digital, designer, underwater watches slither imperiously through my fingers. Ladies' fashion, three Fitbits, a rather dashing nurse's uniform pin-on. Finally, I open the lid of a box to find a silver moon-like disc. I turn it over and a warmth radiates across my chest.

Benjamin James Stanhope.

Few things in my life grant me more pleasure than reuniting property with person, undoing a loss. It doesn't always happen as one might wish; sometimes people complain about how long they have had to wait for their item, some act as if it is an enormous inconvenience to have to come in and collect their own belongings, while other clients rustle suspiciously through a returned bag or briefcase, checking nothing has been stolen. Nonetheless, returning lost items can be redolent with a sense of completion and rightness, a fleeting moment of order and fairness in the world. An unexpected happy ending. All too rare, I fear.

Back upstairs, Mary greets me with a face of hope zig-zagged with ready disappointment.

'It's all right if you haven't got it, love, I know it's a long shot.'

I place the watch on the counter. Her hand flies to her mouth, then reaches for the pocket watch; her fingers lightly trace the curlicues of her nephew's name. Then she lunges and I am enveloped in spearmint cream. I resist the urge to pull away and for a fleeting moment linger in the softness of the wool, the curious delight of another person's laundry detergent.

I disentangle, thrust a form across the counter.

'I will need you to please sign and date this, to record that your goods have been returned to you.'

That pocket watch gives me a spring in my step all afternoon. A timely reminder of good citizenship. Perhaps such a loyal member of the public will hand in Mr Appleby's holdall? Maybe it has already come in?

'Holdall?' Anita shakes her head when I ask her if anything matching its description has crossed her path today. 'No, sorry, Dots, nothing like that. Wish I could help. I've had a shit day. I just had to ask an old dear for the five quid to return her Freedom Pass and watch as she counted through all her coppers to scrape it together. I told her to just get the council to send her another, but she didn't want to trouble them. I could wring bloody Burrows' neck for bringing that charge in. I'm glad we're going dancing this week – I don't half need something to cheer me up!'

'Me too, what fun!' I say, my shoulders sagging.

8

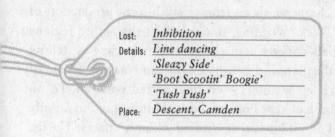

Lost:	_Inhibition_
Details:	_Line dancing_
	'Sleazy Side'
	'Boot Scootin' Boogie'
	'Tush Push'
Place:	_Descent, Camden_

Wednesday arrives with the buoyancy of a week-old helium balloon. There is still no sign of Mr Appleby's holdall or Joanie's purse, so it is looking less and less likely they will come to us now. Should I prepare him if he comes in again, or just let him keep hoping?

My mood is further dampened by the looming visit of Greenridge, Cooper & Price and the fact that tonight, as improbable and disconcerting as it sounds, I am going to a dance class.

Several times over the past few weeks I have contemplated giving Anita an excuse, but then something stops me in my tracks, such as the sight of her nails unvarnished and bitten – most untoward for someone with a Level 3 Diploma in the art of manicure. Then the other day I spotted her exiting the service lift hastily shoving a fistful of damp tissues into her bag. And now she has come right out and told me she needs cheering up.

I change in the Ladies after work, twinning a pair of black elasticated trousers with a long-sleeved leotard. I leave my uniform and brogues in my locker and pop on my special footwear for the occasion, an ancient pair of Minelli character shoes from a sixth-form production of Lorca's *Blood Wedding*, unearthed in the nether regions of the hall cupboard in the maisonette while searching for the dustpan and brush. I also came across a pair of Philippa's leg warmers – an unexpected windfall! I'd no idea Mum had kept hold of these old things of our. Fully attired, I admit I'm rather chuffed with my efforts. The leg warmers give a professional air.

Anita is wearing a leopard-print mini dress in faux suede – her fabric *préféré* – a denim jacket and a pair of elaborately chiselled cowboy boots. I presume she is going to slip on her leggings and dance pumps when we get to class. We take the bus to Camden and make our way to the venue, rather ominously called Descent.

Inside, Descent smells strongly of cider and public conveniences, and pulsates with flashing lights and the thrusting bodies of several dozen people. Anita pulls me through the throng to the bar and orders us drinks. The evening isn't turning out as I expected at all; there is not an elasticated waistband or leg warmer in sight. Instead, the men are astonishingly hirsute and everyone is decked out in at least one item of denim. Cowboy boots are clearly the garb de rigueur for all. I grip my bar stool as the live music starts and people rush to form lines across the dance floor. A rotund gentleman sporting a white cowboy hat and red neckerchief stands at a microphone and calls out incomprehensible instructions – 'Stomp. Kick-cross. Pivot!' – to which the assembled throng in unison begin to strut, waggle their hips, and make wild lassoing movements with their arms, all the while adhering to the line formation. At the end of the number, cowboy hats are tossed skyward, accompanied by some energetic cries of 'Yee ha!' Then the band strikes up again and White Cowboy bellows another mystifying series of actions: 'Heel-touch, two, three, four and kick-cross! Stomp to the front, stomp to the side, and heels, heels, heels! Kick-cross, heels, and stomp!'

'Bottoms up!' Anita says – referring, thankfully, not to another dance move but to the bottle of beer she is handing me.

I gulp a couple of mouthfuls of foam and peer through the mêlée of stamping denim for the doorway, planning a speedy ascent from Descent.

'Fab, isn't it?' Anita smiles. A spray of silver glitter sparkles on her cheeks and her hair has been meticulously coiffed and curled.

'Very . . . vigorous,' I say. 'I don't seem to recall you mentioning line dancing?'

'Too right! You wouldn't have come!'

'But I look . . . ridiculous.' I motion to my leg warmers.

'You look lovely. Thanks for coming with me. You're a pal, Dots.'

'Well, it's—'

'Drink up and let's hit the dance floor!'

Downing her beer at admirable speed, she grabs my hand and pulls me into the fray. I immediately lose her in a tangle of kicking, clicking bodies. I push my way to the back, try and lurk at the end of a row and do my best to just stay in line and in time, but what with all the turning and swivelling the back row soon becomes the front – a dance macabre. I step back and everyone else steps forward, turn left while they go right.

'Sorry,' I cry, as cowboy boots stomp first on my left foot then my right. I try to disentangle myself from the horde but keep getting turned around and kick-crossed back in. Lines of tush-pushing dancers come at me, whinnying and bucking like wild horses at a rodeo. I can't get the steps, they're too fast. The more I try, the more confused I become.

I give up, close my eyes and cede to the stampede.

Lost Property Worker Trampled in Hoedown Throwdown! Achy Breaky Heart Attack! TfL Tush-Push Tragedy!

But somehow I remain upright. Unscathed. Instead the thrum of the music vibrates under the soles of my shoes, pulsates from the energetic whirr of bodies around me. *Step, step, kick, kick, quarter-turn, and stomp!*

From somewhere deep inside me I feel again the lone call of a saxophone on the Pont des Arts on a summer's night. I remember following the sound to the riverbank, grabbing Emile's hand and pulling him into the sway of dancers twirling under the linden trees. Light reflecting on the river water, our bodies wrapped around each other, the soulful siren of the sax, and still feeling the music within me later, dancing to its secret notes all the way back to my *appartement*.

My body recalls and reawakens the memory held in its cells. I open my eyes. My Minelli-clad feet start a duet of their own under me. *Kick-cross and heels, two, three, four and stomp to the front, stomp to the side!* The music hums in my lips, tickles the backs of my knees, vibrates in my elbows. A totally different sound to the soulful Parisian sax, but still it ignites the same desire to move, to give over to the dance. *Cupid Shuffle!* My body finds the rhythm, pulls me with it. *Side shuffle to the left, two, three and kickball change.* I stop trying so hard to get the moves but instead yield to the beat, and soon I am clicking and stamping along with the rest; if not exactly on point, at least with the same gusto.

The jolt of joy at the remembered night on the Seine gives an added élan to my 'Sleazy Slide', my 'Boot Scootin' Boogie' and my 'Tush Push'. What a wonderful dancer Emile was, how close he held me. *Side shuffle to the right.* How warm and sweet-scented the summer air that night. *Grapevine to the right and kickball change!*

'May I?' A cowboy sporting a crimson feather earring offers me his arm. I see other similarly interlinked couples surrounding us. The music cajoles me, my feet tapping already, eager to join in the next number. Why not? I nod. He smiles and loops his arm through mine. The pace picks up and my partner swings me around the room at a dizzying speed.

'OMG! Look at you,' Anita cries, when eventually I emerge and make my way back to the bar where she is perched.

I do indeed look at myself – sweat runs between my breasts; one of my leg warmers has slipped over the heel of my shoe. I mop my upper lip with the sleeve of my leotard. Anita hands me a beer. I take it gratefully – I've worked up quite a thirst.

'Thank you. I must look a sight.'

'You look mega! I couldn't believe you out there, you're amazing!'

'I'm *not*,' I say, half resisting a smile.

'It's funny. I was watching you and thinking how different you look . . .'

'Different to whom? To what?'

'To you. At work you're so . . .'

'Yes?' I look at her quizzically over my drink.

'I think the word I'm looking for is "proper".'

'Anita, I do hope you are not suggesting that my dancing is in any way *im*proper?'

'Oh, no, Dots, I would never . . .' She stops when she sees I am grinning at her.

I take a mouthful of my beer.

'Well, look at me, line dancing, sipping beer at a bar on a work night – how very . . . Wild West!'

'Not to mention dancing with handsome cowboys,' Anita adds with a wink. 'And by the way, if you want to be proper Wild West you have to swig, like this.' She demonstrates admirably.

'I see. Goodness, it's quite a new venture.'

'If not now, when? That's what I say. Ever since I chucked Vince I tell myself, "You've only got one go around the block, Anita – get out there, or life will pass you by. You've got a second chance at happiness, but you have to grab it while you still can."'

I nod, look down at my character shoes, my feet tapping to the music.

'It's like . . . those little fancy soaps and creams you get in hotels,' Anita goes on, gazing philosophically at her beer bottle. 'How you slip them in your bag and take them home.

But then you never use them, you just keep them for best, you know?'

I don't know – I always take my own Pears soap in its plastic travel box. But I nod nonchalantly and hazard a swig.

'Well, if I don't get up and get out there, try new things, maybe meet someone new, then one day I'll wake up, look in the mirror, and best will have bloody been and gone.'

I am still not entirely sure where she was going with the soaps and creams, or what happened to them – although I can imagine they might still be somewhere in the hindmost quarters of her trusty bag – but I am with her in the spirit of the sentiment.

'You have to seize the moment,' I say.

'Yes, exactly. And speaking of seizing – I want you to teach me some of those moves!' She grabs my wrist and drags me back on to the dance floor.

Two highly industrious hours later, I stand at the bus stop in the cold drizzle refining my 'Sleazy Slide' – *Rock, rock, slide, slide, click, click, quarter-half-turn* – until a woman in a conker-brown leather coat passes and cheerfully informs me that the stop is out of service due to roadworks.

I throw caution to the wind and surrender to the Underground.

The tube at this time of night smells of fast food and repressed devastation. Most of my fellow travellers sit mesmerized by their phones but one woman in a plum duffel reads an actual book, held close to her face as if she is stealing the story.

It's been a very long time since I have taken the tube. I notice they have a new design on the carpeted seats, a sort of jaunty Liquorice Allsorts. A woman with olive skin and a Baby on Board badge smiles at me as I take the seat opposite her. She has a sensible satchel and wears a rather fetching indigo bobble hat.

At the next stop a woman with expensive hair and a houndstooth jacket gets on, takes the seat next to me and starts typing on a laptop, slim as a blade. A Chinese couple leave and are replaced by two young women, students probably. One of them wears red Dr Martens. Docs seem to be making a comeback. Despite a few empty seats, the students choose to stand; they sway back and forth with the pitch of the train. One of them, the one with the boots, has a bag on her shoulder. It is half open and my hands twitch to reach over, catch the dangling zip and seal it shut.

The girl sees me staring. I glance away, look up at the adverts – a picture of a bottle of restorative tonic promising verve, energy, 'A new you!' What would that be like? My feet tap out a few steps from the 'Tush Push'.

A new me. It felt so good to dance again. Could I pull off denim? Hmm, that might be a step-pull-change too far, but several of the dancers sported kerchiefs around their necks; I might venture a bandana . . . I had quite a penchant for scarves in France. Flashes from the evening play in my head: stomping and twirling with the throng, dancing with the cowboy, swigging beer with Anita, her saying, 'You're a pal, Dots.' These memories collide with others: hearing that I had been accepted on my MA, the inky water of the Seine, long summer nights, my language classes, Interrailing, Emile teaching me how to make raclette. Could I still remember? I might give it a go. Not really a meal for one . . . Perhaps I could invite Anita, though I doubt cheese-based meals are allowed on all her various diets—

The restorative tonic suddenly shunts back and forth before my eyes as the train screeches to a stop. A couple get up quickly and head to the doors, thinking they are at their station. But outside it is still dark; we are in a tunnel. The couple remain at the doors. They stare intently out of the window into the gaping blackness, willing the train to continue. Most of the other travellers remain tethered to their screen worlds, inured to the fissures and stutters of London commuting. But then the tannoy splutters into life.

'Ladi . . . s an Gen . . . men, on be . . . f of Trans . . . for Lo . . . on I apolog . . . for . . . elay.' The next line comes through clear as a bell. 'We are being held in the tunnel due to a person on the line.'

Sweat prickles my forehead. I can't breathe. My hands clutch at the fuzzy fabric of my seat.

Sellotape.

Inhale.

Sellotape.

Exhale.

The students shrug at each other, then go and sit in the seats vacated by the couple. The one in the red boots opens her mouth to say something to her friend. The friend gets out a bottle of water, gives it to Red Boots.

Safety Pin inhale *Safety Pin* exhale.

I can't breathe.

My glance ricochets around the carriage. The houndstooth-jacket woman keeps typing. Tap-tap-tap. A man in a paint-splattered boiler suit checks his watch. Tap-tap-tap. Baby on

Board's bindi glints like the North Star. I stare at it, try to focus.

Superglue.

Everybody carries on as normal. Houndstooth checks her watch. Tuts. Tap-tap-taps. Time seeps into the Allsorts seats.

Red Boots laughs. Baby on Board shifts her position.

Then, finally, a jolt, and the train moves.

My stomach seizes up. The bitter taste of bile in my mouth.

'You all right, love?' Boiler Suit looks at me.

Suuuuper Gluuuuue, Safetypin. Superpin. Safetytape. I stand up. Everything tips.

'Sit down, put your head between your legs.' A bottle of water is thrust under my nose. I gag.

'Give her some room.'

Sellotape, Sello . . . o . . . o . . . ooo.

'She's going to be sick.'

'Put your head between your legs.'

The train shrieks into a station. I stumble to the doors and fall out on to the cold tile of the platform, suddenly surrounded by wild animals, Leopard, Cheetah, Tiger.

'Is she OK?' A woman in a leopard-print coat paws at me. I stagger to my feet, push through the herds of bodies, claw my way up the escalator. Out. I have to get out. *Safety, Safety, Safety Pin.*

Above ground, I gasp a lungful of gritty London air and stumble through wet streets. I want to lose myself in this city, in its Roman, Victorian, Edwardian layers, in its medieval plague, its Restoration, its World War II Blitz and its bloody Boris Bikes. I want to disappear. Rain slashes down; everything blurs as I flounder forward.

I start to run.

Sellotapesellotapesellotape. My fringe slashes my forehead in wet slats. Directionless, I am carried by the bodies behind, in front, either side of me. A tide of strangers picks me up in a wet woollen wave and sweeps me down streets I don't recognize. I give over to it, relinquish all desire for direction. I just want to keep moving faster, further away, deeper into darkness.

I could have told them, if they had asked, Red Boots and her friend. I could have told them the statistics, all the numbers: that the Jubilee Line has had the fewest since they put in the new doors; that the Northern Line has had the most, 145 between 2000 and 2010. I could have said that the Victoria Line comes out in the middle. The average. But I didn't say. They didn't ask. They just carried on, sitting, tapping, chatting. Laughing. Like it was an everyday occurrence. As if it were perfectly ordinary that someone had just tipped themselves on to the line, into the face of an oncoming train, and been crushed on the track, broken open.

As if that were all right.

A corner, another road, another zebra crossing. Red, orange, green lights gashed with the endless wet of the downpour.

I run so fast I trip.

'Mind yourself!'

'Careful, love.'

'Watch out, for fuck's sake!'

Left, right, another corner, and now my body takes over. It knows the way. It knows to take me somewhere I can lick my wounds, somewhere I can hide, somewhere I am safe.

9

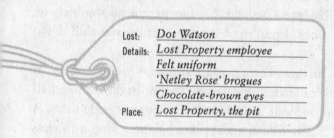

Lost: *Dot Watson*
Details: *Lost Property employee*
Felt uniform
'Netley Rose' brogues
Chocolate-brown eyes
Place: *Lost Property, the pit*

I feel my way across Customer Service in the dark, find anchor at the wooden counter, trace my hand along the warmth of its grain. Holding its familiar shape comforts me; its trusty topography leads me the length of the room. Then on, through the back office to the Ladies where I peel off my raincoat, my sweat-drenched leotard and trousers, and hang them in my locker, put on my dry uniform and my brogues, somewhat steadied by the stolid embrace of felt.

But I need more protection. Like a burrowing animal I need to go deeper, further underground.

In the service lift, I push the button for the stacks but when the doors open I don't get out. I remain immobilized till they close again. I press another button and slowly the lift sinks to the bottom of the building, down to the pit.

I stumble out. It's so dark down here. I knock into something in front of me: Big Jim's chute. I step back to the wall, pat my hand across it till I feel the switch and hit it. The fluorescents come on, their beams flickering half-heartedly over a mountain of unclaimed items – Big Jim's endless Herculean task. I pass the piles of lost things and push through a maze of metal wheeled crates waiting to be filled. I go further, into the unknown gloom of the low-ceilinged basement beyond. My footsteps echo sombrely on the stone floor. I pull my felt closer against the chill down here.

In the furthest corner, shapes loom – dense towers of bookcases lean exhausted against the walls; the bottom half of a suit of armour stands loyally on guard beside them. A mounted puffer fish in a glass box balances atop a faceless grandfather clock. I breathe the composite smell of these strange forgotten artefacts. Bready, slightly stale. In their midst, the low-slung body of a dilapidated mid-century sofa in a shade that can only be described as coarse-cut marmalade. One of its legs is missing and a precarious pile of paperback fiction provides a necessary crutch. Tufts of mottled stuffing gasp out of the seat and an old tartan picnic blanket droops over the back. Goodness knows how long these things have been down here, forgotten remnants from another time. Too unwieldy or defunct ever to be shipped to auction, they have taken root and grown into the building – dislodge them and the whole edifice might cave in on itself.

I sink on to the mid-century, which sighs and settles under me. I shiver, pull the picnic blanket over my shoulders. It releases a thin layer of dust and the scent of tobacco. In the distance, the fluorescents in Big Jim's crating corner continue to flicker. Light, dark, light, dark. On-off, on-off. Here then gone. I close my eyes but under my lids the light continues to judder, like a ribbon of old-fashioned film spooling through a projector. I look at the image it is playing.

It's you, Dad.

Long shot: it is spring. You stand perfectly upright in a field. You are wearing your brown suit, holding your briefcase.

Close up: I see your ears, the hairs on them. They look soft, your ears, pink, vulnerable, as if they are just unfurling like new shoots to the light. I see your feet. A tiny hairline crack appears between you and the ground. I see your tie tip forwards, outwards.

Then I stand and watch you fall.

And it's not a film, because I can't rewind. I can't go back to the moment before *the* moment and press pause. I can't stop you falling.

I have questions, of course. When you lightly snowed sugar over your cornflakes that morning, drank your strong tea from the mug I made you all those years ago in Mrs Bushnell's pottery class, DAD thickly scored into the side, did you know? Did you take an extra spoonful of sugar? Why not? Nothing to lose.

Did you run through what you had planned as you took out your two oval tortoiseshell brushes and smoothed back the badgery hair at your temples, silver-flecked, but still full?

When did you know? Was it when I didn't call you from Paris the evening before? Oh, that's one of my constant questions. I did try to telephone, Dad. But there was rather a troupe of us out that night, you see. I was with Emile.

The streets along the Canal Saint-Martin were full, chairs and tables tumbling outside cafes, people spilling on to pavements, the water of the canal school-uniform navy blue.

I did try to telephone. I promise I did. My phone was out of credit to call England but I nipped to a phone box down a little street just off the canal. Someone was already in it – I can see her now, the receiver tightly cradled between her shoulder and face, distressingly large gold hooped earrings that jangled as she spoke. Every once in a while, she would plunge a hand into her copious blonde mane of hair, shake her head and say, '*Tu n'écoutes pas! Tu n'écoutes pas!*'

I waited, Dad, I waited for ages. But she just went on and on, and in the end I gave up, returned to the light and warmth of the bar, the laughter and chatter of my friends. Emile said to use his phone, but it was noisy in the bar and cold outside, and then I got distracted, Emile catching my hand. '*Ma belle Dottette. Ma choupette.*'

I did try to call, Dad.

Do you remember how, when I was little, I used to get up early to wave you off to work? Force sleep away, push out of the cosy nest of my bed to stand sentinel at my bedroom window. I'd hear the front door close, the crunch of the gravel, then see you in your dark overcoat at the end of the drive. You would disappear for a moment behind the big willow by the front gate. Play a game with me, hide behind the tree till part of you – your arm, your head, your knee, your leg – would suddenly pop out and make me laugh. Then you would appear and I would wave and you would blow me a kiss.

I think about you catching the first train up to Victoria that day, the nasal voice of the announcer intoning last rites: *This train stops at Barming, West Malling, the Lord is my Swanley, Bromley South, I shall not want, London Victoria. London Victoria is the last stop.*

106

Did you rest your head against the smudged glass, look at the outside world scudding by? Goodbye, dear hills! Goodbye, old trees! Why, Dad? Why didn't you get up, get off at the next station, call in sick? Why didn't you pull the bloody emergency cord, Dad?

But you didn't. You sat in the commuter carriage and sped on towards death. At the Underground, you lined up for it, queued with the other commuters as they passed through the turnstile, and obediently filed down into the belly of the tunnel, knowing you would not be going up again. Your final descent.

The display board announced how much time you had left.

Three minutes.

Did you stare at the advert across the tracks for a summer holiday in the Algarve?

Two minutes.

Did the fat man in the mushroom-coloured suit jostle you with his arm? Two schoolgirls with hair in plaits laugh out loud but you didn't notice?

One minute.

Everyone expectant now. Moving closer to the yellow line, getting ready to mind that gap, the thrum of the approaching train palpable in the distance. Did your eyes focus for a moment on the headlines of your neighbour's newspaper?

Pound Sinks to New Low.

Recession Looms.

Wet Weekend Predicted.

Train approaching.

That smell of grit and electricity. The shriek of it. And in that last moment who did you think of, Dad?

Mum, Philippa? Me, your Dot?

Or someone else entirely?

Think of all your steps, Dad: the first upright totter that made Nanna clap her hands and call for Grandpa to come and see; the march up the aisle when you married Mum; the stride into the maternity ward to meet your new daughter, Philippa; the tiptoe as you and I slipped out to watch badgers in the moonlight.

Just one more step. Your last. Into thin air. Into the snorting, careering metal colossus that crushed the life out of you, breaking every single one of your bones.

Your arm, your head, your knee, your leg.

I hope that you were deaf to the screams of the terrified passengers. I hope instead your head was full of music, Dad, notes spinning sweet as candyfloss at 78 rpm, Jussi Björling and Robert Merrill singing together in perfect harmony as you stepped forward with your beautiful flat feet and let go.

That morning I hadn't been there to watch for you at the window. I hadn't waved you goodbye.

10

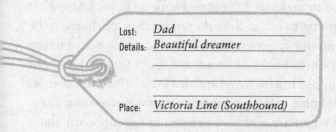

Lost: _Dad_

Details: _Beautiful dreamer_

Place: _Victoria Line (Southbound)_

It's late and I'm hungry.

I make my way back to the mountain of unclaimed items and forage. In a cardboard box, I discover a collection of label-less tins. In the beginning, such odd lost items would make me pause – who would be carrying so many bald tins on public transport? – but after years of logging life-size Spider-Man dolls, harpoons and vasectomy kits, I barely notice.

I give one of the tins a rudimentary shake. My fear, of course, is Pedigree Chum or similar ilk. The contents are loose, liquid. Tinned fruit? It certainly adds a frisson to mealtime. The tins come with ring pulls; for once I am pleased to see them. What else? Further excavations unearth a shopping bag containing a small tub of pink icing-sugar flowers, birthday-cake candles and a box of 'easy-cook' rice ('easy' is entirely dependent on where one is doing the cooking, as my situation tonight illustrates).

Returning to my lair, I spread the plaid picnic blanket on the floor and lay out my tins and sugared flowers. When we went on one of our jaunts – sometimes just down to the tangle of the back garden, sometimes further afield – Dad used to make us Adventure Picnics. I never knew what he was going to bring: domino sandwiches, pilchards to be eaten with our fingers straight from the can, a pot of honey spooned on to hunks of bread torn from the loaf, slices of cake wrapped in a tea towel and tied Dick Whittington-style. We would dine in the garden, adventurers discovering a new land, or on wetter nights sit camped in the cupboard under the stairs, detectives on a late-night stakeout – Holmes and Watson. But sometimes, on a Sunday afternoon, Dad would recoil into himself, a slice of Victoria sponge uneaten in his hand, confusing the plot of The Girl with the Diamanté Hair Bobble with that of The Case of the Home Counties Forger.

Sitting on the floor, I select a tin and open it. Whole peach halves – rather a contradiction in terms, I have always thought, but a happy result nonetheless. As I look about for an implement with which to scoop out the peaches, I notice something glinting underneath the mid-century. I reach and pull out a dusty glass bottle – alcohol of some kind. No wonder foraging has become so popular. I wipe the label: 'Absente'. I give a hollow chuckle at the irony of the word. In the dim light, I try to read the ingredients. Fennel, anise and wormwood. Absinthe! Wasn't that banned? A drink from another time, La Belle Époque. How long has this been secreted down here, gathering dust? I unscrew the lid, which resists at first, but I persevere and it comes off, releasing an aroma of liquorice and jeopardy.

I take a sip, or is it a swig? How does one drink absinthe? Aren't you supposed to serve it with a sugar cube? Would sugared flowers suffice? I crunch a pink nosegay and take another nip. It tastes sharp, acrid. Absinthe, the beverage of Rimbaud, Baudelaire, Zola. I remember reading about them in my class on early nineteenth-century French literature – drinking their potent cocktails in smoky bars in the Latin Quarter of Paris. I take another bitter mouthful.

Paris. My time in France feels so long ago and so happy that it seems to belong to someone else. Graduate school, teaching English to undergrads, exploring cafes and bars with Emile, browsing bookshops on the Left Bank. I thought it would last for ever.

It ended with the sound of my mother's voice on the phone.

'Your Dad's gone.'

I was standing in the office of Professeur Virginie Meunier, Directeur d'Études à l'Université Paris 1 Panthéon-Sorbonne, admiring an extravagant bouquet of white roses on her desk, wondering if the flowers were from her husband – who stared at me from a silver-framed photo, flanked by two ferret-faced offspring – or from a dark-haired paramour. I breathed in the scent of Gitanes cigarettes and amber cologne from the mouthpiece of Professeur Meunier's phone, and decided the flowers were definitely from her handsome lover. I imagined him whispering to her, his words caressing her down the phone line.

My mother's voice had no place in my reverie.

'What? Where?' I asked.

A pause. Why hadn't she called me on my mobile? Why was I in the Director of Studies' office, Professeur Meunier nervously watching me? Honestly. My gaze wandered out of the window, following the perfect topiary of the yew bushes in the garden outside, so ordered, so neat. So French. I traced along their clipped lines to Emile's lecture theatre, imagined him taking down detailed geological notes, biting his lip in that adorable way he had when he was concentrating.

Why had I been summoned from my class on Molière to a phone call with my mother? Why, when I was flying high on my perfect Parisian life?

Then Philippa came on.

'Dad's thrown himself under a train on the Victoria Line.'

She said it as if something terribly embarrassing had happened and we were all going to have to do everything we could to remove the stain, like red wine spilt on the carpet.

Much of what followed remains blurred in the fog of freefall: stark headlines in the local paper; Philippa pink-eyed and pregnant at the funeral, clutching Gerald; Mum silent, ashen, not looking at the coffin. A hum of meaningless hymns and prayers for a God none of us believed in. Friends, relatives, distraught and shifty, their earnest 'We're here for you' belying their latent desire to remove themselves from the stigma of being associated with such a suicide. So violent. So *public*.

Uncle Joe sent flowers from Canada. Florid chrysanthemums, ostentatious lilies. A note.

Gail, Philippa, Dot. We wish we could be there with you. Let us know how we can help, what we can do. We are all so very sorry for your loss.

Your loss. Just ours then, not his. Too embarrassing, too shameful, too much. Not something to be associated with Mum's dashing New World brother. Poor Dad; he was always so chipper when Uncle Joe was around, lit up just talking about him.

At night, the old family house groaned with the weight of the unspoken – Mum and I were still far too fragile to speak the truth. Philippa called in every day but never stuck around long to talk, though she would bring groceries. I couldn't eat, couldn't sleep. In the middle of the night, armed with a blanket and a flagon of Mum's cooking brandy, I'd retreat to the bottom of the garden. There I'd make a nest in the brambles and weeds and hunker down against the cold, slack-jawed in shock, and look back at the house, its facade haggard. I'd drink the brandy and then lie back and stare up at the sky, searching for comfort in familiar constellations. But my thoughts kept returning to how stars explode, become black holes insatiably pulling everything into a cold swallow from which no light can ever escape.

That's how I felt. Swallowed whole, forever lightless. Lost.

Late one night, Philippa came over. She was in her pyjamas, her eyes and nose streaming, her body shaking. I don't know what alarmed me more, the sight of my sister in hysterics or out and about in her nightwear – even in those days she would only open the door to the meter reader if she was in full make-up. It was about midnight and Mum had long since gone to bed. I made Philippa cocoa and put some figgy biscuits on a plate, but when I came into the sitting room she had already poured herself a tumbler of brandy.

'Is that suitable for the baby?' I said, gesturing to her bump.

She stared at me, opened her mouth, closed it, shook her head, and downed the drink in one gulp.

Philippa always seemed so above it all – the mess of our family – as if she came from another world where people wore quality fabrics in clotted creams and school-house blues. A world where nothing was stained or sullied, where everything was clean and crisp and laundered.

As soon as she could, Philippa had left home, got her business degree, then a job in brand management, and then married Gerald. With Gerald, it seemed she had gone overboard deliberately finding herself the complete opposite of Dad. A jovial Tory, a man's man, a proper City chap who could play all the games, knew all the rules, all the codes, and was buoyed up by it, not beaten down. She had swiftly designed a world as diametrically opposed to our home life as she could, with artificial turf, a stainless-steel kitchen, and an alpha male marking his territory with bluster and bonhomie.

Until that moment, seeing her sitting in Dad's old armchair so broken, I never realized quite how much she too felt the desolation of his death. She cried and clung to me, her whole body racked with sobs. I thought she would never stop, would asphyxiate on her jagged breath, choke on her own tears. It helped me, in a way, being able to hold her, soothe her, because just before she arrived I had been face-down on the floor, sobbing into the fitted carpet. Eventually Philippa wrenched herself away from me, wiped her nose on her pyjama sleeve and went back to her own house. I never saw her cry again.

*

A week after the funeral, I came into the kitchen to find the washing machine going full pelt and Mum at the ironing board, pressing the life out of one of Dad's work shirts.

'What are you doing?'

'It's Wednesday,' she said, turning the shirt over and steaming a sharp line along the cuff.

'So?'

'Laundry day,' she said, sending a hiss of steam into the other cuff.

I started at her, still not understanding.

Holding the iron in her hand, she looked down at the shirt lying flattened on the board. 'I wanted to do something . . . normal. I thought it might help. So I went upstairs to get the washing and . . .'

She closed her eyes for a moment, caught her breath. Then she looked at me.

'I found your dad's clothes in the hamper. I couldn't just . . . leave them there.'

She swallowed. I nodded dumbly, about to turn away. Then, on a chair next to the ironing board, I saw a plastic bag. In it were Dad's corduroy garden trousers, neatly pressed and folded, his navy socks paired up, two of his cotton vests, his white handkerchief. Hooked on the back of the chair, one of his light-blue work shirts.

'You're giving his clothes away?' My voice was tight.

'I thought the Heart Foundation could use them.'

She fluttered the shirt up from the board, poked a wire hanger through its collar and buttoned it, as if she was about to take it upstairs to their wardrobe where it would sway clean and fresh till he put it on. But she didn't go upstairs.

She hooked the shirt on the back of the chair with the other one. Pulled his sweater from the laundered pile. Started to iron his shape out of it.

'No,' I gasped. 'Stop it! You can't get rid of his clothes!' I pulled the freshly ironed shirt from its hanger, clasped it to me.

Mum paused, her shoulders sagging. 'He's gone.' Her face a landslide.

He's gone. As if that was a reason!

A tear ran down her cheek, hissed as she pressed it into the fabric.

'Stop it, why won't you stop it?' I screamed, lashing out. My hand knocked a framed photo from the breakfast bar. The glass shattered, sharp splinters scattering on to the kitchen floor. We both stared at the broken mess for a moment and then Mum put down the iron, got on to her knees and started sweeping up the glass with her blue dustpan and brush. I said nothing, just stood there clutching Dad's shirt. When she had cleared all the fragments she picked up the photo, naked now without its protective glass. It was an old one. Uncle Joe took it one Christmas of the four of us standing in front of the tree, all wearing our paper crowns from lunch.

Speaking more to herself than to me, Mum said, 'My mother knew. She told me when I first brought him home to meet them. "He's not for you, Gail," she said. I laughed. What did she know!' She gave a hollow laugh, shook her head. 'He was the love of my life.'

'I knew him better than anyone,' I said, still hugging his shirt.

Mum got up off the floor, carefully replaced the photo on the breakfast bar and stood, staring at it.

'It was . . . complicated,' she said at last, her voice a whisper. A sigh shuddered through her body.

I looked at the broken photo.

'It's my fault,' I cried, and ran out of the room.

I called Emile in tears. He'd gone back to France after the funeral for an interview, but as soon as he heard me he booked a flight and came over. He said I needed to get away, get out of the house. I didn't want to go anywhere but he begged, said it would be good for me. He splashed out on a hotel in London, took me to the theatre, an exhibition, to see the deer in Richmond Park. Mum made the most of my absence and got rid of every single one of Dad's things. His flannel, his Imperial Leather soap, his briefcase, his Sherlock books. The depth and breadth of the evacuation was astonishing. Unforgivable.

'Where are his things?' I shouted when I got back, saw what she had done. I tore through the house, searching for something, anything. 'His records? His record player? How could you do that? They were all I had left to hold on to.'

I only found Dad's pipe because it had fallen down the side of his armchair, along with the biscuit crumbs and two-pence pieces. Not long after that, Mum sold the house and bought the maisonette. No tall trees, no tangled garden. Nothing hidden, no secrets, no surprises. It felt as if she had erased Dad entirely from our life. Home didn't feel like home any more. I could not forgive her.

I returned to Paris because I didn't know where else to go. But everything there reminded me of how happy I had been. I couldn't imagine ever being happy again, and Paris with all its beauty hurt. I stopped returning Emile's phone calls, made excuses when he came around to my apartment, pretended I had work to do. Mostly I sat in the cold rain in the Jardin du Luxembourg, the weather so bitter and sullen it suited my mood. I wandered the antiques markets along the Seine, looked at the old records, held them in my hands.

I sunk deeper into grief and guilt. Louise called me every day but I couldn't speak, didn't want to talk about it. I had no words for it, not in any language.

Eventually I finished the relationship with Emile. We met at a cafe near the Louvre. Touristy, overpriced, with stringently pressed tablecloths and a weaponry of cutlery. Anonymous, anodyne. The perfect setting for what I had to do.

'*Mais pourquoi, ma chère Dottette? Pourquoi?*' he begged when I told him. I groped for words as surly waiters hovered above us but found none good enough, only '*Je suis désolée. Je suis désolée, je suis désolée.*'

For a while, staying in France let me imagine you still at our old home, Dad, out in the garden, checking your tomato plants. Every night I longed to dream of you, of us, off on one of our adventures. But you never came into my dreams like that. Then, as now, when I dreamed of you, you were always falling and I could never catch you.

I failed my qualifying exams, though I knew all the answers. Except to the only question that mattered.

The university encouraged me to stay, to retake, but I found I couldn't. Why study languages when I had nothing left to say? In the end, I returned to England, put the money I had earned teaching towards renting a small flat in London, and looked for work. I saw the advert for the job in the window of Lost Property after spending a morning wandering amongst the collected memorabilia of the Sherlock Holmes Museum on Baker Street.

I eat the remaining peach half with my fingers, take another draught of absinthe. The sharp taste I first experienced has lessened and it's really quite palatable. I pour a glug into the tin, swirl it round with the remaining peach juice, and down it as a postprandial digestif. My head spins in a buzzy rush. What a delicious drink! Perhaps it will become my cocktail of choice? *Just my usual*, I'll say to the barman at Descent, and he'll pour me my Peach and Absinthe. Peachinthe! Excellent mane for a drink – I mean name. Just one more dash then, a nip, a chaser. I pour another generous glug into the peach can. Down the hatch! *Ha.* Quite literally, it seems, as I survey my surroundings. In fact, the contents of my lair appear to have started spinning slowly, a merry-go-round of oddities: there goes the grandfather clock! Hello, puffer fish! I catch sight of Philippa on one spin – how on earth did she get down here? Her arms are going full pelt. A particularly exuberant round of Spray and Wipe? No! On closer inspection, I see she is conducting the London Philharmonic in Mendelssohn's *Lieder Ohne Worte – Songs Without Words*! Da-di-da-di-dum. A favourite of dear old Miss Hyde, who used to perform it – albeit with more vim than virtuosity – as the finale to the annual Christmas 'Notes at Nativity' concert.

Suddenly, a voice brings the music to a halt. 'By Jove, this is a treasure trove indeed.'

I leap to my feet, brandish my picnic blanket before me, a tartan shield.

'Who's there?' I stutter, heart racing like a Derby winner.

Silence. Then the Mendelssohn echoes once more through the pit, and with it . . . the scent of pipe tobacco.

'Ah, Baker Street, so good to be back.' The end of the sentence is followed by an exhale of smoke, which drifts towards me, a spool of unravelled cotton through the dark. A figure steps forward in the gloom.

Only then do I realize it is him.

'The world is full of obvious things,' he says, coming towards me, 'which no one observes. Except you and I, my dear Watson. In the mislaid purse, the discarded wallet, the walked-away-from walking stick – we apprehend it all.'

My mouth goes as dry as a Dirty Martini.

He takes a long suck on his pipe and exhales slowly. I inhale cherry smoke and close my eyes for a moment, open them, and the room takes a few more spins.

'Yours, Watson?' His long fingers gesture behind him to the piles of unclaimed items.

'It's all Big Jim's stuff,' I croak, still clutching the blanket.

He is close now and I can see the curve of his pipe, the bird-wing swoop of his dark hair. His face is so familiar I can barely breathe.

'Big Jim, eh? Sounds like a suspicious cove. Distinguishing marks?'

'He is rather awash with tattoos,' I whisper.

'Indeed! Let's keep an eye on him.' He blows out another swirl.

'I just can't believe . . . it's you.' A shuddering sigh escapes, and with it an extraordinary feeling of lightness and release. I smile.

He smiles back and throws himself down on the mid-century.

'What a pad, old thing! What a hideaway!' He sits with his fingertips pressed together, elbows on his knees, surveying the room. 'One can only imagine what gems and riches languish down here! A miscellany of mysteries and clues.'

'It's a bit in disarray, I'm afraid. If I'd known you were coming I'd have tidied round.'

He pats the sofa, inviting me to sit next to him. I do.

'We have much to catch up on. It's been too long.'

I nod. The smell of him is intoxicating. I move a little closer.

'Oh, Watson, remember our cases? The Ghostly Terror in Tunbridge Wells? The Mystery of the Kentish Carbuncle?'

I nod happily, drape the picnic blanket over me and snuggle down under it.

'A gemstone such as that carbuncle could be secreted quite safely down here.' He surveys the room again. 'But do you know, on closer inspection, I think these environs are more like the den of thieves in The Case of the Back-Garden Burglar. Remember how we cracked that one? It was the heart of winter and we had discovered the blueprint of the underground hideaway . . .' He goes on, but I simply hear the pup, pup, pup of his pipe.

11

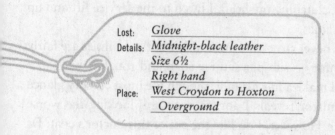

Opening my eyes even a slit causes a groan of pain and a wash of nausea. I cannot claim to have slept well. This is partly owing to the mid-century's narrow frame, but the lion's share of blame has to be apportioned to the absinthe. I try to calm the churning sickness and crushing headache by focusing on the positives – it's quiet as the grave down here and I've never been so centrally located; it will be a handy commute . . . Oh God! What time is it? I pat myself down, searching for my phone, and feel not the familiar nap of my trusty felt but smooth cotton. I sit up sharply, causing my head to pound with pain. I look down at myself and discover that at some juncture last night I changed into what looks like a white lab coat. Where is my uniform? Ah, draped unceremoniously over the half-suit of armour. I stagger to my feet – still clad in yesterday's tights – grab my jacket and retrieve my phone. 8.35 a.m.! Barely any time to sort myself out before staff start arriving upstairs! Thank heavens I am the only one who ever comes in before eight fifty, although NB might be in early and lurking . . . hells bells!

The 'Absente' bottle lies on the floor, its contents significantly reduced, surrounded by a pink powder of smashed sugar roses. A wave of nausea and panic overcomes me and, clutching my head, I lurch to the service lift and up to the Ladies.

It has never struck me previously but the facilities are fairly rudimentary – sub-par squirty soap and rough-hewn paper towels. I make a fair fist of it, though the most cursory glance in the mirror reveals I am (as expected) looking the worse for wear. However, I do like the cut of this doctor's coat: Dr Watson indeed! I close my eyes a moment; a faint waft of tobacco. How long did he stay? Until I fell asleep? What a comfort it was. When can I see him again? My head spins.

Dousing myself briskly in cold water, I start to feel slightly more compos mentis. Brushing my teeth might present a challenge, though where there is a doctor's white coat there might also be a bottle of mouthwash. But more pressing: how can I possibly turn up to work in yesterday's underwear? My phone flashes 8.40 a.m. Even though I don't have the time, I tear off my tights and knickers, plunge them into the sink, and scrub them vigorously with soap and water. I wring them out and attempt to dry them under the hand dryer, which emits staccato bursts of lukewarm air. *Come on! Dry, you blighters!* The tights reluctantly shift from dripping to damp but, despite forceful flapping, the knickers remain stubbornly soggy.

Might there be something in the pit? Bare-bottomed under my lab coat, I take the lift back down and tear through Big

Jim's pile of unclaimed items for something that could serve as underwear. Nothing even remotely suitable. Why on earth did I think it was a good idea to wash my knickers? Day-old pants are at least better than no pants at all! Then I remember. A three-pack of mint-green silk ladies' briefs in an M&S carrier, along with a set of bath towels the colour of sand and a matching floor mat, found on the Central Line. I recall it distinctly because the knickers popped up like an oasis in the desert. I imagined they were a sudden reckless treat flung into the shopping basket at the last moment.

That bag came in . . . about a month ago? Might we still have it? I dash back to the stacks, not even daring to look at the time on my phone. I didn't shelve it when it came in, but it should be here in 'Assorted Bags, Briefcases and Trollies' . . . *Et voilà!* For the first time, I find pleasure in an item not being claimed. The Dijon reveals that under NB's new rules the bag is four days short of relegation to the pit. Strictly speaking, this being Thursday, two of those days are Saturday and Sunday, when Lost Property is closed. Friday is always quiet; people are distracted by the weekend, thinking about what's to come rather than what's gone. One could posit, then, that just one day lies in the balance before the bag will be sent to the pit and then off to Snagsbey's. I hold the packet of knickers in my hand, weigh necessity against integrity. Could I do it? Make use of a bona fide item of lost property? How low have I sunk? Low indeed, because – perhaps goaded by the absinthe still circulating in my system – I rip open the pack, grab a cool silky pair, and before my conscience gets the better of me, retreat once more to the pit where, heart racing, I pull them on along with my damp tights and felt uniform.

As I bend to tie my brogues, I feel a wave of dizziness. I need to eat something after all that alcohol. 8.48. Quick then, quick! I grab a tin, actively relishing the swift ring pull now . . . and this morning's breakfast is . . . *drum roll* . . . tinned prunes! Ah. Bit of a slap in the face with a wet fish, or indeed, a pair of damp tights, but still. I scoop a couple of the fruits out and force them down, shove the opened tin under the mid-century – along with the absinthe, my lab coat and a sweep of sugar-flower crumbs – and hazard a peek at my phone. 8.50. I've done it! I ride the service lift up to start work, if not as fresh as a daisy, at least as resilient as a thistle.

By the time the rest of the staff start to arrive I am in situ behind the counter, labelling and doing data entry as per.

Anita and the beast clank in at 9.01, cutting it fine as ever.

'Dot! What about last night?!' she cries, rushing over to me, wide-eyed.

Can she tell? Is my uniform suspiciously creased? Did someone see me? Can she smell absinthe on my breath?

'What?'

'At the club! You were amazing. Your dancing!'

'Ah. Right.' To be honest, what with more recent events, I had quite forgotten our hootenanny at Descent.

'What else have you been keeping secret, you sly dog?'

Squatting. Consuming lost property. Wearing it.

'Not a thing.' I busy myself tidying a perfectly stacked pile of forms.

'What about your admirer!'

'My what? Who?'

'That chap with the earring you were dancing with? He was tasty.'

'Ah, well, I wouldn't call him an admirer—'

'I would, you lucky thing.'

I look over at her. A slender Milky Way of glitter from last night still traces her left cheekbone.

'Did you have a good time, Anita? Any . . . admirers?'

'No, sod 'em, but who cares! I loved it! And I would never have gone by myself. You really are a pal, Dots.'

I am encircled in a tight embrace. I close my eyes and give over to the reassuringly familiar smell of her hairspray and strawberry lip gloss, the warmth of her affection, until it becomes hard to swallow and my eyes fill. I pull away.

'Better get on.'

I turn back to the computer, focus on the screen. Log and file. Log and file. *Sellotape. Superglue. Safety Pin.*

At lunch-time, I purchase a toothbrush and paste, underwear and paracetamol, but am still too green around the gills to contemplate food.

When I return, Anita immediately spies my bag, of course.

'Dot Watson! Fuck a duck! You've got a dirty stop-out kit! Anything more you want to tell me about last night?'

I am saved by the shrill summons of my phone.

'Did you get my text?' Philippa pierces more than usual. 'Murray Greenridge *loved* the house. Excellent valuation; reckons it will be snapped up for the asking, more if we're lucky. They're doing the pics today – you hadn't forgotten, had you?'

'How could I?'

She steams on.

'They say it will show really well. And I've picked up the particulars of a couple of nice properties for you, cosy and affordable. Shall I leave them when I pop by the maisonette?'

'I didn't know you were popping by.'

'Well, thought I might tidy up a bit before the photos. I've got some time today.'

'No need.'

'I'm happy to help. Just a bit of a wipe-around and . . . clear-up.'

I have visions of the Alpine puzzle avalanching into a bin bag, my guides rearranged in some heinous display centred around Marbella, Klosters and Antigua.

'Philippa, there's really no need for you to clean.'

'Are you sure?' Clearly she isn't.

'Absolutely.'

I stumble through the day, trying to keep occupied and avoid Anita's probing questions. Memories of last night flood in when I least expect it: the smell of the Underground, the lurch as the train stopped, the matter-of-fact-ness of the announcement . . . *due to a person on the line*. I retch, barely make it to the Ladies in time. Afterwards, I run cool water on my wrists, look at my ashen face in the mirror and take myself in hand. 'Keep it together, Dot Watson.' I straighten my uniform and return to work.

A woman in a letterbox-red quilted Barbour holds a black leather glove taut in her hands, palm-side up, towards me.

'I've lost the other one.'

'Do you know where you lost it, madam?'

'I was travelling from West Croydon to Hoxton. I must have taken it off and left it on the seat, I suppose. But it's not like someone would take it, would they? I mean, a single glove is no use to anyone; they only make sense in a pair.'

'May I?' I take the glove. 'Midnight-black . . . size six-and-a-half . . . right hand . . .'

'What?'

'The right-hand glove is the one that's lost.'

'Oh – yes.'

'It's most common, the right – a case of the left hand not knowing what the right hand is doing.'

The woman smiles. 'I almost didn't come,' she confesses. 'I mean, who would bother to hand in a single glove anyway? Who would come looking for one?'

'You have.'

She laughs. 'Yes, I suppose that's true.'

'It's why our mums threaded them with elastic – they knew what was at stake.'

'Right!'

I hand the glove back to her and continue to fill in the form. I feel her standing there, waiting, full of hope. Her remaining glove bares its palm, outstretched and waiting for its partner.

'We need a clear description of the lost glove. Was it absolutely identical to the one in your hand? Did it have any distinguishing marks?'

'No, it was just like this one – they were brand-new.' She turns the glove over so I can see the pattern on its back: a nice criss-cross stitching, the lines ramrod-straight.

I add a row of Xs on to the form, just in case that helps us locate it.

Anita passes by and treats us to one of her throaty chuckles when she sees what I have done.

'Looks like you're writing love notes, Dots!' She arches a brow, clearly thinking back to my 'stop-out' kit.

'It's not a love note,' I say. 'It's a description of the glove.' I turn to the woman. 'I'll just check the computer, see if anything matching your description has been handed in.'

I do a thorough search – it offers up 'plain black', 'butter-cream', 'two-tone caramel', 'leather', 'driving', 'fingerless' – and she stands watching me, holding the singleton glove in her hands. Finally, I have to tell her that there is no match.

'Never mind.' She sighs. 'I suppose it might still show up?' She looks at me hopefully.

That sort of hope demands respect. I recall Mr Appleby's words when he first came searching for his holdall: *I come more in hope than expectation . . .* An ache jags in my throat.

'It might,' I say to the woman.

I watch her carefully fold the lone glove in on itself and put it in her handbag. Unless its partner is found, it will forever be relegated to the back of a drawer, the bottom of a bag, unworn and alone. She leaves and I take a moment to blot my eyes on my trusty felt.

With my emotions every which way today, it's a relief when the final lost umbrella, phone and shopping bag are recorded and the day is done.

'Any plans tonight, Dots?' Anita winks suggestively as she heads to the door.

'Nothing special.'

'Safe home.' Anita blows me a kiss and steps out into the evening.

I carry a crate down to the stacks, and shelve a raincoat and a fedora in 'Men's Clothing'. I wasn't planning to stay

130

here another night, but the thought of going back to Mum's maisonette where strangers have been nosing around and taking photographs is almost too much to bear.

And if I stay, I might see him again.

I wander down the aisle, absently stroking the arms of coats, the hoods of jackets. The anorak with the Polo mints has been collected, I see. The chap would have been glad to get that back. Did he reach into his pocket and find the Baedeker guide to Berlin? Was he pleased? Perhaps he will leaf through it on a clammy bus ride and be cheered by images of young people gathering in Alexanderplatz, drinking schnapps in a bar lit by amber lamps. I do hope so.

Unprepared for a second night in Lost Property, I return once more to the tins, and my lucky-dip dinner reveals itself to be . . . fruit cocktail! The colourful medley is a lovely surprise, but how on earth to eat the contents? Fingers sufficed for the whole peach halves and the prunes but will not do for the fruit cocktail. Hmm, it's hardly swiggable. I am momentarily stumped by the complete lack of cutlery down here. Grandfather clocks and puffer fish abound, but a humble teaspoon? There used to be a few knocking about in the kitchen nook, but since NB requisitioned it there isn't a spoon to be found. A detailed reconnoitre of the pit fails to dig up a single knife, fork or spoon. *And all for the want of a horseshoe nail*, Benjamin Franklin's catchy truism echoes. Come to think of it, we probably do have a whole horseshoe with a bevy of nails somewhere in the stacks, amongst the gymkhana rosettes and curry-combs left on the train from Epsom . . . But what is this? I unearth a chemistry kit from the very bottom of Big Jim's pile. Retreating to my lair, I manage the fruit cocktail most adequately aided by a pair of

131

beaker tongs and a small glass rod. It takes a while, and at times it feels like I am participating in a piece of durational performance art, but I am not in a hurry and it appears absinthe is the perfect accompaniment to a wide range of tinned fruit.

It's so quiet down here! Above me the pavements pound with thousands of people. Roads boom with traffic, red buses thunder, black cabs rumble. The constant metallic hum of chrome and glass scraping and forcing, forever upwards. But here, deep in the bowels of Lost Property, it is so still, so silent.

When I finish my dinner, I count my tins. Twelve altogether, including last night's peaches and this morning's prunes. Did someone lose the contents of an old air-raid shelter on the Bakerloo Line? Mislaid bounty for a Harvest Festival? What is the shelf life of tinned fruit? Does it have a best-before date or does it wait interminably, like that lotus flower in the bog, just longing for its moment to shine? As I think about this, I give the empty fruit cocktail tin a bit of a polish with a corner of the tartan picnic blanket. I get up rather a sheen and soon set to work buffing the rest of the cans. Then I arrange them in a tower formation. Quite a display! It turns out that a tin can be a thing of beauty in the right light. Twelve tins, two empty (I'm only returning to the prunes if I get desperate), so that's . . . nine more meals, which means about four more days, fewer if I let myself have pudding now and then. Not that I am planning on staying here. Of course not.

But while I am here, it's good to keep busy, take my mind off things. The flickering fluorescents, for example. They make the pit rather trippy – albeit compounded by the effects of absinthe – like staring into a film projector or being at a minimalist discotheque. The worst culprit is the one over Big Jim's pile of unclaimed items.

This is the perfect time to put to use the DIY tips I picked up from Mum's TV programmes. I require tools, which the pit is currently sadly lacking. But wait a tick! What about that paint-spattered canvas bag replete with scrolls of sandpaper, lathe, and family of screwdrivers in descending heights that came in a few weeks ago? I know just where to put my hands on it in the stacks. I dither for a moment. After the knickers, it seems I am on rather a rocky road to ruin. Availing myself of items in the stacks is quite a different thing to the unclaimed in the pit. With them, I feel I am offering what might be their last chance for salvation, but the items in the stacks are in limbo, still holding on to the possibility of being reclaimed by their owners. But it would be so good to fix this light, and it would just be a borrow, more like a library loan.

Ten minutes later I am standing on a couple of upturned crates, medium-sized Phillips screwdriver in hand, un-screwing the light fixture hanging above the mountain of lost things, using my phone as a torch to illuminate the tiny fittings. I mentally go over the instructions from the DIY programme.

Does Mum still watch those? Does she sit with the others in the communal lounge or stay alone in her room? Suddenly my phone goes off in my hand. Philippa. To avoid any difficult questions as to my whereabouts, I let the phone take the message and then tap the voicemail icon.

'I just called the house phone but you didn't answer.' Philippa's voice ricochets around the pit, glancing off the stone walls. 'Not home yet? Still at work? I hope they're paying you overtime. Or . . .' There's a pause. 'Are you *out*? With anyone *special*?' Another pause, presumably for her to mouth to Gerald the thrilling possibility that I might be on a date. 'Well, listen, I'm just calling to remind you about those property deets I picked up. There's an adorable cottage for sale very near us. That would be nice, wouldn't it? Anyway, I'll hang on to them. Can't wait to see how the photos of Mum's maisonette come out.'

A prong of silver filament pricks my thumb and a perfect dome of blood is illuminated by the light from my phone, displaying Philippa's name, as if my sister is directly responsible for my injury. In many ways she is.

Occasionally, in the stretch of summer when even those on the outer rim of her circle of friends were unavailable, Philippa would cut her losses and deign to engage with me, five years her junior. One time she came into the garden and found me looking for buried treasure in the potato patch, and commandeered me to go to the swimming baths with her.

The air was parched. Our sandals scuffed the dusty road as we slogged the sweltering mile to the leisure centre. The prospect of the cool dip spurred us on.

It wasn't until we arrived and were getting changed that I realized I'd forgotten my swimsuit.

'What will I do?' I said, standing in my vest and knickers, toes curling on the slimy changing-room floor, my throat tightening with tears.

'I don't know,' Philippa said, pulling on her orange swim cap, covered with its adorable little fishes. 'But I'm not going all the way home and missing my swim because of you.'

She turned and marched off in the direction of the pool. She knew I wasn't allowed to walk home by myself.

Her float lay on the wooden bench. She pretended she only kept it because it was orange and matched her swimsuit and cap. But I knew it was because she couldn't go into the deep end without it. Even at seven, I was a better swimmer. Much.

I also knew that Toby Jackson was trying to get on to the diving team and was training at the pool all summer. Philippa had a big crush on Toby Jackson. She was always going out of her way to bump into him, wanting him to notice her.

I wiped my eyes, pulled my dress back over my head, and trudged upstairs to the spectators' gallery, which smelt of chlorine, and cheese-and-onion crisps. The gallery overlooked the shallow end of the pool, where I recognized some of the girls from my school, the ones with the white knee socks, sharp sandwiches and pierced ears who shunned me at lunch-times. Across the expanse of cool blue water, I saw Philippa and her little fishes. Madonna's 'Who's That Girl' was blasting through the sound system and Philippa sang along, walking purposefully across the slick tiles towards the deep end where Toby Jackson was executing a splashy crawl.

After a while Toby spotted her. He gestured for her to jump in. I watched as Philippa froze, then walked to the very edge of the pool.

Giddy with fear, I stood up, leaned against the railings and got ready to leap over them, rush forward and save her.

'Philippa!'

She pointed up at me.

'Sorry, Toby.' Her voice was amplified across the water. 'Love to, but I'm babysitting my little sister – she just wet herself. I promised her I'd only swim in the shallow end to stay nearby, in case she needs me.'

Whenever I think we might be close, something reminds me how unalike we are. The age difference gives her the upper hand – extraordinary, the tyranny and power that those five years wield. Nonsense, of course, but I feel it, the clout and welly of the older sibling, her capacity to make me feel the same mute heartbreak of unjustness today that I felt up there in the spectators' gallery. And here I am, still spectating from the sidelines as she forges ahead.

I delete Philippa's message, take a short break to wet my whistle with another nip of absinthe – *Where is he? Will he come again?* – and return to fixing the light. It's devilishly fiddly, but eventually I clamber down and flick the switch. The light hums a steady beam. My heart thumps, a punching fist in my chest. The fluorescent illuminates all the forgotten bits and pieces.

Under a man's dove-grey gabardine coat I notice an Anglepoise lamp, still in its box. Why not have even more light! Let everyone have a chance to shine. I unbox the lamp, find a socket and plug it in, focus its beam on a lovely hand-knitted robin's-egg blue scarf. Beautiful! More! A lost torch and a bicycle headlight spotlight a walking stick and a woolly hat, make them glow, luminescent. My cast of scarves, satchels and shopping bags take their places centre stage.

'You're not lost tonight,' I tell them all, spanning my arms wide. 'I adopt every single shivery sock, abandoned book and dear jumper. You are under my care.' Everything around me seems to pulsate with life.

I pick up Big Jim's 1970s retro Toot-a-Loop radio. Unbeknownst to me, as it has always sat in the same dusty spot on a broken crate in the pit, I discover that the Toot-a-Loop is in fact wearable. 'Wear it, swing it, twist it!' direct the words printed along its side. I obey, bending the oblong of plastic so that its two ends meet and form a jaunty bangle. How innovative! I slide it on to my wrist and turn it up. A disco track thrums a low bass, loping rhythm.

I run my hand over a pile of gloves, hover above one – cream leather, butter-soft – then slip it on. A perfect fit. I look down at my two hands, one ensconced in the finest fabric, the other naked, unsheathed. How long will the letterbox lady search for her missing glove? How long will she keep up the hope that one day she will be reunited with her other half?

The owner of this creamy glove never came back for it; nor did the owner of the Spanish-style waistcoat, or the smart tan suitcase with the shiny brass snaps that still has so many places left to travel. The Malacca cane with the silver hare's head, the maroon coat with the velvet collar, the rucksacks, scarves, raincoats, spectacles, books, wedding dress, wash bag. All abandoned, left, forgotten. But it's all right because I'm here, logging and labelling, taking care.

The cream glove, dormant for so long, abandoned, is now animated on my hand. Once more it is able to fulfil its true destiny as a glove. And what a smart glove it is – supple, elegant. Where might one wear such a glove? A day at the races? A picnic at Glyndebourne? A romantic dinner? My fingers reach out, flex, suddenly awake to the possibilities. The leather creaks with excitement. This glove would look rather fetching paired with . . . that maroon overcoat! I pull the coat out of the pile, slip it on. Quality fabric, and what a marvellous swooping length it has! In a coat like this, one would sashay rather than walk down the street, luxuriating in the swoosh of the material . . . I flounce around Big Jim's crates. 'Stayin' Alive' throbs from my radio-cum-bangle. *Swish, swoosh, swish. Ball change. Kick-cross. Pivot.* I hold the skirt of the coat out delicately between my gloved fingertips, breathe in the perfume that lingers on the velvet collar. Rich, musky. A bold perfume worn by a bold woman. If I were such a woman wearing such a perfume, I might seek the dashing companionship of a . . . I peruse the pile of unclaimed garments. Suddenly my gloved hand brazenly reaches in, grabs the sleeve of the gabardine raincoat. A brief introduction and then we're off! A swift tango, perfectly in time. I catch sight of the Spanish waistcoat and without a breath switch partners, take my new *compañero* for a quick Fandango around the pit, switch again to a tangerine silk sarong that twirls out and then back into my arms. One arm looped through the sarong, I link the other with a midnight velvet jacket. How swell the three of us look! The best of chums, we do everything together, always have. Just out for a night on the town. Which town? Take your pick! Singapore? Seville? Santiago? We meet a rucksack-clad student just off to Australia, and change our plans. Sydney it is! Who packed the sun cream? I did! It's here in my tan suitcase with the shiny brass snaps! Sydney is such fun that we keep going: Bangalore, Chiang Mai, Shanghai, all over Italy – Ravello, Monteriggioni, Cefalù. Zambia, Tanzania, Madagascar, Cavalaire-sur-Mer, Conche des Baleines, the Pyrenees! Around the world we spin, me and my dear chums. Finally, we return home to our jobs, our lives, our families, and no one can believe the times we have had. They wonder at all the things we have done, all the people we have met, all the places we have gone!

The whirr of tangerine, velvet, cream slows. Stops.

All the things I could have done, people I could have met, places I could have gone. I gaze around and see – nobody. No one. Just me and a pile of lost things. All abandoned, left, forgotten.

I switch off the Toot-a-Loop, return it to its place. Then I reach for the absinthe and drink deeply, staggering slightly as I make my way, dizzy and disoriented, back to my lair.

'Greetings, old chum!' He is sitting on the mid-century, the picnic blanket draped over his shoulders like a plaid cape. He puffs blue spirals of smoke that curl up into the air.

I beam.

'How completely lovely to see you! May I offer you a beverage?' I join him on the sofa and catch my breath. I proffer the absinthe.

'I'll stick to my pipe, old bean, but most kind. Well, how was your day? Clues abounding? Mysteries solved?'

'A lost glove, I'm afraid.'

'Ah, dashed tricky, single gloves.' He sucks his teeth and nods sympathetically. 'What kind? Driving? Dress? Opera? Fingerless?'

'Marks and Spencer's, midnight-black, funeral,' I say, sinking lower on the sofa, taking a generous gulp of absinthe. Hoping he'll stay all evening.

'Funeral, eh? Suspicious circumstances?'

'I don't think so.'

'Pity. Still, nil desperandum, old thing. It might turn up.' He smiles. 'It really is so good to see you, Watson. Tell me, what events led you to take rooms down here?'

I open my mouth but he holds up his hand.

'Your pen, if I may?'

Slightly hesitant, as I am down to one since Anita 'borrowed' my second best, I unclip my Sheaffer. He tents his fingers together, narrows his eyes and looks at me.

'I'd wager you have been here for some time,' he says.

'How do you deduce that?'

'As I have oft told you, one must never trust to general impressions but instead concentrate on the details.' He points at my jacket. 'The darker patch exposed on your pocket where the pen sits reveals that it – or its predecessor – has been clipped there for quite a while.'

I look to where he is pointing, and indeed a Sheaffer-sized ghost marks the fabric. I feel a strange pang of sadness when I see it.

'The cuffs of your admirable jacket are worn,' he continues, 'but the real clue, along with the general cut of your jib, is the knowingness with which you navigate the aisles, attend to your lost charges, et cetera. You have become a native; ergo I posit that several years have passed.'

'Well done.' I try to muster a smile.

He studies me.

'It's not what I imagined for you, Watson.'

I start to protest, but again he holds up his hand.

'There is nothing wrong with your chosen employ; indeed there is much to be commended in reuniting person with property. It is no small thing, old bean, to turn back time and restore something dear. No small thing at all. And of course, not always possible.' He gives me a sad smile.

I nod. An ache arcs my throat.

'But think of the adventures we used to have!' he goes on. 'You were always such an adept chronicler, and voyager and linguist.'

I toy with my Sheaffer.

'My job keeps me occupied,' I say. 'And really, it's not as if I've been here . . . *for ever.*'

'Of course not, of course not. But see here, what about the evenings? Weekends? Perhaps it is then that you find time for adventuring?'

I think of Mum's old jigsaws and shake my head. 'I suppose I always thought that I would pursue my languages . . . travel . . .'

'Yes, yes!'

'I fancied something in interpreting . . . I used to long to work for the UN.'

'That's right! You did! A most admirable pursuit!'

'But I did not pursue it.' I clip my Sheaffer back on to my pocket, conscious of the faded felt.

He leans forward. 'I have hit a nerve, forgive me. I'm just so dashed pleased to see you. I have thought about you so much over the years, wondered how you are.'

'You have?'

'Of course!'

'I've thought about you too. So much.' I swallow and look at him; my eyes blur with tears.

'My dear Watson. My trusty friend and companion.' His hand reaches out and covers mine. I try not to move, not to breathe, try to keep him there with me as long as I can.

He stays for pudding. Pineapple rings.

12

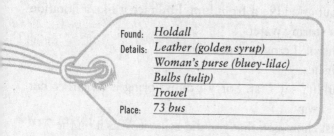

Found: *Holdall*
Details: *Leather (golden syrup)*
Woman's purse (bluey-lilac)
Bulbs (tulip)
Trowel
Place: *73 bus*

Friday: I'm at the counter and, I fear, not looking my professional best. This morning I filched a soupçon of shampoo from a velour travel bag in the stacks. I have been duly punished for taking liberties with other people's property as the shampoo turned out to be body lotion. I admit I'm somewhat sleep-poor and absinthe-rich, and the basins in the Ladies continue to present quite a challenge for a full body wash, even with the correct cleansers. I did my best to rinse out the lotion but have emerged with a lank and greasy coiffure. In tandem with my new *eau d'absinthe* and the dark bags under my eyes, I'm sure I look and smell a little shady.

There is a lull in Customer Service, and I'm just wondering if I could nip to the loo and give my hair another rinse when the door opens and a customer approaches.

I smooth my uniform. Unclip my Sheaffer. Peel off a Lost Item form. Look up – and catch my breath.

My hand flies to my chest. Before me, in the arms of a middle-aged man in a black donkey jacket, is Mr Appleby's holdall.

'Is this the right place for turning in something left behind on a bus?' the man says.

I nod. Beam. Nod again. Then, a slight shake in my hands, I reach out and take it from him. Embrace it like a flotation device in stormy waters.

'You hero!' I croak eventually.

He blushes.

'I wouldn't say that. Sorry I didn't bring it in earlier but I've been away . . .'

'It's just champion that you did bring it. Was it on the 73?'

'Yes, it . . . How did you know that? An old man left it behind when he got off. By the time I noticed, it was too late. I thought it was worth a whirl, to bring it here.'

'You saw Mr Appleby on the bus?' I cry excitedly. I don't know why, but the thought of the man being on the same bus as my Mr Appleby fills me with delight.

The man nods.

'Yes, nice guy. I noticed him when he got on because he helped a woman with her pram, made sure she got a seat, then tipped his cap to her. I remember thinking that was an old-fashioned sort of thing to do, that he was . . .' He searches for the right words.

I find them for him. 'A true gentleman.'

'That's it, a proper gent. Don't get many of those nowadays. So he's already come looking for his bag? You can let him know it's here?'

I beam. 'Yes I can, and shall do directly!' I wish I could give the man something, a medal or at least a garibaldi from

144

the kitchen nook, but sadly I have neither at my disposal so I just thank him again, from the bottom of my heart.

I can't wait to make the telephone call to Mr Appleby but am kept busy with a sudden barrage of lost bicycles, books, and more than one Halloween costume. As I fill out all the various Lost Item forms, I rehearse the call in my head. *Hello, it's Dot, something truly wonderful has happened. I so wanted to be able to make this call, imagined it, feared I might never get the chance and that you would have to go on without the dear comfort of Joanie's purse to hold, to give you succour on the hard days. But I have it! It's here in my hands . . . !* No, no, that won't do at all. *Mr Appleby, Dot Watson here, from Lost Property. Good news! Your holdall has come in.* Yes, something more along those lines. *Really?* he'll say, and I will hear the warmth in his voice, the happiness. And then he'll tell his grandson he has to go up to London. Imagine his face when he comes in to collect the holdall! Perhaps I could take him for a frothy coffee to celebrate? I picture him returning to the coast, reunited with Joanie's purse, holding on tight, never letting go.

Finally, the last customer of the morning is dealt with and I can turn my attention to the holdall. It is just as he said: leather the colour of golden syrup. I unzip it and the sides sigh apart to reveal the contents. There's the newspaper, folded in a neat oblong to the crossword page. The grids are all neatly filled, some of the letters a bit shaky but all the clues answered. There's the trowel and the tulip bulbs – in the dark warmth of the bag a couple of the bulbs have started to sprout, green shoots pushing out. And, burrowed in a corner, the bluey-lilac purse. I scoop it up gently and it nestles in my palm, soft and warm. I bring it to my face. Breathe in a lightness, the scent of violet.

My fingers tremble with excitement as I fill out the Dijon label and tie it to the handle. I am desperate to just make the phone call but proper protocol must be followed. I'll update the file and then I can get Mr Appleby's phone number.

Anita is on the computer and I jiggle from foot to foot as she looks something up for a customer. Why so slow? I could read a biography of Ada Lovelace in the time it is taking her! Finally, she finishes and I take her place, type in 'Appleby'.

Nothing comes up.

I must have spelled it wrong in my excitement. I type his name again, slowly, saying the letters under my breath. Nothing. Nil desperandum! Everything is cross-referenced so that we can search by date and place of loss, as well as surname and item. I try '73 bus route'. Nothing. But that makes no sense! I distinctly remember taking down his details that day he came in, rain-soaked. What date was that . . . early October, because it was all schoolbooks and brollies. Three weeks ago; no, almost four. And he said he thought he had lost it . . . when? That day? A few days before? I check all entries at the start of October. Then I check September. I check every single day and then I check again. Nothing. Not just no holdall, but no Mr Appleby – no register of the claim whatsoever. A glitch in the system. But fear not! That is why we have the hard-copy back-up! Thank goodness NB has not managed to do away with that yet. Paper and pen, tried and true!

'*Ah, ha, ha, ha, paper and pen, paper and pen*' – it is possible that I sing this to the tune of 'Stayin' Alive' as I dash through the back office towards the filing cabinet. Dear Gabrielle looks over and gives me a sweet smile.

But there is no form for Mr Appleby in the filing cabinet. How can this be? I stand there, trying to remember. It doesn't make any sense. After all, he came in not once but twice . . .

Oh no!

After searching for her all over the building, I finally discover SmartChoice in the Ladies, painting her nails citrus-yellow.

'Does this suit?' she asks, brandishing her hands. I am momentarily lost for words, which she takes as approbation. 'I know, right? I never thought this was my colour, but I think I can rock it.' She blows on her fingers.

'I need to talk to you about the gentleman who came in when we had the meeting with Neil Burrows and you were overseeing Customer Service.'

'What man? Ooops, you mean the DILF looking for his Apple Watch, don't you? Anita had a go at me about that too, but I swear to God I was not flirting. The thing is—'

'No, not him. An older gentleman. Mr Appleby. Holdall?'

She scrunches up her face.

'What's a holdall? Like a man-bag?'

I take a breath. 'He came in to give us his change of address. You served him.'

'Did I?' She blows up and down on her nails as if she is playing the panpipes. 'Oh yes, I remember. He was a sweetie.'

'So,' I say, speaking slowly and fully enunciating every word, 'in order to change his information, you would have deleted the old online address.'

'I would.' She nods.

'And you would have added the new one.'

'Ah.' She stops nodding.

'Sheila?'

'The thing is, I might have made a teeny tiny mistake when I was deleting the old address.'

My chest tightens.

'What kind of mistake?'

'Like accidentally deleting the file. Oops.'

'What about the hard-copy form?' I ask between gritted teeth. 'It's not in the filing cabinet – where else might you have put it?'

'Hard copy?' She looks up at the ceiling as if the form might be flapping over her head. Shrugs her shoulders.

'Can't you just google him?'

I turn brusquely and stalk out of the room to hide the tears that have sprung into my eyes.

Despite myself, I do google him and discover a windfall of Applebys, but none who fits my gentleman. I knew SmartChoice was not ready for Customer Service. What can I do?

For the rest of the day I am short-tempered and tense. I snap at Sukanya for speaking too loudly on the phone, admonish a customer for asking if there is a reward when he hands in a set of keys.

As soon as they all finally leave and I have Lost Property to myself again, I retreat to the pit with the holdall. I drink my way through a significant amount of the – alarmingly little – absinthe left in the bottle until he appears. Instead of regaling him with a happy ending, I have to confess failure. He is hugely sympathetic and tuts loudly when he hears about SmartChoice's negligent filing, which gives me some solace. He takes the pipe from the inside of his jacket and tamps down the tobacco.

'Dashed difficult to get the right companion these days.' He shakes his head sadly. 'I have never found anyone like you, Watson. Nobody else matched up.'

A sudden beam of light in the doldrums warms my spirits. An irreplaceable pal? The intrepid duo? Comrades in cahoots, even now? Despite the calamity I smile.

'That's the spirit, old bean, chin up. It's not one of our three-pipe problems.' He takes a long inhale and blows out a ream of curling smoke. 'The night is young! Let the evidence speak to us.' He points to the holdall with his long expressive fingers.

I have another nip of absinthe, open the holdall, take out the trowel, the newspaper, the bulbs and the purse, and lay them on the floor before us. He ignores them and places his hands gently on the sides of the holdall.

'Don't you want to examine the contents?' I proffer the trowel.

His hands move lightly over the contours of the bag, as if he is reading Braille. I settle back on the mid-century. Though he can veer to the vainglorious, I do rather love it when he does this. I take yet another nip of absinthe.

'The owner has an elegance about him.'

'How do you know?' I say, and watch his chest puff, his fingers flex.

'Ah, dear Watson, always seeing and never perceiving. Here!' He delicately traces the curve of the handle. 'The bag is carried always in the hand, never hoisted on to the shoulder, wrenching the leather out of shape. A clear sign of a refined fellow. In addition, we can deduce the owner is right-handed – see the grip of the handle? The large imprint here, from the press of the thumb-pad?'

I nod obediently.

'I surmise that he is a gentle soul . . .' He looks at me and I furrow my brow quizzically, giving him all he needs to sally forth. 'Observe: the stitching is even and pristine, no superfluous tugging on the zip in a hurry or a rage, and the leather lovingly polished.'

I nod.

'Also a tropical-plant enthusiast.' I raise a brow. 'Mark, if you will, this trace of the Madagascar periwinkle, just here on the leather, clearly indicating that he was recently in the Palm House at Kew Gardens.'

I admit I am awed in spite of myself, but before I can say anything he becomes fascinated by the handle.

'I'm not sure,' he says, peering intently at it, 'but I think these white markings might be salt.' He sniffs. 'Hmmm, hard to tell exactly . . .'

He pokes out his tongue and presses it against the leather handle.

At this point in the proceedings I am about to admonish him. I concede that in light of recent events I have had to relax some of my doctrine about the treatment of lost property, but one thing is crystalline – no one is allowed to lick it. Yet before I can speak, he holds up his hand.

'This bag has been to sea, and recently, I would wager.'

'Mr Appleby did mention the coast . . .' I trawl back through my memory. 'His grandson lives there. Perhaps he took the holdall with him on previous visits?'

'Most excellent,' he says, beaming at me, though I rather think congratulating himself. 'What else can we surmise about the gentleman? The crossword reveals an intelligent mind – the general-knowledge answers alone point to that. Like all of us, of course, he can be forgetful, lose things.'

'Not me.'

He stares at me, his eyes luminous, a slight quiver at the end of his nose. The tick-tick, tick-tick, tick-tick of his pocket watch resounds under his coat.

'Is that so?'

'I pride myself on never losing a single thing,' I say.

'I see.'

I nod vigorously, warming to my topic. 'Look!' I proudly reveal my hanky, pinned to the inside of my jacket. 'Every potential loss guarded against. I'm not like Anita leaving a constant stream of things in her wake, SmartChoice losing key data, all my customers letting things go—'

'Dear Watson' – he clears his throat – 'the thing is, one has to look beyond what is obvious.'

I gaze at him, not understanding.

'One can lose things in different ways. One can be out and about living one's life, exploring exciting new pathways – moving to the seaside, for example – and yes, perhaps one might lose a bag en route. On the other hand, one may stay put, everything safety-pinned securely in place, and risk losing so much more.'

I cannot meet his eyes. His voice so solemn, his gaze penetrating. I stare intently at the holdall and feel a strange pull deep down in my guts. I wish he would stop talking like this, stirring away at something inside me, something cold and weighted, churning everything up.

He changes tack. 'Well, Watson, following your line of reasoning, perhaps Mr Appleby isn't concerned about his holdall?'

'Oh, but he is! He needs it. He wants Joanie's purse back.'

'Why?' He pulls on his pipe. Bites down on the ebony-black stem.

'Because it's a . . . portal.'

'Go on.'

'They . . . Objects are time machines, in a way; they can recall . . . the people we have lost.'

'But they can't bring them back.'

'No. No, they can't . . .' I look down at the holdall, nurse it on my lap, stroke its curves. The heavy feeling in my stomach shifts upwards, lodges in my heart. My throat tightens. A rogue tear falls on to the soft body of the holdall. I shake my head, take a quick gulp of absinthe. 'But they can help us feel close.'

A pause. He covers my hand with his, like he used to.

'Indeed they can. So, let us proceed with The Mystery of the Mislaid Holdall without further ado.'

I look up. 'Do you really think we can find him?'

'Watson! Look at your success with The Case of the Imperious Sister – that was a real puzzler. This is a much easier nut to crack! Right, we have deduced *what kind* of man this Mr Appleby is; now let us deduce *where* he is. We already have one excellent lead, the sea salt. Now, we need more. Perhaps there is a secret compartment in the holdall. Some sort of a false bottom?'

Dutifully I pat around the bag, check its underside, but it appears perfectly ordinary.

'Tut, tut, old thing!' he says, leaping up from the mid-century. 'Give it some welly!'

I turn the holdall inside out, shake it vigorously, and a small curl of paper wafts to the floor.

'Aha! What's this?' He points. 'Don't happen to have a magnifying glass secreted in this emporium of loss, do you, dear Watson?'

'I'm afraid not.' I pick up the paper. 'Looks like a receipt. The ink's faded . . . can't make out the purchase or the date, but there's a name at the top, *Judges*, and under it the words, *Old Town* . . . ?'

He claps his hands.

'Well, this is indeed a start, my dear Watson! Judges might be some sort of legal premises – already giving us an inkling that something untoward is afoot! And taking place in an old town? But which one? How old? Perplexing indeed.' He is pacing now, excitable as a dog on the scent. 'But let us remember, not all clues are visible to the naked eye – some exist instead in the *mind's eye*.' He stops, turns to me. 'You said the gentleman in question spoke to you. Can you remember the exact details of the conversation you had? What did he say? Was he in good humour? Did he look shifty?'

'We barely spoke.' I try and recall. 'I can't remember. It was an extraordinary day: Neil Burrows taking over, getting everyone to hold hands in his office . . .'

'Curious indeed. But you must try harder, old bean. Visualize the owner of the bag, see him standing before you. What does he say?'

I close my eyes, see Mr Appleby's kind face, his tweed cap, the perfect darning, his mouth saying . . . what?

'Something about fishermen's huts and a railway of some sort . . .' I hazard.

'Excellent, excellent. And what do you deduce from that? Did you get the impression he was abiding in one of these fishermen's huts, hiding out perhaps?'

I press my fingers to my forehead. 'I remember he said something about a view . . .' He is silent. I take another swig of absinthe. A whooshing in my ears; the room lists. 'Don't go, will you?'

'Dear chum, whatever next! Leave now, when we are so close to cracking our case?'

'Are we? It still feels rather vague . . .' He waves my protestations away. I scrunch my eyes, try to see Mr Appleby, hear his words. 'There was something . . . about how on a clear day you had views from the West Hill, or maybe the West Cliff . . . views across the Channel . . .'

'Well, there you have it!' He clasps his hands, triumphant. '*Judges* and *Old Town*, a place on a cliff or prominence that reveals a vista of the Channel, is where you shall find your Mr Appleby!' He smiles. 'Elementary, my dear Watson!'

I have to admit, I've been waiting for him to say that.

13

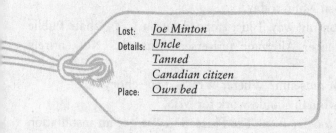

Lost: *Joe Minton*
Details: *Uncle*
Tanned
Canadian citizen
Place: *Own bed*

All night I lie awake, my eyes tracing the strange but increasingly familiar shapes of the pit – the puffer fish, the half-suit of armour, the grandfather clock – my mind trying to piece together the clues in the holdall, solve the mystery of where Mr Appleby could be. Judges, fishermen's houses . . . where is this place? Somewhere on the coast . . . something funny about the railway . . . funicular! Wasn't that it?

Slightly unsure as to what is real and what is an absinthe-soaked hallucination from the depths of the pit, I try to make a plan for the day. Saturday. Lost Property is closed, so I have time to sleuth; where to begin . . .

I am startled from my reverie by the ringing of my phone.

'Where have you been?' Philippa squawks in my ear. I hold the phone at a distance.

'Nowhere.'

155

'Obviously not at home – I left several messages on the answering machine.'

'I didn't get them yet. I was out last night.'

'Again?' A pause. I imagine her eyebrows migrating to her hairline. I quite like catching her off-guard like this. 'Hmmm. Well, where are you now? I thought we agreed you'd visit Mum today.'

'I'm on my way. I just stepped into a . . .' What? Public convenience? Alternate universe? 'Museum.' Not entirely untrue.

'What museum? Where? Why is it so echoey?'

The woman should work for MI5.

'Not too far from The Pines. They've got an installation recreating the . . . sonic experience of life on a submarine.' I can give as good as I get.

'Hmm, well I'm glad I caught you, because I got a call from Auntie Michelle late last night – it was still daytime in Vancouver, of course, but she woke us up. Gerald wasn't best pleased, but in the circumstances, I appreciate she wanted to go ahead and break the news.'

'What news?' My mouth is suddenly dry.

'Uncle Joe had a heart attack. He's dead.'

Uncle Joe. I see his face, hear the shudder of his jovial laugh, how he filled up a room. Took all the oxygen.

'Dot, are you still there?'

'Yes.'

'So I'm afraid you'll have to break the news to Mum when you visit today. I doubt she'll remember him any more than she remembers the rest of us . . .' I can almost hear her lips thinning. 'Still, we have to tell her. I'd go with you, but Sam's got his flute exam then some drama thing, so it looks like I'm going to be chauffeuring him around the Home Counties all day.'

'Do you really think she has to be told? Can't we just . . .'

'Just what?'

'Just not put her through it?'

'She has to be told. He was her brother, she deserves to know. You have to do it, D. You don't mind, do you? You see to that and I'll sort the flowers for Joe's funeral – this Monday, they do things so fast in America.'

'Canada.'

'That's what I said. Anyway, it's a blessing really as it means neither of us is expected to go over at such short notice. Poor Michelle. But he had a pretty good innings, and went in his sleep – at the end of the day we can't ask for more than that, can we? She sent her love, by the way, Auntie Michelle. Anyway, got to go! Enjoy your boats.'

'What? Oh, yes, right. Anchors aweigh.'

It was on one of Uncle Joe's visits that I discovered how Mum and Dad met. I couldn't have been more than eight years old. Uncle Joe's family were over from Vancouver. Auntie Michelle took Philippa and her two girls up to London for shopping and a show, but I had a cold and had to stay home. I didn't care about the London trip; I wanted to go hiking with Dad. 'Just me and Joe this time, poppet,' Dad had said, whistling as he loaded walking boots, maps and knapsacks into the boot of his car. 'Stay home and recuperate – it's probably just a glancing bout of dropsy, picked up from Lady Beatrice in our adventures at Shoscombe stables during The Case of the Chivalrous Sniveller. I prescribe a spot of ice cream and a cosy afternoon keeping the home fires burning. You'll soon feel tippety-top, old thing. You and Mum will have lots of fun.' He reached out to ruffle my hair but I ducked.

Mum stood watching them go, picking at the gloss paint around the door frame. Not looking one bit fun.

But she was. When I wandered into the kitchen later to see if there actually was a spot of ice cream, she asked if I wanted to make chocolate cake from scratch and didn't moan about the mess. She sat in the kitchen curled in her white rattan chair, rereading *Middlemarch* while I clattered about with bowls, measuring cups, a sieve. We had the radio on, musicals from the fifties.

Shall we dance? Cha-Cha-Cha! On a bright cloud of music, shall we fly?

Mum joined in, her voice light, soaring.

'You should be a singer,' I advised, chocolate-lipped.

'I was.'

I stopped in the middle of my labour – industriously cleaning the spatula with my tongue, while sporting the sieve as a hat. 'What?'

She kept her eyes on the page but I could see a pink tinge like coconut ice in her pale cheeks.

'Well, semi-professional. I could have gone professional. Singing is how I met your dad. I was Anna in *The King and I.*'

'And Dad was the king!'

She laughed. 'No, Uncle Joe. Your dad was in the audience the first night, though. And every night after that.'

I begged her to tell me more. She closed her book.

'Your dad wasn't even meant to be there that night. He was supposed to be travelling, but he broke his foot.'

'It was fate,' I squealed, delighted at the romance of it, 'just like in *It's a Wonderful Life.*' Another of my favourites.

'Well, I don't know about that,' Mum said, but she looked pleased.

'It was! Dad is like Jimmy Stewart! If he hadn't broken his foot, he wouldn't have been at the show that night, you wouldn't have met, and everything would have been different. I would not be here.' The thought struck me as disastrous and required another lick of chocolate. 'So it worked out for the best.'

'Yes, I suppose so,' Mum said. Then: 'Of course it did.'

'But why didn't you both go travelling together later?'

'Oh, well, sometimes things don't always . . . work out quite how you imagine they will.'

'They will for me. I have it all planned – first I'll be a librarian, read all the books on the shelves, then I'm going to learn to speak five languages and travel all over the world, and then I'll open my detective agency and solve complex international jewel heists.'

'That sounds wonderful, darling,' Mum said, slightly wistful. She got up and helped me slide the somewhat lopsided chocolate cake into the hot oven. 'There is a whole exciting world for you to discover, to do whatever you want.'

'But what about you, Mum? What about your singing?'

I wouldn't let it rest, barraging her with questions until she went upstairs, me racing behind, to get the big cream album from her bedside table. I followed her into their bedroom. Their bed was a heavy, dark mahogany, covered in a pink bedspread, the wine-red curtains at the windows closed.

Back in the cheery kitchen I snuggled on a stool between her legs, her arms either side of me, holding the album open. I felt part of the world of pictures I was seeing, embraced in the shiny Kodak glow of the past.

It was so cosy – the smell of the cake baking, the toasty heat from the Aga, the crinkle of the cellophane holding the photos in place. Sometimes as she turned a page, Mum lifted her hand and stroked my hair, so gently, before returning to the album.

So many pictures! So many people I didn't know, a sea of faces, carefree and glamorous. But the most radiant, the most captivating, were Mum, Dad and Uncle Joe. I marvelled at configurations of one or two or all of them on trips to the seaside, or snapshots of them clad in elegant evening attire, outside theatres, inside restaurants.

'We were inseparable,' she said, speaking more to herself than me. 'After the show we would always go to this little Italian place and have Chianti and spaghetti . . . Giovanni's. Ha, I'd forgotten. We'd stay up past midnight and dance in the street on the way home. Can you believe it?'

Shall we dance? Cha-Cha-Cha.

The album was stuffed with theatre programmes and flyers: *Carousel, Guys and Dolls, The Sound of Music,* Mum's name inside every one, often at the top.

'*The King and I!*' I shrieked, opening the programme. 'There's your name! There's Uncle Joe!'

'Oh yes, there we are.' Her finger landed gently on the page and lingered for a moment under her name, as if she was trying to locate herself, like the 'You Are Here' spot on a map. 'I was offered leading roles at bigger theatres: Bristol, Birmingham, even London.'

'Why didn't you go? You could have been famous!'

'I chose your father.' Her hand fell away from the programme. 'Then I had Philippa and a few years later you came along.'

The surprise and the *mistake*. The word loomed in my head but I pushed it away. I was having such a cosy time; I wanted it to last, to think only happy things.

'What about Uncle Joe? Could he have been famous?'

'Oh, Joe was just in it for fun. He always knew he wanted to be an engineer. I used to tease him that he just did the shows to meet girls.' I turned, saw that little flush in her cheeks again.

'You must have really missed him when he moved to Canada.'

'I did. But it was right he went.'

The glue on the photos made embarrassing kissing noises as I turned the pages, which made me want to stop turning them. And to keep turning them. Dad and Uncle Joe putting up a tent in the woods, Joe and Mum on stage, Mum in a huge hooped skirt, a bouquet of roses in her arms, Mum and Dad in the snow, flakes falling in front of the camera. A couple of photos skittered out of the album. Mum caught them like petals, tried to press them back in place.

'Who is that?' I pointed to a young woman running out of the sea. Her smooth skin glistened, her head was thrown back and she was laughing.

'Me, of course,' she said, tickling me. 'Why, do you think she looks too young to be your old mum?'

I giggled and wriggled, denying it. I didn't tell her the truth. It wasn't because she looked young, the woman in the photo; I didn't recognize her because she looked so happy.

Dad and Joe didn't come back till late that night. I sat up, face pressed against the window, waiting. I knew Mum was still up too.

14

Lost:	*Mum*
Details:	*Blue eyes*
	Silver-grey hair
	Remarkable singing voice
Place:	*The Pines Care Home*

'*How do you solve a problem like Maria?*' As usual, Mum is singing when I open the door to her room. She is sitting in her armchair, looking out of the window. Rosie is draped on her lap.

'Julie Andrews,' I say, sitting down on the edge of her bed. Mum looks at me, nods.

'Lovely teeth, Miss Andrews!' I say, encouraged. 'And what about that glorious hair that bounces as she runs over those hills?'

'*How do you catch a cloud and pin it down?*' Mum sings.

'Most of us would have to take a bit of care when navigating the Austrian Alps, eh, Mum? Not her, not Julie – arms wide, head thrown back.' I rattle on, trying to hold mind, body and soul together. Truth to tell, a fresh whiff of Alpine air would not go amiss in Mum's room right now. It smells of cleaning fluid and stale talc.

'I'm sure Miss Andrews would approach an escalator at John Lewis in the same breezy manner, wouldn't she, Mum? She's that *type*. Didn't she have such white teeth, Mum? Even, eminently trustworthy. I expect she has very fresh breath: spearmint. There's no excuse for poor dental hygiene nowadays – although try telling that to my new boss . . .' On and on. Anything to avoid telling her the news I have been charged with conveying.

A dull ache starts to throb in my head. Back in the environs of The Pines, I find myself thinking about Dr Chang, remembering the touch of his hands on my face, how he eased the pain. Now there is someone with excellent teeth. Goodness knows what he would think if he could hear me blathering on about the bouquet of Dame Andrews' breath. Probably that it was time for me to be 'welcomed' into The Pines. I could get a room on Lavender next to Mum and we could spend our days singing 'Edelweiss' at the top of our voices, slip into oblivion together. Not a wholly repellent idea. But I can't. For Mum's sake, I have to keep it together.

'Mum?' She pulls at Rosie. 'I have to tell you something. About Joe. Uncle Joe?'

'*How do you solve a problem like Maria?*' Her hands pick at the bedcover as if she is accompanying herself, each pluck a note.

'Auntie Michelle called Philippa last night. It's bad news, I'm afraid.' I take Mum's hand; it sits limp in mine, then jumps out, back to its task.

I exhale.

'He died, Mum. It was a heart attack. He went in his sleep.' I take both her hands in mine this time. She pushes me away and snatches Rosie back, singing louder.

'HOW DO YOU CATCH A CLOUD AND PIN IT DOWN?'

'The funeral is next week. Philippa's sending flowers from the three of us.'

Mum stops singing and turns to me, her face tired. She looks me in the eye and sighs. I nod, stroke her arm.

'Tea time?' she says.

All I want is to go and get her a cup of tea, sit, munch chocolate biscuits and pretend to be Reg the fishmonger, make her laugh.

'In a jiffy, Mum, but first, Philippa wants me to . . . I have to tell you something sad, Mum. About your brother. About Joe. He died, Mum. Your brother died. Do you understand?'

She pats my hand. 'Tea.'

'I'll get you some tea, I promise, but I have to tell you about Joe, Mum. It was his heart.'

'Is Edna coming to do the windows?'

My throat contracts. What can I say? How else can I tell her? *He's gone, Mum! Your only brother. Beloved Uncle Joe. Pegged out. Joined the invisible choir. Shuffled off this mortal coil.*

'Joe's dead, Mum.' She recoils at the loudness of my voice. A drop of my spittle has landed on her collar. I try to wipe it off but she flinches.

'Where's Dave?'

'No, Mum, Dad's not coming. He's dead too, remember. They're all dead: Joe, Dad, Grandma and Grandad. But I'm here, and Philippa – remember? Well, she's not *here* here, she's driving Sam to his music exam, but she's alive. I'm here, Mum. Me, Dot. And I have to tell you about Uncle Joe. Do you understand?'

165

She nods. 'Cup of tea?'

I need to get out of the room. Away from the smell, the sadness. The hopelessness of it all.

'What about a walk, Mum? How's the hip?'

She puts a hand on her leg. 'I hurt it.'

'You did, but it's getting better, the physio is helping. Do you fancy a stroll? It will be good for you. Looks mild out. And I'll fetch you that tea.'

She smiles. Nods.

I bundle her up and take her outside. We settle on a bench across from the apple tree. I tuck a blanket around her knees, prop her stick next to her.

'Back in a mo.'

She clasps my hand. 'With a biscuit.'

'Right you are. Tea with a biscuit. Custard cream?'

She trills a laugh as if we are in cahoots, as if we're having a lovely time. 'Yes, biscuits, yes.'

At the doorway that leads to the dining hall, I look back through the corridor window and see her sitting on the bench, her hands neatly folded, waiting. A bright-eyed blackbird hops at her feet, makes her smile. All she wants is a cup of tea and a custard cream and some peace and quiet, yet I won't stop telling her that her only brother is gone. Over and over again. Why do I bother, when for her we are all already gone, obliterated by the fog of her memory, hidden behind the clouds that roll in, thicker each day? *How do you catch a cloud and pin it down?* Sometimes I feel so sorry for her. Other days I envy her. Is it better to remember or to forget?

In profile, she has a trace of Joe's good looks. I haven't seen him for years. After Dad died, out of the blue, he announced he was coming over to England for Mum's birthday. Philippa called me, demanded I attend.

'Why? He didn't come to Dad's funeral. I don't want to see him.'

'Mum wants us to be there, both of us. I'm doing a lasagne, you can bring pudding.'

Mum had started to make a new life for herself. She had joined a local choir, made friends in the village, got involved with a few parish events. What really filled her time and brought her pleasure was her role as a grandmother. Living nearby meant she could pick Melanie up from nursery every day, and she was always so happy to babysit Sam. She was far more relaxed with her grandchildren than I remember her being when we were growing up.

I think she was happy, though I couldn't completely tell.

Joe filled Mum's maisonette with gifts – dresses, scarves, perfume – and his meaty presence. He bounced baby Sam on his knee and tickled four-year-old Melanie, making her shriek and squirm with delight, her blonde curls bouncing. He complimented Philippa on her kids, her successful husband, her bloody béchamel. He looked so vital next to Mum, with his glossy blond hair and tanned brown skin; he was a thickly daubed oil painting, whereas she was more of a pencil sketch.

Joe and Mum chatted about everything. Except Dad. I resented them both for that.

After lunch Joe suggested Mum should sing. At first she protested, but Melanie jumped up and down, shouting, 'Sing Granny, Granny sing!'

At first Mum's voice was faint. She stared down at her lap, half speaking the lyrics, but then Joe's baritone slipped in under her soprano, and she let the music fill her, her body suddenly awash with the notes. Her pale cheeks pinkened as if the music were a transfusion of life-giving blood bringing light, energy, waking her up. I saw a glimmer of something I recognized from the photo she'd shown me that day, of her coming out of the sea, laughing; a glimpse of the woman she might have been.

At the chorus Philippa joined in. Even Melanie danced around, making up her own lyrics.

I watched them, the perfectly pitched, blond-haired, blue-eyed quartet. Utterly harmonious. And me on the outside, the false note, the broken chord, the mistake.

'Join in, Dot,' my uncle cajoled.

'I . . . don't know the words. I'll see to the pudding,' I said.

In the kitchen, I pressed my forehead against the fridge door, hot tears stinging. If I opened my mouth, a scream, not a song, would come out.

'Your mum looks well.'

Uncle Joe behind me, in the kitchen doorway, blocking out the light, a pile of dirty dishes in his hands.

I turned on the tap, started washing a squeaky-clean glass. I heard the clatter as he put the dishes on the table. Always so noisy.

'And what about you?' he boomed. 'You've got a place in the city, right? That's so great.'

I nodded, watched the scalding water torrent over the fragile body of the glass, saw my hands redden.

'Shall I dry?' Joe said, coming next to me, grabbing a dish towel.

'No need.' I turned off the tap, upended the glass on the draining board, moved away from him to the fridge. I took out the dessert and started to decorate it with blackberries. I focused on positioning each berry upright. The task required my full concentration and disabled all possibility of conversation.

'You remind me so much of him,' he said, his voice soft.

A blackberry fell to the floor and rolled under the table. I ducked down to retrieve it.

'I . . . I know how hard it was for you all, when you lost him. And I want you to know I'm here for you, all of you. If I can ever help, if you need anything, money or just . . . anything.'

I wondered how long I could conceivably stay under the table. I couldn't bear to surface and look into Uncle Joe's disturbingly familiar face talking about my father. *When you lost him.* As if something distracted us and we all got up and walked away, leaving Dad like a brolly hanging on the back of a seat on the bus. *Whoops, silly us! Looks like we lost Dad!*

I left the blackberry bruised and oozing under the table, just another one of our embarrassing messes. There was now a gaping hole in my perfectly positioned family circle of berries. Should I move every other berry along to fill the void? I sensed Uncle Joe watching me, heard him breathing, felt him wanting to make it all better. Needing to.

I never saw him again.

Amidst the noise and clatter of lunch hour at The Pines, I slip to the tea urn and start to fill a cup.

'Miss Watson! Hello there!' Sister Gloria semaphores with two serviettes from the other side of the room. 'Visiting your mum?'

'Just popping in to get some tea,' I say.

'You're very welcome to join us for lunch,' she says, louder now.

'No, thanks.'

'Are you sure?' She semaphores the serviettes more vigorously. 'It's shepherd's pie today! Or shepherdess if you're veggie.'

'Just the tea, thanks,' I say, somewhat perplexed as to why 'shepherdess' denotes meat-free. The silver-white heads of the assembled diners look like a field of cotton, gently blowing in the breeze as they follow our conversation back and forth.

'Well, I know your mum hasn't got much of an appetite, but it's good you're keeping her hydrated.'

I nod, slip a couple of biscuits on to the saucers and head for the door.

'There's space for you both at Mr Diomedes' table if you change your mind.' She flaps her serviette at an old gentleman dining alone, wearing a brushed-velvet waistcoat and corduroy trousers. He pulls the bread basket towards him protectively.

I beat a hasty retreat and head back outside with the teas. The bench is empty. Mum's stick is where I left it.

Cold dread pools in my stomach. Where has she gone? What if she falls?

I abandon the cups on the bench and walk the length of the lawns. No sign. I go down to the Chelsea Pensioner apple tree in case she is hidden behind its outstretched arms. No Mum. Maybe she had to use the loo? I go inside and check the Ladies, then return to her room, check her bathroom. Empty. The cloying smells are stronger here, and I feel a wave of nausea and start to panic. Where is she? Moving faster now, I go to the communal sitting room, occupied by a handful of non-dining residents reading, chatting or napping. No sign of Mum.

My throat tightens and I can hear the thrum of my heartbeat in my ears. Where is she? If she falls it will be my fault. Did the news about Uncle Joe suddenly sink in when she was sitting alone? Is she upset?

How could I have left her? What if she has wandered off the grounds and is lost? Walked out into the busy road, not looking? I pound out of the building to the end of the drive, dash over the road in such a panic I almost get run down by a red Volvo that screeches and swerves. The driver blares his horn angrily, shouts something unmentionable at me.

Tears blur my eyes as I scan the street in both directions. Nothing. I wasn't away that long! How far could a woman with a hip replacement get in that time? Should I alert Sister Gloria? The police? Or – heaven forbid – Philippa? She'd have a field day. I have to find Mum. I turn and run back up the driveway towards The Pines, catching the smell of fear from my own body. *Mum, where are you?*

'Hey, is everything OK?'

Adison Chang DPT. Thank G.O.D.

'I've lost Mum,' I cry.

'I know it can feel like that, but she is still there, inside.'

'No – I have actually lost her. I left her on a bench for a moment, and when I came back she was gone. I can't find her anywhere. I'm worried she went out to the road. I was just bringing her some tea—' A jagged sob catches in my throat.

171

'Let me help.' Dr Chang leads me back into the building. 'Don't worry, we'll find her. I've got a hunch . . .'

I blow my nose and follow him through a warren of corridors, then along a wood-panelled hallway. Large windows on one side look out on to the garden. Doors lead to various craft, music and exercise rooms. I vaguely remember this part of the building from the induction tour. Could Mum have got this far by herself? Despite their focus on the arts, the rooms are all the colour of congealed oatmeal – no pictures on the walls, not even a bookshelf. I can't imagine any of the residents wanting to spend much time here.

He stops outside one of the rooms and I hear a sound. The door is closed but through a circle of glass, criss-crossed with fire-safety wire, I see Mum. She is alone in the middle of the space, singing, her voice soft but pure. Suspended in the round of glass she looks serene, faraway, like an angel imprisoned in a snow globe.

I reach for the door handle, but Dr Chang lightly places his hand on top of mine.

'Why don't we let her finish her song?'

I nod, let my hand drop, still feeling the warm imprint of his. I watch Mum for a moment through the glass. She looks almost happy, lost in her own world, filled with music.

I turn away, sniff as quietly as possible, and engross myself in a sign detailing the fire evacuation procedure on the wall opposite. 'It was my fault,' I say, staring intently at safety drill instructions. 'I had to tell her some sad news. Her brother died last night. I couldn't make her understand, so I said it over and over.' I focus on a picture of a stick man energetically running away from flames.

'It's very hard on families.' Dr Chang's voice is quiet, understanding.

'I didn't even want to tell her. Why should she have to hear it? She's better not knowing. Why force traumatic memories on her, relive his death over and over, after all these years?'

'Sorry, I thought you said he just died?'

I swallow. 'My dad. Mum had to live through the trauma of losing him, but now she doesn't remember. She keeps asking me when he is going to come and collect her. And now Uncle Joe is dead and I'm supposed to tell her that too. But what's the point?' Tears pool in the corners of my eyes. I try not to blink, focus on the fire sign.

'It's hard to see loved ones so changed.' His voice is full of compassion. My chest tightens. I count the emergency exits (six) until I can breathe.

'What is most . . . challenging . . . is that I see her – her face, her blue eyes – so much that is still . . . *her* . . . the Mum I know, but it's a mirage. I keep thinking that if I say this, remind her of that, she'll remember me.' I inhale a ragged breath. 'But she looks at me in exactly the same way when I say her brother is dead as when I ask her if she wants a biscuit – the same way she looks at the nurse who helps her to the lavatory. No, not even the same. Because I think she recognizes that bl . . . oody nurse. She doesn't . . . know . . . who I . . . am . . .' I stop for breath, a deluge of tears spilling on to my cheeks. Dr Chang stands behind me, lightly touches my shoulders and turns me to him. He takes my hand. I remember how he held my head when we first met. The warmth of his fingers. Oh dear, it's all too . . . forward, too American, too *much*.

I pull away, but his grasp is gentle yet firm, and I realize he is not trying to hold my hand; he is . . . opening it. That's the only way to describe what he is doing: unfurling my hand as if it were the head of a flower, spreading my fingers back like petals.

He cups the back of my hand and arches my palm upwards as the pads of his thumbs press down into my soft flesh.

'It might help your mom, if you sit with her, touch her. Like this,' he says gently, circling his thumbs around and around. 'Touch can be a powerful way of inviting the body to open. I believe that our cells hold our memories. That sometimes it's about finding ways to invite the body to open, share its stories. Just applying gentle pressure here' – he presses the joints of my fingers, the pads of my palms – 'can help the body relax.'

His head is bent forward, intent on his task, his thumbs orbiting like friendly planets. His hair smells like Earl Grey tea.

'This part of the body is so tender,' he says, stroking the middle of my palm, sending tremors of warmth pulsing in my stomach. 'It can be receptive to the lightest touch. Then work your way around with firm but gentle pressure, here and here.'

Heat floods my body, radiates out to unknown galaxies. Black holes revert back to the bright stars they once were, pulsing with light, life. I shut my eyes, remember sitting in the Planetarium years ago, head tipped back, staring in wonder at the huge domed roof as different stars, constellations and planets lit up one by one. Mars, Mercury, Saturn. I wanted to open my mouth and let the stars fall in.

'The body is intricately wired – there are places in our hands, our feet, our faces that are connected to our internal organs, our muscles and limbs,' Dr Chang says, his warm, deft fingers travelling the curve between my index finger and thumb. 'Just here. Can you feel it?'

I nod. The sensation is exquisite, almost tender, but there is no pain. He holds my hand in his as if it were something special, then turns it over and stretches it out so that my thumb is in one of his hands, my little finger in his other. It looks like the wing of a bird about to take flight. Just as that thought occurs, he lifts and lowers my winged hand a few times, pulsing it on the air, and then lets go. For a moment, I feel airborne as my hand floats in space, beating with energy.

I am about to thank him when he raises his palms either side of my face.

'May I?' he asks. I hesitate, then nod. He gently cradles my tear-streaked face. His touch is barely perceptible. His fingers, light as butterfly wings, travel around my cheeks. Small circles spiral.

'Ahhh.' The little sigh slips out before I can control it. Perhaps he didn't notice?

I close my eyes, pretend it didn't happen, will him not to touch my hair which, despite several vigorous ablutions in the Ladies, still remains somewhat slick from the body-lotion incident. But after a while I start not to care.

In the other room, Mum works her way through another number from Messrs Rodgers and Hammerstein's *The Sound of Music*. Dr Chang presses a little harder now, and I feel again as if I am tipping forward into his hands. This time I don't pull away. He starts a percussive tapping across my forehead, my eyebrows, back down to my cheeks. Light, staccato, a sudden surprise of raindrops on a summer's day. It feels nourishing. Something cranial, perhaps? Is he reconfiguring my synapses in some way? I hear that's very fashionable now. Very *au courant*. This part of my face must be wired to my brain – yes, it's definitely something cerebral, I can tell. I feel a clearing of thoughts.

'What's that?' I ask.

'Your colon,' he says.

Thank goodness I have my eyes shut. My cheeks turn to hotplates under his fingers. Mercifully he is on the move again.

'*Climb every mountain, search high and low,*' Mum sings.

'These are your lungs.' His fingers press lightly on either side of my nose. 'Here is your spleen.' They travel down to my septum. 'Your stomach . . .' He traces his finger lightly across my top lip, then along the entire length of my mouth. How extraordinarily intimate this touching, this man I barely know navigating my inner geographies, the hidden parts of me. Something deep-rooted inside me releases and sends a solitary fat tear rolling gently down my cheek.

'What's that?' I whisper, praying it is not my colon again, or worse.

His fingers stop, just for a millisecond. He clears his throat.

'Your heart,' he says.

'Did you get those forms I gave you notarized, Chang?' I open my eyes and step back abruptly. A man with a grey moustache stands next to us, looking expectantly at Adison. His room is near Mum's on Lavender. A retired solicitor. Geoffrey.

'Absolutely, Geoff,' says Adison, smiling. 'Be right with you.'

'Good stuff, good stuff, got a client coming to the office today. Need everything signed and sealed.' Geoffrey continues down the corridor.

'Do you think that's ethical?' I ask Adison's shoes after a moment. They are scrupulously clean, extremely well polished, a delicious dark toffee colour.

'What?'

'To play along with him like that?'

He is quiet for a moment, then says, 'I guess I don't think it's about right and wrong – just that we need to be a bit more fluid. Sometimes it can help to step into the world they are in, rather than always forcing them into ours.'

I nod. That makes complete sense.

'I don't want to keep on telling Mum about Uncle Joe,' I confess to Adison's neatly tied laces. 'But I want to . . . respect her, I suppose. Let her know the truth just once, even if I never speak of it again.'

'Then do that. Trust your instinct, Dot.'

I look up at him when he says my name. His face is full of understanding. He smiles.

'Try the pressure points with her. If nothing else, it will be good for her to be touched, to know that you are there.'

I nod, move to the door, and listen as Mum comes to the end of her song.

'*Till you find your dream.*'

Her eyes are closed, her head tilted back, her hands at her chest. The last note hovers for a moment, high and true, then all is silent. She opens her eyes, gazes around, unsure of where she is.

I open the door.

'I'm here, Mum.' She looks uncertain but then gives me a little wave.

Adison and I lead Mum back to her room. I tuck Rosie around her and she starts a gentle plucking.

'I'll just get that tea, Mum, back in a jiffy. You stay put, you hear!'

'I'll stay with you, Gail, shall I?' Adison says.

Mum beams.

'We shouldn't take up any more of your time,' I say to Adison's knees.

'It's my job,' he says, and sits down at Mum's bedside.

Well . . . of course. It's his job. He is just doing his job. What on earth else would he be doing?

I return with three cups. Mum looks happy, sharing a joke with Adison.

'I'll take mine to go,' Adison says. 'Let you two have some time together.'

'Right. I'm sure you have many other patients to see.' I thrust his tea at him, turn and busy myself rootling in Mum's chest of drawers.

'I'll swing by to check on you later, Gail. Goodbye, Dot.'

'Cheerio,' I say, still obviously very engaged with my drawer work.

After Adison leaves, I sit next to Mum on the bed and take her left hand in mine. We have similar-shaped nails; I don't remember noticing that before. The imprint of a parent in their child.

Mimicking the way Adison touched my hands, I press my thumbs into my mother's fragile palms, make circles. Her hands seem so small. I remember her handwriting on the cards she sent when I was at university, her words so big and curling, as if each letter was an embrace. These hands of hers that buttoned my school cardigan, that plaited my hair, that grasped mine as she hurried me to my piano lessons with Miss Hyde, that held me tight till we got all the way across

178

the busy road. Arthritis has forced her fingertips into acute angles now, as if she is forever trying to grasp something that is no longer there.

I take a breath. 'I have some sad news, Mum. Uncle Joe died. I'm so sorry.' I press and circle, opening up the small bulbs of her hands, unfurling them gently. She is humming something and I have joined in, even though I don't quite recognize the song. I follow her notes, let her lead me, make my strokes fit the rhythm of our tune.

'*Wings on your heels*.'

'What was that? Did I press too hard?'

'*And to fly down the street*,' she sings, looking down at our hands.

'Is that *The King and I*, Mum?'

'*And you meet . . . by chance*.'

'That was beautiful, Mum.' I stop rubbing. Grasp her hands tightly in mine.

'Joe is gone,' she says.

'Yes, Mum.'

She looks up at me. We sit for a moment in silence, holding hands.

'Joe is gone to Canada. Is David coming to get me?'

I close my eyes. Breathe. See planets. Solar systems, spinning out to eternity. I stroke her hair. So soft.

'He's just finishing up in the garden. He'll be here soon.'

The lie calms her. Perhaps I should feel guilty, but today I let myself find comfort in her peace. I picture Dad as he might be now, digging in the vegetable patch, then rehousing all the displaced earthworms and snails. I give us both that possibility. For just a moment I allow us to be waiting for a husband, for a father to come and take us home.

179

15

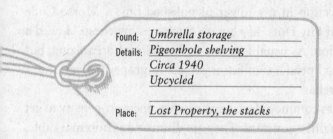

Found: *Umbrella storage*

Details: *Pigeonhole shelving*
Circa 1940
Upcycled

Place: *Lost Property, the stacks*

Sunday, and I still haven't managed to return to the maisonette. If Philippa does indeed pop round, how long will it take her to fathom that I have not been home for the last few nights? Knowing my sister, not long. I keep thinking I'll go back, yet each day it feels more impossible to leave Lost Property despite the challenges my new abode presents: for instance, taking the service lift up to the Ladies in the middle of the night, which is rather scary – I can really see the benefits of an en suite in situations such as these. On the other hand, a jolly nice Wedgwood bowl has made its way down to the pit so I have my breakfast (tinned corn) in style. I can't really relish it though, as my thoughts constantly jostle and chatter. What if Mum wanders off again? Will Dr Chang – Adison – keep an eye on her as he promised? Instinctively my hands go to my face, retrace the pathways his fingers took. I close my eyes, linger for a moment in the memory of his touch, the sparks of heat up my spine, the sense of spaciousness, before I return again to worrying about Mum. Will she remember about Uncle Joe or will I have to tell her anew, relaying his death over and over like a Greek chorus? And where is Mr Appleby? Under NB's new regime, I have a matter of weeks to find him before the holdall is sent to Snagsbey's. I catch my reflection in my tower of polished tins, a Morse Code S.O.S. of tiny Dots. My breath catches in my chest – I need a distraction. As usual I seek it in the balm of organizing, but this time I need a significant project to properly divert me.

Umbrellas.

Seen as commonplace and ordinary, their propensity to get lost remains a constant. They are dismissed as unremarkable, yet the precise service they provide is unique.

The shelves of the stacks are neither long enough nor wide enough to adequately house the umbrellas, so they end up in spilt piles all over the place, as if someone were midway through a game of pick-a-stick.

At the far end of the stacks there is an area that has, over the years, become a catch-all for various odds and ends: mops and buckets, a rickety ladder, a veritable millefeuille of cardboard that should have been cleared out yonks ago. The other day, while searching for a broom, I unearthed a dusty set of pigeonhole shelving from underneath a piece of tarpaulin. I'd guess at its provenance being Baker Street station's ticket office, circa 1940. It comprises sixty-three open-ended compartments, wide enough to house four umbrellas apiece.

First I have to drag it to the only available space with enough room to shelve the umbrellas: an empty nook that abuts the Valuables lock-up. Manoeuvring it halfway across the stacks will be strenuous, and messy to boot. I can't afford to sully my uniform, and my lab-coat nightie is entirely inappropriate for the task, but miraculously a quick rummage in the pit reveals a set of overalls. They are roomy, to say the least, and come with a sharp nip of creosote, but really I couldn't wish for better. When I discover a mint toffee in the pocket, it feels like a blessing. Though the previous occupant wore the buckled straps on the first hole, I tighten them over my shoulders and feel a reassuring sense of safety. The owner had a tendency to rub his hands – her hands? – on the trouser legs; by the size of the oily prints and the general messiness I am going to say 'his', but I don't mean to discriminate.

Back upstairs in the stacks, I dislodge the pigeonhole shelving and drag it to its new position. The wood is splintered and cracked, needs sanding. Some shelves have come loose altogether and require new plugs. Did the canvas tool bag I used to fix the fluorescent light get collected yet? No, still here. This time I barely hesitate before I grab it from the shelf. The longer I stay here the more I start to feel it is home, that these things are not just under my care but mine, because I am the one who pays them attention, the one who does not abandon them.

I set about putting my sanding and dovetailing skills to use, courtesy of my daytime-TV training. The back-and-forth slide of the sandpaper, the sweet smell of the wood, takes me back to France, polishing an antique walnut escritoire I'd discovered at the market at Porte de Vanves. Louise and I wheeled it home in a 'borrowed' supermarket shopping trolley, both of us as giddy and wayward as the off-kilter wheels of the trolley. Our frivolity unravelled into full-on hysterics as we tried to wrangle the desk into my apartment building's tiny lozenge of an elevator. We ended up ascending to the fourth floor with me sitting on Louise's lap as she perched atop the filthy escritoire. The look my neighbour Mme Dechary gave us when the doors opened kept us in fits for hours.

What a thrill, decorating my own place, choosing my own things. Oh, how I loved living in France, loved studying for my Master's degree. Books, books, books and the endless possibility of Europe, one country spilling into the next; getting on a train in Paris in the morning with a steaming chocolat chaud in one hand, a baguette in the other; arriving in Rome in time for a late supper of spaghetti alla puttanesca and a glass of Chianti. I had so many plans: finishing grad school and then taking the United Nations Language Proficiency Exam, a career in interpretation, a job that combined my love of travel and languages.

So many plans. I straighten up, massage my lower back. What would that Dot think if she could see her future – see me here in the Lost Property stacks repurposing discarded ticket office shelving into a repository for umbrellas?

Well, plans change. Anyway, stop malingering, Watson!

When the shelves are ready, I carefully walk around the whole of the stacks gathering up armfuls of brollies, and rehouse them as carefully as if they were children being evacuated from the Blitz. It takes some time, but when the job is done, when order has been applied to chaos and every last umbrella has been attended to, I sit on an upturned crate, massage my aching shoulders, and admire my creation. The double-sided pigeonhole shelving really is spot on, allowing the brollies to be perfectly slotted and easily spotted.

The centre of their bodies balance perfectly on the wooden shelves; their tips nose out of one end, curiously perusing the purses and pearls in the Valuables cage next door, while their flapping canopies extend out of the other end, their wooden handles like branches – birchbark cherry, blackthorn, hazel, chestnut. I colour-coordinated them, so the black umbrellas are housed up top where they roost, a brooding murder of crows. Below them, the coloured brollies resemble a forest of exotic-winged tropical birds. Violet, emerald, sapphire, turquoise. I doubt I'll ever see a hummingbird, but half closing my eyes I can conjure a Crimson Topaz, a Red-Billed Streamertail, a Ruby-Throated somersaulting in the air. I can imagine their song, sweet notes spiralling between the branches as they call to each other.

One afternoon, I came home early after my Spanish A-level and found Mum in the kitchen. Her back was to me and she was standing at the sink looking out of the window, singing. The song was in French; I hadn't heard it before, didn't even know she knew French. Caught up in my own life, I hadn't paid attention to hers, and yet as I watched her, even though I could only see her from behind, I could tell she was transformed. My mother but not my mother, another being, transcendent.

It was an astonishingly lovely song, passionate, full of longing. Sunlight bounced off the droplets of water on her hands, sparkled in the fragments of silica in the floor tiles. I stood and watched her, begging the leather of my school bag not to creak or my tummy to rumble and disturb her. Her voice transported her away from the washing-up in the sink, away from the kitchen, soared her up out of the tree-shrouded house to another world, another life.

Then a dog barked in next door's garden, the sound rupturing the moment, summoning her back. She turned and saw me, gave her head a little shake, jostling herself back to reality. 'Hello, love, you're home early. How did the exam go?'

What happened to that Mum? How did she become the woman with a sadness lodged under her smile? Where did the other woman go, the one in the photos with her head thrown back? The one centre stage who brought the audience to their feet?

I remember I woke that same night to the sound of sobbing. A wretched, tormented wail, full of fear. I thought it was her. Then I realized it was him.

'I can't. I can't.'

'It's all right, darling.' Her voice soothing him. His sobs raw, desperate.

By the time I left for France, she never sang any more and he had stopped playing his records. Everything felt in disarray, out of order. Paris didn't just help me unfurl, it let me take flight. Although not for long.

I linger in the umbrella sanctuary, enjoying the calm until finally my need for food drives me back down to the pit.

After a disappointing carrot-and-pea medley, I decide to do some online sleuthing to find Mr Appleby. The light is better in Big Jim's part of the pit, so I take the holdall and my phone and sit amongst the cascade of unclaimed items. Frustratingly, my phone has run out of battery and I realize my charger is back at the maisonette. Should I go out and buy one? I don't want to risk being seen going in and out of the building late on a Sunday night – most suspicious. All the phones and chargers are locked up in Valuables and of course only NB has the key, so no luck there. I consider the computer in Customer Service, but it's risky now that nincompoop NB is in charge, especially since he is busy upgrading the digital system; he could easily see that I logged in over the weekend and start asking difficult questions. I'll have to wait till tomorrow to continue my search for Mr Appleby.

16

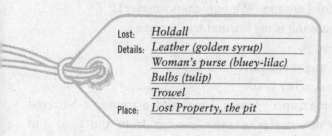

Lost:	*Holdall*
Details:	*Leather (golden syrup)*
	Woman's purse (bluey-lilac)
	Bulbs (tulip)
	Trowel
Place:	*Lost Property, the pit*

I wake with a start. Monday – Big Jim's day in the pit. Didn't Anita mention him coming in extra early to keep up with the accelerating turnover of items? I dress in a hurry and cover my tracks, stuffing my lab-coat nightie under the mid-century along with the bottle of absinthe, now almost empty.

Outside it's freezing. I take a swift constitutional up Baker Street to Regent's Park. The park is dark and ghostly so early in the morning, like going back to a past, timeless London. I feel I'm just as likely to spot a gang of Jacobean highwaymen cantering over the grass as a stockbroker rushing to get to Paternoster Square and put in the early bids. A bevy of Edwardian nannies could clip around the corner of the Outer Circle, en route to the Rose Garden, pushing their orb-faced charges in Silver Cross perambulators. In moments like this the city reveals the layers of its history, especially if one

189

shields one's eyes and blots out the bulbous monstrosities of the modern skyline.

By the time I have taken a turn around the boating lake, the sky has shifted from brooding noir to a belligerent corporate blue, and thankfully the cafe has opened.

'We don't do any of the funny teas,' the girl says at my request for Lapsang. 'We only do normal tea.'

'But Lapsang is my normal tea,' I persist.

She shrugs.

'Well, might you have Earl Grey?'

She shakes her head.

I order a cup of 'normal tea' and a round of buttered toast, which makes a tasty change from the tins, and distract myself from the clamour in my head by leafing through *Hitchhiking in Thailand – Top Tips on Hostels on the Highways*. I keep it in my locker for lunch-time edification. It usually rivets, but today I find I have read the paragraph about the pod-style beds at Stamps Backpackers in Chiang Mai more than once. I'm distracted by thoughts of Mum. How is she? Where is she? Back in the music room, singing away, trying to transport herself to another place? Has Adison been in to see her today? Rubbed her hands? I touch my own; they are rough, peppered with splinters from making my umbrella aviary. Far too rough for Adison to rub, I'm quite sure.

When I strike out an hour later, the park throngs with people: workers engrossed in one-way conversations on their phones, joggers puffing valiantly as they loop the lake. A mother runs hand-in-hand with her little boy who is clad in mottled green. He resists her pull, his attention caught by something in the grass. She drags him onwards, falling in with the invisible beat that speeds Londoners through the chaos and clamour of the city. I, under no such duress, have leave to dawdle and linger, to stoop and marvel at the morning perkiness of a daisy. Perhaps that was what caught the attention of the little boy: the daisy. When we are young we are privy to the intoxicating world of plants. I remember lying hidden in the long grass and brambles at the bottom of the garden, losing hours entranced by how perfectly an acorn fitted its cup, the lustre and curve of a conker. Dad would sometimes join me and we'd stretch out a day way beyond bedtime, green-kneed, searching for four-leaf clovers, both of us fervently wanting to believe in their magic.

I head back to Lost Property in time for start of business with renewed determination to track down Mr Appleby. I may not be armed with a four-leaf clover but I have lived covertly in Lost Property for five nights, survived mostly on a diet of tinned fruit and vegetables, provided sanctuary for the umbrellas, and so I can and will solve The Mystery of the Mislaid Holdall!

I pass a queue already forming at Madame Tussauds. I've never been, but Anita has spoken quite passionately about it. ('I saw Nicole Kidman and Posh and Becks. It's like it's really *them* – you know what I mean?' I do not.) Turning on to Baker Street, I note that no such queue has yet formed outside the Sherlock Holmes Museum – which is, to my mind, a far worthier enterprise.

Feeling determined though slightly duplicitous as I 'arrive' at work, I am surprised to see Anita already in. 'Thought I'd get ahead with some sorting,' she says quickly when she sees me. 'Cuppa?' She hoists a large flask from the beast along with a couple of Tupperware beakers. 'I just took a tea down to Jim. He's been in since the crack,' she adds, somewhat defensively.

'Thank you, no, I had one on the way . . . in. You don't happen to have a phone charger in that wonderful bag of yours, do you?'

The morning flashes by in a whirl of woolly hats, lost wallets and forgotten teddy bears, and I don't have time to collate my clues and extend my search. As well as being busy, Customer Service is also rather tense; the five-pound return fee continues to cause ill will, and a woman who went abroad just as her handbag was handed in falls foul of the month-only hold protocol.

'I'm sorry, we've recently started a new system,' Anita says, as the woman berates her across the counter.

'It's not bloody good enough. I got a letter saying my bag had been found, I've come all the way from Surrey, and you're telling me it's in sodding Tooting? Do you people have any qualifications? Any clue how to do your jobs?'

'The thing is,' Anita says to me after the woman leaves, 'I don't blame her for being pissed off. It's been a nightmare since Brian left.' She reaches into the beast, seeking reinforcements, which she finds in a golden tin of fast-hold Elnett. 'Bloody Burrows,' she says in a hiss of chemical spray. 'That git has a lot to answer for.'

In my lunch break I finally get a chance to turn my attention to Mr Appleby. I grab my phone, now fully charged, thanks to Anita and her champion carrier. I'll have one final peruse of the holdall and that Judges receipt, see if any more clues can be gleaned, and then do an online search of all that I have. On my way down to the stacks, I stop rigid. My hand flies to my chest in horror. I didn't leave the holdall in the stacks. I left it in the pit last night, amongst the unclaimed items. The unclaimed items that are right now being sent to Snagsbey's . . .

Heart pounding, I rush to the open hatch. A vast tangle of clothes and bags are piled around it, ready to go down the chute. I poke my head through the opening. *Please let the holdall still be there, please.* In the pit, Big Jim is slumped on a chair, mopping his forehead with a fistful of packing paper while his Toot-a-Loop wheezes out 'YMCA'. Even his tattoos look exhausted. Despite my panic about the holdall, I am struck for a moment by how odd it is to see Big Jim in the pit. Previously I had considered it wholly his terrain; now I feel as if he has wandered into my sitting room.

The floor around him is covered with piles of lost items. There is still hope!

'Have you seen a brown holdall?' I call, trying to remain calm. 'It was sent down by mistake and I need to get it back urgently!'

Big Jim looks up wearily. Gives his forehead another blot.

'Did you see it?' I ask, desperately scanning the area around him.

'Holdall? Like a big shoulder bag?' he says.

'Yes!' My voice is a high-pitched whinny. I take a breath. 'That's right, sort of syrupy colour?'

He nods.

'*Young man, there's no need to feel down,*' the Toot-a-Loop wheezes.

'It's gone,' Big Jim says.

A punch in the stomach. 'Gone! It can't have gone! Its owner is looking for it, he needs it! Are you sure it's not down there?'

Big Jim shakes his head. 'Went to Snagsbey's in the last van load.'

I swallow a dry swallow. 'But how . . . how can I get it back?'

'Can't. Van went twenty minutes ago.'

'Do you have the driver's number?'

He shakes his head.

'I'll call Snagsbey's directly, then.'

'No one there till tomorrow's auction.'

'But I have to get it back, it's personal property. I have to return it.' My voice cracks. Big Jim lifts his intricately inked paws in a hopeless gesture.

'Sorry.'

Anita finds me later in the Ladies, inconsolable.

'Dots! What is it? Bloody Burrows? Wait till I give him a piece of my mind.' She strokes my back.

'It's . . . not him,' I sob, my face in my hands. 'It's my fault. It's all my fault. Poor Mr Appleby, I've . . . let him down, lost his property. His holdall has gone to Snagsbey's and I can't get it back.' Tears gutter between my fingers.

'Don't you worry,' Anita says. 'Do you know what? He's probably forgotten about that bag already.'

'No. Not him.'

'Well then, how about when he next comes in we give him one of the unclaimed ones? There's a lovely Armani that's due to go down the chute in a day or two. How about I put that by for him?'

I raise my head, stare at her.

'Anita! Mr Appleby doesn't want another bag; he wants *his* bag! The holdall can't be replaced! These things matter.

They have value. Meaning. They are irr . . . irreplaceable.'
My face is wet with tears; I gulp the words out.

'It's all right, calm down, Dots, love. I understand . . .'

'Do you?' I shake her hand off my back. Step away from
her. 'I don't think you do, Anita. "Crap" – I rather think
that was your exact terminology for lost property?'

'I never, I don't—'

'Nothing matters nowadays, does it? It's all disposable,
meaningless. Lost something you care about? Just get
another! Get two! Replace it and move on!'

'Dots, please.' Anita comes towards me, her face hurt,
her eyes glistening. I shove her away and lurch out of the
cloakroom and down to the stacks, where I stand in the
calm of my umbrella sanctuary until I can compose myself.

Eventually I adjust my felt – *Safety Pin. Safety Pin* – and
return upstairs. Anita and her beastly bag keep their distance
at the far end of the counter.

I give a man who comes in to claim his lost jacket short
shrift.

'Please take more care with your belongings or you might
not be so lucky in the future,' I admonish.

Desperate for the day to end, I sweat through the hours
and minutes until I can retreat to the pit.

'I'm looking forward to our one-to-one this evening,' NB
breathes behind me. 'Six o'clock at the Dog and Duck, right?
I've got a meeting out of the office this afternoon, so easiest
if I meet you there. Nice one.' He bustles off before I can
even think of an excuse.

I sink my face into my hands and groan audibly. I had
completely forgotten about the arrangement with NB. Could
this day be any more hellacious? My body longs for the only

things that make sense – the wormwood companionship of absinthe and the smell of his pipe tobacco.

The assault continues when, on my way to the pub, Philippa phones.

'Is Mum OK?' I ask, hoping to heavens Philippa hasn't found out about Mum going AWOL.

'Or you could say, "Hello Philippa, how nice to hear your voice, how are you?"'

'Hello Philippa, is Mum OK?'

'You were the last one to see her on Saturday, and to be honest I rather thought *you* might have called *me*.'

'Right, sorry.'

'Well, how was it?'

'What?'

'For goodness' sake, what on earth is wrong with you? Mum, how was Mum when you saw her?' I can almost hear her rolling her eyes in her head.

'Ah, er, fine.'

'How did she take the news? About Uncle Joe?'

'Fine.'

'Really? Oh, well, good, I suppose. Thanks for doing that.' She takes a breath. 'And there is just one more thing. D—'

'What do you want?'

'That's not very nice.'

'Sorry. It's just, when you call me D, you generally want me to do something.'

'I don't.'

'You do.'

'I don't. Anyway. I actually have some super news, thought maybe we could meet up and talk about it. It's to do with the house . . .'

'No . . . I can't. Not right now . . . I have to meet someone at the pub.'

'Who? Do I know them?'

'Nobody. My new boss.'

'Your boss is taking you for a drink? And he's single, right?' Her voice changes timbre as she digests the news. 'That *is* exciting. Try not to be too . . . *you*, OK? Dot? Are you still there? D? Dot? Hello . . . ?'

I switch off the phone and shove it in my pocket.

NB is already at the pub when I arrive. It's crowded, for which I am grateful. He has commandeered a space for us at a sticky table otherwise occupied by a man in a shiny suit, and a young woman with high hair and presumably low expectations.

He pulls out a chair for me. Instinctively I take a step backwards to avoid the halitosis, but instead I smell something that reminds me of Grandma Minton's cupboard drawers, which she lined with scented floral paper. NB is wearing aftershave.

'G and T? Dry white wine?' he says.

'Just a sparkling water, please.'

'No, no, a real drink, I insist.'

I don't have the energy to argue.

'Wine, then.'

He retreats into the fray at the bar. The clientele is mostly City chaps in packs, clinking beer glasses, slapping each other on the back. The couple at our table are holding hands.

'Young love, eh?' says NB loudly, settling our beverages on cardboard coasters and giving the man a knowing wink, which he ignores.

I take a large gulp of my wine, relish its soothing effects. How on earth did I think I could get through this on sparkling water?

'I'll cut to the chase. We're going to be seeing quite a few changes at TfL. I've been speaking to some of the Crossrail chaps – goings-on there are enough to make your hair curl, I can tell you.'

He clinks my glass boisterously.

'To the future!'

'Indeed . . . Congratulations on your promotion.'

He takes a mouthful of his pint and smiles conspiratorially. 'I'm chuffed, I admit, but this isn't just about yours truly. You and I could be quite a team, Dot. In fact, I have something for you.' He rummages in a plastic bag hanging from his chair, takes out a cellophane-covered box and presents it proudly.

It is a gift set containing a pink oval of soap, a tin of talcum powder and a scented candle. Lily of the valley. For a moment, I wonder if he has taken it from Lost Property.

'Just a little token of my appreciation.'

'Thank you.' I do not want a gift from NB. Neither do I want to be given toiletries that would not be out of place at The Pines.

'We have a lot in common, Dot.'

I try not to let my face show how perturbing I find the prospect of having anything in common with NB, apart from our place of employ. Before I can puzzle out what he thinks this might be, he reaches across the table and suddenly my hand is in his, horribly mirroring the courting couple next to us. I pull away but his grip tightens.

'I've always respected your work ethic. But too much work makes Neil a dull boy!' His thin thumb strokes my wrist. I wrench my hand out of his clasp, wrap it firmly around my glass and take several huge swallows of wine.

'Was there any particular business you wanted to talk about?'

'Business? See, this is what I'm saying – stellar work ethic.' He takes a gulp of his beer and sits back. 'I won't pretend it's not tough being the boss.'

I nod.

'I always hoped I would end up in sports. You might not think it now, but I was quite the athlete in my youth.'

I nod, forbidding my imagination to conjure an image of NB in shorts.

'But there you are – we can't have everything, can we?'

'Well, I wish you all the best.' I finish the rest of my wine in the champion of swigs and shift my weight, ready to make a break, desperate to get back to the pit, to figure out a plan to retrieve the holdall.

'I don't mind saying, I'm pretty pleased with what I've achieved. Stuff's getting shifted a lot quicker at the office, that admin charge has already covered the cost of my new filing software . . .'

Should I call Anita? Apologize? What news did Philippa have? Has there been an offer on the house already? How could I have spoken to Anita like that! But how can she be so glib about Mr Appleby's holdall? These things matter. *Safety Pin.* It's not just 'stuff'. I grip the tacky table edge.

'. . . Work hard, play hard, that's my motto. Yup, things are on the up, I can tell you . . . I was saying to the boys at TfL . . .'

I have to leave. Need to fix things, mop up the mess I've made.

'Another round?' NB stands up quickly, banging the table, causing the man's pint to slosh.

'Oi, watch it,' the man barks.

'Soz, mate.' NB flashes a smile.

'I have to go,' I say.

'What about dinner? They do a pretty good lamb faggot—'

'I need to get home. My mother's poorly.' A vestige of truth at least. He nods acquiescence, but the winds have changed and I note a glint of coldness in his eyes, see him register rejection.

When I get back to Lost Property, I am drained and desperate for the easy company of absinthe and my consulting detective. Surely he'll have a plan for the holdall? Perhaps even some advice about Anita. In the Ladies cloakroom, I brush my teeth, return my toothbrush to my locker, and shove my bag and phone in with it; I don't want any more upsetting calls from Philippa. I descend to my lair in the pit and, still in my uniform, lie down on the mid-century and fall into a short but fitful nap.

I dream I am ten years old, hiking through a forest with Dad. The path ascends from the dark piney cool of the woodland floor to a steep traverse above. The route is twisty, the going arduous. From time to time, we pass other hikers, all heading back down. 'Keep going,' they encourage, 'the view at the top is worth it!' Dad is always a few steps ahead, his heavy grey rucksack listing from side to side with every stride. No matter how hard I try to move faster, I can never quite catch him up. He looks back at me a few times, smiles, then walks on – further and higher. Finally, we break through a copse of straggly trees into the light at the top.

'Come and see.' He turns, his face radiant. He stretches out his hand to me.

From where we stand, you can see for miles – dark-green smudges of other forests in the distance, and beyond them the blue gash of the sea.

I'm thirsty and my legs ache from the climb. 'Is it time for our picnic?' I ask, eyeing Dad's rucksack greedily, thinking of the domino sandwiches, the two chubby iced buns, the cool flask of squash.

'In a moment, poppet,' says Dad, still staring at the view.

I wait. Sigh dramatically. Then: 'Dad, I'm starving.' I pull at the rucksack and suddenly he lurches sideways. His left foot flails out, seeks purchase on a jut of rock in front of him that gives way, sending clods of dirt and shards of stone tumbling down the cliffside, and he lunges again, falls forward, unable to find a footing. For an instant I see the expression on his face, fathoming what is happening, still partially caught in the moment just before when he was looking at the view – his eyes full of rapture, his mouth jarred in fear. I stand frozen.

One of his arms thrashes out. He grabs my hand and together we fall – down, down, down.

I startle awake, sweating. The picnic blanket is twisted around my chest; my heart beats a hollow lament: *my fault, my fault, my fault.* Inhale, exhale. *Sellotape.* I eye the absinthe. It's nearly gone and I know I have to cut back anyway, but I just need a whisper of it on my lips, just enough to see him again, sit together for a while as he pups on his pipe.

Unable and unwilling to get back to sleep, I take the absinthe up to my beautiful new umbrella sanctuary, my aviary of resting birds. Perhaps he will visit me up here; I think it will appeal. My colleagues seem not to have noticed the improvement, but he will. I lie down on the floor, make out the shapes of the wooden umbrella handles – trees I could climb up to get another view, a different perspective. I start to relax.

A noise.

Silence. Did I imagine it? Then another sound, a scuffling, closer this time. *Someone else is in the building.* They are nearby. A rustling, coming directly from the Valuables lock-up. A thief? I can hear boxes being opened. Things being removed. Pocketed. Most definitely a thief, stealing from Lost Property. A clammy chill creeps at the back of my neck.

I recognize a cloying scent and go cold.

'Well, well, well, what have we here?' Another smell, sharp and sour – whisky? – and underlying it something else, something thick, fetid. I gag. I scrabble backwards, feel the press of umbrella handles in my back. The sound of panting, feral, animalistic. He switches on the fluorescents and I see him. I can't breathe. *Sello—*

He lunges.

The absinthe bottle falls from my hand and smashes on the floor and he is on me, the full heat and weight of him pressing into me. Then, faster than I can comprehend, his mouth is against mine, his thick wet tongue rooting past my lips. A hot hand pushes at my chest, ferrets at the buttons of my uniform, rucks up my skirt.

I scream, push him away. He strikes out and there is a clatter like artillery fire as umbrellas crash to the floor.

'No!' I scream again, but my mouth is plugged by his. Panic chokes my throat. He claws at my breast, pulls, then an awful ripping sound. Umbrellas skitter beneath my feet, a sharp crack as a shaft shatters underfoot. I reach wildly, blindly behind me. He pushes me back, ruts his hips against mine; his mouth suckers to my neck.

I scream again and his hand clamps hard against my teeth, forces my head back. Blood in my mouth. I struggle. I wrench an arm loose, clutch wildly, and this time my hand closes around something solid. It is the sturdy curve of a Bark Blackthorn Root-Knob Solid Stick Umbrella. I pull it out and bring it crashing down on the head of Neil Burrows.

A cry, ugly, guttural. He lurches backwards and then forwards again, grabs at me. I lift my rapier, bring it down once more, but harder this time. He groans. Falls forward on to the floor and shrieks. He staggers to his feet and holds his hand up in horror, blood seeping between his fingers. A shard of glass daggers out of his palm from the broken bottle.

'Fuck . . . fuck you . . . you pathetic bitch. Should be grateful . . . Fuck.' He clutches his hand. 'But I've got you. Breaking and entering. Drunk and disorderly. Trespassing. Oh dear, oh dear. Not looking good for you, is it? Not good at all. Fuck, that hurts . . .' He stares at his blood-soaked hand then gives an ugly smile. 'You better hope I don't get you convicted of grievous bodily harm while I'm at it.'

'And will you declare your own crimes at the same time?' I ask, my voice quiet but clear. 'Assault? Theft of valuables?'

A thick globule of spit lands on my cheek.

'Consider yourself fired,' he hisses. He stands for a moment, staring at me. My fingers grip the blackthorn. Bile in my throat. *Sell . . . o . . . tape.* He spits again, misses, the gobbet landing on his own shoe. He turns and walks out.

I stand, shivering, listen to every one of his footsteps, the whirr and hoist of the lift, waiting till I am sure he is no longer in the building.

Then I wipe my cheek and sink to the ground. In my hand, I still clutch the trusty blackthorn. The torn, bruised, broken bodies of umbrellas surround me. Some brollies hang from their shelves, garrotted, swaying. Others, unscathed, lie quietly in their nests, cowed and afraid.

I breathe in the sharp scent from the pool of absinthe on the floor, and long for him to come – *nil desperandum, dear Watson* – rescue me, tell me it will be all right. But he doesn't come. He abandons me once more.

I have to comfort myself. I know how; I have had practice. I close my eyes and imagine that I take a beautiful pair of silver scissors from the torn breast of my jacket; imagine I cut off every single Dijon tag on the umbrellas.

'Fly away!' I whisper.

At first nothing happens.

'Fly away!' Louder now.

Nothing. No . . . a rustle.

Then a sigh, and the lightest breeze as above me wings open. A slither of satin and . . . a Ladies' Everyday with Violet Canopy is the first to go, in a pulse of air that leaves in its wake the scent of Parma violets and a whisper of hope. A curved maple-handled follows, then a domed Birdcage with a translucent body. A phalanx of black collapsibles round up the injured and the broken, and flap to create a pocket of air for them to rise into. Together they swoop through the stacks, up the stairs, then twist and soar across Customer Service, filling it with vibration, colour, life. As one they fly to the exit, the ricochet of their ferules reverberates, and the door opens on to the sooty wet of the city. A brief pause, but no more than that – a fermata before the crescendo – and then in one mad glorious rush they dive into the dark, shake their silky bodies, outstretch their spokes, so long bound, now open, free.

Tears course down my cheeks as I hold on tight to the image, picture them soaring over rooftops and chimney pots, escaping into the midnight-blue of the city and beyond. A magnificent migration.

And now it is my turn to leave.

Slowly, awkwardly, I drag myself upright. I stagger; my feet are pins and needles. I see my Sheaffer kicked into a corner, wince as I bend to retrieve it, feeling the bruises on my body. But worse than the bruises, the sag of my uniform, pulled, twisted, man-handled, and at my breast something flapping loose, torn. I can't bear to look down at it.

I stumble out of my umbrella sanctuary, make my way to the mound of clothes piled at the mouth of the hatch. I reach inside the pile, searching for something soft, something kind. A thin white shirt, elbows worn to threads – yes, that will do. I plunge in again: trousers, voluminous, deep navy. Good. One more thing, a jacket or coat. Through the twist of jumpers, shirts, scarves – a shimmer. I catch hold of it and pull. With a flash of silver it arcs out.

A shiny bomber jacket.

I unbutton my felt, slip out of my pleated skirt. I smooth down the torn breast pocket, then fold the arms around the skirt tightly and tuck the bundle deep into the heap of unclaimed clothes. I push the whole pile down the chute.

'I'm sorry,' I whisper.

In the Ladies, I gather my things from my locker, catch sight of myself in the mirror. Don't recognize what I see. My eyes wide, frightened, scratches on my face and neck, my skin pale. I look like an astronaut in the silvery bomber jacket, its ballooning arms. The owner bagged out the pockets with the press of their hands. I slip my hands into the pockets, copy the gesture and try to feel a little less alone. The trousers are bell-bottomed, huge. I fold over the waist a couple of times and it holds me like a life ring.

Then I walk through Customer Service and at the door I look back at the length of the wooden counter, the neatly stacked pile of Dijon tags waiting for the loss that will come tomorrow, and the next day and the day after.

Then I step out into the night.

The sky is lidded, the air damp and cold, but under my silver bomber my body is numb. I walk with no sense of direction, with the sole purpose of moving, propelling my body forward. Because if I stop, I fear I won't be able to start again; I will stand here, lost in the middle of Baker Street.

After some time, I realize I am heading south, towards the river. When I reach its inky banks I turn left, walk until I reach a bridge, climb the worn steps. Blackfriars. I have always been rather fond of the pink blush of its stone.

A sign on the side of the bridge – ALWAYS THERE, DAY AND NIGHT – and the number of the Samaritans. How thoughtful. But what can I possibly say? I lean over the side and stare down into the dark river, rippling with centuries of history, stories shifting in its watery cells. Does it ever yearn to shrug it off, be washed free of all that it carries? All those memories?

I cross the bridge and walk along the Albert Embankment, following the Thames towards Battersea. Every now and then I stop and stare into the eddies of the water, until eventually the light shifts and the possibility of morning starts to cast shadows on the river.

I find my way to a brightly lit all-night cafe bedecked with violently orange tables and chairs, and order a 'normal tea'.

Then I catch the number 44 to Tooting.

17

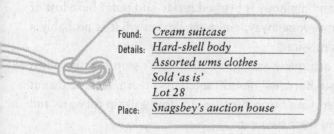

Found: *Cream suitcase*
Details: *Hard-shell body*
Assorted wms clothes
Sold 'as is'
Lot 28
Place: *Snagsbey's auction house*

Snagsbey's suits its moniker well. The Tooting auction house is the last building on a long street that seems to disintegrate the further one travels along it. Shops slouch side by side, spent and shattered. Old paint flakes in yellow-grey scabs; broken red-tiled roofs of derelict houses reveal an embarrassment of cavities.

On first sighting, Snagsbey's itself is reminiscent of a funeral home down on its luck. A black sign with gold embossed writing hangs at an angle: *Established 1896, Mr A. P. Snagsbey Esq.* The building is a Frankenstein's monster – mock-Tudor facade, half covered by a thick metal shutter, with side walls pebble-dashed in an assault of grey and beige. The entrance is down the side, accessed through a black metal gate that swings half off its hinges. A dirty white van idles in the driveway, doors gaping open to reveal a stack of cardboard boxes, a broken enamel bath, plastic bags tied tightly, asphyxiating the children's toys within. A man lolls against the van, a hand-rolled cigarette drooping from his fingers.

'All right?' he asks.

I startle him with an involuntary laugh at the irony. I am as broken and useless as that old bath. I am homeless, jobless, and my body is bruised inside and out. I have lost or pushed everyone away, and now I'm on what is probably a hopeless mission.

I nod brusquely and hurry past. Can't stop because when I do I taste Burrows' mouth, smell his breath, feel the tear at my breast. Can't stop because if I do I will tip forward and shatter on the pavement.

I step blindly into a vestibule that leads to the auction room. A laminated sign shouts the presence of surveillance cameras in operation, and I stare into the eye of a squat lens hanging from the ceiling. I don't recognize myself in its reflection.

The layout of the auction room as a 'house' is manifested inside with an array of pictures – mostly posters of Greek islands or generic English country pastels – hanging on the walls alongside some heavily framed mirrors. Tallboys, dressers and cabinets flank the room, shelves bursting with suitcases, toys and clothes. A motley crew of seats assembled in rows as if at the theatre face a raised stage lined with locked glass cabinets, presided over by a wooden podium with a small gavel on top. See-through bags hang from the ceiling, inside each a pair of women's shoes, suspended in the plastic like goldfish won at the fair.

Everything here sports a lot number. Everything here is for sale.

The auction won't start till 9 a.m., so in the remaining half-hour, viewing is still allowed. I join several men wandering the aisles, most of them dressed in what seems to be an unofficial uniform of grey sweatshirts tucked into shapeless jogging trousers.

People start filling the seats. It is clear that regulars have their territory and the back row is sacrosanct.

A man with pink cheeks like luncheon meat sits, splay-legged, on a blue plastic chair in the far corner. He speaks loudly to a man a few chairs away in the prime position of back row, centre, who sports the regulation jogging-trouser ensemble.

'What's the breakdown of the clientele here? Looks like a pretty mixed bag. Not all in trade, are they?' Luncheon Meat has a strong South African accent.

Jogging Trousers sits back and opens his own legs even wider than his interlocutor's. 'Well, it's like this, see. The people who come here – and I've been coming for years, mate, so I know what I'm saying – they're mostly salesmen. A few members of the public come in looking for a cheap iPad for Christmas.' His head jerks towards a blond man and woman sitting on two soft-backed armchairs a few rows towards the front. They stand out from the rest of the room in their cosy duffels. Their soft golden hair looks as if it smells of apple blossom. They share one catalogue between them and study it assiduously, nodding when the other speaks. There is something about their closeness that makes me want to reach out and stroke them, make them promise to stay together always.

'I come here because I've got a stall down Notting Hill,' Jogging Trousers is saying. 'Regular pitch – gold dust they

211

are, fucking gold dust. Now, tell the truth, there's not much here' – he motions around the room – 'that I would buy for my Notting Hill stall, but I *might* pick up something to pass to a mate of mine who does Petticoat Lane – see what I mean?'

Luncheon Meat shrugs and shifts the crotch of his jeans.

'But having said that,' Jogging Trousers goes on, clearly relishing his role, 'once in a while I've picked up something here – bit of Spode, first edition, quality leather bag – that I've gone on and sold like that' – he clicks thick fingers – 'at Notting Hill for ten times what I paid for it here.' He folds his arms and nods sagely. 'In a place like this, you've gotta know your stuff and be able to sort the wheat from the chaff. You've gotta be able to recognize something a bit special that these numpties' – he gestures to the room – 'don't have a clue about.'

The room fills. I haven't spotted Mr Appleby's holdall yet and search the aisles apprehensively. A few people like me peruse the shelves, but the real bun fight is taking place around the glass cabinets where the valuable items are kept under lock and key. Customers, all male, cluster around them. They sport a different look – men in long leather coats, men in ghutra and thobe, men in tweed jackets who look like they have just stepped out of a mansion apartment in West London, and men in slim-hipped trousers, their sockless feet revealing expensive articulated ankles.

Several of them know each other and call out greetings. The only person who actually seems to be in charge of it all is a thin pallid boy who can't be more than fifteen, with a straggly pubescent moustache.

'When I call your name and open the cabinet you got two minutes to look,' the boy says. 'Just two minutes, right?

212

And as soon as the auctioneering starts, no more viewing allowed.'

The men nod, their eyes locked on the cabinets, alert, waiting for their moment.

As well as selling off unwanted lost property, Snagsbey's deals in bric-a-brac from junk shops and defunct furniture warehouses, and uncollected suitcases from Left Luggage at train stations. Like Lost Property, there is a sell-by date on the storage of luggage. All cases are sold 'as is', meaning with their entire contents. It's a gamble, the luck of the draw, as to whether you end up with a bag that was packed for a jet-set fortnight in Monte Carlo or a soggy weekend hiking in Wales.

Snagsbey's sells stolen goods too, passed on from the police. Perhaps this explains the grim and covert edge of some of the clientele. The auction house also undertakes property clearances and probate valuations, and there is certainly more than a whiff of purgatory about the whole place.

I scan the shelves anxiously for the holdall. There is a violence to the organizing here, if you can even call it organizing. There is none of the finesse of our stacks. Here objects are mashed together, squashed in broken crates, rammed into spaces too small for them. It's the dark flip-side of Lost Property. I recognize the same sorts of items – bags, coats, brollies – many of which once lined our shelves. But where Lost Property is a hopeful sanctuary offering a second chance, the possibility of a happy ending for life's little tragedies, this place is purely opportunistic, a business run for profit. What happy endings can one possibly find here?

'Only one minute of viewing left, ladies and gents, one minute only,' the pubescent boy calls.

I run my hand over Lot 28, a cream hard-shell case brought over from Left Luggage at Paddington. Its label reads 'Assorted wms clothes' and I wonder what might be inside such an elegant case. It is then that I see it – the holdall – and, despite everything, my heart lifts. There it is, squashed between a bulging baize-covered trolley and a parakeet-green plastic case with a broken zip, out of which something yellow and synthetic seeps.

The holdall is lot number 26.

'Take your seats, ladies and gentlemen, the auction is about to start,' moustache boy shouts.

Referring to my catalogue, I see that Lot 26 is part of a section called 'Bagged Goods and Left Luggage'. Its contents are listed as 'wms purse, trowel, veg'. Veg! Someone clearly doesn't know their bulbs from their root vegetables.

The seats have filled up now; indeed there is only one left, in a row near the back. I squeeze into it. Behind me I hear Luncheon Meat say, 'Every woman, however hideous, has a redeeming feature you can compliment.'

Jogging Trousers gives a harsh bark of a laugh. 'Yeah, like, "Your shoes are nice."'

I press my feet under my chair, hollow into the silver armour of my bomber jacket. My body is wobbly from lack of sleep.

A ripple of excitement shivers through the assembled motley crew as, with a sharp click-clack of court heels, the auctioneer enters. She is sixty-ish, angular as a coat hanger, with nicotine-tinted blonde hair scraped into an acute ponytail. Black-rimmed spectacles cover half her narrow face. There is something timeless about her, as if she has been here since Snagsbey's opened in 1896. Her voice, like the rest of her, is sharp-edged – pure London.

'Morning, all. Before we start, a few notes for our new bidders here today.'

The duffel couple smile shyly at each other, as if the auctioneer has bestowed some sort of romantic pledge on them. Everyone else just stares at the catalogues in their hands, antsy.

'Minimum spend is eight quid on all goods,' the auctioneer's voice snips. 'Check your lots before you leave the premises, as mistakes cannot be rectified. Move that front row of chairs forward, Rob, so people can get their legs in the row behind.' Obediently, a man in a grey hoodie orchestrates those sitting in the front row to stand up and shuffle their chairs forward. The auctioneer continues with her litany: 'No moving when the hammer is going, no spend over two hundred quid per person. Right, ladies and gents, here we go.'

Slumped positions shift, tongues lick pencil stubs. A fraught energy quivers. And we're off.

'Lot one, Bose QuietComfort noise-cancelling headphones with audio cable. Starting the bidding at fifteen quid.'

Bidding cards lift and fall like leaves in an autumn breeze and I realize why the back seats are favoured: their occupants have clear sight of who is bidding, on what and for how much. Some cards flap vigorously – the ingénues. The experts barely breathe. Nothing eludes the auctioneer's owl-eyed gaze. She is swift and ambidextrous in her use of pen and gavel as we slice through the first lots.

As she calls each item, the pubescent boy, whose name appears to be Alfie, flits about the room displaying the lot.

A pair of 'his and hers' watches slither between his gangly fingers; the next moment he is on the other side of the room displaying a Kindle in a red fabric case. A magic show, full of conjuring tricks and sleights of hand.

'Lot eleven – who's going to start me off at twelve quid for this nice men's suit, showing at the back?'

We swivel around to see the mercurial Alfie at the far end of the room, holding a Gainsboro-grey suit aloft.

The auctioneer stares us down through her giant specs.

Not a flicker.

'It's down to ten quid. I'm giving it away here.'

Nothing.

'Gents' suit – from up Piccadilly way. Come on, not even eight pounds?'

A sudden waft of white from the Indian gentleman next to me, and bang goes the gavel, swoop goes the pen across the auctioneer's page.

'A tenner for this cupcake stand? Eight for a mini blender, new and boxed – nice little Christmas present for someone,' her voice cuts and slices. 'Pair of wedding shoes, size seven, never worn?' Alfie holds them up. It's strangely unsettling to see the silver high-heeled women's shoes in his lanky boy-hands, feels like a loss of innocence somehow.

'Black carry-case containing air-channel carbon-fibre dual-torsion skis and ski poles – sounds posh – ski season on the way, who'll give me thirty?' The skis go to Luncheon Meat. 'Nice pedal bin?' Alfie snaps to the far corner of the room. As he passes he mutters, 'I ain't picking that up.'

'Just wants a wipe-over,' says the auctioneer, although there is no way she could have heard him. Alfie glumly holds the bin at arm's length.

She controls the room, looks like she knows where dead bodies are hidden. The duffel couple clutch each other. My hands are slick with sweat. I rub my palms against the unfamiliar nap of my trousers, then worry the auctioneer might think I am bidding on the bin. But the bin has already gone, and Alfie is in the middle of the room holding up a bag of assorted ladies' sandals. The threads of his sparse moustache bead with moisture.

'Lot twenty-five.'

My heart pounds.

'Trolley with assorted children's clothes, three tea towels and two belts. Starting the bidding at eight quid.'

The man called Rob bids eight; someone behind raises it to ten. The duffel couple look at each other, nod, and the auctioneer calls out twelve. I am so desperate to get to the holdall I almost bid on the trolley to get it over with, but it goes to the duffels, who look thrilled.

'Lot twenty-six, leather bag . . .' starts the auctioneer. My card flaps before she has finished speaking.

'Please wait till the lot is called,' she reprimands. I dip my head.

'Leather bag containing garden trowel and ladies' purse. I'll start at fourteen, just on the quality of the leather.'

My Indian neighbour flashes his card.

'Sixteen?' says the auctioneer.

I raise mine, then, afraid she has not seen it, wave it more vigorously.

She nods sharply in my direction.

My neighbour brings it up to eighteen, and one of the grey tracksuit men with a heavy gold chain around his neck immediately bids twenty.

I flap my card as if I am fanning a fire and it's back to me at twenty-two, but immediately I feel a flutter behind me, feel sure it is Jogging Trousers, and he has it at twenty-four. My neighbour stops, but Gold Chain raises it to twenty-six. I have it back at twenty-eight. My heart is somersaulting; sweat trickles under my armpits. I lose it again to Jogging Trousers. I see him in my peripheral vision, leaning forward. He is trying to outbid me on purpose. I keep going – how can I not? I flash my card again, try not to breathe. There is a stillness. The gavel hovers.

'Going at thirty-two quid?'

I stare at the inches between the gavel and the table, willing them to shrink with the fall of the hammer. *Please, please.*

Bang.

'Next, Lot twenty-seven . . .'

I close my eyes, exhale. Clamber to my feet unsteadily. Avoid looking in the direction of Jogging Trousers as I start to make my way out.

'Lot twenty-eight, cream shell suitcase, sold as is.'

I turn, flash my bidding card.

At another cafe, thankfully with more muted decor, I sit cradling the blessed holdall in my lap, my newly acquired cream case at my feet. Like all the other customers around me, I peer at the screen of my phone. I tap in the word 'funicular' and find a vast array of funicular railways in countries from South Africa to the Ukraine. I need to limit my search.

What else did Mr Appleby say? A view stretching out to . . . ?

The waitress hovers by my table.

I look up, distracted.

'Breakfast or lunch? We've just started lunch, but breakfast is all day so whatevers.'

My stomach churns at the thought of eating.

'Just a cup of tea, please.' I turn back to my phone.

'What sort?'

'What sort of what?'

'What sort of tea do you want . . . ?'

'I don't suppose you have any Lapsang?'

'Coming up.'

I beam at her. The holdall, my surprise cream suitcase and a Lapsang. Small gifts lighting the dark.

'Going somewhere nice?' she says, looking at my bags.

'I, well . . . I'm not sure yet.'

She cocks her head to one side. 'Mystery trip, eh? Sounds fun. I'll get your tea.'

I return to my research and this time set the parameters to the UK. I'm rewarded with no fewer than seventeen funiculars. They are listed alphabetically. At the top of the list is Bournemouth, which boasts three. I retrieve my Sheaffer from my bag, write 'Bournemouth' on my paper napkin. I put a little question mark next to it. Bournemouth is definitely a contender. I've never been, but thoroughly enjoyed *Discover Dorset!* I picture the travel guide on my bookshelf in the empty maisonette and imagine strangers taking the measure of Mum's little home – Mum's and mine – sizing it up, looking at our things. Poor Mum. I long to speak to her, check how she is, but can't trust myself to call her right now. Can't trust my voice not to break. I don't want to upset her.

Back to business. Should Bournemouth be the mystery destination, *Discover Dorset!* would have come in handy, but as it is I return to the nemesis of all travel guides – Wikipedia – and read on.

Bridgnorth is next, home to the steepest funicular, but isn't Bridgnorth on the River Severn, not by the sea? Not Bridgnorth then; it's good to be able to eliminate at least one. Next is Brighton – a distinct possibility. I list it on the napkin under Bournemouth. Right, moving on, what's next? Bristol. Mr Appleby mentioned views across the Channel – I assumed the English Channel, but could he have meant Bristol? I start to write 'Bristol' on the napkin, but suddenly recall Mr Appleby saying that his grandson had invited him *down* to the coast. I close my eyes, see his friendly face . . . Yes, I am sure of it. Down. And Bristol would have been *up* or at least *over*. Another one to eliminate.

'I can give you a bit of paper if you like.' The waitress hands me my tea and gestures to my scribbly napkin. I nod gratefully. I definitely need more room if I am going to make my way through all seventeen funiculars. She tears a couple of pieces of paper from her pad. I start my list afresh. Oh dear, I feel I'm not getting anywhere fast. I sip my tea and its familiar smoky taste comforts.

The waitress brings a plate of buttered kippers to the man at the next table. I breathe in their pungent fishy smell . . . Hold on, didn't Mr Appleby say something about fishermen's huts?

Excitedly I type 'fishermen's huts' alongside 'South Coast funicular'. The first listing that comes up is an advertisement for Cherry Blossom B&B. '*Perfect for families, this friendly guest house near the seafront is close to all the delights of the Old Town.*'

Old Town! I forgot about Old Town – this must be it! I carry on reading: '*Accessible to all the ancient and modern delights of this part of the 1066 coastline, including the Lifeboat Museum, Flamingo Amusement Park, the fishermen's huts, and the funicular railway.*'

I am getting closer! I grab the holdall, pull out the faded receipt, and once more try to decipher the words. Again I make out the word 'Judges' at the top. Well, a receipt must mean it's a shop of some sort? My fingers shake as I type in 'Judges shop', 'Old Town', 'Fishermen's Huts', 'funicular', 'Cherry Blossom B&B', and hit the Go icon.

I have found him!

I gulp down the rest of my delicious tea.

'I know where I'm going,' I tell the waitress as I pay my bill. 'Hastings!'

18

Lost:	*Employment*
Details:	*Unspeakable*
Place:	*Lost Property Dept, Baker Street*

The train journey through the Kent countryside reminds me of my commute to school. Years ago now, of course, but I remember the swagger and sway of the carriage as it zipped through villages, farms and towns. From the outside, all dash and screech, flashing past. Fast. On the go, busy, busy, can't stop! But inside, the slow sway of locomotion, the easy undulation, the back-and-forth lullaby of the station stops: Maidstone-Bearsted-Ashford-Sturry-Minster.

Pocket squares of Kentish fields slide by under a Tupperware-lidded sky, timeless, sealed. Kent countryside smells sour, fecund, as if something dead is slowly rotting. Hops, of course, I know that now. As a schoolgirl it horrified and thrilled me. If I open the window I know it will smell just the same.

But that was a lifetime ago.

223

I see her, that Dot, her open expectant face ready for a game, aching for an adventure. The name written on the label inside her coat collar is mine, but she is not me. That readiness, that wide-faced grin, belongs to someone else. What's she doing now? Married with kiddies? Circumnavigating the globe in a slim schooner? Sharing a tarte flambée with a friend in Strasbourg? Because she's not here, bruised and untethered under a ballooning silver jacket with no one to reach out, catch her and hold on tight.

I slide open the small window, poke my nose out, and yes, there it is – the smell of hops. Buffets of wind snatch my breath, making my eyes water as the train speeds on towards the sea. Orpington: *au revoir*, dear Lost Property. Sevenoaks: *arrivederci*, sullied uniform. Tonbridge: *bonne chance*, Philippa, Greenridge, Cooper & Price, may you all be very happy together. Robertsbridge: *adieu*, maisonette. Battle: *ti maledico*, Neil Burrows. Crowhurst: toodle-pip, Holmes and Watson. St Leonards Warrior Square: goodbye, dear Anita.

There's still a job to be done. Luckily, I excel at pushing things to the side, footing them under the carpet. It's a family tradition I am well trained in.

At the unsavoury-sounding Wadhurst a bevy of cleaners embark, the words 'Train Presentation Team' emblazoned on their purple uniforms as if some sort of show or skit might be forthcoming.

I glance up through the slats of the luggage rack and am reassured to see the sturdy school-ruler stripes of the leather holdall, and next to it the 'as is' cream suitcase. To all outward appearances I am an everyday traveller, fully equipped for a Grand Tour with my fine array of luggage

– except for the fact that the contents of my suitcase are a complete mystery to me, and my holdall belongs to a man I do not know how to find. Sadly, my guide collection is without a tome on Hastings, but Wikipedia informs me the population of the town is 92,855. So, a challenge. But I have somewhere to stay – while waiting for the train, I booked into the Cherry Blossom B&B for three nights. And I have some clues. Perhaps Judges Bakery would be a good place to start? I may no longer be in the employ of Transport for London, Lost Property Department, but I have a piece of lost property in my possession and I shall do my utmost to reunite property with person. It will be my last official act of service.

Two teenage girls in my carriage look at me and snicker. No doubt I am quite a sight. Sure enough, as they get off at the next stop, one of them shouts, 'Like your jacket, very Ryan Gosling,' and they run off down the platform shrieking with laughter. I confess the reference is entirely lost on me, but I suppose it comes from the same place as those girls in the playground at school all those years ago, as I sat apart eating my sandwiches. A place reserved for those who perhaps don't quite fit in. I grew up thinking bullying would be something I would one day leave behind, but I know now that it stalks beyond the school gates. As a child, I thought taunts about unfashionable shoes, funny sandwiches and butter-fingers on the netball court were solely my terrain. I had no idea my father nursed his own wounds. Wounds that were, in the end, fatal.

Dad and I were at the petrol station once. He used to let me pump the petrol; I loved its fiery smell. A piece of music came on the radio. He spread his long expressive fingers across the bonnet. I always loved watching his hands; they were so graceful, always moving, expanding the air between them as if he were creating whole worlds. It was a piece of opera. *La bohème*, maybe. He closed his eyes, his hands dancing, his face transported.

'Get a move on!' A man's voice, harsh.

Dad started, opened his eyes, looked around, unsure where the voice had come from. A man leaned out of a van. He couldn't see me on the other side of the car. It looked like Dad was just standing there by himself.

'Poofta.' Rough laughter. More than one of them. A pack.

Dad rushed towards me. Tripped.

'Get in the car,' he said.

'But it's not done yet, Daddy,' I said. I'd been watching the counter, excited for all the round zeros when it reached the twenty-pound mark.

'That's enough. Get in!' A shout. He never shouted. Ever. My cheeks smarted as if he had slapped me. I got in the car, crossed my arms, pressed my lips together and didn't speak all the way home.

Back at the house I ran to my room, slammed the door. After a while he padded up.

'Doctor Watson, I need a consultation.'

He peered around the door, pipe between his teeth. I dived into my school bag, spilling books over the bed.

'I'm busy.'

'Ah, are you working on The Missing Pearl of Platts Heath?'

I shake my head.

'The Mystery of the Unkempt Alice Band?'

226

Another shake. He comes closer, strokes his chin.

'I can tell from the noxious shade of yellow' – he picks up my homework folder, mimes holding a magnifying glass – 'that it is nothing less than The Case of the Foolhardy Father.' He brings his forehead to mine. 'Hmm, something's afoot, old bean.'

'Old bean is my line!'

'Indeed it is, indeed it is!' He covers my hand with his. 'Now, I have come upon some very interesting evidence in the Downstairs Cloakroom. Would you care to take a look?'

I did, of course. Always.

Later that day, I thought back to what had happened at the petrol station. *Poofta*. What had the man meant? We used to have a pouffe – maroon leather, tight as a drum with plaited tassels. I think my parents got it on their honeymoon in Barcelona. Mr Tibbles, our adopted cat, used it as a scratching post and was so vigorous that the stuffing seeped out of the scored leather. In the end, it looked so dreadful that Mum got rid of it. Was that what those men were calling Dad? How silly. Part of me knew it wasn't that, of course. I knew they meant to hurt him. I just didn't want to think about that, tried to push it away, but it kept coming back.

In the end, I asked Philippa.

She was in her room curling her hair.

'What?' She frowned when I came in.

'Can I ask you something?'

'If you're quick – I'm going out.'

'What is a poofta?'

227

'What?' She paused mid-curl, till a burning smell alerted her.

'Look what you made me do!' she yelped, wrenching the tongs from the lock of hair, which seemed a mite crispy but not too bad.

'Sorry.'

'Why are you asking that? You are so weird.'

'No reason . . . just, I heard someone saying it about someone.'

She brushed the singed curl of hair. Didn't look at me. 'It means . . . you know . . .'

I shook my head. Downstairs the doorbell rang.

'Oh God, that's Lisa and I'm not even ready, look at my hair! You've made me mess it up.'

'Please, Philippa, tell me.'

'For flip's sake, it means gay. That's what poofta means. Got it? Now get out.'

But I hadn't got it at all, of course.

Philippa was the one who told me Mum and Dad had never planned to have other children after her. She was revising for her GCSEs and constantly in a bad mood. I had done something wrong – borrowed something or broken something or just breathed too loudly – and she had snapped at me and it had escalated into a fight. 'I wish I didn't have to have a sister, especially such an irritating one. Anyway, I think you were a mistake.'

'What do you mean?' I cried. 'I'm not! I'm not a mistake!'

'I wouldn't be so sure,' she struck back. 'Or maybe you were an immaculate conception! Did you never notice Dad sometimes sleeps downstairs? But then you are soooo like him, both of you so . . . ineffectual.'

I sat under the laburnum tree for hours, sobbing, swearing I'd never forgive her, not only for saying I was a mistake but also for being horrid about Dad, especially after I had looked up what ineffectual meant.

Being a mistake haunted me. Was that why Mum sometimes felt so distant? Why Dad spent so much time with me? Because he felt guilty somehow, was trying to put right something he had done wrong, his mistake?

After Philippa left home and I was busy working towards my A-levels, my heart set on getting a good place at university, it seemed that Dad started to give up. His body slumped in the armchair. I could smell sadness wafting off him like aftershave. I pretended he hadn't changed. That we were still Dad and Dot, ready for an adventure, off to have fun. But we weren't.

Nights were the worst. His sobs, her trying to help but sounding defeated. I tried to drown them out, put in my earphones, listened to my language audiobooks.

'David, please, what can I do?'

Per una ragione o per un'altra.

Visto che.

'Please, love.'

Je n'ai jamais eu d'accident.

Quelle sorte de films aimes-tu?

Où voudrais-tu habiter à l'avenir?

'I can't go through it again, love, you need help.'

Que yo sepa.

Habría querido.

Estaría estudiando. Estaría estudiando. Estaría estudiando.

Increasingly I would come into the dining room to say goodnight and find him sitting in the dark, a record spinning, the stylus quietly skating back and forth across the inner edge of the dead wax.

I remember one night when Mum had already retreated upstairs. Dad stared at the record player, silent but for the scratch, scratch, scratch of the needle, a smeary wine glass beside him. He looked up when I came in. Smiled. A compost of mulberry-coloured tannin stained each side of his mouth. I was embarrassed by him. And for him.

'I've done it all wrong, haven't I? Made such a mess.'

'No, Dad! You're perfect.' I had no idea what he meant. I wanted to get upstairs so I could revise for an exam. But Dad kept talking.

'I'm far from that.' He reached for his glass and, realizing it was empty, staggered to the drinks trolley to get another. 'Let you all down.'

'You haven't let anyone down,' I said.

He looked at me.

'My dearest Dot, always so loyal. I'll miss you so much when you go to university. I'm sure you will have a champion time. Lots of chums . . .' He poured a large glug of wine and stared down into the dark liquid in his glass. 'I never did fit in. They don't like it if you are different . . .'

He stumbled back to his chair, stopping at the window for a moment, suddenly fearful, peering out into the dark. He closed the curtains tight, to shut out whatever scared him.

But they were already inside, his fears, his secrets, all looped up in the dark recesses of his tangled thoughts, tormenting him.

He slumped back in his chair. I hovered at the door. Silence stretched between us. I wanted to say something but had no words, didn't know how to reach him. I also wanted to go. To just not be there any more.

'Enough of these doldrums! How about we read a chapter of Sherlock for old times' sake? . . . "The Man with the Twisted Lip"?'

'Umm . . .' I scuffed my toe against the fringe of the rug.

'I've got it!' He beamed, the wine stain giving him a double-rimmed Joker-like smile. '"A Scandal in Bohemia" – we used to love that one! Shall I read?'

'The thing is . . .'

'No – you, you must read, of course! Yes, that's the ticket. I'll just top up the old schooner and we'll tuck in.' He stumbled to the bookshelf, wine slopping in his glass.

'I can't.'

He looked at me.

'What's that?'

'I can't read tonight; I have to revise . . . I would otherwise . . . sorry, I just—'

'Of course, of course.'

'Another time.'

'Jolly good . . . yes.'

I kissed his cheek, feeling wretched at abandoning him, but glad to be able to escape to the steady calm of my books. Clear, straightforward, black and white.

But he couldn't escape. In the end his fear, his guilt, all the things that tormented him, sent him running. Goaded him down to the Underground that day, to the edge of the platform and over.

But there was someone else responsible for that. Someone whose actions sent a spray of Dad's blood arcing up the advert billboard for a summer break in the Algarve, spilling a trail of red on to the thigh of a smiling model in a bikini. Someone who committed an act of betrayal that could only be proved if you followed the trail of evidence closely.

That someone was me.

'Last station stop,' intones the tannoy unnecessarily, as the train shrugs up to its final destination and shudders to a halt.

Stepping out on to the platform in the late afternoon light, I am simultaneously aware of the noise and the silence. Gone is the endless brawl of London traffic, the sirens, the buses, the shriek and screech. It is replaced by a screaming and cawing above my head as orange-beaked grey-and-white gulls circle curiously. *Who is this? Stranger in town! What's in the suitcase? Nobody knows. Where is she going? Nobody knows.*

I follow the gentle slope of the pavement to the sea, crunch across the pebble beach and sit down at the water's edge. The holdall and suitcase hunker by my side – two trusty Labradors, one brown, one cream.

The sea. An art catalogue came in to Lost Property once, full of photographs of people seeing the ocean for the first time – in that moment, the camera clicked, recording the epic encounter. I lingered in the stacks looking at those pictures, at the reflection of light in those eyes, the wonder. There was something awkward, out of control about the people in the portraits, like the wonky movements and gestures of children before they have learned to bring the shutters down on their feelings. That is how those people looked, the sea reflected in their eyes, mouths partly open, a slackness to the skin of their faces as if they had let go for a moment, succumbing to the sheer extraordinariness of it.

For so long my views have been of London, the familiar route of my journey to work, from the blank-faced maisonette to the cathedral of loss. Here, at the edge of the land, there is nothing to be sorted and shelved. Just space. So much space.

The silvered skin of water reaches forever outwards, reflecting back to me my own sense of loss. Felt-less I feel exposed, unprotected. I turn to the west; in the distance, Beachy Head looms, a directionless limb lost out at sea.

Like Dad, I cling to the past to find a safe harbour yet feel increasingly rudderless. I wish I had brought a Dijon label with me. I would tie it around my wrist in a double knot to anchor me. And yet somewhere out here, in this seaside town nestled amongst the rocky cliffs behind me, is Mr Appleby. All I have to do is find him. Then I can return the holdall. Then everything will feel better.

19

Found: *Harriet's luggage*
Details: *Cashmere jumper (charcoal-grey)*
Skirts (2), linen slacks (1)
Oyster silk shirt
Strappy nightie
Place: *Cherry Blossom B&B*

Cherry Blossom B&B is decorated Japanese-style. Apparently the landlady, Mrs Trosley, travelled to Japan once and remained smitten. She greets me wearing a pair of *geta* over her woolly tights, and points out a communal collection in the hallway for guest use. As I have never been at ease with a thonged sandal, I politely decline.

Alongside the *geta* faux pas, I fear that I may have created a spot of awkwardness with the holdall. I didn't let go of it when Mrs Trosley tried to take it from me. It didn't seem right to let a member of the general public handle an item of lost property. We have firm rules about that. Had, rather. I handed her the auctioned cream case as consolation. To her credit, if she was put out she didn't let it dampen her detailed tour of the facilities.

'Sumire and Tsubaki are our family rooms.' She gestures grandly to two doors on the first floor; one with a watercolour of what might at a pinch be an iris, the other a rather showy camellia.

I follow her upstairs, clutching the banister, unsteady and light-headed.

'And on this floor, we have Kiku.' She points to a door on the right sporting a watercolour picture of an elaborate bright yellow . . . swim cap? Aware that I am not totally compos mentis, I keep my observation to myself, which turns out to be the right move as Mrs Trosley translates proudly, 'Chrysanthemum! I'm only an amateur but I was quite pleased with how that one turned out.' She stops at a door at the end of the corridor, a spray of cerise blossom emblazoned at its centre. 'And here's you,' she announces. 'Welcome to Sakura.' She opens the door with a flourish and waves me in.

Despite the largesse of Mrs Trosley's gesture, Sakura is on the small side, but it boasts a perfectly made tatami bed.

'Let me just familiarize you with the amenities,' Mrs Trosley continues, tucking herself into the tiny room beside me. 'Here you have your kettle,' she says, pointing to the kettle. Next to the kettle sits a wicker basket nestling packs of jasmine tea-bags interleaved with matcha sandwich cookies. 'Over here is your television!' She helpfully points to the TV. 'You have two bedside lamps, one on each side of the bed' – she motions like an airline stewardess – 'and in your wardrobe, you will find your complimentary kimono for use during your stay.'

She looks at me expectantly.

'How extremely . . . thoughtful.'

Her smile radiates. 'Well, it's the little touches, isn't it? They make all the difference. Make it feel like home.

Breakfast is served in the dining room from eight a.m. We don't do dinner, but there's plenty of nice restaurants on the prom if you fancy a bite later.'

When she finally leaves, I do what I have been longing to do since I left Lost Property: I wash. The hot water supply at Cherry Blossom B&B is blessedly bountiful and I stand under the steaming torrent, soap and rinse, soap and rinse, again and again. I try not to look at the mosaic of bruises on my wrists and arms, the murky green mound forming on my thigh. I wish for the abrasive assistance of a loofah so that I might exfoliate every trace of Neil Burrows from my skin, but instead make do with vigorous sweeps of the cherry-pink guest flannel, and stay under the cleansing heat of the water until my flesh is scarlet and the en suite as steamy as a subtropical forest on Yakushima.

I emerge eventually, swaddled in towels, and heft the cream shell case on to the low tatami bed. Before springing its silver clasps open, I close my eyes and will the suitcase not to be packed with attire chosen for the Costa del Sol in August. My wish is fortuitously granted. It looks like I'm equipped for a nice weekend at a respectable four-star hotel in the Cotswolds: two smart but unfussy skirts, a pair of blue linen slacks, a silk blouse in a very nice shade of oyster, and a charcoal-grey cashmere jumper. There is a complicated nightdress, satin with lots of straps, that I slip modestly back into the case along with the silky underwear, but everything else I hang up.

Other treasures in the case include a small bottle of designer perfume and some luxurious-looking face cream, which I lay out in the bathroom along with my toothbrush. I discover a well-thumbed *Pride and Prejudice*, sensibly inscribed with 'This Book Belongs To: Harriet' on the inside cover. Yes, I can see her as a Harriet, the strappy nightie notwithstanding. *Thank you, Harriet.* To all outward appearances I am now a professional woman on a brief sojourn to take the sea air and reread a classic romcom over coffee and cake on the prom. Delightful.

I take Joanie's purse out of the holdall and sit with it on my lap. I stroke the tiny golden orbs of the snap closure, circling it like Adison's hands on mine, coaxing it to open up, unlock, tell me how to find Mr Appleby.

'Where is he?' I try to summon clues from the creases and curves of its soft body. *Concentrate on the details . . . look beyond the obvious.* Finally, exhausted by the events of the past hours, I fall asleep still clutching the purse.

I wake at 3 a.m. clammy with sweat from a nightmare in which I am running through the Lost Property stacks wearing a pair of Mrs Trosley's wooden Japanese slippers, which make me slip and slide on the stone floor. Neil Burrows is chasing me, flapping scabby pink wings and rattling his key set. 'Nobody's coming to collect you!' he squawks, his halitosis breath warm on my neck. 'Nobody wants you! You're past your sell-by date. Left on the shelf! Your dad left you! Squawk! Your mum's forgotten you! Squawk! Your sister says she won't pay the five-pound charge! So it's down the chute, into the pit and off to Snagsbey's with you!'

In the pink Sakura bathroom, I splash cold water on my face and the back of my neck, and stare at myself in the mirror. I am unravelled. My brown eyes look lost in my pale face; bruises shadow my neck and arms. I brush my teeth then smooth Harriet's cream on my temples, across my cheeks, under my chin, massaging it in small soft soothing caresses. Perhaps I can cover all traces of myself, escape into the clothes and contents of Harriet's case and become someone else, able to walk away from my own tormented thoughts. Because who am I now? With no job to go to, no home to go to, no Mum to remember me? *Down the chute, into the pit and off to Snagsbey's!* Neil Burrows' face lurches in my memory. I can smell him. I retch.

Craving more security than Harriet's strappy nightie can provide, I wrap the complimentary kimono about me and get into bed. The sheets waft a light fabric conditioner scent – cherry, of course. I turn on the kettle next to me and make a cup of jasmine tea, eat my way through three packets of matcha sandwich cookies. I am grateful for the small comfort these things give me.

I try to get back to sleep, but am too scared to close my eyes in case I dream of Neil Burrows again. I lie awake, my heartbeat jerky, my breathing fast, until light filters through the bamboo blind and the smell of frying bacon becomes overpowering. I pull on one of Harriet's skirts and her cashmere jumper, and join my fellow guests downstairs.

It appears there are just a handful of us residing at Cherry Blossom B&B: an older couple, silently eating their way through an extensive meal of eggs, bacon and what looks like seaweed, and at another table a mother with two small children. Thankfully Mrs Trosley has not followed her Japanese theme to its zenith and made us sit on tatami mats on the floor – in normal circumstances nothing would delight me more than sitting on the ground around a low Japanese *horigotatsu*, but today my body feels too bruised and achy to manage that. Along with the full English offered on the handwritten menu there is also a tamagoyaki option, which

I take small secret pride in recognizing (from my trusty copy of *Japan – Culture Smart!*) as a complicated type of omelette.

'Finish what's on your plate first before you take more!' the mother says, swatting at the jammy hand of her little girl. The woman is wearing a maroon mohair jumper, and each time she moves, tiny spores of mohair spiral off into the air. Her son is laboriously eating a bowl of Rice Krispies one at a time with his fingers.

'Kids,' she says, looking at me, shrugging her furry shoulders.

I hunch over, study the menu, willing her not to talk to me. I can't remember the last time I ate something substantial that wasn't tinned. Eggs? My stomach twists. Perhaps just a piece of toast and a cup of tea. I notice they have Earl Grey.

They'll be arriving at work now in Baker Street. It's past nine, so even Anita will be clanking in with the beast on her shoulder. Will they miss me? What will Neil Burrows tell them? What words will he use? Trespasser? Thief?

Sellotape.

'We're off to Eastbourne,' says the man to Mohair Mum. 'We're doing the South Downs Way. Expecting a bit of rain, but it's so much quieter this time of year.'

Normal conversation, normal life. Wholesome holidays, chitchat. Yet I can barely sit at the table and manage breakfast.

Superglue.

When my toast and tea arrive I scuttle back to my room with them, heart pounding, breathless.

I sit on the bed, focus on my breath, cup my hands around my tea and cherish its warmth, its comforting bergamot smell. I take my time with it.

Breakfast finished, I pull on my silver bomber, pick up the holdall and head out.

As I leave, I pass the beaded curtain that separates the guest quarters from the Trosleys' private rooms. I hear a chink of dishes, the radio promising a cold day, rainstorms later. What is the etiquette with a beaded curtain? I give it a quick rattle before popping my head through. Backstage, the kitchen and the small sitting room are quite ordinary. Mrs Trosley has put all her design flair and Japanophilia into the guest rooms. She is at the sink, elbow-deep in suds.

'How can I help?' she asks.

'Might you have a map? Sorry, I didn't see any out front.'

'Of course.' She wipes her hands on her apron, leaving tiny snowballs of foam on the fabric, and takes a bundle of maps from the dresser. 'I keep forgetting to put them out – people just seem to use their phones now.'

'Thank you.' I retreat through the beads.

'Plans for the day?'

'Oh . . . I'm heading to Judges.'

'Best cheese straws in Sussex. Was your room all right? Sakura is my favourite.'

I feel I am being complimented in some way.

'You've made a . . . remarkable guest house.'

She beams.

'It was my fantasy, a B&B by the sea. And I've always loved Japan. And pompoms, of course.' She points to what I took to be a knitting basket full of fluffy cream wool but turns out to be two Pomeranian puppies, fast asleep. 'We've been here for twenty-seven years now, me and Mr T. Wouldn't be anywhere else.'

'Actually, perhaps you can assist?'

'I will if I can.'

'Do you happen to know an Appleby? A John Appleby?'

'Appleby?' The Pomeranians wake and bounce over, barking at me like little alarms going off.

'Taro, Takeshi, back to your bed, you naughty lads! Such busybodies. Appleby . . . no, that's not ringing any bells, sorry.'

'Not to worry.' I retreat from the barking. 'Have a lovely day.'

'Always do! Every day I wake up and say to Mr T, aren't we just the happiest of the happy.'

Outside the front lawn shivers with frost. Ahead the thin blue line of the sea is like a margin in an exercise book.

Aren't we just the happiest of the happy? The happiest of the happy!

Is it possible, such happiness? The Trosleys have found it, apparently. Who else? Not my parents. Philippa and Gerald? Yes, in their own way. Not Anita, not yet. Mr Appleby and his Joanie – absolutely. And me?

I walk to the sea, drawn once more to its edge, and watch the endless froth and splutter of the surf. Boisterous waves return over and over, as if they have some tidbit of exciting news to impart but are forced to retreat just before they can share it.

My phone buzzes crossly. I take it out of my pocket and see a ream of messages and missed calls from Philippa and Anita. I can't bear to read them, listen to them. I can't face knowing what Anita might have heard about me. And I simply don't want to know what Philippa has to say about the house sale. I can't think about that. Not right now.

242

Focus on the case in hand, Watson. One must know how to look or one misses the important clues.

I check the map, get my bearings, then make my way back to the prom.

I walk along a cobbled high street of shops and seventeenth-century cottages – one with a blue plaque commemorating a visit from Dante Gabriel Rossetti and his muse Lizzie Siddal. Amidst a bevy of antiques dealers and artisanal shops, the white-and-blue awnings of Judges Bakery announce its nautical heritage like a stripy Breton shirt. Through the window, I can see the interior thrumming with eager customers. Behind the counter two women move fluidly, reaching up to shelves loaded with round, oblong, domed loaves, stretching into the window display case to retrieve garlic, fennel and parmesan sausage rolls. A sign proudly declares that Judges has been *Serving fishermen and their families since 1826*. An endless miraculous bounty of loaves and fishes, feeding the population of Hastings from then till now, disciples clamouring for their daily bread.

I open the door and step inside. The deliciously comforting aroma of fresh-baked bread brings tears to my eyes. I can't tell if I'm hungry or if I just want to cradle a warm rye loaf in my arms. One of the women serving, the older of the two, has an abrupt ponytail and a faint streak of flour on her forehead. Her hands move non-stop, taking in orders fast and furious – 'Your usual, Susie?' 'Sliced?' 'Just sold the last spelt round, but I've got a nice walnut, will that do you?'

I wait for the queue to subside, admiring the shelves of smoked mackerel quiches, lime and sea salt brownies, and rose and pistachio meringues. Mum would like the meringues. At the back of the shop a tiny cafe boasts a few tables, already occupied. In the corner, four women share three seats between them, sipping from steaming mugs of tea and biting into doughnuts that spill out what must be entire pots of jam. Their conversation is light, overlapping, sugar-sweet. Part of me longs to go over and tuck in alongside them.

'Anything else?' Ponytail asks, when I take advantage of a lull in the morning's rush and purchase a mini quiche.

'Do you, by any chance, know a man called John Appleby? I think he might be a customer.'

She pauses a moment, my change in her hand.

'Older gentleman, tweed cap,' I go on, adding hopefully, 'kindly.'

She hands me my coins, slides the small quiche over the counter.

'I don't think so . . .'

'Never mind. It was a long shot.' I turn to leave.

'Hang on. There's a couple doing up a house on the West Hill. Leila, aren't they called Appleby? She gets the gluten-free linseed? Arty.'

Leila nods. 'Yeah, I think so.'

'Do you know which house?' Hope flutters in my chest.

'I think it's one of the Victorian terraces up on the hill.' She points westward. 'I don't know exactly where, but I know she's up on the hill because she always makes a joke when she comes in about liking our bread so much it's worth the walk back up. That's it, sorry I can't be of more help.'

'Sorry? You've been magnificent!' I cry. Ponytail and Leila exchange a look as I beam at them and head out, bolstered by this new titbit of information.

Outside, day-trippers brave the cold to have chips on the beach. Seagulls hover, beady-eyed, waiting for their chance for a stolen snack. A rocky cliff towers above me, in its middle two wooden cabins moving up and down in sync with each other, suspended on tracks leading to the top of the cliff. *West Hill looking down over the fishermen's huts . . . there's a funicular railway . . .*

Things are looking up indeed! The funicular will take me to the top of the cliff, and maybe there, finally, if my run of luck holds, I might find Mr Appleby. I enter an ornate ticket booth, purchase my fare and pass through the old-fashioned turnstile. I feel as if I am going back in time.

I drop my change from the ticket back in my purse and wonder how soon I will start running out of money. Burrows will terminate my pay. I have a little put by in my savings account, but how long will it last? Working in Lost Property for years hasn't exactly left me in the highest tax bracket. Well, I can't worry about that now. Onwards and upwards, Watson. Quite literally, as it happens: the wooden coach ascends the almost vertical hillside, passes through a tunnel and emerges at the clifftop.

As I disembark, the wind puffs my jacket out and snatches the breath from my mouth. The view is so dramatic, the sea zipped up to the horizon. A wire fence at the cliff edge warns walkers against getting too close. In the distance a lighthouse flashes safety – the ever-fixed mark.

The fresh air makes me dizzy. I sit on an exposed bench by the ruins of a castle. Perhaps it is wise if I eat something before I continue with my mission. It has been some time since I have eaten anything substantial, and if indeed I am about to find Mr Appleby and return his holdall I want to present myself properly, professionally. The mackerel quiche is delicious: smoky, salty and sharp.

A woman and her toddler play, battling against the wind. The child wears a bright yellow all-in-one and keeps slipping in the muddy grass. The mother laughs and picks her up. The child is getting muddier by the second but the more she wallows, the more they both laugh. The mother runs behind a castle battlement and for a moment the child stands there, arms starfishing out in the yellow suit. She has two red ribbons in her hair that snap and spiral in the sea breeze like propellers. She looks about her, rooted, computing the absence. The not-thereness. Her mouth wavers, ripples and drops open.

The mother's face pops up. 'Peek-a-boo!'

The little girl runs towards her, her face now a mess of happy tears.

'Did you think Mummy had gone? Here I am!'

It takes a moment but then the little girl recovers and trundles off to hide behind the stone rampart, her yellow arm poking out.

You were excellent at disappearing, Dad – in the long grass and brambles at the bottom of the garden, behind the old dresser in the garage. You even hid in the coal bunker once. I searched for you for ages, gave up in the end, sat sobbing on the grass. Inconsolable.

'Sorry, old thing,' you said, coal dust sparkling on the hairs of your hands.

'I thought you were gone.'

'I'll never leave you, dearest Dot,' you promised.

For so long I believed it was just a game we were playing.

'Now, where can she be?' The mother makes a show of looking for the yellow-clad girl behind the castle information sign, its letters already half lost to the salty sea air. She passes me and winks, as if I am also now involved in the game, in cahoots, keeping the secret.

'Where can she be?' the mother calls. 'Is she under this bench? I bet she's under this bench.'

Half-suppressed chortles from beyond the thirteenth-century ramparts.

'She's here,' I say, standing up, pointing. The remains of my quiche fall from my lap. A seagull, amber-eyed, swoops down and snatches it.

The girl sticks her bottom lip out, starts to cry.

Dot Watson, how could you? You fiend. You lowlife.

I blot my eyes fiercely and walk to the cliff edge. Below, tall inky-black fishermen's net huts are flanked by blue, orange, grey boats. In the distance, Beachy Head's forlorn arm reaches ever outwards.

I'm getting closer.

20

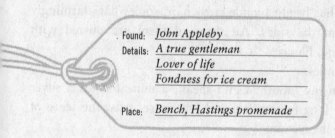

Found:	*John Appleby*
Details:	*A true gentleman*
	Lover of life
	Fondness for ice cream
Place:	*Bench, Hastings promenade*

I hug the holdall to me, turn away from the cliff edge, and walk till I see a Battenberg row of pink, yellow and white Victorian terraced houses. I feel sure this is the street. But which house? The end terrace is boarded up, paint flaking, neglected. Its rose-flushed neighbour has a For Sale sign in the garden. Further along are two smart houses, one cream, one custard, then, next, a marzipan with scaffolding up one side. The woman in Judges mentioned building works . . . could this be it? Next door is painted bone-china white; a tabby cat washes itself in the window. Beyond that house, another split into two flats. A further crescent of pastel Victorians line the other side of the road. I cross over, walk along, turn, check the view. Beachy Head is still visible, but the fishermen's huts are obscured. I retrace my steps to the first row.

The marzipan house is covered with the grey woody arms of winter wisteria. Mum loved wisteria. 'It demands loyalty,' she used to say. I follow a breadcrumb trail of white powder to the front door. Ring the bell.

A young woman answers, a miniature Dachshund wriggling under one arm, a baby wriggling in the other. The woman has bright blonde curly hair, somewhat alarmingly shaved at the sides. All three of them are dusted with something. Flour?

She smiles.

I open my mouth. Can't speak, a mute fool in a silver jacket. I long for my felt uniform, its security, the sense of purpose it gave me.

Three pairs of eyes stare.

I take a breath and try again.

'Sorry to disturb. I'm looking for Mr Appleby. I have some property to return to him.' I gesture to the holdall.

The woman wrinkles her nose. A silver stud sparkles on one side.

'John?'

'Yes, John, this is his—'

A high-pitched beep starts going off behind her.

'Oh, bloody hell, what's that? Come in, will you?'

I follow her into a kitchen dominated by wall-to-wall cupboards painted in a shade that can only be described as egg-yolk. A laptop is open on the scrubbed pine table and, like everything else in the room, it is liberally doused with white powder.

''Scuse the mess. I'm behind with my deadline, but some unhinged part of me decided my column would be better if I finished the plastering.' Ah, mystery solved.

The beeping continues.

The baby grabs for a slab of butter on the table. The woman whisks her away.

'No, Flora! She's been crying all morning. *Who's* done a pop-pop? Anyone going to own up to it?' She shrugs up the dog and the child, who both wear expressions of complete innocence.

She disappears out into the hallway and I hear her bellow upstairs, 'John . . . !'

She returns without the dog, grabs a broom handle and gives the smoke alarm a sharp knock.

'That's better! Tea? Sit down.'

I perch on a powdery chair. She grabs a brown tea-pot and gives it a ruminative swirl.

'Hmm, I'll make fresh.'

Footsteps on the stairs. I get up, clutch the holdall to my chest, my heart thumping. A chance to reunite person with property one last time. To reward hope when hope seems lost.

A young man in a T-shirt that declares *There is No Planet B* comes in.

'Hi . . . ?' he says.

Suddenly dizzy, I totter.

'Becks!' The man grabs my elbow and guides me to an armchair.

'I'll put sugar in your tea. You look like you need some sugar,' Becks says.

'I do . . . apologize, how embarrassing.' I catch my breath. 'I don't mean to take up your time. I'm looking for John Appleby – senior?'

'Grandad? Oh, what a shame. I'm sorry, he's not here.'

I feel numb. 'But I came as fast as I could . . . would have come quicker . . . but his file got deleted . . . then there was Snagsbey's . . .' I blot a rogue tear with my silver arm, which again fails in the task, thoroughly lacking the absorbency of my felt.

'Drink this.' Becks thrusts a cup of sweet tea into my shaking hands.

'I'm too late. I'm so sorry.' The tears spill now and I don't bother to staunch them. I have failed again, messed up, let him down.

I am wrapped in a warm blonde cloud haloed with plaster dust.

'Christmas crackers, hon, don't cry! He's just out on his walk. He'll be down on the stretch of prom by the pier.'

I recognize his tweed cap from across the road. He is sitting on a blue wrought-iron bench, looking out to sea. The road is busy; there's a pedestrian crossing further up but I can't wait. Look both ways. Cars and motorbikes flash by.

Come on, please.

I step out but a bus lurches by, pinning me back on the pavement.

Come on!

A sudden gap – I take it and dash across the road.

I stand behind him for a brief moment, grateful for the chance to return what has been lost. To perform one small act of repair. Then: 'Mr Appleby?'

He turns and looks up at me, confused. Then his face clears, that smile.

'Why, it's the Lost Property lady.'

'I've come to return your holdall, sir.' I gasp, still breathless from my dash across the road. I place the holdall in his arms and feel the sudden emptiness in my own.

'Well I never!' He holds it in his hands for a moment and then slowly unzips it. 'Would you look at that,' he breathes, 'the tulips are sprouting.' He reaches in. 'Ah.' And I know he has it.

My body exhales.

It is done.

The purse sits in his palm, a lilac heart. Light glints off the clasp. He opens it, closes it. A chirrup. We savour it together.

After a moment, he says quietly, 'Mustn't let the moths fly out.' And gives a little chuckle.

'Sorry?'

'Something Joanie always said when she closed her purse. A little joke – I can't even remember when it started, or why, because she was generous to a fault . . .' A tear glistens in the corner of his eye but he is smiling. 'It was just a funny thing she always did. She'd pay for whatever she was buying and then, just as she dropped the change back in her purse, she'd snap it closed really fast and say, "Mustn't let the moths fly out!" and she'd give me a cheeky little wink.'

He is quiet, staring down at the purse in his hand. He nods his head slowly – again that soft, sad smile – and the tear caught in his eye escapes and runs down his face. She is there for him once more, his Joanie. In that moment he can see her hand holding the purse, her face smiling at him. He can hear her voice again, catch that cheeky wink.

He slips the purse into his pocket, picks up the holdall and turns to me.

'I was having a bit of a sit-down halfway through my constitutional. Care to join me for the second half? You look like you could use some company, if you don't mind my saying.'

We walk along the beach. The cold is biting, the water vivid. Out on the horizon small boats bob.

'Fishing,' he says, following my gaze. 'They still have the original net shops further along. It's the largest beach-launched fleet in Europe. Well worth a look . . . Whoops!' He stumbles a little on the pebbles and I take his arm, and together we stroll in silence.

'Fancy you coming all that way,' he says eventually. 'Can they spare you at work?'

'I . . . I'm no longer in the employ of Lost Property.' The words are vinegar in my mouth.

He doesn't reply. We stop, look out to sea for a moment. Another boat, closer to shore – I can see two people, a man in a dark cap and a younger lad in a bright red jumper. Gulls swirl above the boat, hopeful, intent.

'Well, change can be invigorating,' says Mr Appleby. 'John and Becks – my grandson and his wife – want me to sell up and move down here.'

'Will you?'

'I think so. We all need to keep moving forward, don't we?' He looks at me then back out to the horizon. 'When we real-ized that Joanie was dying, I was inconsolable. I just wanted to go with her. She took my hands in hers, looked me right in the eyes and said, "Live, my darling. Always choose life."'

We walk on, our feet crunching over the pebbles. The light shifts on the water, turning it from green to silver to blue grey. I can't see the boat any more; perhaps it has come to shore, bringing in a catch of fish for supper. For the first time in days I feel strangely at ease, walking next to Mr Appleby, comforted by his presence, his arm in mine. The holdall swings from his other hand, returned to its rightful place at last.

Two girls race past us down to the water's edge, shrieking as they dodge the surf. One picks up a long strand of seaweed and gives chase to the other, both laughing, squealing with joy.

'Life gives us so much,' Mr Appleby says, 'chance, excitement and hope. But woven through it all is loss. If you try to pull out that thread, the whole thing unravels. Loss is the price we pay for love.'

Under a charcoal sky the sea darkens, denim-blue. Cuffs of white foam edge the waves that rush forward – then slowly recede. Again and again.

Mr Appleby turns to me, smiles. 'Now, what about an ice cream? My treat.' Despite the weather, a pink-and-yellow ice-cream van sits purring up on the prom. We walk over to it. 'Two ninety-nines, please.'

We take our ice creams to a bench overlooking the sea.

'Joanie was always a city girl, said she wanted to be in the thick of things. Loved the museums, the art galleries. But I've always been more of a country lad myself.'

'Do you think you'll be happy here?'

He takes a lick of ice cream, savours the taste, dabs his mouth with his hanky.

'Do you know, I think I will.'

I walk Mr Appleby back to the wisteria house.

'Please stay for tea. You'll get a kick out of Becks, and John makes a great flapjack.' Part of me longs to go with him, sit in the warmth of that yolk-bright kitchen, eat a flapjack and receive my own light dusting of plaster.

'I won't. But thank you.'

'I still can't believe you came all the way down here to return my holdall. I never knew TfL were so thorough. I'll stop grumbling about the ticket prices!' He winks and squeezes my silver arm. 'Thank you, my dear Lost Property lady. Thank you for bringing Joanie's purse back to me.'

'Just . . . doing my job.' Suddenly I realize that it is over. I wish I had said yes to the flapjack, to make the moment last just a little longer. But I am sure he was only being polite. There is nothing else to say except farewell.

I head out towards the cliff path with no idea where I am going.

'Miss Watson? Dot!'

I turn, see Mr Appleby hugging the holdall, waving.

'Always choose life.'

21

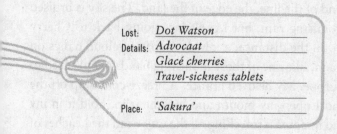

Lost: _Dot Watson_
Details: _Advocaat_
Glacé cherries
Travel-sickness tablets

Place: _'Sakura'_

I walk upwards along a steep path that eventually takes me to the clifftop. I sit on a bench, look out to sea. Overhead a skein of brent geese fly in a perfect phalanx. They've probably just arrived from Siberia, across the Baltic Sea. Hello, up there! In the V-formation they can fly further than just one bird could flying alone, taking turns in the slipstream. I watch until the arrow disappears over the horizon. What is my flight path, my trajectory? I have no idea.

I feel none of the elation that usually comes with reuniting a really meaningful lost item with its owner. That's it. My job is done. There are no more tags for me to fill, no more shelves to sort. My umbrella sanctuary has no guardian. Did anyone even notice it? Did they see the disarray it was left in, or did Neil Burrows hide the evidence? Will the woman come for that leather bag with the mismatched lipstick? Will the letterbox lady's glove be handed in before she has given up searching for it? What will Anita think of me? Does Big Jim suspect I was squatting in the pit? What has Neil Burrows accused me of? Breaking and entering, trespassing? My reputation will be as sullied as my uniform. Perhaps I have already been replaced by a temp from SmartChoice.

I am bereft.

The end of the line, the edge of the land. The sky is bruised now, promising rain, but I can't face going back to Cherry Blossom. In the distance, a low dark strip of cloud hangs on the horizon, like one of those mourning bands people used to wear. Europe. My beloved France. A breeze comes up off the coast and I open my mouth and breathe it in, hold it in my lungs and imagine it travelling all the way from the beaches of Nice, across the snowy mountaintops of Grenoble, through the cedar forests of the Dordogne, the roofs of Paris. I lick my lips and I taste the possibilities. Writing travel guides in a lemony kitchen in Avignon, teaching English in Madrid, curating an exhibition of lost treasures at the Etruscan Museum in Rome. I remember looking up Emile on the internet one night, just after Mum moved to The Pines. He's married with children, living in Grenoble. And where am I? Sitting on a windswept cliff with nobody waiting for me.

A pain deep inside whiplashes up from my stomach, tightens around my lungs and heart, rips through my throat. 'Why?'

The word reverberates out of my mouth and across the clifftop. 'Why?' I shout again. It brings me to my feet and I shout out to sea. 'Why, Dad? Didn't you know that you were taking me with you when you jumped?'

A woman on the cliff path hurries her two children away from me – 'Quickly, don't stare.'

Darkening now, the moody sludge of grey-black in the sky asserts its presence as a storm about to break. The bomber jacket billows out; the wind might take me up and off to sea. I wish it would. But I remain rooted, and wonder suddenly what on earth I am doing out here staring into the emptiness.

After you died, Mum insisted that we went to therapy, all three of us. But we didn't know how to do things as a three; we were lopsided and off-kilter. We only knew ourselves as double acts: Philippa and Mum, you and me. The psychiatrist, Dr Scott, had sharp shins sheathed in taupe tights. She talked about you being a lost soul and used words like 'neurosis', 'troubled' and 'paranoid'. Mum nodded and cried; Philippa twitched and twisted her wedding ring. Sandwiched between them, I stared parched-eyed at Dr Scott's desk, taking in her black-and-yellow pencil, striped like a wasp, her careful box of tissues, a roll of Sellotape. I focused on my breathing, and the dependable glossy roundness of the tape, its honey-gold layers holding on tightly to each other. I marvelled at how complete it was – a golden bracelet, a child's stencil for the sun, the rings around Saturn. I concentrated on that sun, those rings, and it helped me not hear Dr Scott, helped me stop seeing you crushed on the track, your beautiful dreams spilling out. Every time she said unravelling words like 'depressed' or 'repressed' or 'obsessed', I thought *Sellotape*. Later I added *Safety Pin*, *Superglue* – safe words, solid words, words that kept everything together.

There were so many things I wanted to ask you, Dad.

But everything was opaque. In those last few years, before I left home for university and after, there was a distance between us. Too old to hide in our make-believe worlds, we were exposed. We talked as if we were doing a complicated crossword where all the clues were cryptic and the answers were always in next week's paper.

Five across, ten letters. Clue: A sadness, or subsidence, glacial?

D dot dot R dot S dot I O N.

Morse Code in black and white. Give me a clue, Dad. Give me a bloody clue.

I was ready to protect you, to fight with you. Only you didn't want to fight. You gave up. I'm still here, Dad, waiting, watching, vigilant as ever. But who is there left to save?

Good old Watson! The fixed point. The lighthouse, always there, signalling safe harbour. But as it turned out, I wasn't your supportive sidekick after all, was I? That was the red herring! Aha! Didn't you spot it?

I thrust my hands deep in my pockets and trudge onwards, tracing the cliff edge, looking down at the chasm below.

You're just like Dad!

Maybe Philippa was right; perhaps it is in the DNA after all. Perhaps this is how it was always meant to be. I walk out to the very edge of the cliff. The wind is strong here, whips my hair in my eyes. Under my feet a few crumbles of rock loosen. I watch as they fall – so fast! – into the froth of sea churning below and I see the way ahead. I finally understand the flight path I am on and it comes as a relief.

I turn away from the edge of the cliff and head back to the prom with a growing sense of purpose.

The drugs available from Kwik Shoppe are: children's Calpol, VapoRub and travel sickness tablets.

260

The picture on the packet of tablets is of an aeroplane, gliding in a Mediterranean-blue sky filled with chubby clouds. Below the plane, a white sailboat scuds through foamy water. Quite a big adventure for such a small box – bodes well, I suppose. I pop it in my basket.

Next – adult beverages. The cider comes in unattractive bulbous plastic bottles. I give it short shrift and eye a six-pack of beer in treacle-hued glass, remembering the 'Hop Picking in Kent' jigsaw I left for Mum at The Pines. I wonder how she is. I should have said goodbye before I left. My eyes fill. I shake my head. No, don't think about that now. Focus on the job in hand, that's the spirit. Something bright catches my eye – advocaat. Perfect. I take a yellow bottle and in the surprisingly well-stocked baking section find a tub of glossy glacé cherries. Next to each other in my basket they look like a sunset in a 1970s romance.

'Coo-ee,' Mrs Trosley calls as I enter Cherry Blossom. 'Mr T and I are just clocking off. Anything you need before we go out?'

Benediction, absolution, forgiveness?

'Do you happen to have any cocktail sticks?' I ask.

'Guest lounge, top dresser drawer, in with the playing cards and the *shogi* board. Help yourself.' Mrs Trosley emerges through the beaded curtains. Her hair is balanced in a chignon, affixed with a pair of ebony chopsticks, a Mikado-yellow silk scarf tossed about her throat. 'We're off to a party.' A dab of face powder nestles on the tip of her nose. 'My niece is getting engaged. Anyway, make yourself at home. The other guests all checked out this morning, so it's just you.'

Just you. The words follow me upstairs like an accusation.

In my guest room, I sit at the tiny dressing table and make ready. Courtesy of the Trosleys' complimentary Wi-Fi (password: Ikebana) I find the music I need. But I don't play it yet; I'm not sure why, but I think there should be an order to these things.

I pour a tumbler of advocaat, spear two glacé cherries with a cocktail stick, drop it in my drink. I watch it crest the frothy surface like a life raft before it sinks below.

The bamboo blind beats a solemn tattoo at the window. I take my cocktail over and look down into the neighbouring garden. A barbecue grill hunches under green canvas and a swingball set stands in the middle of a handkerchief of lawn. Two tired plastic racquets lie discarded on the ground, yellowed grass poking up through their slats. Creosote flakes from a small garden shed.

How hard Mrs Trosley has tried to create a world removed in every way from the blank-faced semis that flank Cherry Blossom. You have to admire a woman like that, a woman who creates – a bamboo screen here, a complimentary guest kimono there – a home, a life that manifests her fantasy. I raise my glass to the fortitude of my landlady. *Aren't we just the happiest of the happy!*

My first sip of advocaat transports me back to Friday nights when exciting shapes bulged from Dad's faded leather briefcase – ovals that crackled when poked with an eager finger. Cadbury Creme Eggs.

Elbowing and pushing, Philippa and I would race to the front door when we heard the scrunch of Dad's footsteps on the drive, run out into the crisp evening air, eager to hug him, desperate to get our hands on his briefcase.

How extraordinary that the dip of a tongue into sugary fondant could bring such pure happiness.

I return to the dressing table. Open the box of travel sickness tablets. The pills are like little white buttons.

Travel sickness tablets may be taken one hour before embarking on your journey.

I unbutton a row. Hold them for a moment in the palm of my hand. Then tip them to my mouth, swallow.

I refill my tumbler. Replenish my cherries. Unbutton another row.

Do not use if you are sensitive to Meclizine.

Do not use if you are sensitive to Hydrochloride.

Do not use if you are sensitive to Lactose.

What if you are just sensitive? What if you are sensitive and raw and sad, and your felt uniform has been defiled and discarded down Big Jim's chute, and you have nothing left to upholster you?

Some loss cannot be tagged and shelved. It persists. Howling and hollering.

Loss is my constant companion. By day it clings to me; at night it wraps its long limbs about me. What else can I do but hold it tight? I am both anchored and unmoored by its fidelity.

And so each day I lose you anew.

Unbutton. Swallow.

Unbutton. Swallow.

Unbutton. Swallow.

When taking travel sickness tablets, do not operate heavy machinery.

I should write a note . . . how remiss . . . I pick up my Sheaffer, take a blush-pink sheet of Cherry Blossom headed notepaper, and write . . . what? What's left to say would fill a whole library. What's left wouldn't fill a Lost Property tag.

I think again of what Mr Appleby said and write just two words –

L o v e

L o s s

– and see how one is already half the other, twinned in an endless duet.

It's time. I press play on my phone.

'Beautiful dreamer, wake unto me.'

Your music fills my room. It is yours. It always was. I know that now.

The music comes back from the past to tell me your secrets, reveal that our evenings in the orange-curtained-dining-room-that-was-our-ballroom weren't ours after all. They were just yours, your way to transport yourself to another place, another possibility, another person.

Not a Dad and Dot thing.

Just Dad.

Or, to be exact, Dad and Uncle Joe.

Did you know I saw you that evening? Even though you had ruffled my hair and sent me to bed. I was there, hiding behind the orange curtains, watching you with him.

I saw you as you slipped our record on and asked him, 'Remember this?'

Heard the chink of your cocktail glasses, the familiar hiss and swish as the record started to spin, the earnest click and thrum of the slow arm moving across, the crackle as the needle searched for its place.

'Beautiful dreamer, wake unto me.'

I saw the way you turned your head, looked at him.

'List' while I woo thee with soft melody.'

I saw the slow move of your arm. Searching for its place. Finding it.

'Beautiful dreamer, awake unto me!'

I didn't think, then, of how you were betraying Mum. Standing behind those curtains, a cold draught coming from the conservatory doors at my back, their handles digging into my spine, all I could think was how you had betrayed me. Every one of our Dad and Dot evenings when I sat with you, sang with you, spun with you in our waltz, our cha-cha, our tango, you were dreaming of being with somebody else. I was there so Mum wouldn't nag you, 'What are you doing alone in the dark listening to old records?' I was there so you could say, 'It's Dad and Dot, love, having a jig,' so you could push her away and be left to your dreams of him.

Unbutton. Swallow. Legs heavy. Head woozy. The taste of advocaat sweet on my lips. Something salty too, cheeks wet. Salty and sweet and heavy and sad. And the next day, your hands fumbling as you tried to train the sweet peas out in the garden. Uncle Joe on the plane back to Canada and your heart breaking. And me, slipping into the dining room, going through all your records and taking 'Beautiful Dreamer' out of its soft white waxy sleeve, carefully, just as you had shown me.

I held it gently by its edges, slowly lifted it up to the light, blew the softest breath across it, lowered it, moved the tone arm over, letting down the stylus so tenderly that the diamond just kissed the body of the record. Then I pressed hard and scored it all the way across. One long pure line scarring every single note.

I watched you the next time, as you carefully slipped it from its sleeve, lowered it gently. Watched your face as the stylus scraped and stuttered over that scratch. Worse than broken because you kept it, but you could never play it. A constant reminder of what was lost. Like all those bloody single gloves. Like all your beautiful dreams.

That was the first time I betrayed you.

The second time was far, far worse. I hadn't planned to do it and after it happened I couldn't take it back. So often I have unravelled time back to that moment – the moment before – and tried to make it come out differently. I have willed it so hard that I wake with my teeth clenched, my hands balled into fists, and the sound of my pulse loud in my ears.

The first time I hurt you, when I scratched your record, it was out of a sense of betrayal. The second time it was out of loyalty.

Unbutton. Whoops, dropped it, travel tablet adrift in the nap of Mrs Trosley's carpet. Never mind, here's another. Swallow. Sakura spins.

I was home from France for the weekend and the family were all at Philippa's for Sunday lunch, commandeered to celebrate your wedding anniversary. Tasteful streamers and balloons bobbed in the sitting room and Philippa had made a two-tiered cake with your names on it. We sat down at the table and Gerald opened a bottle of Bordeaux.

'This is rather a nice little vintage, comes at rather a nice price too,' he said. 'Bet you'll miss all those fancy French wines when you move back, eh, Dot? When is that, must be soon now?'

There was a lull in the conversation and I felt all eyes upon me. I had hoped to avoid the subject, not make it part of your celebration, maybe venture it later on when my plans were more clear, but now it was out . . .

'Well, I have been thinking of . . . staying on . . . travelling . . .'

'You should,' Mum said. 'Why not? It's what you always wanted.'

'Look at my princess crown!' little Melanie shrieked, running around the room, a nest of streamers piled atop her blonde head.

'Sit down at the table like a big girl,' Philippa said.

'Let's make a toast,' Gerald boomed. 'To Dave and Gail and all their years of married bliss. Here's to many more.' He reached over and patted you on the back. Hearty pats. Which in Gerald's world was akin to a full body hug.

We raised our glasses. Mum smiled, took your hand. Your lips trembled.

'Can you carve please, Gerald?' Philippa said.

Later, as the others were finishing their coffee and cake in the sitting room, I followed Philippa into the kitchen to lend a hand with the dishes before I left to catch my train. Of course, they were already done, lined up in glinting battalions.

'Nice party,' I say.

'Hmm.' Off went the Spray and Wipe.

'What's wrong?'

'Nothing, only, Dad seems very . . . emotional.' Her lips peeled back over her teeth as she said the word.

'Nothing wrong with—'

'Shhh.' She put her finger to her mouth like a schoolteacher.

I drop my voice to a whisper.

'Nothing wrong with showing your feelings,' I say. 'He's just very expressive.'

'I don't like Melanie seeing him drunk.'

Melanie had spent most of the party sitting on the sofa, happily dressing the cat in a crown matching hers.

'It's a celebration, Philippa, surely he is allowed a drink? And anyway, Melanie strikes me as a very robust toddler.'

'You're so defensive of Dad. Always have been.'

'I'm not. I haven't. It's just that Dad's fine. You don't know him like I do.'

'I know enough.'

'What's that supposed to mean?'

She paused. Rubbed at an invisible mark on the stainless-steel counter-top while she chose her words. 'I know he's drinking too much, I know that Mum is at her wits' end with his moods, and I know that the neighbours think he has a screw loose.'

'And I know he is fine.' My voice was louder now as I defended you. 'He is just sensitive. And who cares what the neighbours think!' Granted that last remark was completely wasted. Philippa's belief in the opinion of one's neighbours is on a par with Catholics' belief in the Eucharist.

'Typical.' She rolled her eyes, shook her head. Trilled the 'what on earth are we going to do with you' laugh she keeps for me. 'Just go back to France, D, off to your bohemian life.'

I watched her swishing around her kitchen, caught her reflection in the gleam of her appliances. Always the upper hand, the last word, the supercilious put-down. And suddenly I was back, standing in the spectators' gallery at the swimming baths all those years ago with Toby bloody Jackson in the deep end and Philippa in her fishy costume ridiculing me, pointing me out, the girls from school laughing. That moment. That stupid, childish, ridiculous moment flooded me. I felt the shame of it, the hurt of it, and I wanted to strike back. I had imbibed quite a bit myself; we all had. But still, there was no excuse for what I did next.

'I know things about Dad you have no idea about.'

'Don't be such a drama queen.'

'I do.'

'Oh D, you're being ridiculous.' She shook her head, picked up a bowl of leftovers and opened the door of her giant American fridge-freezer. 'You don't know anything that would be news to me.'

'I do.'

'You don't. You really don't have a clue.'

'I know he's gay. I saw him, him and Uncle Joe.'

Philippa swung the door of the fridge-freezer closed and there you were, standing in her kitchen entryway looking straight at me.

My legs shuddered under me; a slick sheen of sweat coated my body. A sudden heat flooded my bowels. I felt sick.

Mum appeared at your side with your coats.

'We're off, girls. Thanks for a lovely spread, Philippa.' She came over to hug us goodbye. You followed. 'Safe journey back to Paris tonight,' she said to me.

'Dad, I—'

A scream from the other room and Melanie ran in crying, a gash on her arm, blood, bright red, dripping on to Philippa's pristine floor tiles. Philippa yelled at Gerald to get the antiseptic cream, and at me to get a cloth. Melanie, over-sugared and shocked, screamed louder, goodbyes were said in a blur, and suddenly you were gone.

All the way back to France that night I went over and over that moment. When did you come into the kitchen? What did you hear?

Soon though, I got caught up in my own life, preparing for my MA thesis, making plans to spend the following summer in Italy. When it came into my head, I felt the same sick shuddering guilt and self-loathing I felt when it happened. I convinced myself that you did not hear.

When I called a couple of weeks after the party, Mum sounded bright as usual but said you couldn't come to the phone.

'He is a bit under the weather. He sends love.'

'I'll call back in a day or so.'

'OK, love.'

I put the phone down. Then I called Philippa.

'This is a surprise. How is *la vie française*?'

'*Vachement superbe*, thank you. Look, Philippa, is Dad OK?'

'What? I haven't seen him since the party, but I popped around today to give Mum some of Mel's baby clothes for her neighbour and she was fine.'

'Did she say how Dad was?'

A pause. 'I thought you called to speak to me, Dot. To ask *me* how *I'm* feeling. Or perhaps ask after your niece? Melanie? She ended up having to have a tetanus jab by the way, after the party. It can give you a fever, being scratched like that.'

'I'm sorry, that's horrid. I just wondered—'

'You know, it's actually a thing, cat-scratch disease. Something to do with flea faecal matter.'

'Oh dear. Poor little Melanie.'

'Yes, well, she's fine now.'

'Good, send her my love . . . So Dad didn't—'

'There you go, on about Dad, yet again. Honestly. I'll tell you what about Dad – Mum actually looked awful when I stopped by this morning, like she hadn't slept all night. Anyway, I've got to go. Was there anything else?'

'No. Sorry.'

A week later you were dead.

And it was my fault. I betrayed you.

I'm all unbuttoned now and so tired. I rest my head on the table, see Dad's lips singing *'Beautiful . . .'* and feel a sense of loss I can put a shape to, but not a name. I look at the empty box of tablets and imagine that I am on that tiny aeroplane, staring out of its oval window. The sea glints below. I am high up, heading into the soft woolly clouds, so white, so forgiving. Into the blue sky I go. What kind of blue? *Mediterranean!* That's it . . . Up, up and away. It's so *'Beautiful . . .'*

22

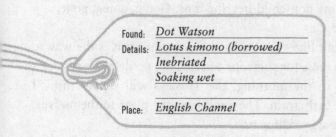

Found: *Dot Watson*
Details: *Lotus kimono (borrowed)*
Inebriated
Soaking wet

Place: *English Channel*

On fire . . . sweat wet . . . wretched retch . . . loo . . . quick, quick! Yuck. Wipe mouth . . . hot . . . so hot! . . . clothes off . . . water . . . need water now! . . . face in mirror, still here. Cherry lips, something on cheek? How long asleep? Oh no, loo again . . . hot, boiling hot . . . need a dip . . . a dippety-dip, just the ticket . . . dippety-tickety . . . whoops, better pop something on or . . . what's this? . . . something silky . . . a kimono?

Downstairs. Outside. That's better.

Ahhh. Breathe. Salty air.

Night's sharp as glass. A night to wash your sins clean.

Not a soul out and abouty . . . no one to show my kimono off to, kimonoshow . . . so comfy! So pretty . . . somonopretty, all lotus flowery.

There's the sea – I saw it first! Down the pebbly beach . . . Shhh! You pebbles are so loud!

Sea.

Toes in, feet in . . . Ahh . . . Deliciously cold. That's better, there, there. All better.

Go further.

Gone my father's feet. Gone my mother's ankles.

Go further.

Gone my non-child-bearing hips. Going, going, gone.

Simple.

Why not like this, Dad? This is better. This is the way to do it: no mess for someone to clear up, no delay to anyone's journey. In the morning, the Trosleys will simply think I took the early train. They will have the place to themselves, cook tamagoyaki for two.

And me? I will disappear. Not a trace. Not a dot.

It's my turn, my time. Water up to my tummy now, and stark naked under Mrs Trosley's silk kimono with the lotus pattern bought authentically in Japan. Open my arms wide, open my mouth wide to catch the stars on the way down, open wide to the sky and the sea.

Let myself fall forward.

Here I go.

Slap. Hard. Cold.

Salt in mouth.

Choke, splutter, I am pushed upright by the pummel and thrust of the water, open my arms, try again, walloped up, eyes smart, skin stings, hurl forward, full force, harder now, another smack back up. Sharper. Colder. Harder. Water in eyes, up nose, chokes throat.

'Please just let me go!'

I wade in further. Deeper. Liver-deep now. Lung-deep. Heart. Deep and dark and cold and black.

Try again. This time I tip backwards.

I float.

Above me, more stars than I have ever imagined: Hydra, Capella, Pegasus – old friends, beloved stories told in fragments, fractured poems in the sky.

The lotus kimono unfurls about me like petals. *The lotus seed waits in the mud of the bog.* How do I know that? I forget. *It waits hundreds of years for its chance, and when its chance comes, it takes it, and blossoms.* I am out here with the lost mariners, the shipwrecked and the sea-swallowed. I am a lotus flower, unblossomed. I open my mouth and let the stars fall in.

Water fills my nose and mouth.

What happened?

My kimono, once so buoyant, is now lead-heavy and pulling me down. I must have drifted deeper. How far out have I come? My legs thrash, kick towards the murky surface, but I am pulled down again. Suddenly I don't want to die. My heart pumps. Mum's face, the soft blue of her eyes. Philippa in my arms after Dad died. Anita at the dance, that streak of silver on her cheekbone, *You're a pal, Dots.* Adison Chang's hands, how they sent a long-forgotten current through my body. Snaps of light.

I kick out again.

But my body is tired, so terribly tired.

The heavy drape of the kimono wraps itself around my legs, drags me down. I splutter to the surface, gasp for air then sink again. I feel the pull of the current, stronger here. It's so cold. Under again I flail, struggle. Lungs bursting. Heart in my ears, pounding.

This is it.

Pulled under again. No stars down here.

Fight to the surface. Gasp for air.

I'm so frightened. Was this how it was for you, Dad? Were you frightened like this?

I don't want to go.

Under again, my legs flailing beneath me, falling deeper. Struggle to the surface, seize air into my lungs, heave my aching arms through the water.

No, please no.

Please.

Come on, arms, come on, heart, lungs, muscles. Come on, Dot!

Nil desperandum, Watson.

I strike out, pull forward. Again. Over and over, strike out, pull forward. Every fibre of me shrieks with bloody-minded effort, refusing to give up. My legs cramp below me, violently, dragging me down again.

Try again. Try harder. Slice my arms through the water, wrench me up, heave me forward, upward, onward.

Choosing life.

Mr Appleby was right.

In the distance, a looping string of lights – land. Shallower now, calmer. I turn on my back. My hands scull me through the water, I follow the curve of Orion's Belt back to shore.

I am hungrier and colder than I remember ever being in my life. Pull myself to my feet. Wobbly. I skid and stumble on the pebbles, half crawl back up to the prom.

Everything is dark and shuttered. Where am I? I don't recognize anything. I must have drifted down the coast. I start to shake. Where am I?

Then I see it. A small gleam of light, beckoning me . . . Religious light. A lighthouse? A church?

Zeus's Fish and Chips.

I walk towards it, one hand on the iron balustrade to keep me upright.

'Fuck's sake!' a girl in leather squawks.

Close now, I shield my eyes. It's small, but oh so beautiful.

'She's like, totally wasted!' a boy in leather caws.

Their sounds hurt. I reach the van, clutch its side.

'Oi, you two, on your way,' Zeus thunders.

The leathers stuff white parcels in their jackets, weave away up the prom, two black crows.

'Good evening to you,' I say.

Except it comes out, 'Ggggggeeeeoooooouu.'

'You all right, lady?'

'A bag of your finest chips, please.'

I hear, 'Bbbbbbfff innestsssssttiiii pppppeeze.'

My teeth bang together, run loose in my mouth. I try to point. My hand ricochets wildly up and down.

'Chips?' says Zeus.

I nod.

'Salt? Vinegar?'

Nod again. Can't stop nodding. Every part of me nodding, shaking, rattling as I watch Zeus's hands circle in the spit and sizzle of the fiery heat.

He leans down from above.

'Here, lady.' Places fire in my hands.

Pick up chip. Can't close fingers. Try again. Hand shakes. Drop chip. Please, oh please. Claw fingers. Grab again, grab harder. Catch one.

Oh
Golden skin
Heat exploding
Salty lips
Oh
Greasy fingers
So . . . Oh
More . . . More . . .
Such. Soft. Potato.
Warm tears spill.
'Thhhank y-yyou, Zzzeus.'

'Here, take this.' A sheepskin coat wraps around me. 'I'll close up now, lady, take you home.'

23

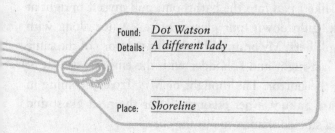

Found: *Dot Watson*

Details: *A different lady*

Place: *Shoreline*

The scent of cherry blossom. Has there ever been a more exquisite aroma? The soft patter of rain on the window. Could Bartók's *Music for Strings, Percussion and Celesta* sound sweeter than those raindrops? I bathe in its glory until other sensations, far less pleasant, start to nag, poke then engulf. The delicate timpani drowned out by the throbbing of a bass drum that seems to be located directly in the centre of my skull. The drummer energetically fills every nook of my cranium with pulsating, throbbing, excruciating sound.

I peel back the bedclothes. My mouth is salt-encrusted; my body judders, awash still with last night. Last night. I piece the events together from a debris of scattered clues: empty blister packs of travel sickness tablets, yellow dregs of advocaat, a damp mound of sheepskin coat.

Mum, Philippa and the kids. How could I? After everything, how could I?

Light pulses under the scrunched blossom of the lotus kimono on the floor. I watch it for a moment, transfixed, wonder if the flower is about to bloom. Then I realize it is my phone. I crawl across the tatami bed and down on to the floor. Animal-like I pad into the bathroom, pull myself upright at the sink, gulp down four glasses of tap water along with two painkillers. My body still holds the memory of the same actions last night and I shudder with the embarrassment of it, with the horror. The thought of Mrs Trosley coming in to prepare Sakura – her favourite – for the next guest and finding a suicide shames me to the core.

A screed of text and voicemail greets me when I retrieve my phone. Philippa, Anita, Philippa, Philippa, Anita, Philippa, Anita. And then, The Pines.

Heart pounding, I play it.

'Hi, it's Adi, Adison Chang, from The Pines.' I grab the sheet from the bed and cover my nakedness. 'I was just with your mom, and she was asking for you.' My hand shakes so much I drop the phone. How kind of him to let me know. I mean, of course I know he is just doing his job. I replay the message. '. . . with your mom, and she was asking for you. By name.'

Despite my wretched state it doesn't take long to wash, dress and pack Harriet's cream case.

Mrs Trosley is sitting at her kitchen table practising calligraphy in a journal when I poke my head through the beaded curtains.

'I'm checking out early,' I say. 'I have to go and see my mum.'

'Is she OK?'

'Yes. No. I don't know.'

280

Mrs Trosley puts down her pen, gets up and empties a bowl of oranges into a string bag.

'Take her these.' She presses the bag of oranges on me. 'In Japan they believe oranges bring luck. Have a couple for yourself too – you look a bit peaky.'

Outside, the rain has eased off and patches of blue have lured a few intrepid dog walkers. I breathe deep: coal fires and fresh sea air. The smells calm me, distract from my pounding head. The sea is tranquil, azure. So different from the dark danger of last night.

I trace the length of the prom till I see a small white sugar cube: Zeus's van.

When I arrive, Zeus is pulling up the hatch; raindrops splash on to my bomber jacket where they sparkle like diamonds.

'Five minutes, love, I'm not quite open.'

'Thank you,' I say, handing over his sheepskin fleece.

He turns, narrows his eyes, then widens them as he recognizes me.

'I can only imagine what horrors I presented you with last night. The coat is a bit damp, I'm afraid, though I did try my best with the hairdryer . . .'

'You look . . .' He gestures softly to his face. 'Like a different lady.'

'Do I? Well, that's a relief!' I hand him some money. 'For the chips.'

He takes my hand, closes it, turns it over and kisses it.

'Lady, for you Zeus's chips are on the house, always.'

Half an hour till my train departs. I head down the pebbly beach to the shoreline. Sit at the water's edge, Harriet's case next to me. A shipping-container barge hulks on the horizon, taking precious possessions to new destinations, fresh starts. To my right the breach of Beachy Head, hooded in mist, hovers in the distance. I shudder, my body remembering the dark chill of the water.

The abrasive buzzing of my phone interrupts my reverie. I answer immediately before I even see who it is – has something happened to Mum?

'Where the hell have you been? I've called you a million times, left goodness knows how many messages.'

'Philippa—'

'I almost went to Lost Property looking for you.'

My tummy flips as I imagine Philippa storming up Baker Street, confronting Neil Burrows and him telling her . . . what? That I've been sacked? That I broke into Lost Property? That I'm a trespasser? I imagine SmartChoice standing at the counter in some hairband of an outfit, cleaning her nails with a Dijon tag, and nodding disparagingly as the inventory of my crimes is revealed to my sister.

'Anyway,' Philippa is saying, 'as it was I had to take Sam to the orthodontist and couldn't get up to town, but honestly, Dot, I've been worried about you.'

'Really?'

'Didn't you get my messages?'

'Sorry, I've been on a . . . staff awayday.' Not wholly a lie.

'Days, surely.'

'What?'

'Away*days*, you mean – I've been calling since Monday night. It's Thursday.'

'Is it? I mean, it is, yes, of course it's Thursday, why wouldn't it be? The thing is, it was less of an awayday and more of a . . . retreat.' Again, at least a soupçon of truth.

The gulls caw overhead.

'Where are you? Are you at the seaside?' Honestly, MI5 have really missed a trick. 'Because if it's Whitstable I could get there in about fifty mins? We could catch up.'

Goodness! What have I done to deserve this change in tune?

'Lots to tell you – Sam got the drama prize, he's actually rather good, he's dying to show you his medal, and oh, Murray Greenridge says they have a second viewing lined up, young couple, very keen . . .'

'I don't want to talk about the house, Philippa.' I might have guessed that was what she wanted to 'catch up' on.

'All right, but I need to know what's going on.'

'With what?'

'With you.'

'I'm fine.'

'I popped around to Mum's . . .'

Bugger. What did she see? Post unopened, no sign of life?

'D, is something the matter? What's going on with you?' A different register in her voice; a note of concern that disarms me.

I grab a couple of pebbles, close my hand over their smooth round bodies, rattle them together like dice. What is going on with me? I stare at the sea – the clipped white wing of a sailboat swoops in the distance. Again I see myself out there, last night, in the dark, in the cold, dragged down by Mrs Trosley's kimono, sucked under over and over, the water closing above me, pulling me down until I couldn't breathe. Until I thought that was it.

Philippa would have had no idea until she got the call. *Hello Tonbridge, Tango, Oscar, November, Bravo?* The police on the other end of the line, breaking the news, just like all those years ago. My sister standing in her polished hallway, gripping the banister, her hand slick with sweat as a voice said things like 'suspected suicide', 'next of kin' and 'bereavement support line'. Philippa saying, 'I see', 'yes' and 'thank you', then afterwards being immobilized in her spotless sitting room, marooned on her sleek floorboards until the pane of glass in her front door rattled and the children arrived home from school. Her having to tell them. Their faces. Melanie. Sam.

My throat tightens. 'I'm so sorry, Philippa. I never . . .' I grip the stones, press them hard into my flesh.

'Oh . . . well . . . it's OK, Dottie, I was just worried, that's all. When are you back?'

'Actually, I'm on my way to The Pines.'

'Why? Is Mum OK?'

Has Mum asked for her too? What if she hasn't? Adison just mentioned me. I don't want to get her hopes up. 'No, I mean, yes, fine. I just thought I would pop in.'

'Good, she'll like that. Try and bring her something nice, D, not one of those dreadful jig—'

'Must dash, train to catch, bye!'

I toss the two pebbles into the sea; they disappear with a gulp. A heroic beam of winter sun pushes its way between the clouds. I close my eyes for a moment, lift my face to its caress, and listen to the froth and jostle of the water, its gasps and sighs.

I understand something: when Dad jumped it was not because he didn't love us, his family. He just needed the pain to stop.

I reach into the bag of oranges and take one out, marvel at the colour, its perfect shape. Peeling off its coat in one complete spiral I eat the juicy fruit, watching the gulls freewheeling and cawing above. The silver of my bomber jacket glints in the wintery light. I throw the last segment of orange up into the sky; a gull swoops down and grabs it.

'For luck,' I say, and turn towards the rest of my life.

24

Found: *Maria Callas*
Details: *My Heart Opens at Your Voice*

Place: *Back of wardrobe*

Although the journey back to The Pines takes just over an hour, it feels interminable. I get a taxi from the station and bite my lip at every red light. I run up the driveway and towards Mum's Lavender corridor, Harriet's cream case bumping against my leg. As I reach the door to Mum's room, it opens and Adison comes out. He smiles when he sees me.

'Is she all right?' I gasp.

'She's good, I've been with her the whole time. She was a bit panicked at first. She didn't understand where she was.'

'Is she lucid? Does she remember the fall, why she's here?'

'No, and it's a lot to take in. I went through the basic facts with her, and she is calmer now.'

I imagine him holding her hands, being gentle.

'Thank you.'

'She'll be glad to see you. She's still asking for you.'

'And Philippa?'

'No, just you.'

My heart pounds hard in my chest as I open her door.

She is at the dresser, going through the drawers. She looks up when I come in.

'Mum?'

'Thea?'

'No Mum, it's me, Dot.'

'Thea,' she says, and smiles.

Tears spike my eyes. 'It's me, Dot. Do you want me to get the nurse?'

'Dot.'

A pinprick of light in the shadowy room.

'Mum?'

'My Dorothea.' She looks right at me. She sees me.

She comes towards me and takes my hand. Her touch is gentle, a bird alighting on a favourite branch, and bird-like she starts to sing.

'*Dorothea, my lovely Dorothea, the sweetest girl I know* . . .' I have heard her hum the melody before but never the words. She stops, strokes my hand. 'I always wanted two little girls,' she says, smiling at me. 'Didn't think we'd have another, but I always hoped. My two lovely girls.'

Not a mistake?

'*The sweetest girl I know.*'

She stops singing. Has she gone again?

'Mum?'

She looks at me. 'My prize,' she says.

Outside, the apple tree's bare branches shiver in the silver-grey chill of the day. All of its years it has stood, outstretched, offering its gifts – fruit, shade, a trunk to lean

288

against – always there in the background, holding out its arms, waiting patiently to be paid attention to.

I look into my mother's eyes and see her, holding us up and doing every day what I had been too frightened to do – staying open to love even when it seemed so impossible. And one night he had come to her and loved her in the way she needed. Longed for. And from that love came me. Dorothea.

One more syllable than Philippa.

'Oh Mum, I have missed you.'

'Are you going to take me home, love?'

'I wish I could. I wish I could.'

She points to the dresser drawers. 'All my clothes. Why are all my clothes here?'

'You're living here, Mum, for now. Remember what Dr Chang told you?'

She nods slowly.

'Shall I call Philippa, tell her to come in, bring the children?'

'In a bit, love. Philippa is fine. I want to see you.'

We sit on her bed, side by side. I can't stop looking at her, staring at her face, seeing her see me. I don't want to blink, don't want to miss a moment, like a gorgeous sunset on a day you never want to end.

There are so many things I want to say, ask her, but also I just want this, to be by her side, holding her hand and her knowing that we are together.

'Can I get you anything?'

She squeezes my hand. 'Do you know what I fancy?'

I swallow, clear my throat. 'I'd put money on a cup of tea?'

She shakes her head, points to the top dresser drawer.

I get up, go over, and inside find a family-sized box of chocolate liqueurs.

'Secret admirer, Mum?' Maybe Gerald brought them in when he visited with the kids. I can't imagine they are from Philippa.

'And the puzzle,' she says.

I retrieve 'Hop Picking in Kent' from the drawer and we do it together; she hands me the pieces and I find their places. We eat our way through the entire box of chocolate liqueurs and it turns out she is particularly fond of the Bristol Creams. We 'cheers' each chocolate before we bite into them, laugh as their insides spill down our chins. The puzzle pieces become sticky, and the hop fields of Kent take on new geological formations.

I don't ever want to leave her room but eventually I notice her face is pale, her eyes tired. I know she needs to rest. Reluctantly I get up, clear the puzzle and the twists of foil from our Bacchanalian 'pub crawl' off her bed.

I kiss her goodbye. She touches my cheek, holds me there.

'I remember you had lots of plans.'

'What?'

'When you were a little girl, lots of wonderful plans.'

I smile. 'I did. I wanted to read all the books in the library, open my own detective agency . . .'

'Travel the world.' She keeps hold of my cheek.

'Yes.'

'Don't forget your plans, love.'

I nod, not trusting myself to speak.

'And make sure you're eating properly – you're too thin.'

Such a normal thing for a mum to say to a daughter. And so completely extraordinary. My eyes fill. I smile, cover her hand with mine.

'I will. You too! Which reminds me . . .'

I empty the bag of oranges from Mrs Trosley into a bowl. Their zesty scent brightens the room.

'See you later, Mum.' I go to the door.

'Dorothea?'

The tears of sadness and joy that have filled my eyes all afternoon spill down my cheeks. I blot them away, turn to her.

'Yes, Mum?'

'Can you bring me something from home?'

'Anything.' *Please, God, not the dustpan and brush.*

'My music, can you bring me my music? It's in my bedroom, top shelf of the wardrobe. If it's not too much trouble.'

'Mum, I'll bring you the whole bloody London Phil-harmonic if you want!' She smiles, chuckles and then gives a big belly laugh. I join in.

I can still hear her laughing as I walk down the Lavender corridor.

It is the sweetest sound.

The maisonette feels chilly and nervous when I step inside, like the last person waiting to be chosen for the netball team. Philippa must have been in and collected the post recently as there are only a couple of missives lying on the mat – the water bill and an advert for a Stannah stairlift. I wonder if she suspected I hadn't been there for a while. Perhaps that was part of the worry I heard in her voice on the phone at the beach. What on earth would she say if she ever found out where I have been living? What I have been doing?

In the kitchen, I see my sister's hand in the mirrored sheen of the appliances. I open the fridge, peek in the freezer compartment, half hoping to see a pair of Mum's spectacles staring back at me, but there is only an empty ice tray.

I wander into the sitting room, turn on the TV for company. A woman with painfully blonde hair is making lemon meringue pie.

'Well, Jenny,' says the male presenter, 'it looks like you're off to a great start with the peaks you've got on those egg whites – am I right or am *meringue*?' They both hoot. I think about how Mum would kick her leg if she were here. Perhaps she will start to get better now. Maybe even come back home.

A huddle of naked coat hangers shiver gently when I open the doors of Mum's built-in floor-to-ceiling wardrobe. I climb up on the bed to check the top shelves. I pull out the spare pillows and toss them on to the floor. Feel further in the wardrobe, not sure what I am looking for exactly. The old sheet music she used to keep in a folder? Is this it? I pull out a soft, peach-coloured crocheted bag. No music inside but instead a family archive of baby booties, certificates for piano exams, a school prefect badge, a random photo of me as Gandalf in the school play gripping a silver cardboard staff, Mother's Day and birthday cards from Philippa and me. I had no idea she kept all these things. I think of my character shoes, Philippa's leg warmers, and feel a pull in my throat, thinking of Mum holding on to these pieces of our lives. Her bag, my Netley Rose shoebox – these deceptively humble containers that store such precious memorabilia. They go unopened for years until one day we bring them into the light, needing to touch the treasures within. Needing to remember again.

I continue my search. Under a set of spare towels, I discover her photo album. I think deep down I always knew Mum would have kept it, that she couldn't have got rid of all those memories of happier times. I have thought about looking for it over the years, but was never sure I could bear seeing those faces smiling at the camera, oblivious of the loss that lay ahead. I sit on the edge of the bed and carefully turn through its sticky pages. The old pictures of Dad, Joe and Mum, the theatre programmes, then other more recent pictures she has tucked in at some point, different configurations of the four of us: Christmas, summer holidays, lolling in the back garden. We look fine, normal. But when I peer closer, I see Dad caught between a smile and something else.

I find a photo of Philippa and me in a wheelbarrow. I don't remember ever seeing this picture before, but as I look at it I remember the moment, the ride in the silver chariot. Dad is pushing; you can only see his hands. Philippa and I fill the frame. I am about three years old and Philippa is behind me, gap-toothed. The two of us wear the matching canary-yellow dresses Auntie Michelle sent from Canada. Scratchy nylon, an overabundance of frills with sticky-out skirts. I adored them.

I close my eyes, feel the slipperiness of the silver metal, its thrilling sun-baked heat, the bump, bump, bump of the wheel over the stubby lawn. Another sensation: something tight around my tummy, secure, anchoring me. A belt? I open my eyes, check the photo. Philippa's arms are wrapped around me, holding me. Bump, bump, bump. Swooping and swerving along the path, thinking we might topple any moment and spill out into the flower bed, the two of us shrieking and squealing with a heady combination of joy and fear. I wanted it to last for ever. 'More, Daddy, more! Again!' But when I look closer at the picture, I see it is in fact Mum's hands on the wheelbarrow. She is the one making us fly over the grass, the one pushing us forward.

The more I look at the family pictures piled in my lap, the more I realize how often she is cut out, behind the lens, stepping back to make room for us. *Two lovely girls.* Poor Mum – all that time, all that patience, waiting to be seen. An audience of strangers at the theatre had given her more attention than Dad and I ever had. They got to their feet, applauded her. Encore! Encore! They begged for more of her.

My two parents, caught in an uneven two-step, him wanting to be lost and her wanting to be found.

No wonder now she lies in bed, forgetting, depleted after holding on to so much for so long. Exhausted from the energy spent buoying us all up, and from carrying the weight of the loss of the thing she most wanted but could never really have.

Another picture. Their wedding: Dad so young, a boy really, his face all angles, his mouth uneven, untidy. Hopeful. The two of them together, holding hands at the front of the church, wanting to give it their best shot. I put that photo in my pocket.

A photo of Mum and Joe arm in arm outside Giovanni's. Unlike Philippa and me, they look so similar – same colouring, same smile. I turn to the last page: Dad and Joe staring happily into the camera, Snowdon shadowed and majestic behind them.

In the photo Dad's arm is outstretched; he is taking the picture. Uncle Joe's arm is around Dad's shoulders. He is, in that moment, where he most wants to be. They look a perfect match, the two of them standing there in their climbing togs, a pair. The right glove finding the left.

I see now how, because he could not have his other half, he chose another, almost the same, with the same smile, the same blue eyes, the same enchanting voice. Similar, but not quite a match.

Tears blur my eyes but I make myself look. I don't know if the love was reciprocal, but since that night behind the curtains I've always imagined it was. There was something in his touch, the way it landed, the way Joe's body seemed to move towards it. How he closed his eyes, dipped his head a little. And the look between them.

As if it wasn't the first time.

As if this was a dance they had done before, a dance that always started like that; silence, the move of an arm across, a pause, a shift as it finds its place. A feeling of thrilling exploration and a long-awaited homecoming.

I imagine them setting off early that day in the mountains so they could start the climb by dawn. Music playing on the car radio. Uncle Joe driving, one-handed, singing; Dad boyish, laughing. Hiking all day, taking in the high scent of grass and earth, the endless bounty of summer, unfettered and out in the beauty of it all. The soft roll of the thick socks, then the release of feet on to cool grass as they picnicked. Fresh bread, pickles, beer, the view stretching out below.

Climbing higher. Up there where the air itself is thinner, their lungs expand, they take in more oxygen. Dizzy, they reach out, steady each other. An excuse to hold on tighter, closer.

Then the descent. With each step, closer to another reality.

Despite everything, I want them to have had one perfect day together when life was theirs, there was no fear, no sense of being watched or spied on. No disguise, no pretence, just two beautiful dreamers, walking in a warm silence under a forgiving sky.

I put the album on the bed. I will take it with me when I go and see Mum; perhaps it will help her keep remembering. No sign of the sheet music though. I climb back up, and on tiptoe I reach as far back in the cupboard as I can. I feel the hard edge of something – large, solid. I coax it forward with my fingertips and pull it into my hands. I know what it is before I even see it. The shape of its body is as familiar as my own: my father's record player.

I was so sure Mum had let it go, given it away with the rest of his things because it must have been the most painful; it was such a part of him, fragile, old-fashioned, from another time.

I pull it down, lay it on the bed. Inside the pocket in the lid, his records. I lift them out, look at them, their names old friends. There is one I don't remember. Maria Callas, 'Mon coeur s'ouvre à ta voix'. Maria. Is that who Mum has been asking for? Not a nurse at The Pines, but Maria Callas? Is this the music she wants? As if in answer, as I slip the record out of its waxy cover, a blue square of paper falls out on to the bed.

I leave it there for a moment, not sure if I should look, if I even want to see what is written there. I lift the record player to the dressing table and plug it in. Then I pick up the Maria Callas, purse my lips into a kiss and blow across the body of the record, gently lower it on to the player. The hiss. The crackle. The infinitesimal pause, like an inhale, and then . . .

I close my eyes, give over to the searing beauty of the music. I remember it . . . but how? From when? Then I have it. That day in the kitchen when I startled Mum. This was the song she was singing. It is the only time I can remember her singing it. The thought of her that day, transported, her voice so unbearably lovely. Almost as if she already knew the sadness that was to come.

I return to the bed and unfold the piece of paper. Communion wafer-thin, it seems capable of flight. Folded for so long, it has almost become individual squares, both one piece and four different entities at the same time. Like a family.

My Nightingale,

I am downstairs listening to our music and thinking of you. You have held on but I can't, not any more. It is worse than before.

I close my eyes and hear you singing. My heart opens at your voice, my darling, it always has.

I'm sorry I could not love you as you deserved. But I did love you. So much.

I always will,
Your David.

I fold the letter up, slip it back into the record sleeve. Listen to the music filling the room. The music that shelters in its notes the fragile beauty of my parents' love.

Joanie's purse, Dad's pipe, Mum's record – ordinary objects, extraordinary objects, objects that contain in their bodies a memory, a moment, a trace of a life lived, a person loved. Portals that we hold in our hands, willing them to transport us back to those we have lost, if only for a moment.

I overlooked so much, missed so many clues that were right in front of me. How unwavering my mother's love for her husband, who could not fully return it; how loyal she was to me, the daughter who could not see her, even though she was always there, quietly encouraging me, pushing me forward. And how in the end, she was the one to come back and find me; even through the fog of her dementia she reached out and called my name.

So much loss. But so much love too – imperfect, compli-cated, but love nonetheless. I pack everything up and carry it downstairs. I relish the heaviness of my load – so many things here to help her remember, to help bring her back to me. In the hallway, I pack them into Harriet's cream case to take to The Pines.

I wander back into the sitting room. Jenny and her mer-ingues have been replaced by a DIY decorating programme. A man called Nick with a fulsome beard cheerfully shares tips on creating your own wallpaper. The King Charles Spaniels sit patiently on the mantelpiece; across the coffee table the Alpine mountains gleam.

I think of the time Mum and I shared here, the home we made together for a brief period. I close my eyes and remember her voice, pure and true and unwavering. And deep down I feel the stirrings of something that, if not exactly happiness, is at least hope. And with that hope comes strength.

I take out my phone and call the police to make a charge against Neil Burrows.

25

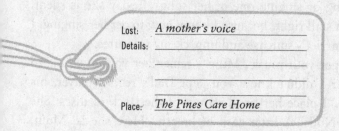

Lost: *A mother's voice*
Details: _____
_____
_____
_____
Place: *The Pines Care Home*

I feel a flutter of excitement in my chest as I wheel Harriet's suitcase up the driveway of The Pines. I can't wait to see Mum, show her the things I found, play the Maria Callas. I'm thankful I don't have to go to work. That I can be with her, sit with her, help her keep remembering who she is.

The first thing I notice is how quiet the room is. Mum is lying in bed. She hears the door open and turns towards me. I smile.

'Hello, Mum.'

Her face is cloudy and I know already that she does not recognize me, that she has gone.

She shakes her head. 'Sorry.' Her voice is a whisper. Her breath comes in small sudden gasps. Like someone who keeps remembering something exciting they have been wanting to say but never gets to say it.

'I've brought you some treats.' I bustle about, blithe and brisk, suddenly understanding why Sister Gloria always seems so spirited: as those around you start to pale and recede you become more animated, as if you might resuscitate them with your verve and vigour.

I realize why it is so quiet. Usually when I come in Mum's humming or singing one of her songs. Today she is silent. But that's all right, because I know how to get her singing. I open Harriet's suitcase and unpack my treasures.

'I've got your music, Mum – remember you asked me to bring it? I didn't know you kept Dad's record player, his records.' I place her hand on top of the stack of discs. She smiles. Nods. A little gasp of breath. 'Here she is, Mum, here's Maria.' I slip the Callas out of the waxy jacket. '"*Mon coeur s'ouvre à ta voix*". Remember, Mum? I found it, just where you said it was.' Another gasp.

I set the record spinning, help the needle find the groove. I look at Mum as I wait for the first notes to spill. I don't want to miss the look on her face when she registers the music, connects to it. I want this to be the key that unlocks all the happy memories of the days when everything seemed possible, when she had a handsome suitor and whole auditoriums stood and called for more of her.

'Tea?' she gasps.

'Soon, Mum.' I take her hands in mine, rub them gently as if I am trying to press the notes into her palms. 'Listen. Maria Callas, Mum, remember.' Less a question, more a request. A demand, a beseech. Please remember, Mum, please come back! Please let me find you somewhere, I don't care where, which moment – our day in the kitchen making cake, your head thrown back laughing on the beach, your wedding, pushing Philippa and me in the wheelbarrow. Please, Mum, pick one, any one. Remember Maria. Remember me. Please, Mum, any memory, even a sad one – at the ironing board steaming your sorrow into his shirts, the day I went back to France after Dad's funeral. I'll take anything. Just a moment when you see me again, Mum, your Dot. Your Dorothea.

She pulls at Rosie.

'Look, Mum, remember Miss Hyde, my piano lessons. Here is my Grade Two certificate, see? You kept it. Or what about these, Mum, little adorable knitted booties. Were they Philippa's or mine? Did you make them, Mum? I bet you did, such beautiful stitching.'

She coughs, shakes her head.

I seize the photo album, splay it open on the bed. 'Look, here's the four of us – you, me, Philippa, Dad – remember that day, Mum?'

Her breath rattles in her chest; she turns away.

'It's all right, Mum. It's all right. I'll get the tea,' I say, desperate to bring her something she actually wants.

She's sleeping when Adison comes in. Callas sings on.

'How is she?' he whispers, standing at the foot of Mum's bed.

'Far away.'

'She knows you're here.'

'She knows someone is here – a nurse, a neighbour, a visitor. Not me.' I am grateful that he does not argue.

'This music is incredible,' he says after a while.

'"Samson and Delilah". Maria Callas.'

'What is she singing? Do you know?'

'*Mon coeur s'ouvre à ta voix.* My heart opens at your voice.' He looks at me, puts his hand to his chest, breathes the music in.

'I know,' I say. 'It's exquisite.'

He nods and motions to the record. 'What is she saying now?'

'*Comme s'ouvrent les fleurs aux baisers de l'aurore . . .* that means *like the flowers open, to the . . .*'

He smiles. 'Go on.'

'It's something like *the flowers open, to the kisses of the dawn.*'

'Something like that, huh?' he says, nodding slowly. He looks at me.

I take a breath. '*Redis à ma tendresse les serments d'autrefois, ces serments que j'aimais!* Umm . . . *Repeat to my tenderness these promises from the past, these promises that I loved.*' I blot a few sudden rogue tears. 'Sorry.'

'It's OK.' He comes over. Sits next to me.

'I just . . . I thought if she heard this, of all things, she would remember.'

'Remember . . . ?'

'Anything. Everything. Me, Dad, her life.'

'If you want to, you could leave the record player here,' he says. 'I can come in and turn it on sometimes. Maybe later on today – or tomorrow morning – she might connect with it.'

I nod.

'Time can be kind of elusive for dementia patients,' he says, 'but windows can still open – unfortunately, hardly ever when we expect them to.'

'Thank you for all the time you spend with us . . . with Mum, I mean. She really responds to all the work you do. I'm so glad you saw her the other day when she was lucid – I'm glad you got to meet her.'

'Me too. I wish you had been here the whole time. I called you right away.'

I look at him. His face is so kind.

'Thank you.'

'She talked about you.' He smiles.

'She did?'

'Yes, you and your sister and Mr Toddles.'

'Toddles?' I frown, puzzled. *Who on earth is Mr Toddles?*

'I'm pretty sure she said Toddles.' He nods. He looks so serious in his crisp white medical coat. 'Mr Toddles,' he says again.

'Mr Toddles,' I repeat. A snort.

He nods. 'Definitely. Mr Toddles.'

Another snort, louder now, erupts into a chuckle.

'Unless it was maybe . . . Mr Tiddles?' he says, smiling broadly. My goodness, the man has dimples! Whatever next?

'Mr *Tiddles*, you say. Ah, well that throws a whole new light on things!' I guffaw. Despite everything I can't help it. Laughter whinnies out of me. He plays along. Puts on a grave face. Cups his chin, slowly strokes his lower lip with his thumb.

'Hmm, well, now I come to think about it, it could have been Mr Toodles.' He tries to keep his face serious, but I see the corner of his mouth twitch. He bites his lower lip but can't help himself – a laugh slips out.

'TIBBLES!' I cry. 'Mr Tibbles, our old tabby cat.' The two of us hoot with laughter.

Eventually I catch my breath, shake my head.

'Mr Tibbles, of course. I'd forgotten his name there for a moment. But Mum remembered. Brava, Mum.' I look at her face, surrendered to sleep. Her inhales sound like little gasps. I imagine her chatting to Adison, telling him about her girls. The scene is so ordinary and yet so unimaginable. I want to ask him more but am suddenly shy.

'She said you loved to dance,' Adison says.

'I did.'

'Do you?'

I shrug, then nod.

'That you lived in France?'

'She remembered?'

He nods. 'She's proud of you.'

I turn away.

The record ends. Mum's breathing ruptures the silence. I get up, blot my face, replace the needle in the groove, restart the aria.

'Perhaps once more,' I say, 'just in case.'

'Good idea.' He smiles, reassuring. 'You never know.'

We listen to the music for a while.

'I wanted her to remember,' I say finally, my voice quiet. 'I know she can hear the music. I see her fingers moving to the notes but she doesn't remember, she doesn't sing along. Is her voice gone? Without her voice, I worry she will . . . disappear too. And I'm not . . . The thing is, you see, the thi . . . thing . . . is . . . I'm just not . . . ready for her . . . to go.'

I sob silently, then noisily. Adison takes my hand. But he does not massage it, or find the pressure points. He simply holds it in his own. His touch is warm. Safe.

'So trembles my heart,' Maria sings, 'ready to be consoled, by your voice that is so dear to me!'

My mother's voice so dear to my father. Her voice so dear to me. And now my heart breaks because I know it has gone, and that without her voice she will go too. I scavenge my memory to try and recall everything – every sentence, every song – wish I had paid more attention.

So many lost years, lost opportunities for life, for love. Poor darling Mum. We left her, all of us, over and over, left her standing in the kitchen, suspended in the frame of the door, unmoored in the hallway. And when we finally turned, remembered who she was, that she belonged to us, by then she was lost. She was unable to find her way home, lost in the space between the sitting room and the kitchen, not knowing what went in the fridge and what went on the bookshelf. She no longer recognized the daughters she had waited for, so patiently, for so long. Poor Gail, suddenly a stranger in a strange land with no guides. Perhaps that was why she got all my guidebooks down from the shelves that day. She was trying to find her way back.

I go to The Pines every day and sit with her for hours. We play records and I rub her hands and tell her stories, become Reg the fishmonger, Mrs Knight with the baritone timbre and the Irish terrier from next door.

Adison stops by. So kind. At first I'm embarrassed when he catches me snapping invisible braces as I pretend to deliver halibut, but he just smiles, sits on the bed and talks to Mum, takes her hands. She always looks pleased to see him. Her lungs have become congested, but I watch the pain ease from her face as he massages her poor body. Sometimes I'd swear

I can see energy and light radiating from his palms, but I wonder if it is just wishful thinking.

This morning I'm wearing the grey cashmere jumper from Harriet's case. It is indulgently soft. I read to Mum and watch as Adison moves his hands over her body, working on her hip, then massaging her chest in cycles of friction, quick kneading and percussion, moving her into different positions. But always with so much care.

'He's very good at his job, isn't he, Mum.'

'Yes,' Mum gasps.

Adison's white coat is pushed up to his elbows and I admire the elegant articulation of his forearms, his strong hands, so deft and gentle as they do their work.

'I like spending time with people,' Adison says. 'In the hospital you don't always get to spend enough time. All finished for today, Gail. Thank you so much, you did great.' He rolls his shoulders, eases out his back. 'I like to get to know my patients.' He smiles at Mum. Then he turns to me, a shiny dark wing of hair half falling over his face. He brushes it back. Looks into my eyes. 'And their families—'

'Halloo!' Philippa bustles in, bearing a large potted hyacinth and a basket of prunes. 'Heavens, are you wearing perfume?' she says as she knocks her cheek to mine.

'Oh, it's nothing special.' I may have dabbed on the tiniest soupçon of Harriet's scent this morning.

'Hmm, smells expensive,' Philippa says. 'Dr Chang, how's the patient?' She kisses Mum.

'Well, today I've been focusing on pulmonary drainage, and decreasing inflammation—'

'Jolly good.' Philippa nods. 'How are you feeling, Mum?'

'I'll get out of your way, let you enjoy your visit,' Adison says. 'I'll swing by later, Gail, if that's OK, see how you're doing.'

Mum wheezes.

'He won't be around long,' says Philippa knowingly. Adison has barely left the room. 'Clever chap. Asian, right?'

'Asian American,' I correct her. 'What do you mean? He likes it here. He was just saying how much he enjoys his job, spending proper time with his patients,' I add proudly.

'Handsome man like that working in a care home long term? No offence, Mum, but mark my words, not for long.'

I take a vicious bite out of one of the prunes.

26

Found: _Travel guide_
Details: _Frommer's Forty-Eight Hours_
in Rome
annotated (see: tiramisu)

Place: _Leather handbag (broken clasp)_

'Dot! Bloody hell! I don't know whether to hug you or slap you,' Anita says, as I arrive at Lost Property to meet her for lunch. 'I've been watching the door and it's had me that distracted, I gave a man who came in to collect his briefcase a shopping bag full of demerara sugar and elasticated support tights.'

Lost Property has been transformed under Anita's short tenure as manager. The kitchen nook in the back office has been re-established, and when she proudly points it out to me I see half a Dundee cake, moist and fragrant, next to a coffee maker, percolating chirpily to itself. Overturning all previous Burrows rulings, she has added a clause that staff are permitted to distribute uncollected brollies at their discretion. I note that personal possessions are now permitted throughout the building. Each to her own.

Anita's office is covered in a bricolage of files, paperwork and folders liberally sprinkled with make-up brushes, pots of lip gloss and tubes of mascara. It is as if she has managed to take up residence in a giant version of her trusty bag.

'I'm sorry . . .' I begin.

'Dots, I feel awful . . .' Anita says at the same time.

We both stop. Start again.

I hold up my hand. 'I'm sorry for behaving so abysmally that day.'

'What day? When?'

'In the Ladies, I was so upset about losing Mr Appleby's holdall. I . . . pushed you. I'd just . . . I'm so—'

'No! It's my fault. When you didn't come in the next day I was beside myself. And when you didn't take my calls—'

'Sorry, I just couldn't—'

'And then when that creep came in with that big cut on his head, his hand all bandaged . . .'

'I'm not sorry about that.'

'Too right! Turns out he was on the fiddle with Snagsbey's as well as everything else – taking a cut of the proceeds from the auctions. I knew he was up to something, little git. TfL have given him the heave-ho. Not even waiting till the trial – I suppose there will be a trial?' Her eyes soften as she looks at me. 'Will you have to testify? I'll come with you, love.'

'Thank you.' It is not a prospect I relish. But I will do it.

'All right, we don't have to talk about it now. But I'm here for you, Dots,' Anita says. 'Let's talk about something good! Like when are you coming back?'

'Coming back?'

'To work. Ooh, guess what? We're moving premises!'

'Lost Property, moving? Where?'

'South Kensington! How bloody brilliant is that? Ten minutes to Harrods!'

'But what will happen to this place?' I look round, can't imagine it being anything else, anywhere else.

'No idea. TfL have probably got plans for it. Or it will just become another Starbucks. But that's another reason you need to come back to work – you have to save me from blowing my salary at the Clarins counter!'

It feels good to laugh together. Anita reaches over and takes my hand.

'Come back soon, Dot. We're lost without you. I'm trying to run this place while still helping out on the counter, and anyway, truth is . . .'

'It looks to me as if you are doing a first-class job.'

'Well, I'm doing my best, but it's not Lost Property without Dot Watson.'

'Anita . . . I'm not coming back.' I surprise myself with the words and Anita stares at me, equally shocked.

'What? No! Really?' She squeezes my hand.

'Really.' And as I say it I know it is true.

A phone call comes through and Anita gesticulates to meet her in Customer Service in five minutes. As I get up to leave I notice my second-best Sheaffer amongst the make-up and files on her desk. I smile. It has found a good home.

I nip to the stacks to bid a quick hello to Big Jim. I instinctively avert my gaze as I pass the umbrella sanctuary, but a cascade of colour lures me back – daubs of almond, lemon, a flush of damson, violet, chartreuse; umbrellas in an assemblage of coordinated shades.

'I . . . tidied up a bit.' Big Jim hovers at the threshold.

313

I trace the curve of a maple handle with my fingers. 'It's lovely.'

He ducks his head. 'Yours.' He hands me a soft bundle. My uniform. 'Thanks for fixing the light,' he says.

'You knew?' He strokes the tail of the scorpion tattoo. I notice his fingernails are buffed, pink and shiny. 'But you never said anything?'

'Your business,' he says, and retreats back to the pit.

The uniform is neatly folded. I daren't look too closely in case he has gone the full Boo Radley and stitched the pocket.

Back upstairs, I stand behind the counter and wait for Anita.

'I wonder if you can help me?' A woman, dressed in a well-cut vintage sage two-piece, smiles across the counter. Atop her head a nut-brown cap perches snug as an acorn.

'I don't actually . . .' I look around. SmartChoice – who has had eyes on stalks since I set foot in the building – is 'busy' with a customer. I lick my thumb and forefinger, pick up a Lost Item form.

'What have you lost?'

'It's rather what I've found,' she says. A familiar copy of *Frommer's Guide to Forty-Eight Hours in Rome* slowly slides across the counter.

We both look at it intently, studying the picture of the Colosseum on the front.

'Ah,' I say.

'Yes,' she replies. There's a pause. 'I came in a while ago and collected my handbag.' Fine leather, broken clasp, Liberty-print hanky, odd lipstick. 'And when I opened it, I found that this travel guide had been put inside. It seemed

'. . . deliberate.' She keeps her gloved finger pressed on the corner of the guide.

'I see.' I fiddle with the Lost Item form. She tilts her head to one side, her little acorn staying perfectly in place on her auburn bob.

'I went.' I look up. Meet her gaze. 'To Rome, for the weekend. I did it all. St Peter's Basilica, the Colosseum, even rented a bicycle and took a spin around the Borghese Gardens.'

'Oh.' I duck my head, pretend to write something on the form. I can't believe it.

Rome, by all means, Rome. She'd gone. She'd really gone. How thrilling. I feel my pulse quicken.

'Went to Pompi's on the Via Albalonga,' she says, still pinning the guide with her finger, a challenge somehow. 'Seeing as it was underlined three times.'

'Did you try their tiramisu?' My hand arrives at my mouth too late to stop me.

'So, it *was* you.' She gives the guide an affirmative tap. 'I knew it! Are you on some sort of commission with the Italian tourist board?'

I smile, shake my head. It's really rather discombobulating, the intensity of her stare.

'Delicious, like licking velvet,' she says, 'the tiramisu.' Again, that look! 'Did you know that the word tiramisu translates as a pick-me-up? Apparently, it's an aphrodisiac. You should try it.' Another slow pause unfolds, and for some reason my cheeks toast under her gaze. 'Late October was the perfect time to visit Rome – only a few tourists but still warm enough to go without a jacket most days. It was just what I needed.' She smiles. I seem to have folded the

315

Lost Item form into a tiny concertina. Hopelessly I try and smooth it out. She watches.

I take a breath, then: 'Sorry, I have to ask – the lipstick, it wasn't yours, was it?'

'What lipstick?' she says.

'Red-Hot Poker. It was in the bag . . .'

She gives me a curious smile. 'No, not my colour or my brand. Cheryl's. My ex. She borrowed the handbag – hence it getting lost – which caused the overdue fight that ended the relationship.'

Aha!

The woman leans closer. Her voice is low, intimate.

'*Grazie.* And if you ever fancy trying that tiramisu, give me a call. I left my number in the guide – you'll know what page.'

Anita and I lunch together at the Italian next door. I spend most of my energy trying to control a sudden desire for tiramisu which seems to surround me, chalked on the specials board, listed in the leather-bound menu, and sitting sumptuous and sweet under a glass dome on the counter.

After lunch I accompany Anita back into Lost Property and, while she is engaged in a rather intense conversation with Big Jim in the kitchen nook, I slip down to the pit.

I pass by the crates, loaded with unclaimed items. I can't imagine this place not being Lost Property any more. What will happen to the building? It has stood here almost a century housing lost items and now will be lost to history, another sedimentary layer in this city that keeps changing, trying to keep up with itself, roaring into the future yet steeped in the past.

One day, archaeologists will dig through the sedimentary layers of Lost Property and wonder at the people who lived here. What will they surmise, as they unearth mountains of single gloves, skeletons of prams and carcasses of mobile phones? As they carefully stroke the spines of desiccated umbrellas with their little brushes. *What kind of people were these?*

In my old living quarters, everything looks normal, just as it was: the puffer fish still presides atop the grandfather clock, the mid-century still astoundingly upright despite its missing leg.

For a brief period, a woman lived down here, surviving on foraged items mislaid on the Northern Line.

There is a difference between a fall and a jump.

Dad jumped. He willingly propelled himself from this world. I fell, sunk into the bowels of Lost Property, lived in its underground memorial. Dad's jump was executed in an instant. My fall took years. But both are over now. Like a lost umbrella, I found a sanctuary that could house me. But brollies can't fulfil their function shelved and dormant in a basement. And neither can a linguist, a traveller.

'Goodbye,' I whisper.

27

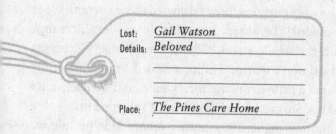

Lost: _Gail Watson_

Details: _Beloved_

Place: _The Pines Care Home_

It's dark when I get to The Pines, the late-November sky is pricked with stars and a low calm moon glows. The taxi drops me at the gate and I stare up at the constellations till the two amber prongs of Philippa's Audi headlights nose across the driveway.

We walk down the gravel path, but just before we get to the main door she puts her hand on my arm.

'Can we wait a moment?' she says. I look back up at the sky while she searches for a tissue, clears her throat.

'See there . . . that star?' I point. Philippa looks up, puffy-eyed. Nods. 'Capella. It appears to be just one star, very bright, but it's actually a cluster of four stars, organized in two binary pairs.' She sniffs.

I have a memory of her, long ago, one Christmas Eve. She was nearly ten, I was five, and we were both so excited. She still just about believed in Father Christmas, and having a younger sibling meant she could let herself believe a little bit longer. 'What if he doesn't come?' I said, running into her room, anxious and bleary-eyed. 'What if he doesn't know we moved? What if he can't find us because of the tall trees in the garden?'

'Go and look out of the window,' she said. I pulled back her peachy silky curtains (how I'd envied those curtains). 'See that big moon?' she asked. I nodded. It was huge, creamy, and lit up the whole street. 'That's how Father Christmas will find us, don't worry,' Philippa said. I smiled hopefully and shivered a little in my nightie. 'Come on.' She opened up her blankets. Surprised and delighted, I snuggled in.

Now another night sky. Another moon. Side by side we stare at the constellations; at the way the sky looks on the night our mother has died.

Sister Gloria greets us. Makes us tea.

'Stay as long as you like,' she says.

I don't recognize any of the other staff on duty – the night team, all starting their shift. Did Adison get a chance to say goodbye? I suppose I won't see him again now.

Mum is lying on the bed, her eyes closed, her head tipped back a little, revealing the length of her throat. It looks sculptural, the dip of it like a secret hollow she could hide in. I touch my own throat, feel the same dip. Trace upwards and find the same jawline.

Someone has brushed her hair; it puffs out on the pillow. A thin sheet covers her. I open her chest of drawers and pull Rosie out. Threads of cotton fall like pink petals.

Philippa starts to say something but then stops. I cover Mum with Rosie and bend down, kiss her cool cheek. The bedside lamp throws a harsh glare on her face. I switch it off and we sit in the semi-darkness either side of her.

'I kept hoping she would get better.' Philippa's voice. 'I know that doesn't make any sense, but still . . .'

'Me too.'

'I hated it that she couldn't remember us, but I prayed that the things she did remember – or think about – were happy.'

'She kept thinking Dad was going to come for her.'

'I know.' We are silent for a while. I reach out in the dark and touch Mum's cheek. The percussion of Philippa's bracelets clatter together and I know she is touching her too.

'She loved him too much.' Her voice tight.

'He loved her too.'

'Not enough.'

'As much as he could.'

The moon casts our silhouettes on the walls.

'I wish I had been here,' Philippa says. 'I hate that she was alone.'

'Sister Gloria said she went in her sleep. That she wouldn't have felt the stroke, it would have been fast.'

The record player lies open. Maria Callas is silent. I imagine Mum listening to the gently spinning record, the lyrics soothing her as she slipped away. *Ready to be consoled, by your voice that is so dear to me!* Her David, the boy she knew from long ago. Full of hope.

Philippa gives me a lift back to the maisonette.

'Do you want to come in?' I ask as she pulls up.

'No. But can you wait a while?'

'Of course.'

We sit in her Audi parked outside Mum's old house, neither of us quite knowing where to go, what to do. Not wanting another ending, another goodbye.

'Do the children know?'

'No. I'll tell them tomorrow. Well, today now, I suppose. Give them the day off school. Make pancakes and eat them in bed, all crawl under the duvet together.'

'That sounds nice.' I wish for a moment I had brought Rosie with me.

'It will be Christmas soon,' Philippa says. 'It seems unbelievable.'

'Then a whole new year,' I say.

At the same time we both let out an exhale, knock wet cheeks against each other. I open the door and get out.

She rolls down the window and we look at each other for a moment, then Philippa drives away.

I watch a pink dawn rise on the first day of my life without my mother.

28

Found: *Philippa*
Details: *Missing shoe (expensive, blue)*
Fierce
Filthy
Sister
Place: *Cow field, Kent*

Mum's funeral is well attended. I recognize several people from Kent Dementia Support, some staff and even a few residents from The Pines. Sister Gloria gives me a view halloo from the pew. I smile but steer clear in case she initiates one of her booming conversations across the aisle. I am touched by her presence nonetheless. I scan the church for Adison but don't see him. I do see a handful of Mum's friends from our old neighbourhood and several from her life in the maisonette. The local choir she belonged to sing 'Abide With Me' as people find their seats. I spot Anita in the middle of a row, *sans* the beast but *avec* Big Jim, which I have to admit isn't a complete surprise. He looks perfectly normal in the light of day after all, most substantial. I scan the rows; the service is due to start in five minutes. Aunts, uncles, cousins and second cousins – or first cousins once removed? – whose names I can't keep straight fill the pews. The vicar enters and the congregation stand. I spot Adison slipping in at the back. He sees me and gives me an exquisite smile. Some people can chat for ever and say nothing; others can give you a whole world with just an expression.

Gerald is up at the front with the children. I give Melanie a kiss, squeeze Sam, breathe in his salty puppyish smell. His eyes are red-rimmed, poor darling. I join my family on the pew: Gerald, Melanie, Sam, Philippa and then me, the punctuation mark on the end. Dot. Dorothea.

Everything goes smoothly. Philippa, the children and I sob. Gerald sits tensely and focuses on reading the order of service over and over. Midway through, Philippa and I mop our faces and get up; she reads W. H. Auden's 'Stop all the clocks' and I do Emily Dickinson's 'Because I could not stop for Death' – admittedly not as popular a choice, but it seems to go down all right. The only real moment of tension is when the Shipping Forecast comes on, which raises more than a few eyebrows. People start looking around, puzzled.

'What the hell?' Philippa hisses, wet-faced, leaning towards me.

I lean in and hiss back, 'It was on the playlist you read me down the phone.'

'No, it wasn't.'

'Yes, it was.'

'I said Mum wanted "Abide With Me", "Wind Beneath My Wings" and "Sailing By".'

Ah. Well, at least we retained the nautical bent. And, as it turns out, there is something surprisingly comforting about hearing the vicar say a prayer, followed by 'Cromarty, Dogger and Finisterre'.

'She won't mind,' I whisper back. Philippa shakes her head crossly and returns to her upright position, and I shift uneasily, thinking of the musical compilation I have made for the end of the service – a sort of mourners' promenade. No doubt my sister will have a few bon mots about that. It's challenging feeling like I'm in trouble, even at my own mother's funeral.

We've arranged for a buffet of cold cuts and finger foods – expressions I have never relished – at Philippa's at four o'clock. I imagine she will be in a hurry to dash back and spend the time steaming the doilies or origami-folding the napkins, but after we have thanked all the mourners she grabs my hand.

'I need some fresh air. Come with me, will you? I can't go back and be the hostess with the mostest right now. I can't breathe. I need to be away from all the . . .'

All the hugs and the sympathy and the well-wishes. Neither of us are good with that and we have already lived through it once. Her eyes are red, her face haggard, and I've no doubt I look just the same. I nod.

She instructs Gerald to go home and lay out the buffet – I see a flash of fear pass over his face – then stalks off around the back of the church on to a footpath.

I follow.

After a few hundred yards, she stops and turns to me. Usually I see Philippa against the backdrop of her own life, serene, in control. Out here in the countryside she looks less substantial, fragile even, like the spindly sweet peas Dad was always training up bamboo poles. She looks older too. I see Mum in the blue of her eyes and fight the desire to take her hand.

'Which way?' I say, squinting into the wind that buffets across the downs. Signs for a public bridleway point in two directions: up towards the Weald and then across a field, down towards a few houses that mark out a hamlet.

'Up,' she says, marching forward.

The wind pummels us, snatching our words away, for which we are both grateful. We push on, upward, heads bent. Philippa wears her grey silk headscarf tied under her chin like the Queen. The loose triangle of it against her skull flaps like a broken wing.

'Keep up, D!'

'It's freezing out here!' I gasp.

At the top of the Weald the wind is stronger, but we stop and take in the view. The fields stretch out and away. There is not a soul around.

'Just us,' I say, into the wind.

'What?'

I try again, shout, 'JUST US.' She nods and another meaning surfaces. We used to be four: the top hat, the wheelbarrow, the race car and the Scottie dog. Now it's just us, Dot and Philippa searching for traces of our parents in each other's faces. Mum in her eyes. Dad in mine. Imprints of our parental ghosts.

'It was a GOOD FUNERAL,' she shouts.

I nod, shout back, 'Mum would have LIKED THE SONGS.'

Philippa leans closer so that we can stop shouting. 'I'm not sure what the vicar thought when the overture of *The King and I* played as people walked out of the church.'

Shall we dance? On a bright cloud of music, shall we fly?

It was perfect.

326

'It was nice how many of the staff from The Pines came,' Philippa says.

I nod casually.

'Sometimes I wonder . . .' Philippa trails off.

'What?'

'I wonder if she willed it. Mum. The dementia.'

'That's not possible.'

'I know . . . I just wonder if it was a relief . . . to forget.'

'Forget what?' I know, of course, I've thought it too. I just need to hear her say it.

She looks at me for a moment. I arm myself for a barrage of Spray and Wipe but it doesn't come.

'Forget about Dad. How he broke her heart.'

I look away, watch a herd of cows wander across the adjoining field.

'I never understood the violence. It was so unlike him,' I say.

'He had to make sure . . .' She pauses. It looks as if she is going to say something more but she seals her lips and glances out over the fields, her eyes squinting.

He had to make sure. Was that it? As stark and simple as that? I remember how, years ago, at lunch one day Philippa found a little slug in her salad. She shrieked and made a fuss. Dad came over and gently scooped up the slug on a paper towel, took it to the sink, washed the salad cream off it and deposited it on a bush outside. 'Off you pop.' It often struck me how tender he was, which always made me wonder how he could have chosen such a violent end. Now I understand.

'If I hadn't gone to France, if I had stayed . . .' I say.

'You were right to go!' Philippa says, turning to me, her eyes bright, fierce. 'Mum sacrificed her life for him. We didn't want you to. Dad held on too tightly.'

'That's when things get lost.' I say it quietly but she nods. I have a memory, more like a physical sensation, of snuggling in front of the TV to watch another old black-and-white film with Dad, but secretly wishing I could watch *Freaky Friday* instead. I remember listening yet again to a record with strange mournful lyrics when I yearned for something cheerier. Pop, even? Guilt twists in my stomach.

'You were jealous because I was his favourite,' I say before I can stop myself.

'Jealous? I felt sorry for you.'

'Sorry? Why? I was happy.'

'You were too . . . tethered. I wanted you to go and have fun, play with friends your own age, be a little girl.'

'You never wanted to play with me. What about that time we went swimming? You just wanted to see Toby Jackson.' Am I shouting?

Philippa stares at me, her face a puzzle of shock, surprise and utter confusion.

'*Toby Jackson?* The boy at my school? Is that who you mean? That Toby Jackson?'

I nod fiercely. My whole body suddenly floods with anger.

'Yes, Philippa, *that* Toby Jackson. You were there showing off in your fishy swimsuit, afraid to go in the deep end, said I wet myself . . .' Tears stream down my cheeks. 'So *you* didn't look foolish. You used *me*, humiliated *me*, betrayed *me*.' I am screaming at her now, my hands clenched into fists, my face contorted.

Philippa puts her hands on my shoulders and turns me to her.

'Betrayed you? What? Over Toby? That's bonkers. But Dot, if that's what you need me to say, I'm sorry . . .'

'No!' I yell at her and the rip of anger zigzags through me, twists into what it really is, guilt and pain. So much pain. I feel it in my stomach like a wallop. 'I'm the one at fault. I did it. It's my fault. I betrayed him.'

'Toby?'

'What? No! Not bloody Toby. Dad. I betrayed Dad. And he knew, he heard me. In your kitchen. And that's why he did it. It's all my fault.'

She shakes me. 'D, stop it. Stop it. You're upset, let's go back . . .' I tear her hands away. 'Calm down! Shhh!' She reaches out again but I push her away. The wind slashes the tears across my cheeks.

'He heard me,' I gulp. 'At the anniversary party. I told you he was gay. I told you about . . . about him and . . .' I choke over the words. 'Don't you remember? He heard me and then he . . . killed himself.' I gag, bend forward, retch into the grass.

Philippa holds my head, pulls my hair from my face. When it is over she rootles in her pocket. Gives me a hanky. I grunt. Hold it to my face. Smell L'Air du Temps.

When I finally stand upright she is looking out across the field again, her face pink against the muddy green of the landscape.

'It wasn't your fault, Dottie,' she says quietly, still not looking at me.

'It *was*. He was so unhappy. They used to talk at night.' I swallow. 'Mum and Dad. He was so . . . desperate. And she would plead with him.'

'I know,' Philippa says.

'You do?'

She turns to me now, her jaw tight. 'I lived in that house too. Why did you think I changed bedrooms with you?'

'I thought you wanted the bigger room.'

'Charming. Well, maybe I did. But I also wanted you to have the room further away from theirs. So that you wouldn't hear them at night.' She swallows, looks away. I see her struggling for the words. 'So you wouldn't hear him crying. It was too awful.'

I look at my sister. How much I thought I knew – know – the imprint of my own sibling. I share her DNA. I know her habits, her particular scent, the triptych of moles beneath her left earlobe. I know the way she will react to a joke, answer the phone, the piece she will always pick in Monopoly (race car). How is it, then, that I can remember the most intimate details about Philippa – when she first got her period, the cuts around her ankles when she started to shave her legs – yet suddenly I can turn around and see an entirely different person?

'I was desperate to leave home, to get away,' Philippa went on, still staring out at the landscape, not looking at me. 'Desperate to get out of that house. It was all so . . . so bloody sad. And I wanted you to get out too. To get on with your life. Be happy.'

'But I was happy.'

How could Philippa's version of our childhood be so different from my own? As if we had lived in two completely distinct realities, even though we spent them in bedrooms separated only by a partition wall. I wore her old clothes for the first fourteen years of my life. We sat next to each other at the dining table eating fish on Friday, a roast on Sunday, every week of our childhood.

We stand side by side in silence, both staring ahead. Bruised clouds scud across the sky.

'Then why?' I say eventually. 'Why did he do it?'

'I don't know, but I know it wasn't your fault.'

'How do you know that? You don't know . . .' My voice cracks.

I see her chest rise and fall under her coat as she breathes in and heavily out. The wind plasters a strand of hair across her face. It has brazenly escaped from the strict confines of her scarf, but she pushes it back and turns to me. And then she says slowly, clearly, 'I know because it wasn't the first time.'

'What?'

She shakes her head. 'Let's leave it.'

'Tell me.' I barely mouth the words. Then I scream them. 'Tell me!'

She swallows. Inhales.

'It wasn't the first time. He'd tried before. Pills. I don't know exactly. I overheard them one night. Mum begging him not to do it again, begging him to get help, him promising he would. I never got the full details. Mum wouldn't discuss it.'

'Mum knew that you knew?' I can't breathe.

'Not at the time, no. Later. You had gone back to France, after the funeral. I think she felt guilty, that she should have . . . stopped it. And I told her I knew – about the time before. The times, maybe.'

My legs crumple under me and I fall.

I land with a thud on the soggy ground.

'Why didn't you tell me?' I cry. I wipe my running nose with the back of my hand, smearing mud across my face. 'Why didn't Mum tell me? I would have stayed.'

Philippa stares down at me and says softly, 'That's why.'

'What do you mean?'

'Mum wanted you to go, to have your life. She knew Dad was already lost, she was saving us.'

Philippa looks at the damp patch of earth next to me, sighs, then pulls her raincoat tightly under her and joins me on the ground.

'Why did he leave us?' I ask.

She turns to me. Her face is so sad. 'I don't know.' She tugs the sleeve of her coat over her hand and carefully dabs the tears streaking my face.

We sit, our silence broken by my inelegant sobs. From where we are on the hill we can see the church. A small black line of cars arrive; another funeral.

I try to piece it together, all that she has said. A jigsaw of facts, but not a straight edge amongst them. I can't take it in. Instead I look out across the Weald, to the horizon, the sky that particular granite cast of winter. The ancient oaks stand naked, exposed. Their delicate skeletal shapes are beautiful in the silvered light, revealing both their vulnerability and strength. There is a truth to those bare branches, like there is in a pencil sketch – clear lines, no blurring, no colouring in. A stark awareness of what has been and what is to come as the tree waits, holding out for the promise of spring again. I look at the outline of my sister silhouetted next to me, the shape of her, and see – in her angles, her edges – her truth.

'We'd better get going,' Philippa says eventually, hoisting herself up. 'I told Gerald I would only be ten minutes. Everyone will be at the house now. I know he'll forget to take the cling film off the sandwiches and he won't remember to put the oven on for the savoury puffs. Christ, look at my shoes!' Her expensive-looking dark-blue satin pumps are rimmed with mud and grass. My old brogues are not faring much better. 'I think that might be a short cut,' she says, pointing across the neighbouring field.

Returning once more to obedient little sister, I follow, my footsteps tracing hers, her words looping in my head. *It wasn't the first time.* Oh, Dad.

We climb a stile, up and over. Halfway across the field, Philippa slows her pace.

'What is it?' I ask.

'I think that cow looks a bit . . . cross.' My gaze follows her pointing finger and indeed, in the middle of the field a large stocky beast is staring at us, snorting through flared nostrils and tossing its head. Its large, *horned* head.

'I think that cow is a bull. Let's give it a wide berth, keep walking slowly, no sudden movements. Actually, I think you are meant to keep it in your sights. So turn around – and walk backwards.'

Philippa nods, reaches out and takes my hand. In sync, we lift a foot and step backwards, then another foot, then another. There is a slurping, wet sound. Philippa's right foot is submerged in a cow pat.

'This is a nightmare!' she yells, and pulls her foot out, but the pump remains interred. 'Now what?'

The bull snorts, his nose wet, wide black nostrils flaring open and closed.

'Leave the shoe, Philippa.'

'Do you know how much they cost?' She reaches towards the shoe to pull it out. 'I am jolly well going to—' Whatever she was jolly well going to do is lost as the bull gives another snort, louder now, and rolls its eyes, revealing a lattice of red veins. He ducks his head, paws the ground.

'Maybe you're right,' she says, her hand retreating from the cow pat's stench. The bull dips its head again. 'Dot!' Philippa grabs my arm.

'It's all right, just nice and slow now, one big step at a time.' In slow motion, we back away down the field. I take a moment to look behind us; the gate seems far away. I cover her. 'Keep going, make your way to the stile.'

'But what about you?'

'I'm coming. You go first, I'll follow.'

'Dot!'

'Go, Philippa!' I hear her slowly pacing backwards, one-shoed. 'That's right, you're almost there . . . keep going . . . nice and slow, that's the ticket.' I sneak another peek; there are just a few feet now between my sister and the gate. I start to move, catch up. The bull looks so ferocious and so full of life in every one of its terrible, powerful muscles. Heavens, is he deliberately turning to show me how big he is? Really, really big.

'Dot! Come on!'

I see Philippa peripherally, already halfway over the stile. I see her mouthing my name. I feel as if I'm trapped in a slow-motion film, silent except for the whoosh of my blood. Adrenaline rushes helter-skelter around my body, the jolt of the fight-or-flight hormone. Flight is obviously the better option in this situation.

The bull glares at me, flicks its tongue and rumbles, 'Rrrrrrumph . . . rrrrrummmph.' I don't move. Realize I can't.

The bull steps closer, tossing its head up and down. I stand frozen. The freeze reaction. I forgot about that one. Fight, flight or *freeze*.

334

It wasn't the first time. He had to make sure.

The communion wafer-thin letter I found amongst his records.

It is worse than before.

Poor Dad. Poor Mum.

And poor Philippa. Little Philippa hearing that through her bedroom wall. Keeping it to herself all that time, a young girl protecting a younger girl. All the secrets. How could I have missed it?

The bull paws at the ground, glaring at me. I can't move. I am powerless, stuck in place, a needle in the groove of a scratched record.

'Run, Dot! Run! For fuck's sake – RUN!'

I hear her.

I uproot my family-tree feet, and bid them move. Suddenly they are not my father's feet, not my mother's ankles; they are mine, all mine, and they are running hell for leather. Fast. Faster. I trip. Fall forward. Imagine I hear the bull behind me, its hooves thundering closer. Too close.

A murderous cry rips through the landscape.

'GET AWAY from MY SISTER, you BASTARD, or I will RIP your FUCKING BOLLOCKS OFF!'

Philippa as I have never seen her, ferocious, wild, epic.

I feel a violent tug on my elbow, then my shoulder is almost dislocated from its socket as she drags me backwards on to my feet again.

'Run! Run!' she screams, grasping my arm harder now. We run. We don't look behind us. We slide and skitter over the mud, spraying it up in a fan, hearts pounding in our chests, breath sawing at our throats, the sound of our blood in our ears. Our eyes are fixed on the stile, safety. Philippa pushes me up and over first and then hurls herself after me.

Both of us lie in the field, catching our breath.

I look across and see my sister, her hair flecked with black, sludge trowelling around her décolletage, coating her legs like a mud wrestler. Still, her earrings glint merrily in the light, pristine. I start to laugh.

'What is so bloody funny?' she gasps.

'Sorry, it's just . . . you look . . . so . . . pretty.'

She lifts her arms and for a moment I think she is doing Spray and Wipe. But she brings her hands to her face. Mud streaks her cheeks. She is crying.

'I thought . . . you were just going to . . . stand there. Let that, that . . . beast just trample and gore you. I can't lose you too.'

'You didn't lose me. I'm fine . . .'

'You're my little sister. It's my job to p-p-protect you.'

'You did! You saved me!'

'I thought that you would be all right when you went to university, to France, but then, after Dad, I thought . . . I thought I'd lost you.'

I reach out and take her filthy hand. 'You haven't lost me. I'm here.'

We lie in the mud, hand in hand on the damp ground.

After a while I say, 'If we make an entrance at yours looking like this, I fear people will think we have both rather lost the plot.'

'Sod them.'

I smile. And then a chuckle ripples and shudders and bursts out from every part of me – full, deep, breathless, all-encompassing laughter. Philippa shakes her head.

'Look at me! I haven't looked this shit – and I use that word in its most literal sense – in . . . my whole entire life!' Her face crumples for a moment, and then starts to reshape itself; a crack in the cheek, a crinkle around her eyes, and she joins in. We lie on our backs in the muddy field, roaring until we can hardly breathe, until our stomach muscles burn with pain.

Game, set and match, but this time we're on the same team. Two *oeufs*: the surprise and the mistake. Two gifts, two daughters. Rivals, allies, sisters.

'Remember when we put on that show for Mum and Dad?' I ask later, as Philippa – still one-shoed – drives us, tear-stained and filthy, back to her house.

'*The King and I*,' she says, flicking the indicator with a grubby hand.

'You do remember!'

'How could I forget? I had to be Yul Brynner!'

I don't know how I persuaded Philippa to don a swim cap to play Yul Brynner to my Deborah Kerr. I think it was something about the day itself; school had finished, the summer holidays stretched ahead endlessly. Dad was off work for a fortnight, and we were heading to Devon at the weekend. The weather was perfect. All of us spent the day in the back garden, Philippa sunbathing, Mum tucked into one of her novels, me helping Dad harvest his tomatoes, the creak of canvas, a nip of lime cordial in the air, time slow and sweet as honey.

Later we stumbled inside, sun-tipsy and relaxed. Mum and Dad pottered in the kitchen making supper, the soft cadence of her laugh infusing their conversation as the earthy perfume of sliced fresh tomatoes wafted through the house.

'Let's put on a show for them!' I said to Philippa. '*The King and I!*' I couldn't believe my luck when she said yes.

'Really and truly? With costumes and everything?'

'Why not?' She glanced towards the kitchen. Mum was singing something jolly, Dad joining in the chorus. She smiled. 'I'll help you with your outfit if you like.'

To recreate Miss Kerr's swooping satin-hooped ball gown, we pinned an emerald-green bedspread around my plastic hula hoop. The slippery silky folds of the fabric cascaded over the curve of the hoop, trailed along the floor. It was absolutely gorgeous.

'How do I look?' I asked Philippa, busily tucking her hair up under the swim cap to emulate the bald pate of Yul Brynner. She snapped in the last lock, turned to me, slowly appraised me up and down. I shifted, nervous.

'Just like Deborah.'

A moment of complete happiness.

We made tickets, a programme, set up cushioned chairs in front of our 'stage'. It was all busking, play-acting, making do. Halfway through the King and Anna's thrilling waltz, Philippa trod on my skirt, dragging down the material to reveal a section of plastic hula hoop and my bare legs in grubby socks beneath. But it didn't matter. We just laughed, and at the end, Mum and Dad stood up, clapped and clapped. 'Encore!' they shouted. We reset the record, played 'Shall We Dance?' again and again, and they joined in, Mum singing and the two of them dancing beside us in an elegant duet.

I picture the four of us, dancing, laughing that summer night. Caught up in a rare moment of happiness. And I see the care interwoven between us all. My care for Dad, Mum's care for her girls, wanting us to be free, to fly. *My two lovely girls*. And I see Philippa caring for me. I remember the evening I was at hers, when she told me about putting Mum's house on the market. How she stood in her doorway, Spray and Wiping as she watched me leave, and realize that it was not because she didn't want me *there*, with her, but because she wanted me to be *elsewhere*, to return to a place where I had been happy. To go back to France, get on with my life.

Shall we dance? On a bright cloud of music, shall we fly?

Streaked with mud and much, much worse, we sneak into Philippa's house the back way through the utility room, leaving a mess on the lino never before seen at my sister's abode. We clean up as best we can, seizing the opportunity of a fresh pile of folded laundry on top of the washing machine to change outfits. Philippa finds a pair of Melanie's flat pumps and twins them with a cerise two-piece, rather jolly for a funeral but better than what she hands me: Sam's tracky bottoms and a baggy T-shirt proclaiming *Save the Elephants!* I look dubiously at the illustration – a herd of the noble beasts traversing the savannah across what will be my chest – and am about to protest, but she pulls the top over my head before I can say anything.

'We can hardly go through in that,' Philippa says, pointing to our mucky pile of funeral clothes on the floor. 'And anyway, nobody will notice what you're wearing.'

There she is, my sister.

People spill from the living room into the kitchen. I'm stunned, then mortified to see Adison standing by himself in the corner of Philippa's living room, a totally incongruous vision. He sports a tasteful soft charcoal jacket with a grey triangle of linen handkerchief poking from his top pocket – sombre occasion-appropriate, but stylish. Hideously aware of my filthy brogues, not to mention the tribe of proboscideans gallivanting across my chest, I go to greet him. As I draw near, I sort of hunch my shoulders forward to try to make the elephants less . . . *elephantine*.

'Dot, is your back OK?' Adison says when he sees me. 'I can give you an adjustment.'

Much as the idea of Adison adjusting me appeals, I shake my head and fold my arms across my chest to obscure the worst of my teenage boy ensemble. Adison steps closer, puts out his hand and takes mine. That whiff of bergamot.

'It was a real privilege to know Gail,' he says.

'Thank you. I know she appreciated your work. Thank you so much for—'

'Miss Watson, how are you holding up?'

Adison's hand slips from mine and Sister Gloria envelops me in a cushiony hug. 'We all miss your mum. She was such a lovely lady. Did you see the flowers? Everyone chipped in – the catering staff, Mr Petrie our chiropodist. Everyone had a nice word about her.' I smile, thank her. How strange to think about all these people who had, for a brief while at least, such an intimate knowledge of my mother. I doubt I'll see any of these familiar faces beyond the funeral. Sister Gloria leans in and I brace for another hug, but instead she sniffs lightly at my hair and makes an indeterminate expression before taking a small step back. It's true I didn't give much attention to my coiffure after narrowly avoiding death by bull, but I wouldn't have put Sister Gloria down as a stickler for the finer points of grooming.

'We're a great team,' Sister Gloria is saying. 'I used to work in hospitals, all go, endless paperwork and accounting for every cotton swab. But what am I saying? I am sure you know all about it – aren't you in the medical profession yourself?'

Philippa strikes again.

Adison has politely stepped away and immediately been swooped up by Anita and Big Jim.

'Have you sampled Philippa's Emmental puffs?' I ask Sister Gloria. 'They're delicious – I'll just nip and get you some.' I abandon her and make my way back to Adison.

Anita is looking rather flushed (owing to Gerald's generous pours and/or the proximity of Big Jim) and is holding forth.

'We've even got two funeral urns in Lost Property, shelved under "Miscellaneous". Really – you name it, we have it . . . Sorry, Dots, didn't see you there. Didn't mean to say that about the urns, what with your mum and everything . . .'

'No, no, it's all right. The flowers the office sent are glorious.'

Anita beams.

'Jim chose them. Those birds of paradise – lovely, aren't they!'

'Thank you, Jim.'

Big Jim tickles the head of his snake tattoo in acknowledgement.

'I was just saying how much we are going to miss you at work,' Anita says.

'I'm sure,' Adi says, and smiles at me.

There is a pause during which Anita slowly looks from Adi to me and back again, and then, just in case there was any doubt whatsoever, says, 'Looks like we're not the only ones to have a soft spot for our Dot, eh, Jim?'

'Didn't you say you were going away for Christmas?' I splutter, my face reddening. 'How lovely, where was it again?'

Anita slips her hand into Big Jim's paw and beams.

'Tour of the Greek islands. I can't wait.'

I remember the guide I slipped into her bag that time and catch Big Jim looking at me, swear I see the hint of a twinkle in his eye.

Meanwhile, Anita has turned her attention back to Adi. 'Anyway, like I was saying, there is no one like Dot. Have you seen her dance?'

Adi shakes his head, looks at me and gives a slow smile. 'No, but I sure would like to.'

My cheeks reach combustion point.

Anita winks at Adi. There really is no holding that woman back.

'You should,' she beams. 'She is a-ma-zing on the dance floor. Never know what our Dot is going to do next – or wear, come to that. Is that a herd of elephants?' She peers at my chest.

'The thing is, it's not my—' I start.

'Auntie Dot.' Melanie comes over. 'Mum sent me to get you – Uncle Robbie and Auntie Linda are just going.' I have no idea who these people are and begin to proffer an excuse, but Melanie, every inch her mother's daughter, takes a firm grasp of my arm and leads me over to the far side of the room where a sweet-faced couple are talking to Gerald. She deposits me before giving me a cursory look up and down and crinkling her nose.

'Why are you wearing Sam's T-shirt?'

Robbie and Linda are followed by a brood of similarly unknown or 'honorary' relatives and well-wishers. When I finally have room to breathe, Sam envelops me in another of his deliciously uncomplicated puppy hugs.

'I'm so glad you're here, Auntie Dot.'

'Me too.' I kiss his straw nest of hair. I see myself out in the Channel in Mrs Trosley's kimono, swallow, and squeeze him harder until he wriggles away.

'Pooh, you pong, Auntie.'

'Oh dear. Do I?'

'But you look brilliant in my T-shirt. You can keep it if you want.'

'Keep it? Well, I . . . How sweet of you.'

'I've got an epic picture of Pompeii to show you later!' he says, skittering off.

I give my left arm a quick sniff. It's true Philippa and I only did a rudimentary clean after the bull episode. Hmm, yes, I do detect a distinct odour of *la campagne*, but it's not coming from this arm. I duck my nose further into my other armpit and take a big sniff.

'There you are.' Adi stands before me, immaculate.

'Oh, tippety-top,' I say. 'I was just . . .' What? Smelling myself? 'Thank you so much for coming. Did you have one of Philippa's puffs? They're simply delicious,' I gabble. I've longed to be with him all afternoon, but now that he is in front of me I just want to disappear.

'Like I was saying, I really valued getting to know your mom.' I nod. 'And you, of course.' He looks at me intently. I wrap my arms tighter around the T-shirt. 'I wondered if I might give you my number?'

'I have it.'

'You do?'

'Yes, The Pines . . .'

'Oh, I meant *my* number – my cell phone.'

'Oh. Yes, of course.' He writes it down and hands it to me. 'Thank you.'

'Just in case I can . . . help.' He reaches out. Maybe he will touch my face again. 'You have something in your hair . . .'

I wrench my head away, fearing he has spotted a clot of cow pat. *Oh God, please no.*

'Sorry,' he says, pulls his arm back.

'No, it's not that, it's just—'

'Gerald, this is the physiotherapist I mentioned who was so good with Mum.' Philippa deposits Gerald at our side and sallies forth to a fray of other guests.

'San Francisco, right?' Gerald says, shaking Adi's hand. 'Surprised the tech world didn't snap you up. They probably pay ten K a massage at Google. Are you settled here in England?'

'I'm doing a research project – looking at the benefits of physiotherapy and haptic techniques on dementia patients.'

'What's that in plain English?' Gerald says, with what he believes to be a manly guffaw.

Adi smiles, exposing those marvellous teeth.

'Basically I'm studying the power of touch. I'm investigating a variety of medical procedures along with more holistic methods: reflexology, Feldenkrais, shiatsu, reiki, EFT – that's Emotional Freedom Technique, it's—'

'Jolly good, jolly good.' Gerald starts to look for an escape route; all this talk of touching and emotion is unsettling him.

344

'The Pines gives me so many amazing opportunities for applied research. I've been collecting some case studies.'

Gerald nods.

'Well, thanks for all the care you gave Gail. The family appreciate it. Must just go see if Philippa needs my help.'

'Research?' I say, as Gerald swiftly departs.

'What?'

'Case studies?'

'Yes . . .'

'So my mother, is she – was she one of your case studies?'

'No. Well . . . yes, but . . .'

Just doing my job. What else? How foolish I have been to have thought otherwise.

'Well, so kind of you to come to Mum's funeral. I see you take your research very seriously . . .'

'Dot, I—'

'Yoo-hoo!' The trumpet call of Sister Gloria heralds across the room. ''Fraid we have to go now, no rest for the wicked. Big AGM tomorrow – need to pick Dr Chang's brains about a few "hands-on" strategies.' She chuckles at her joke before remembering where she is. 'Lovely funeral, you did your mum proud. Don't be a stranger now! Come and see us any time. You are always welcome!'

Several other guests also choose this moment to leave, and I lose Adison in a mêlée of coats and cling film-wrapped dishes.

Philippa invites me to stay over and I accept gratefully. She insists we leave her to clean up alone and we all know better than to argue. She sends me upstairs for a bath: 'Have a good soak, relax, and make sure you get that cow shit out of your hair.'

After some vigorous ablutions, I change into the pyjamas and dressing gown she has laid out on the spare bed for me. As I fold the tracksuit bottoms, the piece of paper with Adison's number falls out. Why did he bother giving it to me? More 'research'? I hold it for a moment then scrunch it up.

I linger upstairs for a while as the events of the day churn. Mum's funeral, Philippa's revelation about Dad, the conversation with Adison. I want to bury myself under the bedcovers, but eventually I rally and join the family downstairs in the sitting room. Melanie is on her phone and Sam is playing a game on his iPad, but they drift away from their screens when I come in. Sam sits next to me on the steely sofa and Melanie lolls against Philippa's chair, flicking through old photos.

'Look at this one,' Melanie says, pointing to a picture. 'Granny was so beautiful! I definitely take after that side of the family.'

'I liked it when Granny would come and stay at the weekends, before she got poorly,' says Sam. 'She'd help me learn my lines for drama. And she made the best cheese on toast.'

'She did love cheese,' I say, and Philippa gives me a look.

'What's your best memory of Granny, Auntie Dot?' Melanie asks.

'Goodness . . . well . . . let me see . . .' The chocolate cake? The day I saw her singing at the window? Her cheering 'encore' after Philippa and I performed *The King and I*? Another memory comes to me, forgotten after all the years, but now I recall it vividly.

It was sports day, and I had made a mess of the three-legged race with Penny Pavey, but redeemed myself by being placed second in the egg and spoon with swotty Jane Stevens. Mum was thrilled, made such a fuss of my medal. Then they called for volunteers for the last race, the parents' sprint. It never even occurred to me that my mother might race, but at the last minute as parents crouched at the starting line, she threw off her sandals and joined them.

The whistle went and I watched open-mouthed as she raced down the track, her turquoise frock flying behind her, her legs strong, muscular. And the look on her face, so full of life. I wondered at her, so fast, so vivid, leaving the other parents far behind, her hair falling out of its ponytail, her arms outstretched, breaking through the finish tape. Glorious.

I wake in the middle of the night, moonlight pooling on my sister's parquet. I was dreaming about Dad, and for once he wasn't falling. We were driving back home from a ramble but before we turned into our street, Dad stopped the car and turned off the headlights. The night was perfectly clear. He motioned for me to get out and we lay back on the bonnet, side by side. 'See those three bright stars,' he said, pointing up. 'Orion's Belt. The sky is full of stories, Dot – you need never feel lost. Just look up at the stars.' I was cuddled into his coat, and when I wake I can feel it as fully as if it had just taken place, the warmth of him holding me.

I wrap myself in the duvet and go outside. It is bitterly cold. I take the cover off one of Philippa's garden loungers, lie back, look up.

Hello, Dad.

I remember when I was about to start my MA in France. I was excited but also nervous about the term ahead. I wanted to do well, make you proud. I was standing in the hallway putting daffodils in a vase. I wanted to tell you I loved you. To make sure I didn't go without you knowing. I wanted to say: 'You have always been a mountain.'

I had my words all ready, lined up, single file like shiny-headed schoolchildren in the corridor. All present and correct! My 'You' and my 'Have', my 'Always' followed by 'Been', 'A' and 'Mountain'. But at the last minute, I faltered, sending my words collapsing into each other. 'Ouavewayseeenmotn.'

'All right, old thing?' you said, ruffling my hair as you walked by. I nodded.

You called out to me from the kitchen. 'What about a spot of lunch? I could fix us a plate of domino sandwiches – remember?'

Everything, Dad. I remember everything. The Adventure Picnics, our Holmes and Watson escapades, the shape of the air that was the space between my feet in your wellies, your fingers as you tamped your tobacco. Your lips puckered, singing, '*Beau . . . tiful.*'

In the kitchen, I heard you whistling as you made the sandwiches, a long sad note that seemed to be so far away. Like the sound of a distant trumpet, like the crushed head of a daffodil. *Ooooooooo.*

Hear me now, Dad: you have always been a mountain. Soaring and magnificent, even though I know that life always seemed too garish and jagged and abrasive and unkind. When all your colleagues were stamping on each other's necks to make money, you were rescuing a slug, giving it safe passage on a magic carpet of kitchen towel.

I think of you now, darling Dad, high up there in the stars, making your own constellations.

They were kind people, both my parents, despite their sadness. Looking back, I see them as gentle souls, like plants, in a way. Some of their leaves pumped with chlorophyll, others hopelessly shrunken, crowded out by more forceful growth around them that blocked their light.

29

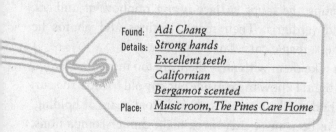

Found:	*Adi Chang*
Details:	*Strong hands*
	Excellent teeth
	Californian
	Bergamot scented
Place:	*Music room, The Pines Care Home*

Philippa was right: it is a seller's market. The Bevans will move into the maisonette in the new year. The money from the sale will be split between us. Gerald has been delivering unfathomable monologues about financial portfolios, clearly worried that I'm not to be trusted with such a large sum of money. I hear them as background noise. What resonates most deeply is the knowledge that, when I'm ready, my mother has left me enough money for a place of my own, that she is still providing shelter and security. Even now she manages to extend her invisible care. I mistook her hands on the wheelbarrow for my father's. But I see her now, fully in frame. I see all her attention, her love. I am grateful for the brief time we spent living together here. Not chums purely through proximity. Not at all. Two people who cared for each other. Mother and daughter. Gail and Dorothea.

I wish I could thank her for all that she has given me. But I will make the most of it. I will put myself centre stage as she wanted, I will do what I have most longed to do. What I once planned to do.

Travel.

My guides cover the maisonette's living-room floor, transforming the taupe surface into a rainbow of ambers, blues and verdigris. Their maps, pictures and photos lie before me, a magic carpet of possibilities.

I can't take them with me – there are too many and I want to travel light. I know them inside out, my old friends; the curl of their bodies, their spines softened from years of holding. They have been my trusty week-night dinner companions, my weekend breaks. But I know that just as objects cannot replace people, guidebooks are not destinations.

However, I will never forget their ability to inspire, to educate. In homage to the magnificent Phyllis Pearsall, I fashion my own A–Z of sorts, selecting favourite pages from my most beloved guides: the section on the Alpujarra villages from *All Things Andalucía!*, the photograph of the Earth Pyramids of Euseigne, the page with the marginalia of shooting stars next to the bistro in Lyon famed for its onion soup. It will be the guide for my journey.

I will start in Holland – rainy February days entranced by the Rembrandts at the Rijksmuseum – then move on to France in time for spring – Paris then the Dordogne, maybe look into some translation courses in Montpellier. Then on to the wilds of the Camargue, Marseilles – I might pop in on Louise, that would be rather nice, then Avignon before taking the train to Italy. *Avanti!* I'll travel through Tuscany,

Abruzzo, right down to Catanzaro, the ball of the boot, then over to Sicily with its gin-clear water. I'll summer in the Greek islands. Think of all the postcards I can send to Sam and Melanie! I'll return via Spain – or should I go the other way? – come back through Croatia and Switzerland . . . A float down the Rhine at Basel? Well, I don't have to do it all in one trip, after all. There is the next, then the next . . .

Sister Gloria greets my taxi at The Pines.

'Goodness, looks like you've got the whole world packed up in there!'

'Indeed.'

'Well, it's good to see you, and such a nice idea. Those rooms could all do with a bit of cheer, especially Music. Anything to give it a lift will be much appreciated.'

'Thank you for letting me do it.'

'Of course. You're looking very pretty, if I may say so. New dress?'

I nod. Inspired by Harriet, I have purchased a cobalt-blue dress. Astonishingly soft, cashmere, quite figure-hugging. It is a fabric with which I could become rather smitten.

The music room is empty and heartbreakingly silent when I enter it. I wouldn't mind Big Jim's Toot-a-Loop radio right now. Noisily, I lay out my tools: ruler, craft knife, paintbrush, level, chalk, wallpaper paste, spray lacquer. Sadly, I am *sans* a wallpaper-smoothing tool – something Nick, the gentleman on the TV programme, stressed was crucial. I will have to make do, but it's a tad frustrating because I know exactly the shelf in Lost Property where I could lay my hands on one.

353

I have already pre-selected the choicest photos and writings from my guides, carefully cut them out. On the TV programme a whole sitting room was wallpapered in animal pictures. I have decided on a collage in a one-metre band running along the wall at around average torso level, so it can be enjoyed easily by wheelchair users and foot travellers alike. Following TV Nick's precise instructions, I make a chalk line first, then choose different sized pages and alternate black and white with colour to make things 'pop' and 'give contrast'. As I paste each picture, I carefully smooth my ruler across the surface to eliminate air bubbles.

I order the pages not by geography or alphabet or author; instead I curate my travel exhibition through the sensorial and experiential. I start at the doorway with a feast of restaurants and eateries – in Amsterdam a cluster of canal-side cafes, rustic bistros in the Languedoc, aromatic Cachaça bars in Porto Alegre, the tiny backstreet cafe in Bangkok with the lemongrass chicken and coconut rice, betel stalls in Bangalore, a sugar sprinkle of Italian gelaterias. I splice street maps with photos: steaming dishes of spaghetti, pungent salads, piquant aperitifs; include recipes of local specialities: slabs of yellow cheeses in the Alpes-Maritimes, spice stalls in Mysore, a garlic festival in Gilroy, California, market stalls in Valencia with tomatoes so plump and red you can smell them.

After tempting the taste buds, my sensorial voyage continues along to the next wall – a brisk walk after all that fine dining! I create a collage of forests, parks, mountains – more maps, more photos – wildflowers in the spring, the view from the Matterhorn, the Atlas Mountains of Morocco, the Black Forest in winter, lavender fields in Provence, the flower market on Dal Lake, Kashmir, golden curves of beaches, cliffside walking paths, vistas, elegant parks; a bricolage to spark imagination and memory. I leave a pot of map pins in case people want to mark places they like or have been – or want to go.

I start on the third wall, a collage of spiritual and architectural delights: churches, temples, towers, statues, fountains and follies; the blue-and-white ceramic tiles that line the streets of Puebla, Mexico, the Teotihuacan ruins at sunset. As I carefully smooth the wrinkles out of the Temple of Heaven in Beijing, my first visitor, a woman in a coral velvet jogging suit, fresh from yoga in the movement room next door, comes in to investigate what is going on. She swiftly sticks a pin into Santiago de Compostela.

'I first walked the Camino de Santiago when I was eighteen,' she says, tracing a picture of the pilgrimage with her finger. 'It's where I met my husband. We did a week every year after that on our anniversary – after five years we'd done the whole thing. Funny how I can just run my finger along it now, and it's just a few inches, but you wouldn't believe the blisters on my feet at the end of it!' She laughs. 'We loved it.' She lingers, retracing her steps, remembering.

As the paste dries, I go over the pages with spray lacquer and give them a protective finish. By the third wall, my head is a little spinny. Did TV Nick say anything about intoxicating fumes? I don't recall. Perhaps I should take a little break?

'Dot.'

Adison stands at the doorway in an olive-green jumper and black jeans.

'Oh, hello. I . . . didn't think you were supposed to be in today.' I have not returned any of his calls.

'Oh, right.' He dips his head, causing that silky fringe to fall forward. I wish he wouldn't do that. Especially when I'm already feeling a bit giddy . . .

'Wow – it looks awesome in here. Can I help? Seems like a pretty big job.'

'No need. I am sure you have lots of your own research to be getting on with.'

'Dot—'

'And may I just say that the word "awesome" has its origins in the late sixteenth century and refers to being "filled with awe", usually in respect to standing in the presence of something daunting or experiencing something truly inspiring, something fundamentally profound and life-changing. Something akin to a religious experience. It gets bandied about far too much. Especially by Americans. Perhaps, *perhaps* it can be attributed to Maria Callas's voice, but it is certainly not appropriate for a wall collage – though I have done my best.' I pick up my brush with a dramatic flourish, smartly turn back to my project, and lose the high ground by stumbling backwards in a dizzy spin.

Strong arms catch me.

'I'm fine. Just a smidgeon too much glue.'

'It reminds me of the first day I saw you.'

'When I established a pattern of embarrassing myself?' I pull away but he doesn't quite let go.

'Dot, what I said the other day about my work . . .'

'Yes, your "case studies".'

'Your mom was my patient, and yes, my work with her did inform my research, but I do this work because I want to help dementia patients.'

'I'm sure we are all most grateful, Dr Chang.' I move away.

'Listen, please. I liked spending time with your mom and I am so sad that she died. I did everything I could to try and ease—'

'I know you did—'

'And I want to learn more, so I can offer more. I know how hard these stages of life can be, I really just want to help . . .'

He is so close now. The curve of his mouth, his cheekbones, the passion in his face. I breathe him in, see the dip of his collarbone under the soft neck of his jumper.

'I know,' I say quietly.

He steps closer still.

'Dot.' His voice is a caress.

'Adi . . . I—' A sound. We both startle apart, turn towards the door.

'Just thought I'd come and see what all the fuss is about up here.' Geoffrey. My nemesis. Camino de Santiago has clearly been busy spreading the word.

I step back and vigorously daub my brush with wallpaper paste, while Adi intently examines a cluster of women's clothing boutiques in Milan. Geoffrey enjoys a slow and lengthy perambulation of the whole room before dedicating his focus to a section on essential vocabulary that I have pulled from the backs of the guides.

'It's funny what sticks,' Geoffrey says. 'I can't for the life of me remember the address here, but I can say "I would like a room, please" in Croatian and Turkish.'

Geoffrey is followed by the Lemon Jacket woman who wheels her husband over to the cafe section, pointing to photos of dishes and reading out lines from recipes. I imagine them outside a trattoria perusing the menu before they enter and dine on penne all'arrabbiata, sitting opposite each other at a candlelit table.

Camino de Santiago herself reappears with a group of friends and authoritatively leads them around the room like a tour guide.

Adi comes over, takes the ruler from me.

'I may as well make myself useful. What if you compose, and I smooth?'

We start on the section I have left till last; (my favourite) rivers, lakes and boat trips: Venetian canals, a Thai river cruise to Ayutthaya, the Chobe river in Botswana, the Nile, of course, Lake Malawi, the Rhône, the Danube. We work side by side, sometimes joined by helpful or curious residents who make suggestions, select choice places or just peruse the collage, dipping in and out of treasures, sharing memories. Finally, they all go off to the dining room for supper, and Adi and I are alone again.

'Looks like there's room for just one more,' says Adi, 'any last favourite?'

'This one, I think.' I carefully press the final page into place.

Then, amidst cathedrals, temples, mosques and yoga shalas, I reach out and caress his face, retracing the touches he gave me when my mother stood in this room, filling it with song. My fingers traverse the arches of his eyebrows, the bridge of his nose, his temples.

Adi closes his eyes, smiles, his mouth a delicious curve. So delicious, in fact, that I move closer to that face, to that mouth, to those lips. Press my mouth to his. The sweetness of his lips . . . so . . . oh, so . . . what's the word? I kiss him again, harder now . . . The exact right word? I feel his mouth on mine, the warmth of his tongue, his arms close around me, strong and kind and safe.

Ah! I have it, the word for this kiss that sets me spinning around the globe.

Awesome.

EPILOGUE

The giddy, light-hearted rain that has flirted against roofs and windows all morning takes a moment's reprieve, giving way to a cadet-blue sky. It's the perfect interlude for an hour's cruise on a Bateau Mouche.

The city drifts either side of me in unabashed splendour; the Gothic extravagance of the Musée d'Orsay, the seductive curve of the Île de la Cité, the hopeless romanticism of the Pont Marie, lined with tender-eyed strangers who gaze down dreamily at the boats passing underneath. The tradition, though its origins are highly suspect, is that you must kiss the person sitting next to you as your boat goes under the bridge, and make a wish. The Pont Marie, or 'lovers' bridge' as it is known, was the last image I stuck on the collage in the music room. I know, I know, but it seems I can't help myself, because really, is there anywhere more enchanting than Paris in the spring?

The person next to me is equally captivated by the city's charms and takes endless photographs, clearly filled with delight at every building, bridge and passing bateau.

'I can't believe I never came here before. It's spectacular!'

We are so close that if we were both to turn our heads and face each other, there would be nothing for us to do but kiss.

So we do.

It is only when the captain clears her throat, rather pointedly, that we realize the boat has docked and all the other passengers have disembarked. Giggling like children, we jump off, race down the jetty.

The captain's voice behind us calls, '*Madame?*' I turn. '*Votre parapluie?*' She waves my black collapsible brolly in the air. '*Avez-vous perdu votre parapluie?*'

I throw my head back. Laugh.

'What's she saying?' Adi asks.

'It appears that I have lost my umbrella.' I grab his hand and we run into the city.

SONG CREDITS

Lyrics on p. 45 from 'More Than A Woman' by the Bee Gees (lyrics by Barry, Robin and Maurice Gibb)

Lyrics on pp. 158, 160, 326 and 339 from 'Shall We Dance' from *The King and I* (lyrics by Oscar Hammerstein II and Richard Rogers)

Lyrics on pp. 163, 164, 165 and 166 from 'Maria' from *The Sound of Music* (lyrics by Oscar Hammerstein II and Richard Rogers)

Lyrics on pp. 176 and 177 from 'Climb Ev'ry Mountain' from *The Sound of Music* (lyrics by Oscar Hammerstein II and Richard Rogers)

Lyrics on p. 179 from 'Hello Young Lovers' from *The King and I* (lyrics by Oscar Hammerstein II and Richard Rogers)

Lyrics on p. 193 from 'Y.M.C.A.' by Village People (lyrics by Jacques Morali, Victor Willis and Henri Belolo)

Lyrics on p. 264 and 265 from 'Beautiful Dreamer' by Bing Crosby (lyrics by Stephen Foster)

Lyrics on pp. 296, 302, 304, 307 and 321 from '*Mon cœur s'ouvre à ta voix*' from *Samson and Delilah* translated to English by Chloé Déchery

ACKNOWLEDGEMENTS

The journey of writing this book began in San Francisco and ended in London. Novel writing, like a transatlantic move, is challenging, thrilling and leaves you feeling a tad jet-lagged. What made the journey possible was the collaboration and support of many people. I would like to take this opportunity to thank them all.

First to the glorious and impeccable Judith Murray, whom I'm honoured to call my agent. Thank you for finding Dot Watson. Huge thanks to all at Greene & Heaton, especially Kate Rizzo and Alisa Ahmed.

Thank you, Sally Williamson, my fantastic editor, for all your generative feedback and expert guidance. Thank you, Darcy Nicholson, my acquisitions editor, for believing in *Lost Property* and supporting it to the hilt. Thanks to Claire Gatzen for your attentive copy-edit. Deep gratitude to the incredible team at Transworld for making this book happen.

Thank you, Victoria Blunden for your excellent suggestions and all your help.

To first readers: Christine Paris-Johnstone for being the best sister a girl could ever have, and Alex Hyde and Jane Sillars for your generous insights and friendship.

To Sara Houghteling for your inspirational writing class at Stanford University.

To Sabrina Broadbent and the hugely talented group of fellow writers in the Faber Academy class of 2018–19: Claire Anderson, Jacob Bushnell, Lucy Crane, Jo Franklin, Farah Halime, Kate Anthony, Eric Harberson, Greg Jarvis, Weiwei Lu, Timothy Murphy, Francesca Quinn, Grania Read and Philippa Wood.

With special thanks to Ericka Waller for your super feedback on an early draft and your own wonderful *Dog Days*.

To Lauren Rusk for a sharp-eyed read.

To Domnita Petri, my California writing pal.

To Adi Chang.

Heartfelt thanks to my family – Tony and Juelette Paris, for your endless love, belief and support that makes possible more than you can ever know.

Mike, Jem and Lucy Paris-Johnstone for all our creative adventures!

Virginia and Paul Resta, Jerry and Barbara Hill for your love and generosity.

To Lou Kuenzler for your astute advice and for being such a treasured friend over all these years.

To Claudia Barton, Caroline Bevan, Jen Harvie, Debbie Kilbride, Ali McArdle, Eliz McArdle, Emmy Minton,

Gretchen Schiller, Margaret Stevenson for all your support and encouragement.

Thanks to the employees at TfL Lost Property Department (formerly of Baker Street) for paying such very good attention.

To the writers, both long-beloved and newly met, whose extraordinary words and worlds provided such succour in the 2020 lockdown, and helped me through my own battle with the COVID-19 virus: Lucy Atkins, Kate Atkinson, Clare Chambers, Sara Collins, Bernardine Evaristo, Joanna Glen, Kate Gross, Rachel Joyce, Toni Morrison, Ingrid Persaud, Kiley Reid, Anne Tyler, Sarah Waters and Evie Wyld.

And most of all, thank you Leslie Hill for tirelessly reading, editing, then re-reading every single blooming draft. I am so grateful to you for your brilliant insights, your deep intelligence and your unfaltering faith in this book and in me. I could not have done it without you.

With thanks to everyone at Transworld for bringing *Lost Property* to publication.

Editorial
Sally Williamson
Katrina Whone
Vivien Thompson
Judith Welsh
Lara Stevenson

Copy editor
Claire Gatzen

Publicity
Alison Barrow
Hayley Barnes

Marketing
Julia Teece
Ruth Richardson

Production
Phil Evans
Cat Hillerton

Sales
Tom Chicken
Deirdre O'Connell
Laura Garrod
Emily Harvey
Gary Harley

Design
Irene Martinez
Marianne Issa El-Khoury

Contracts
Rebecca Smith
Shaikyla White

Operations
Mariana De Barros Van Hombeeck

Q&A WITH THE AUTHOR

Dot is such an unusual main character, with many facets to her personality. Did someone in your life inspire you to create Dot?

I worked briefly at the Transport for London Lost Property Office at Baker Street some years ago, doing research for a theatre project called *Lost & Found*. I was touched by the level of care and attention the Lost Property staff gave to the customers who came in looking for their lost items. For the staff it didn't matter what had been lost, whether it was a diamond ring or a teddy bear with one eye and half its stuffing missing; value was apportioned equally. No loss was too small, each carried within its shape and description possible heartbreak for the one who had lost it. This level of care, of attention being paid, inspired the novel and the character of Dot Watson, who appeared to me practically fully formed one day. As soon as I had Dot's voice, I knew I had my story.

What I love about reading and writing fiction are the imaginative worlds one enters. I love the freedom to create a character called Dot Watson who wears a felt uniform and savours the word 'Sellotape'! Having said that, I would like to think there is someone like Dot out there, especially in these times; someone who pays attention, takes care of lost things, and who now and again slips travel guides into our pockets encouraging us to pop over to Rome or Paris or Seville for the weekend.

Your descriptions of the Lost Property Office and London are vivid and real. How did you go about researching these settings for your novel?

Setting is hugely important for my writing, perhaps partly because I am a theatre-maker – the first thing I need to know about a show is where it takes place, which might be a theatre but which might also be a canal barge, a bomb site or a secret garden . . .

The cavernous basements of Lost Property, Baker Street are filled floor to ceiling with objects all hoping to be found, each sporting a mustard-coloured tag. It was an extraordinary place to be, surrounded by loss, and creatively most inspiring. I would have been able to imagine the lost phones, brollies and shopping bags that fill the shelves without spending time *in situ*, but I would never have guessed at the false teeth, the two-and-a-half hundredweight of sultanas, or the jar of bull's sperm! Truth is indeed stranger than fiction.

I was particularly struck by the textual and gestural language around loss. Each day people from all walks of life would turn up at Lost Property, queue at the counter, and when their turn came, try and describe the items they had lost. I was taken by the detail of their descriptions: 'It was the District Line going from Embankment.' 'A shiny metallic bag, blue. *A gift* bag.' 'It was a claret from the Médoc – I can't remember the Château – 1996, I think ...'

All that informed Dot's attention to detail.

You write so beautifully about how our memories of the people we love are tied to objects. Was there anything that inspired the story behind Mr Appleby's search for his wife's purse?

I have always been fascinated by how even the most everyday object – a pipe, a bag, a small purse – can contain in its body a memory, a moment, a trace of a life lived, a person loved. Objects can unlock stories, relationships, whole worlds.

Objects can be portals that allow us to time travel back to the past, to the place or person they recall and let us linger there with them, if only for a moment. That is what the little bluey lilac purse is for Mr Appleby. We all have them, don't we? The things that remind us of the people we love.

What does a day of writing look like for you?

I wrote *Lost Property* during a transatlantic move between San Francisco and London, so each writing day was quite different and some were pretty hectic. Lockdown life has been something else entirely. Mostly I have worked from the top floor of my Victorian house, which faces out to sea. I start around 8 a.m. and clock off about 6 p.m., and during that time I try to make sure I get out to a yoga class or go for a run or hop on the cross-trainer. Or at least walk down-stairs and back with the incentive of a cup of coffee.

Do you have any routines or items that help you to focus when writing?

I like to listen to music when I write and usually it's music that plays a role in the novel in some way. When I was writing *Lost Property* it was Maria Callas singing 'Mon Coeur S'ouvre à Toi Voix'. My current book has a protagonist who is partial to the film *Brief Encounter*, so I have been listening to Rachmaninoff's Piano Concerto no.2 op.18. Listening to Callas or Rachmaninoff on repeat can leave me an emotional wreck by the day's end. Happily, it looks like my next book calls for Elvis Presley and a dash of Latin ballroom – thank goodness!

2021 has been challenging for many reasons and reading can really help to transport us to another world. What are three books you've read this year that have lifted your spirits?

Three? THREE?! I've had to create more shelves for the books that have flooded in this past year, a whole life raft of them.
The Island of Missing Trees by Elif Shafak for its beauty and generosity, *Lessons in Chemistry* by Bonnie Gamus for its atomic wit and the character of Elizabeth Zott, and *Dear Reader* by Cathy Rentzenbrink because opening this book feels like suddenly making a new friend and visiting lots of old beloved ones besides.

If you could have dinner with three authors, living or dead, who would you choose and why?

These kinds of questions are always so delightfully wild, aren't they? Embracing that spirit then, I'd love to invite Flannery O'Conner, Carson McCullers and Tennessee Williams because they are all such poets on the theme of the Misfit. I imagine a queer romp of an evening laced with dark wit and well-mixed cocktails.

Can you tell us a little bit about your next book?

My next book is set on an allotment and it's about female friendship, adventure and how it really is never too late to fall in love.